Buried Away

By Kamery Solomon

Praise for *The Swept Away Saga*

"Amazing! The best way I can think to describe it is **Pirates of the Caribbean meets Outlander!** There is action, adventure, romance and so much more! You will not be disappointed!"
~Heather Garrison, *Amazon Customer*

"Kamery Solomon never disappoints a reader in her ability to tell a great story. She has proven she's not a one trick pony and capable of writing across genres. **Highly recommend reading** any and all of her books."
~Lisa Markson, *The Paranormal Bookworm*

"This book has so many twists and turns that **will keep you reading all night long**. I love the characters and the mystery. The author does a fantastic job weaving every part in this story that will leave you wanting more. I highly recommend!"
~Laura Collins, *Amazon Customer*

"I was pulled in right away and **I did not want to put the book down**, nor did I want the story to end . . . a must read!"
~Holly Copper, *Amazon Customer*

"This is the book you **MUST** be reading **NOW!**"
~Julie Engle, *Amazon Customer*

"This is a story I will read time and time again."
~Angie Angelich, *Book Banshee*

"What else could you want?!"
~Vonnie Hudson, *Amazon Customer*

Other Books by Kamery Solomon

Forever
Hell Hall (A Halloween Novella)

The God Chronicles
Zeus
Poseidon
Hades
Adrastia
Exoria

Dreams Novels
Taking Chances
Watching Over Me

The Swept Away Saga
Swept Away
Carried Away
Hidden Away
Stolen Away
Buried Away
Taken Away (A Swept Away Saga Origins Story)

The Lost in Time Duet
Finding Freedom

Buried Away

By Kamery Solomon

For Kysee
Thank you for all of your help and support ♥

Eric Ray
Present Day

There was something about staring down the barrel of a gun that made me feel like I couldn't breathe. It was akin to gazing into an abyss, a black hole of uncertainty, and the face of the grim reaper all in one. My mouth went dry, hair standing up on the back of my neck, all thoughts focused on the cold, hard metal threatening me with death.

However, watching as the pistol aimed at the woman I was falling for caused little beads of sweat to surface at my hairline, my knuckles turning white as I held her to me.

This moment was worse than when I'd seen Michael Greene crushed to death in the Treasure Pit. Ghastlier than the moment I'd learned of his daughter, Samantha's, passing, learning she'd drown in the very same hole. Perhaps even more shocking than when I accidentally discovered she'd not died, but traveled back in time instead, only to be joined by our fellow treasure hunter, Mark, later.

None of those things mattered at this moment, though, as I watched my twin brother direct his firearm toward Rebecca O'Rourke—one of Samantha's descendants and the woman who made my heart do strange things I'd never felt before.

"Kevin," I muttered, my chest heaving as I stared

at him with wide eyes. "This is ridiculous. She's not armed!" Reaching forward, I tried to push his wrist down, to take the focus off the woman I believed he might harm. Standing partially in front of her was the only comfort I could give myself, shielding her with my body as we both stood inside the tiny, brick room, Kevin outside the barred entrance.

Shrugging me off, Kevin gritted his teeth, shaking his head. "I have my orders, Eric. She stays down here, in the cells. Besides, she'll be with her fellow Dogs." He snorted, the derogatory term leaving his lips in a sting that suggested he truly despised the group. "I'm not about to let her slip by because you don't want me to follow protocol. Now, get out of there, or I'm going to be forced to shoot her."

Throwing my hands in the air, I stepped back, unable to comprehend a single second more of his absurd behavior. "How do you know what the Black Knight's procedures are?" I half laughed, shaking my head at the ludicrous nature of it all. "You've only been one for what, a month? It's not possible for you to have such deep-rooted hate for Templars already!"

Sighing, he raised an eyebrow, focusing on me. To his credit, the firearm never left Rebecca's position, his finger resting on the trigger. Whatever training The Black Knights of The Order of the Templars had given him, it appeared ingrained, despite the short amount of time he'd spent with them.

If I was honest with myself, there were several indications he was not the same person I'd always known. His clothes, which had been so bright and teenage-like before, aged him somewhat now. Gone were the fandom tees, replaced instead with a plain, gloomy shirt covered by a dark brown, leather jacket. Jeans that had once bore stains and rips were now clean and pressed, meeting the top of his laced boots. I'd never seen him wear anything other than tennis shoes before, save some steel-toed footwear when he was working with us on Oak Isle. He'd also grown a short beard; the chocolate covered stubble mixed in with a few strands of red. The matching locks on the top of his head were parted and styled like something you'd see in a *Great Gatsby* movie, giving off more of a mobster vibe than this whole kidnap-you-and-your-girlfriend-and-lock-her-in-the-dungeon thing he had going on.

I didn't know if anyone would recognize us as identical twins at first glance anymore, he had changed his appearance so much.

The silence between us grew thick, stretching on for minutes. While I didn't want to believe my brother would shoot Rebecca, something in my gut whispered it was still a possibility. There was no way I was going to back down until I knew she was safe from harm.

"Er," Kevin started, lowering the weapon and motioning for me to leave the cell. "Come on, man. I understand you don't want to leave her down here. Hell, I don't care that you two have been boning each other, even if she is a Dog. But my orders are to bring you to Kinkade. If you don't get out of the cell because of her, I'm going to have to take care of her, understand?"

Gaping, I continued to stare at him, not sure if I should start with correcting him on how close Rebecca and I were or my horror at the callous way he threatened her. How had things changed so quickly?

Only a day ago, Rebecca and I had agreed to run from the Templar Knights and be together. We were going to find Pandora's Box and keep it safe so no one else could travel through time with it. Now, we were both prisoners, and my brother was suggesting he could kill her.

"Eric," Rebecca muttered, taking my hand in hers. "Go. I appreciate you wanting to stay with me, but I can take care of myself. Trust me." Wrapping her arms around me, she hugged me tightly, kissing my cheek. Her lips went to my ear, faint instructions zipping through them. "Find out everything you can about this place and the people who run it," she hissed with authority, her face hidden from Kevin. "Whether or not we get out of here is up to you now."

Pulling back, she rubbed her thumb over my jaw, smiling sadly, a picture of nervousness and caution replacing the strong, determined woman who had just ordered me around. "I'll be fine," she stated, insecurity in her tone.

"See?" Kevin smiled, jerking his head toward the exit once more. "She's a big girl, Eric. Let her face her demons on her own."

Furrowing my brow, I frowned, unable to help the sense of dread and unease I felt at leaving her behind. We'd spent most of our time together since she saved me from being taken by the Black Knights the first time. I'd known I cared for her after only a few days, but it wasn't until being kidnapped from her room in Rome that I'd realized I was possibly falling in love with her.

What if I left now and never got the chance to tell her?

Steeling myself, I nodded, grabbing her hand and squeezing her fingers for a beat. Not giving a damn about where I was or what was going on, I swept her into my arms again, pressing my mouth against hers.

All the things I wanted to say to her, the promises I wished to convey, flooded into the action, my body reacting to hers in a way I'd not expected. A heat sprung between us, my fingers digging into her back, tongue swirling with hers, breath hot and quick. She fit perfectly against me, responding in kind, sending shivers along my spine as she clutched me in return.

I'll get us out of here, I thought, wishing she could hear it. *I will be the soldier you need me to be. I'll find out all I can. We'll take down the Black Knights together if we must. I won't leave you in this cell forever.*

I love you. God, how I love you, Rebecca. I'm coming back for you, come Hell or high water.

Kevin cleared his throat, pulling me back to the moment at hand and I stepped away, staring into her eyes.

"Go," she muttered, her lips red and swollen. Somehow, her gaze conveyed she knew all the things I'd wanted to say, filled with trust and confidence.

Nodding, I turned, straightening my shirt, and calmly strode from the cell. The clang of bars closing rang in my ears, and I stiffened, unable to look back and see her as a prisoner.

"This way." Kevin moved past me, putting his weapon in his shoulder holster under his jacket. With Rebecca locked away, he suddenly seemed more like himself, an air of relief present in his every step.

Moving down the narrow hallway, I marveled at

the number of cells built into the walls. They seemed to stretch on forever, leading off into the darkness, housing the Templars captured from Washington D.C. when the Black Knights attacked their headquarters. Rationally, I knew they didn't go on for all eternity. New York City was on an island, after all, and the things hidden beneath it had to stop at the water's edge.

Didn't they?

Shaking the idea I could get lost in a labyrinth that somehow encompassed the entire east coast, I watched my feet, finding it difficult to look at any of the prisoners kept here.

"How did you guys find this place?" I asked Kevin instead, hoping to drown out the silence surrounding us.

Continuing to lead the way, he snorted. "Everyone knows about the abandoned subway tunnels under New York. It pays to have someone on the city council help keep a good portion of them blocked off."

"There aren't any tracks here." Confused, I stared at his back.

He shook his head. "No, this is an old sewage runoff. It was closed in the seventies. We've connected a few abandoned places over the years and claimed some buildings above ground. It's a literal maze to get through, but you figure it out eventually."

"How long did it take you?" The bitterness in my voice surprised him, and he stopped, turning to face me.

"What's your deal?" he demanded, folding his arms.

Flabbergasted, I laughed. "My deal? You're working for the bad guy, Kevin!"

Anger flashed across his features, and he rolled his eyes. "You've been misinformed, Er. The Black Knights aren't doing anything wrong—it's the Templars that are corrupt."

"Yeah, that must be why they blew up your headquarters and endangered countless lives. Oh, wait! They didn't do that. The Black Knights did!" Scoffing, I met his glare, not believing he was that obtuse about his actions. "Come on, Kevin. What did they tell you that made you choose sides so quickly?"

"I've been a Black Knight for almost five years, Eric." His voice rose over mine as he rubbed his brow, sighing.

My mouth fell open as I stared at him, an electric buzz ringing in my ears. "What?" I whispered.

He shrugged, letting his arms fall to his side. "I was approached when we were still in high school. You know those early college classes I took? There's a test they give the students, like a prescreening for admittance to the organization. And I passed."

Floundering, I took a step back, closing my eyes. "You were one of them this whole time?"

He sighed again, and I heard him shift, his boots scuffing the floor. "I was supposed to continue helping with the Pit and, if we discovered any treasure, report back to my supervisor."

"Who was that?" I asked sharply, afraid someone else I'd trusted had been deceiving me for years.

"Professor Stephens," he replied. "Once it was clear we wouldn't be able to work on Oak Isle any longer, because of Michael and Samantha's deaths, he decided I would be of more service if I came here, to Headquarters."

Shaking my head, I met his gaze once more. "There's no way. It's not possible for you to have done something like this and me not know. We shared everything, Kev! You're my brother and my best friend! How could you keep a secret like this from me?"

Eyes narrowing, his nose twitched as he folded his arms. "Everyone always lumped us together. We did share everything, but I wanted something that was my own. Sue me."

Laughing without humor, I matched his stance, glaring at the ground for a beat. "Did you know?" I prompted, biting the inside of my lip.

"Know what?"

Raising my head, I let out a breath. "Samantha and Mark traveled through time and are stuck in the past."

It was almost funny. The longer I thought about it, the angrier I became, feeling as if my entire world was crashing down on me once more.

"Did you know that when you were working side by side with them, pretending to be their friends?" I continued, letting a small amount of the fury I felt into my voice. "Were you aware they would suffer and be in pain, torn from the people who loved them? That they would spend their lives fighting the organization you belong to, working with the Templars, doing their best to make the world a safe place?"

Frowning, he held a hand up, silencing me. For a beat, he seemed far away, his eyes vacant as they peered down the tunnel. Sucking in a breath, he glared at the wall, his head tilting to the side as he swallowed, confusion evident in his features.

Surprised, I stepped toward him, realizing the

truth. "You didn't know?"

Glancing at me, he came out of the fog. His voice clipped as he ground out his answer. "No! How the hell would I have known *any* of that? How do *you* know it?" A myriad of emotions clouded his face—pain over the loss of our friends, anger and surprise at my words, and confusion as he tried to sort through it all.

"They sent Scott letters . . ." Touching my throat, I cleared it, trying to keep my voice from breaking. He had accepted what I'd said so easily as if there were no reason for me to have lied to him. There wasn't, of course, but I was thrown off by the absence of his doubt. "I found them by accident, and he told me everything. Rebecca picked us up and took us to D.C. right after. She was worried Black Knights were coming for us and wanted to take us to a safe place."

A shock going through me, my eyes widened as I grabbed his shoulder. "Where is Scott? Is he alive? Do you guys have him?"

Swallowing hard, he nodded, waving at me. "He's here."

Not satisfied with such a short answer, I continued to press him. "Is he hurt? Do you have him locked in a cell down here? What are you planning to do with him?"

"Geez, Eric!" Pushing me, he ran his hands through his hair, messing up the gangster style of it. "He's fine! His leg broke during his extraction, but that's it. He'll be as good as new in a few weeks. However, he failed to mention to me that the time travelers the Black Knights have been trying to track down were Sam and Mark!"

"Where is he?" I wasn't going to stop until I had

all the answers I wanted.

Growling, he glared at me, unhappy with my pestering as he tried to absorb the information I'd given him. "He's upstairs, with Kinkade. If you'd shut up for more than three seconds and let me think this through, I'll take you to see him."

"What then? Will I be locked up down here, too?"

"Damn it, Eric!" He roared, turning on me in an instant, towering over me in a fury I'd never seen in him before. "You aren't a prisoner here, don't you get that? We *saved* you from the Templars! *I* rescued you! If it weren't for me, you'd be locked in one of their prisons by now, no thanks to that woman you so obviously are in love with back there. She'd turn on you in an instant if she didn't think she needed your help. That's what Templars do! They steal and lie and cheat their way through everything, just to keep the treasures of the world hidden from those who should have them. The Black Knights exist to try and stop their reign from destroying our history. If not for my organization, we would have no clue of the past. How do you not get that? We aren't the bad guys—the Templars are!"

Holding my ground, I stared at him, grinding my teeth before replying. "If that's the case," I said carefully, "why did they keep the truth about your friends from you?"

Pausing, he pursed his lips, his features flickering with doubt as he backed off. "I don't know," he admitted. "But I intend to find out."

Kevin led the way up a staircase that ascended out of the underground tunnels and into what appeared to be an apartment building. The doorman nodded to him as we left an exit labeled as a janitor's closet, not thrown off at all by the emergence of identical twins from what should have been a small cubbyhole.

Right off, I could tell we were in a higher-end establishment. Marble floors, decorated with gold filigree, flowed across the space. Pillars twisted elegantly from ground to vaulted ceiling, the stone edifices framing large windows that looked over the city street on one side and a lush garden on the other. Furniture that looked like something out of a couture magazine rested in the nooks and crannies, business-attired individuals residing on the pieces. They talked on cell phones and typed away on laptops, each of them oblivious to those around them. Opposite of the double-doored, glass entrance, a pair of elevators waited, the dials above each one showing which levels the machines were on. The numbers moved without stopping as I watched, seeming to give the entire building an air of hurried activity.

Heading for the lift nearest to us, Kevin pressed the button to call it down to the first floor, shoving his hands in his pockets as he waited.

"This is your headquarters?" I asked, glancing at the people seated along the walls. Were they all Black

Knights? Was I standing in a lair of endangerment, offering myself to the wolves if I so much as stepped wrong?

My brother nodded, stepping to the side as the elevator arrived and spilled a flood of people out into the lobby. Motioning for me to go in first, he waited for me to comply and then stationed himself beside the control panel. To my surprise, he opened the compartment housing the emergency phone, lifting the piece to his ear.

"Kevin Ray for Kinkade," he stated, pausing for a beat before hanging up.

A second more passed and the elevator began to move upward, driving straight to the top. Apparently, there was a way to sidestep the hustle and bustle of this place when you wanted to.

Toeing the black carpet, I swallowed hard, the beat of my heart thrumming in my ears. There was a small part of me that felt safe with my brother. He wouldn't hurt me, I was sure. However, the grandeur of the building, coupled with the small platoon of business-people below had set off an uncomfortable bubbling sensation in my stomach, like I was about to be thrown in the lion's den for dinner.

Glancing at him, I bit my lip, a wave of unrecognition washing over me. Did I know who he was at all?

"Five years," I mused, leaning against the handrail and folding my arms. It was hard to picture my brother knowing something about all of this for that long and never saying anything to me. "How did you keep anyone from finding out?"

Sighing, Kevin glanced over his shoulder at me. "I

started out as a junior initiate," he admitted, grinning sheepishly. "Which means I had nothing to do with the actual organization other than them knowing my name and location. They said I was in a prime position to watch the Treasure Pit for a time. It was certain there was a Templar cache down there, but there was no way to get to it. For about the first three years, I didn't do anything. I forgot I was a member at all, now and then. I was doing what I'd always done, helping out the team on Oak Isle, hoping to find something cool in the end."

His shoulders slumped as he faced the doors, a hitch entering his voice as he continued. "When it looked like Michael had made his breakthrough and was going to get to the bottom of the Pit, I called it in and let them know. After he died . . ." His voice trailed off, his head dropping as he stared at the floor. "I thought my membership would fade into nothing. Everything I did ended. There was no place for me among the Black Knights."

"Until Sammy decided to keep working in her father's name," I added for him.

"I was promoted to a full-time member that summer," he continued. "There was a ceremony and everything. I told everyone I was going hunting, but I came here, to the city."

"But Samantha died, and the state cut off access to the island," I continued, at last grasping where he was going with the story. "There was no point in keeping you in Maine, not when your chance to get the treasure was virtually gone."

Clearing his throat, Kevin fell silent, gazing at the doors in front of him. "Exactly. Professor Stevens suggested I move here to continue my education and be of better service to the group. So, I did. They gave me a nice apartment, good pay, promoted me to Master's Assistant, and I get to finish my degree for free. I know more about Oak Isle than anyone else here, so I guess it was a natural fit for me to help the higher-ups with everything."

The lift slid to a stop before I could answer, the doors opening with a soft *ding*. Kevin exited without another word, not looking to see if I was following him. He knew I had nowhere else to go.

Stepping into the room with caution, I peered around, once again baffled by the elaborate nature of it all. Immaculate wood floors spread across the ground, covered by thick, dark red rugs. Clawfoot furniture with delicate floral patterns printed on white fabric sat arranged around the space, and a considerable desk flowed out of the floor in front of a giant window. Wispy, white curtains hung on either side, mirroring the other two windows in the room. Built-in display cases housed everything from artifacts to decorative plates. Rather than appear overcrowded and messy, each shelf seemed to have a theme and order, giving the entire apartment a well-organized and beautiful feeling.

A man who couldn't have been older than his late forties sat behind the desk, not in a suit, but dressed for any regular occasion. He smiled at me, standing as I entered, his black hair catching the light of the sun behind him. Slightly more round in the middle and tall, he appeared friendly enough but had no chance of holding my attention—not after I saw the man resting on the couch.

"Scott!"

Propped up on the flawless furniture, Scott appeared to be better than I'd seen him in a while. His legs spanned the entire seat, the left one in a cast and resting on a fluffy pillow. The aged look he'd gained while kept at the Templar's compound had diminished somewhat, the smile on his face as wide as any I'd ever seen him wear. Even his clothes looked happier and more comfortable, the light green polo shirt and tan slacks bringing in an air of normality to our situation. Chuckling as I hurried over to him, he waved, welcoming me into a tight, one-armed hug.

"It's good to see you, Eric," he said. "I knew Kevin would be able to bring you back."

"You look so good," I confessed in surprise, pulling back to inspect him again. "I was worried you were locked in a dungeon somewhere, or dead. How did you survive the explosion?"

"I was in my room when the blast occurred, on the other side of the mansion," he reminded me. "I was being taken out by the Black Knights before I knew what had happened."

Frowning, I glanced at his leg. "They did this to you?"

He shook his head. "I tripped. It all happened so fast. One moment I was at the top of the stairs, the next I was at the bottom, unable to stand."

"We take excellent care of our guests, Mister Ray."

Turning, I stared at the other man for the second time.

He was smiling, but the friendliness of his voice and actions didn't reach his eyes. Moving around the edge of the desk, he strode over, offering a hand in greeting as I stood.

"Joseph Kinkade." He introduced himself with warmth, taking my palm in his firm grasp and shaking it before I'd decided if I wanted to or not. "It's a pleasure to meet you, Eric. Kevin and Scott have a lot of good things to say about you."

"Thanks," I said with hesitation.

I'd been so sure I was being brought up to be lectured and told how things were going to work. Instead, I found Scott entirely at ease, and Kinkade seemed to be content with small talk.

"It's a high compliment," the man continued, releasing me but staying where he was. "I know if Kevin says anything about someone, it's the truth. In the short time since I've met Scott, I've come to realize that about him as well."

Frowning, I furrowed my brow as I glanced at the three of them. "What's going on?" I pressed. "What are you not telling me?"

Kinkade laughed, the sound booming over the chuckles of my brother and elderly friend. "Nothing. Why? Should something be happening?"

Flabbergasted I stared at all of them. "I was brought here at gunpoint, forced to leave the woman I love in a cell upon threats of her death, and now I'm up here. You're seriously going to tell me that nothing is going on?"

Kinkade's smile diminished some as Kevin cleared his throat and Scott stared at his leg.

"We rescued you from the Templars," Kinkade said. "That's all. It was wrong of them to take you from your home in the first place, under the guise of protection. Even more so for the O'Rourke woman to take you all the way to Rome. She stole you not only from your life but your country as well. That doesn't sit right with us here."

Snorting, I took a step back, not believing one word of it. "It doesn't sit right with you—the group that kidnapped Scott and got him involved in a firefight that could have killed him?"

"That was a misunderstanding," Kinkade started, only to be interrupted by Scott.

"The people who took me in Arizona were a rogue group, Eric," he stated. "They had no authority to act in that manner and have been disbanded from the organization for their actions."

"As soon as I heard of the conduct which they had displayed," Kinkade confirmed. "I know it seems like a far stretch, but I am still a very new Grand Master here. The previous authority condoned heathen activity. I do not." Frowning, he went back to his seat, sliding up to his desk and pulling a stack of papers out of a drawer.

"Grand Master?" I questioned. "Like—what's her name—Lucy? The Grand Master of the Templars?"

At the mention of her, Kinkade visibly stiffened, a dark cloud of anger moving across his features. "Lucy Cavanaugh," he confirmed. "The Pretender. It is because of her that myself and my men have been branded Black Knights at all."

When I gave Scott a confused look, he shook his head ever so slightly.

"Cavanaugh tried to steal the treasure for herself," Kevin added, adamant in his accusation. "Started selling it off to the highest bidder under the guise of protecting it by splitting it up. In truth, she doesn't care what happens to any of it. She only wants the money she can get from it."

"That can't be right," I objected. "I mean, sure, there were things for sale in the Mansion, but not all of it. Rebecca told me they move it around to keep it safe. They buy it off black market dealers."

"You can never trust anything a Dog says, Er," Kevin replied, his voice bitter. "Especially one from the inner circle, which is what your girl is."

My anger flared at that, and I glared at him, surprising myself by growling. "Don't call her that," I warned him. "Her name is Rebecca, not Dog. She's also Samantha's great-granddaughter, going back about twelve or thirteen generations. You should show her some respect, if only for that reason."

Kevin's eyes widened in surprise as he looked at his leader for confirmation.

"He'll have told you your friends are the time travelers who used our missing Pandora's Box, of course." Kinkade sighed, rubbing his eyes.

"It's true then?" Kevin pressed. "Rebecca O'Rourke is a descendant of my friend?"

"Yes." The Grand Master met his gaze. "Unfortunately, that isn't going to hold any sway over her sentence."

"Sentence? What sentence?" Panic flooded into my system, the word setting off all kinds of alarms. It made me think of trial and punishment, of things that they had no business involving Rebecca in.

Kinkade looked at me, the tiniest bit of apology in his eyes. "Rebecca O'Rourke has been sentenced to the same punishment as her leader, Lucy Cavanaugh, for participating in treasonous acts—by not protecting the treasures of this world at all costs."

Fuming, I folded my arms. "And what punishment is that?"

His features became stony, anything personable about him disappearing behind a wall of authority.

"Death."

The color drained from my face, the word hanging in the air like a stink that wouldn't go away.

"You can't be serious," I whispered, glancing at Kevin, hoping he would contradict Kinkade's statement. When Scott remained silent, the panic in me burst free.

"No!" I shouted. "She hasn't done anything wrong! You can't have a trial without her present, either, it's not right! She hasn't even had a chance to defend herself!"

"Eric." Kevin shook his head, motioning for me to be quiet, but I couldn't stop.

"Her whole life, she's only done what her dad wanted her to. She doesn't want to be a Templar anymore—she agreed to run with me before Kevin showed up and ruined it all. Rebecca was going to leave The Order on her own." The words poured out of me like a flood, my voice rising as I hurried to the edge of the desk and placed my hands on it, leaning over the top toward Kinkade. "You can't kill her," I refused breathlessly. "It goes against everything you stand for."

The Grand Master snorted, raising an eyebrow. "And how do you know what that is?"

Pausing, I floundered, trying to come up with something. "You want to protect your treasures, don't you? Isn't human life a treasure in and of itself?"

"It's not the same, Eric," Kevin said behind me. "Rebecca O'Rourke was at the very center of the corruption in the Knights Templar. She had an active hand in the executing of it every day."

"No, she didn't!" I insisted, on the verge of complete hysteria as I faced him. "She was their secretary. Her job was a punishment for an accident that got her brother killed. Her father told her straight to her face what a failure she was. I swear, whatever it is you think she's doing, she had no hand in it."

"How would you have access to any of that information?" Kinkade interrupted. "What are your sources?"

"She told me," I stated lamely, facing him once more.

"So, it's her word versus our evidence?" Kevin pressed, not realizing how his question was tearing my heart to shreds.

Focusing on Kinkade, I took a deep breath, trying to calm down enough to articulate what I wanted to say. "She hasn't even had the chance to defend herself," I stated again, well aware of the desperation I'd displayed. "If you have any honor at all, you will recognize how wrong that is."

He pursed his lips and shook his head, standing once more. "You speak of honor as if you know what it is," he started. "But, in truth, you have no idea the depth of the situation you now find yourself in."

Moving around the desk, he pressed a button on the phone in the corner, pausing for a moment as he waited for someone to pick up on the other side.

"Yes, Mister Kinkade?" a female voice said through the speaker.

"Have the car brought around, will you?" he asked in a polite manner. "And have someone help Mister Williams back to his room."

Confused, I glanced at Scott, noting the pale color of his skin and the worry in his eyes. "You're going somewhere?"

"We all are, Mister Ray," Kinkade replied. "Save Scott. His leg won't easily allow him to travel with us yet and I think he would probably appreciate more rest."

"I would, thank you," Scott said, his voice quiet.

"You can visit with him again when we return," he continued. "We shouldn't be gone more than a few hours."

Motioning to the elevator that had brought us up, he opened a panel in the wall, revealing a small closet. Removing a jacket and pulling it on, he strode to the exit, waiting for me and Kevin to join him before pressing the button to take us down.

I'd been shocked into silence. It was as if my initial outburst was the only amount of words I'd been able to come up with to defend Rebecca. We moved downward without stopping, same as the ride up. With each floor we passed, more desperation filled me, until I found myself blinking back tears, surprised further by the reaction. If the other two men noticed, they said nothing, waiting in the quiet for us to reach our destination.

As soon as we made it to the ground floor, there was a flurry of activity around us, making it clear why Kinkade had remained in his penthouse, rather than come down and meet me when I arrived. People swarmed him, handing him papers, asking him questions, confirming information, some of them speaking in languages I didn't understand. Through it all, the Grand Master moved with ease, answering in kind, redirecting people, and signing forms he'd barely glanced over. As we walked by the front desk, he confirmed three appointments with them without stopping, pausing only a moment as the doorman opened the exit to the street for him.

Waiting at the curb was a black town car, the back, passenger side door open and waiting. The driver greeted us all, making small talk with Kevin before shutting us in.

With a start, I realized Kevin wasn't just a Master's Assistant in this place; he was the Grand Master's Assistant. That was why everyone knew him, why they opened doors and sent him wherever he wanted without question. He was the top lackey of the organization, the gopher who did the dirtiest work.

My opinion of him slipped ever so slightly, despite the fact he was my brother.

"Where to today, Mister Kinkade?" the driver asked, his thick Brooklyn accent present in every word. He watched us in his review mirror, the top of his black hat brushing the roof of the car as he waited for an answer.

"The Vault, please, Robert," Kinkade answered.

"You got it, sir."

As the car pulled away from the apartment building, Kevin pressed a button and raised the privacy screen, shutting the driver out of the rest of our conversation.

"Tell me, Eric," Kinkade said, pulling a pair of leather gloves out of his pocket and putting them on.

"How do the Knights Templar work?"

Hesitating, I glanced at the two of them, receiving no help from my brother. "Is this a trick question?"

Kinkade laughed, peering out his heavily tinted window before meeting my stare once again. "No. It's a test of your knowledge of our organization. You seem so sure of how it works, but I wonder if you understand it even a fraction of a percent."

I drew back, frowning as a slight trickle of offense crept over me. However, I recognized this as my chance to gain information I didn't have, and I wasn't about to let it go without a fight. "Templar Knights protect the treasures of the world."

"How?"

Sighing, I leaned back against the seat, watching the cab next to us as we moved with traffic. "It's in vaults, isn't it? Like the one beneath Oak Isle?"

He nodded. "That's how they did it in the past. However, with today's technology, it's not as easy to bury something in the ground and hope that no one ever discovers it. Things that are precious need more protection than that."

Thinking it over, I nodded. "Which is why the Mansion on O Street is—was—filled with artifacts. The knights were keeping the treasure as close as possible, to watch it."

"No." Folding his arms, Kinkade pursed his lips, pausing a beat before continuing. "The Templars you knew were selling the treasures, rather than protecting them. The profit they gained from such sales went to their leaders, padding their pockets until they were wealthy enough to not care about what really mattered."

"Which was what?" I questioned.

"The wealth of the world lies in its history, Eric," Kevin said softly, answering for his master. "Every piece of it, no matter how inconsequential, is important. Somewhere along the line, the Templars lost sight of that. They placed a few items at the highest value and forgot about the rest."

"I don't understand," I confessed. "What items did they think were more important?"

"Every culture has their gods and the relics they left behind," Kinkade replied, picking the explanation back up. "The Greeks had Zeus's lightning bolt, the Aegis, Hercules's headdress, Icarus's melted wings, and so on. Norsemen left us Thor's hammer and belt, magical swords and boats, and the Native Americans hid a treasure they believed their gods would feast upon one day. From the mysterious realms of the unknown to the pyramids in Egypt, each culture has revered a handful of items and kept them safe, until they came into the ownership of the Knights Templar during the crusades. But, above all these, are the artifacts the Templars held most dear. They were things that brought them closer to God and reminded them of their commitment to the cause."

Not following, I shrugged.

"The Holy Grail," Kevin supplied. "A piece of the One True Cross. The Ark of the Covenant. The blood of Christ himself."

Eyes widening, I stayed silent. I knew there were incredible things in the Templar's treasure, but it had never occurred to me that it could be things like *that*. The stories had always been just that to me—stories. To hear that these items not only existed but someone living today possessed them was almost unfathomable.

"All other artifacts fell to the wayside over time," Kinkade continued. "Things that should have never been forgotten and destroyed were. To our knowledge, the cache underneath Oak Isle is the only one that remains unbothered after all these centuries. Until your team almost got into it, that is."

"That's why we need Pandora's Box," Kevin butted in. "So we can go back and stop the corruption from ever happening. Lucy Cavanaugh branded us all as Black Knights, but it was only because members began speaking out about selling off the treasure. In truth, it is she who broke the covenant she made with The Order."

"And what are you planning on doing with all of this treasure?" I asked, not sure if I believed the pair of them yet. The blatant selling and purchasing of items had happened right in front of my eyes, and Rebecca had told me of her trip to buy an object off the black market, but I hadn't witnessed any genuinely greedy people while I was at the Mansion. Not so far as I knew, anyway.

Kinkade smiled, the car rolling to a stop. Not waiting for the driver, he opened the door and stepped outside, answering my question as he did so.

"We're giving it back to the world we stole it from."

Sliding out of the seat, I stepped onto the sidewalk, staring up at an iconic building, one I'd seen in several television shows and movies, making it impossible for me to mistake it for anything else. Past the broad expanse of sidewalk, stone steps paved the way to the center of the long, two-story building, handrails spaced across the area to assist those climbing up. A pair of pillars rested between each of the three arched windows, the glass inside them and in the center doorways catching the afternoon light in a way that made them seem to glow with magic. On top of the pillars, a thick block rested, giving them a Roman feel. But, above the block, there sat stones stacked together in a pyramid shape, as if contradicting the idea of the design's origins. The rooftop peaked every few feet along the edge as well, creating a ruffled sort of pattern that touched the sky. In truth, the edifice was as much a work of art as the things that were inside it.

The outside was swarmed with people as well, a few sitting on the steps, others walking to and from the building with smiles on their faces. Banners under the arched windows detailed exhibits that were on display inside, the sheer magnitude of it all causing a ripple to move over my skin. Glancing back at my companions, I gaped at them, not believing where we had ended up.

"Welcome to the Metropolitan Museum of Art, Eric," Kinkade said, a broad grin covering his face. "Or, as I like to call it, The Vault."

"You keep all of your treasures . . . in a museum?" To say I was surprised was an understatement. How had they kept themselves a secret? Resisted the Templars taking their goods, when it was all right here, on display?

"Of course," Kinkade replied. "This wealth belongs to the world. What better way to give it back to them than through an avenue where it will not only be protected and cared for but provide funds to keep it that way?"

Confused, I glanced at Kevin. "But, this place has

been open since I don't know how long."

"Eighteen-seventy," he supplied, smiling. "There's not much money can't buy, including this place. When we split from the Templars, we took this—and all of New York City—with us."

Thrown off by his use of the word "we," like he had somehow been part of this since its beginning, I shook my head.

"Come," Kinkade said, moving toward the stairs. "Let me show you what your Templars have been throwing away and what we have been fighting to protect."

It was breathtaking. The marble floors, arches, pillars, and every other piece of architecture had been made to truly leave those who laid eyes on it in awe. However, the building itself was nothing compared to the artifacts inside it. Statues, paintings, pottery, clothing, mummies, and a complete Egyptian temple waited for eager patrons to view them. Employees stood by, waiting to answer any questions you might have. Never in a million years would I have thought a place such as this belonged to a secret organization.

Kevin and Kinkade allowed me to view it all uninterrupted, for whatever reason. Perhaps they wanted me to feel the magnitude of it on my own. Maybe they didn't want to speak about their organization out in the open. Either way, I was grateful to be left alone for a time.

Conflict roiled inside me with each step I took. Rebecca's face, locked behind the bars of her prison, kept flashing through my mind, as well as the Grand Master's promise she would soon be put to death. How was no one upset by this? Even Scott had seemed to accept it without question, like it wasn't even worth arguing over.

Besides my own issues, the idea of the Knights Templar and the Black Knights kept throwing me for a loop. How could they both claim to be in the right? It seemed to me that each side had their fair share of secrets and I was certain I'd learned almost none of them. In the back of my mind, I still had a feeling that I should get as far from both organizations as quickly as possible.

But how? Despite their insistence I had been rescued, I knew the Black Knights wouldn't allow me to leave on my own. I was as much a prisoner here as I'd been at the Mansion, only this time it was my brother following me around instead of a beautiful woman.

Rebecca. I cringed again as the knowledge of her current position shot through me. She was trusting me to get her out, to help us all escape, but I had no idea how to do it.

Come Hell or high water. I curled my fingers into a fist as we left the building.

I would get her out. I had to.

"What did you think?" Kinkade asked as soon as we were all back inside the car.

"It's impressive," I admitted. "And everything is well taken care of."

"One of our utmost priorities," he agreed, pleased with my answer.

"I don't understand why you brought me to visit," I confessed. It had felt a little like he was bragging about all the things he'd been able to do, but I knew there was more to it than that.

Nodding, He leaned forward, resting his hands on his knees. "I wanted to prove to you the Templars are not the honor-driven group you believed them to be. Did you ever see their artifacts taken care of the way ours are? Did they hold their relics in high esteem, recognizing each of them as special and unique? No, they did not. They do not, and they will not."

His voice turned gruff as he shook his head and leaned back in his seat. "Lucy Cavanaugh wants to brand my men and me as Black Knights for refusing to bow to her treachery? Fine. We are Black Knights. So long as it distances us from the horrible actions she has taken, I do not care what they call us. Knights protect their treasure, and that is what I am doing."

Raising an eyebrow, I remained silent, knowing my true impressions wouldn't be appreciated by the present company. In my mind, Kinkade was as bad as he was making the Templars out to be. He wasn't giving the world its history back—he was making those who could afford to pay to see it. That wasn't teaching anyone anything out of the goodness of his heart. He was lining his own pocket, even if he was doing it by sharing his artifacts with the more fortunate.

Waving his hand in dismissal when I didn't reply, Kinkade yawned, as if he were bored with the whole affair.

Glancing out the window, I realized we weren't heading the way we'd come from, my stomach twisting in on itself. Rebecca was under the apartment building. If we didn't go back there, how was I going to find her in the maze beneath the city? How would I find the entrance to it?

"Where are we going?" I asked as nonchalantly as possible, glancing at Kevin in the seat beside me.

"You'll be staying with your brother for the time being," Kinkade answered, gazing out at the busy street. "As my extra space is currently occupied by Mister Williams."

Stiffening, I tried to keep my surprise and discomfort from my face but didn't entirely succeed.

"Don't worry," the Grand Master ordered, chuckling some. "We own many buildings in the city. If you want to contact your friend, you only need to have the front desk call him."

Hesitating, Kevin cleared his throat. "What about my classes?"

Kinkade shrugged. "Take him with you. I'll send word to the professors to expect him."

Kevin nodded, relaxing, and leaned back in his seat. "It'll be like at home, right Eric? Us sharing a room, going to school together. All we're missing is a pizza parlor to run."

He laughed, his master joining in and I half-heartedly chuckled, hoping it was enough of an agreement.

While Scott was definitely on my list of worries, Rebecca clouded my every thought. I needed to get back to her, to somehow break her and the other Templars free before they were all subjected to an untimely death.

Even worse, I was afraid they would execute Rebecca and not tell me. She could be dead right now, and I wouldn't know it. They all could be, for that matter. Why would the Black Knights tell me of their workings beneath the city? It was obvious I was a prisoner. The only thing I lacked was a cage.

Well, that wasn't true, either. I *did* have a cage, or rather a babysitter. Kevin was being ordered to keep me with him. Spending that much time with my brother wouldn't have bothered me. But spending time with a man who was practically a stranger? I did have a problem with that.

The more I considered it, the worse my situation seemed to become. I was the Templar's only hope. Scott's only hope.

Rebecca's only hope.

Steeling my nerves, I swallowed hard, folding my arms. There was no other choice.

I was going to have to escape and somehow free them all tonight.

"So . . . this is actually a dorm?"

Surprised, I faced Kevin, having expected his apartment to be an undercover thing, not a resident hall at New York University. We weren't all that far from campus, according to Kinkade. The Third Avenue North Hall was only a ten to fifteen-minute walk from the Washington Square building. Combined with the vast amount of amenities the complex provided— including a courtyard, game room, dining hall, performance space, and more—it was a college kid's dream for a living space.

The apartment itself was very nice, too. There was a kitchen and living space, as well as a shared bathroom and bedroom. Kevin's roommate was gone, but his things were strewn across his unmade bed, marking him as the sloppy one of the pair. On the other side of the small room, my brother's things looked immaculate, arranged neatly and with a clear order. The rest of the apartment had been tidy, too, I remembered, right down to the dishes in the drainer and the covers on the couch. Kevin had never struck me as a neat freak when he lived at home, and I found myself wondering if this place had maid service to clean up after the students.

"Of course it's a dorm. What did you think it was going to be, a Cold War bunker?" Kevin laughed, sitting at the wooden desk at the foot of his bed. As with the rest of the place, his books were stacked in one corner, his papers and pens tucked into a drawer, and an empty wastebasket sat on the side closest to the door. Across the way, the matching desk looked like a small bomb had gone off on it at one point.

Shrugging, I remained where I was, positioned between the two mattresses, turning my attention to the window in the center of the wall. Outside, I could see the courtyard, filled with tables and students milling around, a couple bikes locked into the provided racks. The New York City Skyline stretched out beyond our building, and I was struck with the feeling of being trapped again. It was as if the skyscrapers were the bars of my cell, the world closing in all around me as the light faded from the sky.

"Are you hungry?"

Kevin, not seeming to notice my inner turmoil, went about rearranging his stuff, the sound of a zipper occurring twice, accompanied by a dull thud of a bag full of books hitting the floor.

"I don't know," I answered, the words quiet.

It was hard to think of food when I knew about the prison beneath the city.

Pulling the most recent image I had of Rebecca to mind, I closed my eyes, fighting the thought that it could have very well been the last time I would ever see her. I hated that it was a memory of her locked in a cell.

Pushing away the bars and brick walls around her, I focused on only the woman. Her dark hair had been loose, for once, the curls tumbling down her back and cradling her heart-shaped face like the hands of an angel. Wide, round eyes, eyes that shined like light on the ocean at sunset, watched me, filled with confidence and trust. Pink lips smiled at me, hiding her perfectly white teeth. Her black business suit was a little worse for wear, after being carted from Washington D.C. to Rome and then from Rome to New York City in it, but she still looked stunning. She was the most beautiful woman in the world and the most terrifying all at once—I knew she could kick the crap out of me at any given moment and not break a sweat.

She hadn't fought back when Kevin showed up and took us, though. There'd been no fists flying or kicks delivered as she was shoved into her cell. For some reason, whether she'd known she couldn't win or she didn't want to risk either of us getting hurt, she'd allowed herself to be taken and locked up. She was buried beneath the city, locked in a suffocating box by her worst enemies.

And she was trusting me to get her out.

Clearing my throat, I steeled myself, knowing I had to do something and quick. If I was going to rescue anyone tonight, I needed to figure out how I was going to get down there first.

"Actually," I started. "I am kind of hungry. After we get food, will it be possible at all for me to go see Rebecca and at least let her know Scott and me are okay? I don't know how to get back to headquarters from here, so you're going to have to take me."

Kevin shook his head, distracted by something on his phone. "You don't have to go back to headquarters to get down to the cells. You can get in through any subway or sewage tunnel, you only have to know what you're looking for."

Nodding, I didn't reply. If I asked too many questions, he would realize what I was trying to do. I'd just have to hope I could figure out what to look for while I was down there.

Rising, Kevin left the room, motioning for me to follow. He led the way into the kitchen, grabbing a couple granola bars out of one of the cupboards and tossing one to me.

"Snack on this," he ordered. "We have class in about twenty-five minutes, and then we can go out for dinner. Sound good?"

My nose twitched, annoyance at how long it was going to take to get out of his ever-watchful presence filling me. "Yeah, that's fine."

He paused at the tightness of my voice, raising an eyebrow, and shrugged. "Come on, we've got to go, or we'll be late."

Within moments, we were both on bikes—also provided by the Black Knights, it would seem—and were making our way toward Washington Square. The thought of making a run for it entered my mind more than once, but Kevin seemed to know this, staying close to me and continually checking to make sure I was following. As it was, we were seated in the lecture hall, enjoying a cool bottle of water by the time the professor arrived and began.

He was a small man, with thick-rimmed glasses and a yellow button up shirt that made him look like the silliest of nerds from television. His voice was commanding, filling the space with ease as he arranged all his paperwork across the desk at the front and began writing on the blackboard.

"Welcome to World Mythology," he stated, drawing something beside the word he'd scrawled out. "In continuing with last week's lecture, we will be discussing Roman mythology and the symbolism within it. Now, does anyone know what a *caladrius* is?"

Kevin's hand shot into the air immediately, like Hermione Granger in a potions class.

Startled, I gave him a somewhat surprised and annoyed look, which he ignored.

"Mister Ray." The professor pointed to him, adjusting his glasses as he looked up the curve of the room to my brother.

"The *caladrius* was a bird that lived in the king's household. It was believed to heal the sick and injured by absorbing the sickness into itself and flying away, dispersing the ailment into the wind."

The professor nodded. "Very well put, Kevin. And what kind of bird was it, really?"

Another student raised their hand and was called on.

"It's not known which bird exactly," she answered. "However, due to the all-white color it was said to have, many scholars have suggested it could be the dove."

The professor smiled, gesturing to the blackboard, where he had drawn an outline of a dove. "That is correct."

Class continued much in this manner for the next

hour, myself battling between being completely enthralled by what they were studying and bored out of my mind as I counted the seconds until I could escape. By the end of the lecture, I'd heard more about birds and their place in Roman society than I'd ever cared to.

"Wasn't that great?" Kevin asked as we walked our bikes to a nearby café. "Professor Whitlock has a way of making history come alive."

"Yeah," I replied offhandedly.

As we passed an entrance to the subway, I felt the hair on the back of my neck stand up. This was it. If I was going to escape, I needed to do it now, when Kevin was least expecting it. He was still rattling on about class, staring at a girl as she walked past, her smile flashing in his direction as he nodded his head toward her.

Seizing the opportunity, I turned, shoving my bike against his and almost knocking him over. The clatter created a commotion on the sidewalk, people trying to jump out of the way as the cycles went wild, Kevin stuck in the middle of it.

Breaking into a flat run, I headed for the tunnel, jumping down the stairs, shoving people who cursed at me out of the way. The attendant shouted as I jumped over the turnstile, but I didn't care. A train was waiting at the platform, doors open wide and welcoming me to freedom.

"Eric!"

Kevin's voice echoed through the small, tiled space and I glanced over my shoulder, startled to find him almost right behind me.

The doors on the train began to close, and I pushed

myself to move faster, sliding through them into one of the passengers with a hard smack.

"Watch it, man!" He glared at me, shoving me into another passenger as he shook his head.

"Sorry," I said breathlessly, trying to shrug away from the person who had caught me as we all began moving.

"What the hell, Er," Kevin muttered in my ear, his grip tightening on my arm. "You're going to screw everything up if you can't just trust me for a while!"

Freezing, I blinked in confusion, not understanding what he'd said.

"Come on." Yanking me around, Kevin towed me to the nearest pair of seats. Thankfully, the compartment was empty in the back. As we sat down on the black rows of connected chairs, the conductor said something unintelligible over the speaker, "map" the only word I could pick out among the bunch. There were a couple of them placed along the walls, between the windows and ads, but I didn't care in the slightest.

"What do you mean I'm going to screw everything up?" I asked, dropping my voice when he hushed me and glanced around.

"Look." He sighed. "I couldn't say anything before because they bug all of their buildings, okay? We all have a part to play. I've been doing mine the best I can since I got here."

He might as well have been as muddled in his speech as the driver.

"What are you talking about?" I pressed, a brief blossom of hope blooming in my chest as I watched him.

This man looked and sounded more like my brother. He'd kept secrets from me—more than I'd thought—but there was something about the way he was behaving and speaking now that felt familiar.

"Are you not a Black Knight?" I asked, not willing

to wait for him to answer my previous question. "Are you a Templar? What plan do you have? How can I help? Are you going to break everyone out?"

Holding his hand up, Kevin hushed me again, his eyes flashing dangerously. "Will you be quiet?" he hissed, gaze darting around the train like he expected someone to burst from the wall and shoot us. "I'll answer your questions. And for God's sake, keep your voice down. Kinkade has spies everywhere. I'd expect him to have someone following me, especially since your arrival." Smirking, he punched me in the shoulder. "But we've lost them now, what with you running off like that."

Shrugging, I didn't know what to say. All I wanted was for him to answer my damn questions and say he would help me get Rebecca out of here.

Sensing my impatience, he swallowed, looking around the space one more time before continuing. "I am a Black Knight, but I'm not loyal to them."

"So you're a Templar spy?"

He shook his head. "No. *Caladrius* is the only organization that holds my loyalty."

Raising an eyebrow, I folded my arms. "You mean the bird from your class?"

Chuckling, he leaned forward, his voice so soft I almost couldn't hear him. "The bird is the symbol of the organization. We consider it poetic."

"Why?" I considered what I'd learned at the university as he watched me, a grin on his face. "The bird steals sickness and heals the people it afflicted," I said. "So you're . . . stealing something from the Black Knights?" It popped together in less than a second after that. "Stealing their treasure?"

Kevin nodded in excitement. "Just as the caladrius healed those who were sick in the past, we heal them today—from the infection of greed."

My mind raced, absorbing the information he was giving me. "How?" I pressed. "Won't they catch you? Lump you in with the Templars?"

"It would be best if they did, should we ever be caught," he confessed. "Caladrius has members in both sects. We consider ourselves the True Knights. If captured, we go to the grave to protect the secret."

Raising an eyebrow, I frowned. "Then why are you telling it to me?"

Scooting closer, he smiled, enthusiasm rolling off him. "Professor Whitlock's drawing of the dove? That's the signal. Tonight, Caladrius will storm the tunnels beneath the city and free all the Templars. We can't continue to operate as we have if the Black Knights think their enemy is defeated. We'll be discovered in a manner of days. Plus, we have members who were captured and are locked away. We can't leave them to die if we can help it. And we can."

Relief filled me in an instant. "I want to come," I demanded, standing in my eagerness to get off the train and do something right then.

"Whoa, slow down," he stated seriously, grabbing my hand and pulling me back into my seat. "You can't go down there right now. Kinkade gave me strict instructions not to let you out of my sight."

"You're not going?"

For the first time, his eyes darkened somewhat. "No. I can't blow my cover. It was a stroke of pure luck that Kinkade picked me to be his assistant. We've never been able to get another spy in at that high of a level with the Black Knights."

Leaning back in his seat, he sighed, as if the weight of the world were on his shoulders. "I think Kinkade was hoping I'd be able to tell him something about the Treasure Pit he didn't know. They want whatever's down there, Er. That's why they've treated me so good. I'm the only inside man they have for that job. We have to protect it from them. Somehow, we need to get down there and move it, before the Templars or the Black Knights can get their hands on it."

"That's great," I replied, brushing all that to the side. "But what about tonight's raid? I have to be there, Kev. If only to make sure Rebecca makes it out okay."

As soon as I said her name, his expression fell, and his gaze turned toward the floor. A sense of despair washed over him, making the brightly lit train feel dim for a brief moment.

"She's really Sam's granddaughter?"

Pausing, I realized this was the first time he was able to talk to me about it. He'd been playing his part, as he put it, and was forced to set aside the knowledge of his friends for the time being.

"Yes," I answered.

"And Mark's?"

Surprised, I shook my head. It hadn't occurred to me that he would think they were together like that. But, if I ended up stuck in another time and only knew one other person from my own . . . I could see where the idea could start.

"She married a man from that period. His name was Tristan. He was a pirate and a Templar." Thinking back to the letters I'd read at Scott's and the things I'd learned about the pair from Rebecca, I felt confident adding the next part. "She was happy with him."

"What about Mark?" He cleared his throat, the talking about his departed friends choking him up.

"I don't know," I confessed. "He was with them, but I don't know if he ever got married or had kids or anything. He became a Templar, too. Rebecca said they all played critical roles in the history of the Knights."

Meeting my stare once again, he smiled. "You're in love with her, aren't you?"

"Yes," I answered without hesitation or doubt. The realization may have come on suddenly, but I'd done nothing but reaffirm my feelings to myself since our forced split.

"I could see it on your face the moment I first saw the two of you together," he confessed, laughing. "Sorry about breaking that up, by the way. If I'd known you two were making out, I would have knocked first."

Blinking, I sat back in my seat, folding my arms. I felt like I had whiplash from all of Kevin's different behaviors. For the past two days, he'd been acting like a different man, causing me to question our whole relationship. Now he was back to teasing me and speaking as the brother I'd known my entire life.

"I'm going down there," I told him, focusing once again on my end goal. "I don't care what you have to tell Kinkade. If she's going, so am I."

Exhaling, he rubbed his face, sitting up straight. "I know. I insisted on being the person to kidnap you for the same reason. You're my brother, and I love you, Eric. I couldn't let anything happen to you, despite trying to stay in good standing with Kinkade."

He fell silent for a moment, the only sound between us that of the train flying over the tracks below.

"Kinkade be damned," he finally muttered, standing as we slowed to a stop. "We're both going. That's Sam's family down there, and we're going to save them for her."

My palms were sweating too much to keep a good grip on the gun I held. Tightening my grasp, I tried to breathe slowly, the beat of my heart screaming in my ears.

It was dark in the tunnels now, only the most needed lights glowing. It gave the prison an almost haunted feel. Now and then, I could hear a train rumble by in the distance, dust shaking from the ceiling onto our heads as water dripped somewhere.

Ahead of me, Kevin peered around the corner, using a penlight to signal to someone on the other side of the shaft. After a few moments, he grunted in frustration, looking behind both of us and trying the light in that direction.

"What's going on?" I whispered, attempting to remember the four quick fighting moves he'd shown me over the past five hours. With any luck, I wouldn't get destroyed when we ran into the guards.

"Something's wrong," he whispered back fiercely. "There are more guards on duty than there should be and the prisoners that were sharing cells are all in individual lockups."

"They know we're coming?" Fear spiked through

me, and I gripped the weapon harder, glancing over my shoulder as I wondered if someone watched us at this very moment. It was no secret I was a terrible shot, and the odds of me remembering how to punch or kick anyone well enough to get out of this alive were slim. There was no chance I was going to chicken out and run, though. Not without Rebecca.

"I don't know." He squeezed his eyes shut, rubbing his temple, and let out a long breath. Staring at me, he pressed his lips into a thin line, the executive decision on his face before he said anything. "Get ready," he ordered, flashing his penlight in both directions, the same message beaming out in quick succession. "We're going in."

Without another word, he raised his pistol and dashed around the corner, the sound of his boots on the concrete echoing through the tube.

A gunshot sounded up ahead, followed by the cry of the man it had hit, and the entire area burst into sound and light.

Blinking, I tried to adjust my vision to the sudden influx, the bright, incandescent lights overhead buzzing with life as they revealed the small group of soldiers invading the cell block.

Well, a small group of soldiers and me.

Up ahead, three guards ran toward Kevin and me, causing my panic rate to increase exponentially. It felt like I was going to have a heart attack and die before any actual clashing took place.

Remember the plan.

Kevin's words echoed in my mind, time slowing for a moment, my breath noisily moving through my head. Still, I could remember what needed to happen, the instructions the only source of comfort I had at the moment.

The block is one straight wall of cells, all of them on the right side. We'll attack from three points: both ends and the middle. You and I have the center.

Right, we had the middle. Kevin's contacts with Caladrius had been more than happy to add us to the sting because they needed more than one man in each spot. Rebecca fell in the center section as well, which meant I could personally make sure she made it out alive.

Kinkade and the other Black Knights will be gathering for a weekly meeting in their Temple, beneath Saint Patrick's Cathedral. That means most of the members will be several miles away and fewer guards at the checkpoints. Three checkpoints, three guards, ten of us, max. We'll be in and out before they know what's happened.

But, there were three times the guards there should have been, making us the outnumbered ones, not them. What did it mean? Were we discovered? Was the entire force of Black Knights waiting to discard us like a used tissue?

Kinkade isn't expecting me at the Temple tonight, because I'm watching you—and I know the code to unlock all the cells. Even better, there is a remote open button in the guard shack. Once we have the sentinels taken care of, we can clear all the chambers at once and make a run for it. You take Rebecca and go with the others. I'll get Scott and meet you at the rendezvous.

Rendezvous. I could do that. I could wrestle an entire brigade of expertly trained warriors, break open a hundred cells, rescue the woman I loved, and meet up with yet another secret organization who could claim they saved me.

Not.

As the guards ran toward us, I knew the time for doubt and hesitation was over. I'd promised Rebecca I would get her out and I'd do it now or die trying.

Aiming the best I could, I fired one round, gasping in surprise when it hit the far right guard in the shoulder. I'd been targeting for the one on the left, but I'd take anything I could get at this point.

It wasn't enough to stop the man, a grimace covering his face as he jerked back but kept running toward us all the same.

Kevin shot then, three rounds in quick succession, dropping the woman that had been on the left.

One down, two to go.

Swallowing hard, I fired again and missed completely, the bullet ricocheting off the concrete.

They reached Kevin first, a fist fight of epic proportions breaking out as they wrestled over each other's guns and tried to gain the upper hand. It was almost like an out of body experience, seeing it all happening in front of me, zooming closer and closer until I realized it was my own feet carrying me toward the fray, a crazy shout of determination on my lips.

Whacking the closest guard with the butt of my firearm, I dropped him to the floor, following up with a kick to his face. Blood spurted out of his nose as it crunched beneath the force of my foot, and he made a half gurgling, half maniac sound as he grabbed me around the ankle and pulled me down with him.

Stars exploded in my vision as my head bounced

on the ground, my attacker continuing to pull me toward him, getting on his hands and knees as his blood seeped into the leg of my pants. Panicked, I kicked again, bending one of his fingers back at an odd angle.

Howling, he jerked away, grasping the wound, looking like an undead zombie as blood continued to pour from his nose, down his face, and all over his gray, uniformed shirt. Reaching for me, his hands closed around my neck, squeezing as he lifted me up and slammed my head into the ground again.

"Use the gun, Er!" Kevin shouted from somewhere overhead. "Shoot him! *Shoot him!*"

Struggling for air, I gasped, hands trembling on my firearm. I turned it around, hoping it was pointing the right direction. All I could think was that I needed air and to get out from underneath my captor somehow. He banged my head on the ground again, and my vision went black for a few seconds, the back of my head stinging as it scraped across the concrete, skin splitting open.

Kevin was still screaming, unable to come to my aid.

It occurred to me that I had never killed a man before.

The sound of a pistol firing echoed through space and the man towering over me jolted. For a beat, nothing happened. He only stared at me, dripping blood into my already hazy vision as his hold on my neck loosened. Then, he toppled over, his lifeless body bleeding out onto the floor.

Breathing heavily, I shoved him aside, throwing the pistol by the wall with him. I couldn't even remember pulling the trigger; it had happened so fast.

My head spun, pounding and screaming at me as I reached back and touched the spot where it had split open near the crown of my head. It was a small cut, thankfully, but I felt like someone was digging their fingers into my skull, ripping the skin apart.

Suddenly, my stomach heaved, and I threw up the tiny bit of food I'd eaten ahead of time. The action pulled at my wound more, and another wave of stars passed through my vision before I was able to sit up and clear my throat.

Glancing over to Kevin, I saw him still wrestling with the last guard, a significant cut on his cheek. They seemed pretty evenly matched, blocking and jabbing at each other. Finally, the guard stumbled slightly, giving Kevin the opening he needed.

He grabbed the Black Knight by the hair, shoving his head into the bars of the cell in front of them repeatedly until the man's body went limp and crumpled to the floor.

Nodding, Kevin sucked in a breath, wiping at his cut and staring at the blood from it on the back of his hand before jerking his head toward the guard shack down the row. "This way."

He hurried toward the small cut out in the wall, flinging the door open and going inside before I'd gotten to my feet.

"Eric?"

Freezing, I turned toward the sound, back the way I'd come. "Rebecca?"

She was a few cells back, her body pressed against the bars as she tried to see where I sat, one hand reached out to me.

A buzzer sounded as all the cell doors opened at once, swinging out into the wall in unison and setting a flood of people free.

Struggling to my feet, I pushed through the stream of bodies running down the tunnel, following Kevin's instructions as he waved them toward the other end of the cell block. They all knew they had to get out as soon as possible, or risk capture again.

I didn't care, though. There was only one person I wanted to see.

Suddenly, she was there, throwing her arms around me and kissing my bloody face as she held me to her.

"This was a stupid plan," she said over and over again, layering kisses across my lips. "Why would you do something like that?"

Wrapping my arms around her waist, I hugged her, feeling like I could take a full breath at last.

"We gotta go, Eric!"

Turning, I nodded to Kevin. The rest of the prisoners were disappearing around the bend in the tunnel, headed toward the abandoned subway station that would lead them all to freedom. The train waiting there would at least get us off the island and to the rendezvous point.

"You good?" my brother asked, concern on his features as he watched me, held up by Rebecca.

"I'm good," I replied thickly, my voice cracking as the soreness from my strangling took over.

"I'll get him out," Rebecca added, tightening her hold on me.

"And I'll get Scott," he agreed.

She nodded, grabbing my hand and pulling me

along in the direction we needed to go as Kevin ran toward the stairs that would take him to the headquarters building and Scott.

"Kevin?" Rebecca called before he disappeared.

He turned, a questioning expression on his face.

"Thank you," she said quietly.

The train took us to Queens, subtly slipping onto the open tracks and joining the rest of the subway system. Caladrius must have had their connections in the city, too, because the sudden presence of an extra machine on the line caused no problems. When the rail had gone as far as it could, we all disembarked our cars and got on an actual, above ground freighter. It felt like we were fugitives from a horrible war, running to a place where we could find peace. In a way, that's what we were. I knew we were lucky—the rescue could have been a lot worse. Without Kevin's help, it would have been a disaster.

As the night hours rolled by, I filled Rebecca in on what happened during our time apart. After a while, I found myself nodding off, resting my injured head on her shoulder. The worry I felt for Kevin and Scott was now my primary focus with her back at my side, but I had no way to reach either of them and make sure they had made it out alive. As it was, I was left with the gentle sway of the train and my love to comfort me, the entire group quiet as our journey continued.

We arrived in the Adirondack Mountains the next morning, finding the heavily forested area covered in a fresh coat of snow. It was an untouched wonderland, one we followed our Caladrius companions through without question. The Templars among us didn't enquire as to where they were headed, giving us more of a refugee feeling.

On and on we trudged, hiking up the mountains, shivering through the cold. Many of us didn't have jackets and those that did rotated them between users, sharing what little warmth they could. Just when I believed I wouldn't be able to go any further without something to warm us all up, the entrance to a mine shaft appeared, accompanied by a group of people welcoming us inside.

Clutching Rebecca's icy fingers in my own, I stumbled inward, shuffling down the long shaft until we reached a more massive cavern. Crates stacked around the walls, lanterns lit here and there, and several other mine shafts led off in different directions. In one corner of the space, someone was offering food and hot drinks, the entire room a camp for us escaped prisoners.

"Would you like a blanket?"

Turning toward the feminine voice, I stared at her, not comprehending.

"I can look at your head, too, if you'd like. You've taken quite the beating."

"That would be wonderful," Rebecca answered for me, her voice weary. "Has anyone else returned besides our train yet?"

The woman shook her head. "We don't get much reception out here," she said apologetically, "and this was a sting mission. There won't be any news until Peter's heard from all the agents he sent in."

Something about that name stirred my memory, and I held up a hand, stopping her. "Peter?"

"Peter Smith," she answered. "The leader of Caladrius."

"*What?*" Rebecca gaped at her. "Are you sure?"

The woman laughed. "Positive. Do you know him?"

Rebecca snorted. "I'm the secretary for The Order. Of course I know him."

The woman's eyes widened, and she examined the two of us with a new understanding. "Rebecca O'Rourke?"

"That's correct. This is Eric Ray."

"Oh!" Clasping the blanket to her chest, she motioned for us to follow her, turning and starting toward one of the other mine shafts. "Come with me. Peter will want to see you both right away."

Exchanging a glance, Rebecca and I both kept our surprise silent. Peter Smith hadn't seemed to like me when I met him, and it was pretty obvious he hadn't cared for her either. The fact that we were going somewhere now that our names were known was suspicious at best.

"I thought Peter was a Black Knight," I whispered as we made our way down the tunnel, making sure not to let our guide hear. "He was acting really strange before the explosion at the Mansion. I assumed he was in on it."

"I did, too, after you told me about that," she agreed. "But you didn't see him while we were in the city, did you?"

I shook my head. "No one said anything about him. I'd almost forgotten he existed."

She pondered this for a moment, a small frown gracing her face, causing her forehead to wrinkle. "If he's the leader of Caladrius, that means they were in on the explosion as well and didn't do anything to stop it. They let it happen."

"Why?"

Sighing, she shrugged. "I don't know. I suppose we'll have to ask him ourselves."

Our guide stopped a few feet in front of us, gesturing to what looked like another small shaft with light coming through it. "Right through here," she said confidently. "I'm sure Peter'll be more than happy to hear you made it out alive."

Not liking how stale the air felt down here or how the walls seemed to close in around me, I nodded, towing Rebecca behind me as we went on without our guide. After a moment, this shaft opened into a cavern as well, though it was much smaller than the first. Lantern hooks dug into the stone walls, electric lamps hanging from them and making the space almost as bright as it was outside. Supply crates also lined the edges of the area here, leaving room for one round table in the center.

Standing beside it was Peter, his head bent over several pieces of paper in his hands. He'd abandoned his smart business suit for suitable weather attire, the fur cuffs on his boots and jacket making him look like he was settling in for the long haul. At the sound of our footsteps, he turned, smiling when he saw the pair of us.

"Ye're alive!" he exclaimed in his thick, Australian accent, setting his things down. "I'd assumed the both of ya dead in the bombing until Kevin told me he was going to get ya."

"Yeah. It was nice of you to not warn anyone about that," I answered coldly. "You could have saved a lot of people from dying, you know."

His grin faltered at that, showing he at least had the decency to look somewhat ashamed of his actions. "I wanted to warn everyone after Kevin told me what the Black Knights were planning." Clearing his throat, he resumed a more business-like approach. "I knew if I let it slip, we wouldn't be able to stay in operation. As much as I hate to admit it, Caladrius needed that bomb as much as the Black Knights did."

"How could that possibly be true?" Rebecca interjected. "If your so-called mission is to rescue the treasure, you did nothing but blow it to pieces." She stared at him in disappointment. "All of that history and knowledge is gone. It's destroyed, because of people like you."

Peter smiled, moving around to the other side of the table from us. "I always thought ya would be a good candidate for recruitment, Rebecca," he said easily. "But I knew with yer past, and the position yer father held, it was too risky a venture. Then, at least."

Confused, she raised an eyebrow. "You wanted me to join your group?"

He laughed, nodding. "Aye, I did. Lucy never did appreciate yer full potential, but I could see it right from the start."

She looked somewhat taken aback, her gaze flicking toward me as if this were strange behavior.

"I want to show ya something," he announced, stepping beside one of the stacks of supply boxes. "If ye'll let me?"

She nodded hesitantly, gripping my fingers. "What is it?"

He grinned again, and for a moment I thought he was going to open one of the boxes. Instead, he pushed the whole lot of them aside, revealing a hidden tunnel that stretched out into the darkness. Grabbing the lantern off the hook beside him, he crooked his finger, motioning for us to follow him.

A feeling of great importance passed through me as a soft current of air from the hidden shaft moved past me. Whatever was down there, it was huge. And I had a feeling I knew what it was.

Rebecca, appearing to be on the same current as I was, moved forward, following him with caution, her fingers still wrapped in mine.

Peter, moving on with confidence, continued to address us over his shoulder. "The Knights Templar of old had one goal alone: to find and protect the treasures of the world. Everything was of equal importance in their eyes, no one religion holding sway over another. They knew the gods of old, and the new gods were all true, some the same. So, whenever they came across something of value and importance, they buried it away, to protect it."

He glanced back momentarily, as if making sure we were still behind him, and continued. "However, they also understood that such a treasure was too great for any one man to possess, or one organization. For that reason, they split the items up, hiding them all over the world. Only the Grand Master knew each location, and he could only discover it by the use of a unique, encoded map.

"Over the centuries, as technology advanced, the map became ineffective. Instruments could detect the caches from the sky or by merely testing the soil. The Knights believed they needed to reclaim the treasure from its hiding places, bring it all together, and protect it in new ways. At the same time, new artifacts were being created every day, as the world continued to grow and mature. Things that were once considered holy had long been stricken from earthly records, forming a portion of the treasure that seemed unneeded in the eyes of its protectors. This was how so much of the cache came to be sold, ruined, and lost.

"Enter Lucy Cavanaugh and Joseph Kinkade." A hint of bitterness crept into his tone as he spoke of the opposing masters, his dislike for them evident. "Both good in their way. Both bad in many others. For years, I stood by and watched them destroy our treasure. Sold for profit. Put on display to line their pockets. I'd joined The Order to protect my heritage, not see it auctioned off to the highest bidder. So I decided to do something about it."

"You formed Caladrius," I stated, shaking my head. "An organization that would keep it from them both."

"Yes." Stopping, he turned to face us, the outline of a door in the wall behind him. "I began gathering like-minded people to do what we promised in the first place. We needed the Mansion bombed to clear the air. If the Templars and Black Knights think they're the only ones in the fight, they won't be searching for the third man. Many of the people who were a scourge to the cause were wiped out. As sad and vulgar as that seems, it needed to happen." Frowning at our shocked and disgusted expressions, he shook his head. "The treasure comes first. Always."

"That makes no sense," Rebecca argued again. "Because you blew up the artifacts inside the mansion, not to mention the records of The Order. How much history did you sacrifice so you could keep pretending you're the good guy?"

"That and Lucy Cavanaugh is here, in your mine," I said in an off-hand manner. "We rescued her with the other prisoners."

He smiled, shaking his head. "Did ya?"

Pausing, I glanced at Rebecca, suddenly realizing I'd not seen the Grand Master at all during our trip.

"She's not here," Rebecca said, horror dawning on her face. Facing Lucy's former second-in-command, she almost shrieked at him. "We left her behind?"

He cleared his throat, a pained expression in his eyes. "No. Lucy was hung in the Black Knight's Temple last night during the escape. We had hoped to save her and send her back to her people, but it was too late. When we heard of the execution time, we decided we would rescue the others during it."

Rebecca took a step back. "You traded her life for all of ours?" The anger grew in her tone with every word until she was shouting at him, the betrayal in her voice striking me. "What about The Order? The rest of the treasure? Any of the oaths you swore when you became a member?"

Straightening, Peter ran a hand through his hair, pursing his lips. "I've kept every oath I made," he said confidently. "And as for yer treasure—here."

Pulling a key from his pocket, he inserted it in the door behind him. The lock turned over with an audible click, and he pulled on the cumbersome entrance, revealing the black room beyond. Stepping inside, he ushered us along, letting the darkness consume us as he moved around, searching for something. When he found it, at last, there was another click, and a flurry of bulbs turned on overhead, lighting the most magnificent sight I'd ever seen.

The cavern was vast, perhaps as wide as the base of the mountain it was concealed in. Electric lights were wired through the space, humming as the sound of a generator buzzed from somewhere in the room. Pathways laid out on a grid system stretched down rows and rows of crates, statues, boxes of gold coins, shelves of parchment, and every other type of artifact I could imagine. Ahead, I could see a statue of an Egyptian pharaoh, arms crossed over his chest as he held his staff. Across the aisle, a case of what looked like Greek and Roman masks sat, displaying the intricately designed faces.

With slow steps, I walked into the cache, gazing at the wonders of the world, buried here in the mountain. Some sections were empty, no indication of what was supposed to reside there. Others were missing pieces that were represented by pictures or descriptions of the artifact. The sheer amount of it all made my heart flutter with excitement, to think of the knowledge and history contained here.

"My missing files," Rebecca said quietly behind me.

Turning, I found her bent over a stack of boxes labeled "Records of The Order of the Knights Templar—Mansion on O Street." Immediately, my eyes went to the painting of my friend Samantha and her husband, on display beside the documents.

"They didn't destroy them," Rebecca continued, her voice catching somewhat. "They've saved everything. The artifacts from inside, the records . . . somehow, they got it all."

"We'd been switching the real things out for fakes for a while before the bombing," Peter supplied, still standing beside the door. As we looked back at him, he grinned. "Like I said. The treasure comes first."

A figure appeared in the doorway behind him, and he turned to greet whoever it was, leaving Rebecca and me to continue perusing.

"So many empty spaces," she muttered. "They intend to bring it all here, don't they?"

"I think so," I agreed.

"To protect it."

She sounded conflicted and in awe at the same time. I knew, whatever she'd been expecting to find down here, this was not it. At least, not this much.

Retaking her hand, I smiled reassuringly. "It looks that way."

"Great news!" Peter called from the entrance, moving toward us as his messenger left. "Kevin made contact. He and Scott made it out before the shit hit the fan. They should be here in a couple of hours."

Relief filled me, and I sighed, the weight of their fates lifting off my shoulders.

"Is that what I think it is?" Rebecca suddenly piped in, pointing to something behind me.

Turning, I looked at the grainy photograph. Taken from a security camera, the still appeared to be the backside of a hotel lobby desk. Someone had zoomed the image in on a box beneath the counter, revealing an old looking vase covered in Greek markings.

"Pandora's Box," I breathed.

Facing Peter, my eyes widened. "Caladrius isn't the one who stole it from the hotel in Arizona?"

Pursing his lips, Peter frowned. "No. We thought

it was the Black Knights."

"And they said it was still missing," I added, a completely new sense of dread filling me. "That means, if you don't have it, they don't have it, and the Templars don't have it—"

Rebecca inhaled sharply, catching on at once. "There's someone else who knows what it is and could use it."

"Which means it isn't safe," Peter added, also understanding my meaning.

Shaking my head, I looked around at everything once more, swallowing the lump in my throat. I wanted so badly for this whole ordeal to be over already, but my conscience wouldn't allow it now.

"We have to find it," I stated. "Find it and keep anyone from ever getting it again."

"Peter!"

One of the men I'd seen ushering the refugees into the mountain burst through the doorway, out of breath and with a red face, his expression one of confusion, uncertainty, and awe.

"What is it?" Caladrius's leader turned, frowning and folded his arms.

The man bent over, putting his hands on his knees, trying to catch his breath. When he was finally able to string more than two words together, he shook his head, straightening. "You're never going to believe who showed up on one of our surveillance cameras in Maine."

He removed a tablet from inside his jacket and offered it to Peter, licking his lips as he shrugged.

Peter's eyebrows rose in a flash, his nose wrinkling as his frown deepened. "Is that who I think it is? How is that possible?"

The messenger made a motion halfway between a nod and a shrug, his eyes flicking toward me.

"Who is it?" I asked, almost dreading the answer. I didn't like thinking about bad things happening in my home state. No doubt, they were probably in my hometown, too, sniffing around where they shouldn't be.

Peter turned to face me again, holding the tablet out.

Surprised, I took it from him, turning the pad around so I could look at the picture right side up. In an instant, my fingers tightened around the screen, knuckles turning white, and I all but pressed my nose on the glass, straining to find something that would explain what I was seeing. There was nothing to suggest the photo was fake, though. The image on the screen was real.

It felt like my heart stopped in my chest as I stared at it, frozen.

"Eric?" Rebecca's hand rested on my shoulder, pulling me away from the photo. "What is it?"

Swallowing hard, I turned the screen toward her. "It's Mark," I said hoarsely.

"What?" Snatching the tablet, she examined the photo as well, confusion and concern on her face. "Are you sure it's him?"

"It's him," I stated breathlessly. "No doubt about it. Mark's come home from the past."

Samantha O'Rourke
1700

The wind blew through my hair softly, brushing the wayward strands of my plait against my cheeks. Inhaling, I closed my eyes, savoring the scent of salt in the air and allowing my body to adjust itself to the sway of the ocean waves beneath us. It had been some time since I'd been on a ship, especially one of this size, and it was apparent my sea legs had gone on vacation.

All those past voyages had been worth it, without a doubt. Whenever I went over all the things that had transpired over the last five years, I knew I wouldn't have changed the path my life had taken at all. I may have traveled through time and fallen in love with a pirate and Templar Knight, but it had brought me my beautiful baby boy. Even with the painful memories I'd gathered— precisely concerning our nemesis, Thomas Randall, and his place in our suffering—there was never a second thought given to whether or not I should have gone a different way.

Still, standing here now, it was hard not to admit I would miss the life I'd lived for the last year. It was a quiet one, uneventful and perfect.

Staring at the Irish coast, I rested my hands on the smooth railing, brushing my fingers over the gold inlay. Rigging stretched up on either side of me, the formerly white ropes now brown from use and almost constant sunlight. Beside the salt from the sea, I could smell tar and gunpowder, the deck freshly sealed and cannons anchored every few paces, already loaded and ready for combat should the need arise. The boatswain's whistle sounded, followed by the clanging of a bell, and the great, white sails overhead tumbled down, catching the air and filling in a mere moment. With a gentle tug, we began to move with more speed, leaving the harbor.

Tristan, my husband, sang a quiet song behind me. His voice rose and fell with the water, carrying on the air in a whisper filled with love. While not the most practiced man, I enjoyed the executing of it, smiling to myself as the Gaelic nursery rhyme continued to entertain those who heard it.

Turning, I looked across the dark wooden planks, catching sight of him on the steps leading from the bowels of the vessel. His black boots were scuffed, a few specks of fresh tar stuck to the sides, tan breeches and white shirt still mostly clean, if not a bit wrinkled after the ride from our seaside cottage to the main harbor. In his lap, our son sat, giggling as Tristan clapped the boy's hands together, playing with him.

A wide grin covered my face. My boys were handsome. Anyone with eyes could see that. There was something about watching Tristan as a father that was insanely attractive, too. Every time I saw him with our Michael, I felt like I was swooning, falling in love with him all over again. All I wanted to do was run my hands over his firm muscles and taste his sweet lips.

However, finding time to be alone had proven difficult with a child. We took our moments where we could, but it was never enough.

Then again, I never had enough as it was. Our year in Ireland had been the honeymoon we never got, in many ways. Now, heading back into the mess the Knights Templar had created, I felt as if the wind were changing again in our lives, pulling us apart once more.

There was one thing I was always certain of, though. I was his, he was mine, and we'd created a son to share. If every bad thing that had occurred in the last five years came back full force in our future, I would still be happy for that one reason alone.

Stepping away from the railing, I chuckled, moving toward them as the busy crew of the boat continued to work around us. The skirt of my plain dress swirled over the deck, picking up tar flecks of its own, but I didn't mind. Much to my surprise, I'd come to find such outfits relaxing, despite the horrible stays I had to wear with it. The clothes I'd worn in Ireland weren't bulky like the gowns I'd had in Paris, built with a million layers. After a few weeks, I found myself preferring them to my pants and vests, especially when my baby bump grew more pronounced. After I'd delivered, I seemed to do better in the dress, too, and so I'd kept wearing them, accepting my part as a woman of the past.

"Come here," I said with a sweet voice, holding my hands out for the baby as I stopped in front of the pair.

Standing, Tristan passed the child to me, ruffling his short, black hair with affection. It raised off his head like a bird trying to take flight, the mop never entirely tamed, no matter what I attempted to do to it.

Gathering my son into my embrace, I kissed his

chubby cheek, snuggling the round, little man.

"He's doing well on the water?" I asked, a bit of hesitation in my voice as I tucked a hair behind my ear.

"Of course he is," Tristan assured me. "He's an O'Rourke! We were built for the sea, weren't we, Michael?" Chuckling, he leaned in and tickled his son's chin, grinning as the baby laughed and reached out for him.

Sighing dramatically, I gave the boy back to his father, laughing. "Fine," I said to the baby. "Stay with your dad."

Tristan grinned, taking Michael and kissing him. "We love ye, Ma," he said, a heavy dose of teasing in his tone as he looked back at me.

Rolling my eyes as I smiled, I turned back to the view. Ignoring the pang in my chest as the island slipped into the distance, I hummed the same tune Tristan had been singing to the boy, reaching out and putting my fingers in his embrace with one hand and toying with the white stone of my necklace with the other. An air of foreboding hung around me, my mind unable to quiet the nervous inklings that filled it.

Sensing my apprehension, Tristan adjusted his grasp on the baby, wrapping his free arm around my waist and pulling me close.

"We'll be okay, right?" I asked quietly, fear seeping into my words.

He hummed in the back of his throat, his nervousness showing for a split second. "Ye know I'll do whatever it takes to keep ye safe."

"I know." Pausing for a moment, I let the sounds of the riggers calling to one another fill the air, accompanied by a few cries from the mainland birds. I had more I wanted to say, the number of things on my mind like a tidal wave coming in to destroy everything else. However, there was only one thing I was uneasy about right then. "What about Michael?" I finally asked, my voice trembling.

Tristan hugged both of us tighter, and I felt more than saw his smile as the baby cooed against his shoulder. "Randall is out there, waiting for us," he answered. "His branding of Cal only proves that. He must have done something in Paris, too, for The Order to send for us. The snake wants to fight, and he is willing to do whatever it takes to make us comply, even if it means hurting a baby. We will simply have to trust that our son is safe in our care."

"We can't take Michael with us," I responded, my voice rising as I realized what he was saying. "It's not safe!"

What was he thinking? We couldn't take a child into battle! He couldn't live on a pirate ship or traipse across countrysides! He was only three months old, for God's sake. I was still breastfeeding him the majority of the time, too. What if the stress caused me to stop producing milk? Michael could starve to death if he weren't lost at sea, taken by animals, kidnapped, or killed by someone first.

That train of thought affected me the way it would any mother, and I promptly started crying, blinking and sniffing as I tried to get the reaction under control.

Tristan held me tighter, kissing the top of my head as I leaned into him, my mind swirling with worry. "He's not protected without us, lass," he whispered, brushing his fingers across my waist. "If Randall knew he was left behind—"

77

"He'd swoop in and take him like he did to me." The icy edge in my tone made Michael fuss, and I moved to soothe him, taking him from Tristan and kissing the top of his head while I rocked him back and forth.

Grimacing, I bit my lip, feeling another onslaught of tears trying to break free. Yes, Thomas Randall had kidnapped my unborn child and me. Unfortunately, I was the only one who made it back home. Who was to say the bastard wouldn't try and steal another baby from me? I'd believed we'd managed to rid ourselves of him at last, when Tristan became excommunicated from The Order of the Knights Templar for disobeying orders, and they took the villain into their possession. I wasn't even sorry for the shame it had brought to our name. All I wanted was to be done with the monster and move on with my life.

There was only one problem; Randall couldn't die. With the blood of several gods in his system, he possessed a power unlike anything else. Combined with his sharp mind, the magic in him could destroy entire civilizations.

And he'd tried.

Villages burned, vessels sank to their watery graves, men perished, and treasures vanished, all in the name of Thomas Randall's ambitions.

Honestly, it was a relief to leave the organization that kept pitting us against the beast. In my mind, it was better to let someone else deal with him. Was it the more evil of two pathways? Probably. But I'd lost enough, as had Tristan, and we were ready to be finished.

But, no. An emissary from the Grand Master had

been sent to our home, asking us to return. Randall had escaped, and the proof lay in Callaghan's burned house and the bastard's initials carved into his chest.

Thinking of Tristan's adopted brother, I felt another pang of sadness. Everyone had believed him dead after he was accidentally taken to the Otherworld—another cunning plan put in place by Randall. When we discovered him alive, Tristan was overjoyed. Now, he was near death again, and it was all our fault.

Tristan growled, bringing me back to the moment at hand. "I'll not let him take either of ye," he declared fiercely. "Never again. It doesn't matter what the Grand Master says. This conflict with Randall ends now. I don't care if I have to go to hell and back to get it done."

My brow furrowed as I looked up at him, worried. I'd never been one to shy from a fight before, especially one concerning Randall, but being a mother had changed that. I would do whatever it took to keep our child safe.

Even if it meant sailing the ocean with a crew of unruly pirates, child in tow.

Grasping my arm, he leaned his head on mine, closing his eyes for a moment as the weight of what we were about to do settled around us once more.

"I swear to ye, Samantha Greene O'Rourke," he said, his voice sure, "all will be well. If it is not, then may death claim me, for I will not cease until I have made this world a safe one for ye and our children. As God as my witness, I will make it right."

Inhaling deeply, I nodded. "And I promise I will be by your side through it all."

Stepping back, I stood up straight, tightening my hold on Michael. I'd made the promise out of habit, having always insisted we would be together. However, this was different now. As I thought about it, I knew the risks we were taking. This was life and death. We were a family, damn it, and we would stay together, no matter what happened. This pain and suffering had gone on long enough. A rage that burned like a thousand suns filled me, and I pressed my lips into a thin line, resolved to do whatever was needed. "We need to stop Randall," I continued. "He wants us to come battle him? Fine. Let's show him what it really means to face down the O'Rourkes. I swear, he will regret the day he first heard our names."

Leaning in, he caught my lips with his, sealing the oaths with a kiss. The embrace turned heated as he lingered, his tongue slipping into my mouth and creating a sensation that was almost sinful inside me. In an instant, I remembered all the nights we'd been robbed from each other after the baby was born. Perhaps, if I could get Michael to lay down in our cabin for a few moments . . .

As if the child knew what I was thinking, he began to cry, and I pulled back, looking down at him.

"He's hungry," I said, unable to hide the frustration in my voice. "I'll go to our cabin and feed him."

His desires obviously having gone the same direction, Tristan made an impatient noise in the back of his throat. "You could give him something from the galley," he suggested, running a hand down my side.

Snorting, I grinned, staring up into his handsome, green eyes. "I would love to," I replied honestly, "but if I don't feed him soon, I'm liable to explode."

The crying had signaled my breasts to make more milk, making me feel like I was about to spring a leak.

What luck I had.

Groaning in feigned annoyance, Tristan smiled, nodding for me to do what I must. "Go feed our son. I can wait a little longer if I have to."

I snickered, the jest lifting the mood considerably, and kissed him on the cheek. "Come find me in half an hour," I whispered in his ear, feeling a slight thrill as he grasped my hips and held me against him.

"Make it fifteen minutes," he growled, stealing another kiss from my lips.

Michael cried louder as he squished between us and I laughed. "Twenty-five?" I asked, walking backward so I could continue to look at him.

"Twenty is all ye're going to get," he shot back, his eyes shining with happiness.

Giggling, I turned around and flitted down the steps to the next deck. Our cabin was located under the captain's. After weaving through a few hammocks and darting around the edges of the galley, I shut myself inside and sat down on the small chair in the corner. Quickly, I slipped the hem of my top down, releasing the breast that felt the most full and offering it to Michael. He latched on right away, cuddling with me in comfort, and I sighed with relief, leaning back in my seat.

The smell of roasted chicken flitted through the walls from the kitchen, making my mouth water. I loved short voyages because it meant there would be fresh food instead of hard tack and oats for days and days.

Closing my eyes, I replayed the conversation I'd had with my husband, surprised to find that our promises had lightened my spirits. We would always have each other, and we would both do whatever it took to protect the other. If anything, our time together had more than proven that. We'd battled pirates, undead armies, sea monsters, and the fae of the Otherworld, winning each fight. In the end, Thomas Randall would be no different. I knew it in my bones.

"Ouch! Watch it with those wee fingers, aye? Yer ma says those silly strings gotta stay in there until a proper physician has a look-see."

Callaghan chuckled as he scooped Michael off his lap and passed him back to me, wincing. He was doing better now that we were off the ship and in our new Paris accommodations, despite the stitches I'd crudely laced through the cuts on his chest right after we'd discovered him to be injured. Unfortunately, the initials carved into him made it hard for him to wear a shirt still, as well as move around without suffering a searing pain.

If it hadn't been for his apparent lack of interest and high levels of discomfort, I imagined the city woman would have flocked to him when we walked to this place from the docks. He was still as handsome as ever, with chin length, curly, black hair, a dazzling smile, and a body to boot. His banishment in the Otherworld had done nothing to fade his attractiveness, I'd been told, and I half feared what life would become like once he was up and about, wooing women and breaking hearts.

Groaning, Callaghan adjusted himself on the bed, laying a hand on his chest and partially covering the large "TR" now permanently etched into his skin. He looked exhausted, the angry red cuts unclothed, the stitches appearing like horrible mutilation. His skin seemed an unnatural shade of white, almost as if he'd seen a ghost that robbed him of all his color. The brown blanket covering his lower half did nothing to help the sight, serving only to make him look like one of my white shifts.

"How are you doing?" I asked, my worry for him rising as he collapsed back the rest of the way.

"I'll live," he replied, somewhat unconvincingly. "I've lasted this long, haven't I?"

"Ye'd best be careful sayin' stuff like that," Tristan responded in kind. "I think ye've tested fate more than enough for one lifetime."

His brother snorted, rolling his eyes. "Try a hundred. Five hundred years in the Otherworld does a number on yer ability to stay alive."

Smiling, I shook my head. Callaghan fought for his life in the Otherworld for so long. It was normal for him to poke fun at that fact all the time. That was how he dealt with regret and pain, I'd come to realize.

Callaghan O'Rourke was a man who liked to laugh at himself, even if he didn't find his situation particularly funny.

"Ach, the warning's the same, be it one life or one hundred." Tristan grinned, scooting his chair beside the bed and knocking his brother on the shoulder, not jostling him enough to cause any pain. "Ye've got us this time around, too. We'll not leave ye to yerself in yer hour of need, will we Sam? Michael?"

Grimacing, Cal laughed. "I'd prefer it somewhat at the moment," he admitted. "Makes me uncomfortable to be unable to defend myself. My instinct says I'm only safe when I'm truly alone, though my mind knows I've escaped the Dark Isles for good."

The confession stung me. It was so easy to forget Cal was more scarred on the inside than he was on the outside. Tristan often shared his sorrows with me about how different his brother was since his accidental banishment. The naïve, young man who had entered the space had left a warrior full of nightmares.

"You are safe in our company," I reminded him. "There are no beasts who hunt you here. As for being left alone, you can count on me hovering over you until a real doctor can come in and look at you. I'm still not convinced you don't have an infection."

Snorting, he stared at the ceiling. "A 'real doctor,' eh? What can they do for me that ye haven't already?"

Raising an eyebrow, I adopted my "mom voice" and addressed him with sternness. "Callaghan O'Rourke," I started, enjoying his shocked expression. "You will see a doctor, and you will like it. I have just the one in mind, and I intend to send for him as soon as we're all settled in here."

Tristan cleared his throat at that and crossed his arms. "Mark?" The way he said his name let me know he didn't think that was a sound idea. The pair of them had parted on not very good terms—not to mention the fact Mark was not afraid to tell my husband he was in love with me.

Biting my lip, I nodded, resolving not to back down. "Mark is the only person here who has modern experience with medicine. I don't trust the doctors from this century. They're a bunch of crazy quacks, for the most part."

Cal laughed, enjoying my observation, and adjusted his head on the pillow to look at me better.

"Fine, fine. Send for yer fancy doctor friend. Surely my brother can stand one visit from the man, aye?"

Tristan frowned but nodded all the same. He knew Mark would be best for Cal, no matter how much he didn't like him at the moment.

"Good," I announced decisively. "I'll have a message sent in the morning. Does that work for everyone?"

The men muttered their agreement and Tristan stood, gathering me into his arms for a quick kiss.

Out of the corner of my eye, I watched as a cloud crossed Cal's features as if a forgotten memory plagued him. In an abrupt change from our conversation, he asked if he could speak to Tristan alone.

"Man to man," he said, winking as if trying to downplay the seriousness of whatever it was he wanted to share with his brother.

"Sure," I answered in surprise. "I'll feed Michael for a bit."

Smiling at the two of them, I backed out of the small room and into the hall, taking a seat on a bench beside the door. Within a few moments, Michael had latched and was sucking away, relieving the pressure in my breast.

Sighing, I glanced down the hall, listening to the sounds of the cook in the kitchen below as he prepared dinner. This house was much smaller than the ones we'd previously been put in, but very lovely all the same. The Templar who'd brought us here—John Roberts, the same young man who fetched us from Ireland—warned us the servants didn't know The Order ran this house and that we'd best not speak about it in front of them. Everything was paid for, and despite the secrets we had to keep I'd quickly become comfortable with our temporary surroundings.

There were only two rooms, both upstairs, and a sitting room and kitchen below. No stables or servant's quarters, but I enjoyed feeling like we were alone at night. It helped somewhat with being thrown back into this life of luxury and constant service. Everything was decorated in whites and pale blues and yellows, giving the entire building a cheery outlook over the somewhat grim streets of Paris. Noises from outside flitted through the open windows, bringing to mind the many memories I had of this place.

As I sat there, appreciating the city and its charms, the men's voices flitted through the closed doorway, muffled somewhat, but still understandable.

"Do ye think women will appreciate a scar such as this?" Cal hesitated as if he dreaded the answer.

Tristan laughed loudly, amused. "If the past is any indication, women won't care what ye've got written on yer chest, so long as they had a chance to see it naked."

Biting back a snicker, I rolled my eyes. I'd not have expected Cal to be one for "guy talk," but I understood why he needed it now.

Chuckling in kind, Cal exhaled, a sense of relief in the sound. "One can never be too careful when assessing such things," he asserted. "Especially when he has a brother who does nothing but drool over his wife, reminding him of his unmarried and womanless status."

Tristan snorted. "Can ye blame me? I've not only a pretty one but a fierce heart as well."

"That ye do."

Silence spread between them and I smiled, happy to hear them speaking so effortlessly. For the past couple days, our conversations had been strained by the brand on Cal's chest. Every time I laid eyes on it, a river of guilt filled me. The mutilation had been a message for Tristan and me and Callaghan's body had been the unfortunate vessel for it. I'd believed him dead when I first saw it, blood dripping from him as he tumbled to the earth. Even worse, there was no sign of Randall at the scene of the crime, the villain disappearing in the smoke of Cal's burning home. However, whenever I attempted to broach the subject of apology, I found I didn't know what to say.

Tristan had confided as much in me. He didn't know how to make it right, if that was possible. His brother would live with the scars for the rest of his life, and it was our fault.

"Do ye think they mean to reinstate us?" Cal asked suddenly, his voice dropping so much I almost didn't hear it. "They want our help, don't they? Grand Master MacDonald wouldn't have sent for us if he didn't think he needed our assistance."

Leaning closer, I struggled to listen, knowing it was wrong to eavesdrop, but wanting to hear Tristan's answer at the same time.

"Aye," Tristan replied, his voice weary. "Whether or not he'll reinstate us is a mystery to me. He wants us to do something, though. I suppose Randall left just as loud a calling card for me in Paris as he did at home."

Cal snorted. "He'd have to do something rather large to outdo this, don't ye think?"

"I shudder to think what that bastard is capable of," Tristan admitted. "And we've no way to kill him, not with all the blood he's ingested."

"We need to rob the gods from him," Cal agreed. "I have not the faintest idea of how we can do that. Do ye?"

My husband sighed. "None at all."

Grief pricked my heart. There was so much wrong in the world right now, and it felt like we were facing all of it. It was my fault, too, or at least it felt like it. Randall had once said he wanted me. He'd plagued my nightmares and kissed me, using the powers he'd stolen. If I hadn't ever traveled to the past, would he have become the monster he was?

Before I could continue that train of thought, Tristan spoke up again, his voice twisted and filled with pain.

"I am sorry, Cal. For everything. If not for me, ye would have suffered none of this."

"If not for me, ye mean," his brother retorted. "I'm the one that introduced ye to the fiend, after all. I've no one to blame but myself for how things turned out."

"Wherever the blame lies," Tristan conceded, "I intend to be the one who sets the monster right. For all our sakes."

"And I'll be right there with you, brother."

There was a sound like the clasping of hands and Tristan's chair creaked. "Sleep," he ordered. "Ye'll need all the rest ye can get, more than that if ye plan to meet with the Masters once they send for us."

Footsteps sounded in the room, causing me to look back at the door in time to see it open and Tristan poke his head out.

"Mind if I join ye?" he asked pleasantly, his smile sending a thrill through me.

"Of course," I replied cordially, scooting over to make room.

Chuckling, he sat beside me, gazing at our child as it suckled at my breast. "He eats more than a horse, methinks. No wonder the lad is calling ye away from me at all hours."

Snickering, I nodded. "Yes, Michael has quite the appetite, but all growing boys do. I'm not complaining. I've been able to eat as much as I want and not gain any weight at all."

Well, at least I didn't think I'd gained anything. We didn't exactly have a bathroom scale for me to use. My clothes had gotten a little looser. However, whatever weight I'd lost on my body had gone straight to my boobs. It was almost impossible to lace them into a bodice these days, and I often felt like I looked like I had work done on them.

Tristan, on the other hand, loved them and had told me so on many occasions. That was another thing our year apart from the Templars had done—we'd grown closer in ways we'd never been. Before, there was another fight, or a ship we needed to board, or a great and mysterious treasure that needed protecting. In Ireland, it was only us. He fished and I ran the house. Before Michael was born, we spent our nights together and the days visiting, bringing in the nets and setting traps together. After the baby, we learned how to live with the new addition to our lives. I couldn't hardly remember what it was like to not have a child all the time.

I could have lived in that seaside cottage for the

rest of my life, the happiest woman on the face of the planet.

Now, it felt all of that personal growth and love was at risk. We were back among pirates and secret societies, thrust in danger's path, ordered about like soldiers.

"Promise me," I said suddenly, grabbing his hand and squeezing it. "Promise that we won't forget what it was like in Éire. That we'll still be as close as we became. That The Order won't pull us apart like it's tried so many times." Tears began to gather in my eyes as I smiled and remembered the time with fondness. "Promise we'll still look at the stars together, and you'll laugh at my Gaelic, even though I know I'm getting better at speaking it. I want to hear you singing Michael to sleep at night and laughing with your brother as you play cards. I want to have impromptu picnics and sit wrapped up in front of the fire with you. Take me for long walks in the surf, feed me god-awful food you know I'm not going to like. Dance with me on our anniversary. Play with my hair."

My voice broke as my lips trembled and a tear escaped down my cheek. I could only whisper the next part, my heart thumping in my ears as I continued to crush his fingers in my grip.

"Don't turn into the Templar who's never home," I muttered. "Don't leave us for secret missions. Don't stay out all night for meetings. Don't be gone all day, fluffing foreign dignitaries and attending parties at the palace."

Squeezing my hand equally as hard, he touched the side of my face, resting his forehead on mine and closing his eyes as I continued.

"Be the man I fell in love with and continue to fall in love with every day. Be *mine*, not The Order's."

Using his thumb to wipe the tears from my cheek, he kissed me softly, careful not to squish the baby between us as he did so. "*Grá mo Chroí*," he whispered against my lips. "I am yers, always and forever."

The words soothed me, as well as having finally confessed my fears in returning here to him. He was right. Nothing was going to come between us and the feelings we'd nourished and grown together. We were each other's *Grá mo Chroí*—the loves of our lives.

Adjusting the lengthy piece of fabric I'd tied around my body, I held my arms out to Michael, trying to ignore Tristan's suspicious face.

"Ye're sure ye've tied it on there right?" he asked again. "He's not going to fall out?"

Frustrated, I nodded, pulling at the strap I'd created over my shoulder. "I mean, I think so," I assured him, somewhat unsure myself. "I didn't ever learn how to wear a baby sling, but I saw lots of moms do it in my time. They do it in this time, too, just not exactly like this I think."

"Why don't ye get a sling like they have in this time then?" Cal asked from his bed, grinning when I glared at him.

"Because we only have enough money to either feed yer lazy arse, or buy the bairn a sling," Tristan responded, chuckling.

Still, he hovered nearby as I slid Michael into the pouch I'd created in the wrap across my chest. It wasn't stretchy, like the carriers I'd seen in my own time, but it seemed to work fine. I tightened the knot by my hip, pulling the fabric until I felt confident Michael would be safely cradled for as long as I wanted.

"There," I said, taking a few steps to make sure it didn't all come undone at once.

"How does it feel?" Tristan sounded more curious

than concerned now.

Relaxing, I faced him with a smile. "Good! I think Michael likes it, too." Smiling down at the child, I watched as he drifted back to sleep, snug as a bug, his head on my breast.

"What lad wouldn't like to be wrapped up and resting on a woman's bosom?" Cal muttered under his breath, earning himself a chuckle from his brother.

Grinning, I shook my head. It was good to see him sitting up and with more color to his skin, but his wounds were starting to turn red around the edges, and I feared if I didn't get a doctor here soon he would get ill.

"I suppose I'm off," I said, bouncing slightly to test the carrier one more time.

"Are you sure ye don't want to send the messenger after all? Or for me to come with ye?" Tristan asked for what was at least the tenth time.

"I'm sure," I replied, the words firm. "Mark will be happy to see me, and I assume he'll have no problem coming over to check on Cal, since he can't get out of bed that much yet. The last thing I need is the two of you picking a fight. Which is why—"

I grabbed his hand and pulled him toward the door. "You're going to go to the market or the docks or somewhere for a while and not come back until tonight."

He raised his eyebrows, opening his mouth to protest, but I stopped him with a kiss before he could.

"It's only a couple of hours," I reminded him. "You could use the air after being cooped up inside all day yesterday and last night, and it's what's best for Cal. You and Mark didn't part on the best of terms and

I'd rather he be a doctor than try and work things out with you first."

Defeated without uttering a single word, he sighed, grabbing his jacket off the end of the bed where I'd left it.

"She's got ye trained well." Cal snickered, shaking his head. "But I do appreciate the thought, Sam. I'll try and get cleaned up a bit before ye return, savvy?"

"Aye, and I'll spend time down at the docks," Tristan added, a hint of regret in his voice. "Perhaps there's fresh fish to be had for supper or an odd job I can do to make some coin."

"It's odd that The Order put us up here but didn't pay for anything other than the house and staff, isn't it?" I asked, remembering times gone by when we had more than enough provided to us without a single question.

"We're not Templars anymore," he reminded me. "We're lucky they've given us a place to stay at all."

Snorting, I rolled my eyes, not impressed with the politics of the group yet again. "Well, good luck at the docks. If we finish early, I'll come down and get you."

He ushered me into the hall as I waved to Cal, and the two of us walked down the stairs, going out the doorway and onto the narrow front steps that led to the cobblestone street.

Grabbing my waist as I stepped away, Tristan pulled me against him, layering kisses across my lips long enough for others to stop and look. "I love ye, Sam," he whispered.

"I love you, too," I replied, blushing. "I'll see you in a few hours."

Nodding, he released me, taking my hand and kissing my knuckles before turning and strolling down the street, whistling a nursery tune.

Grinning like an idiot, I went my way as well, weaving through the crowds of people in the direction the cook had said Mark's house was. He hadn't recognized the name at first, but after an hour or so, he'd informed me he'd asked around and discovered the location of my friend's in-home practice. It wasn't too far from us, and I'd instantly decided that a walk would do me good.

The idea for Michael's sling had come later, when I realized I had no stroller to move him around in, like the tiny bassinet Tristan had fashioned for me back home. It was a familiar concept, both in my own time and this one, and I'd soon found myself trying to work out how to wrap and tie my new shawl into something useful. It had taken all night, but as I walked across the pathways and pushed through crowds of gossips and merchants trying to sell their wares, I was more than pleased with how it had turned out.

Resting my hand on the precious bundle on my front, I smiled at those I passed, adjusting the straw hat I'd donned to help keep the sun out of my face. At last, after about a thirty-minute walk, I reached the address the innkeeper had given me.

Confused, I stared at the home in front of me and then the paper in my hand, double checking I was in the right place. This was no mansion with beautiful gates and a courtyard like I would have expected Mark to live in, being taken care of by The Order. Instead, it was a tall, skinny thing, almost no better than a shack, with only one window on each of the three floors. The front door was propped open, a few people milling about, and I suddenly realized it was an apartment complex.

Hesitating, I scanned over the somewhat dirty men laughing at the entrance, watching as another man appeared in the doorway, pushing past them and walking down the street. Perhaps the innkeeper had been wrong? When I'd last lived here, Mark was staying in an elegant estate, complete with servants and his carriage. He didn't live there now—I knew because I'd asked about the place beforehand and was informed that a Lord, his Lady, and their three children now resided there.

Swallowing, I held my wrapped baby a little tighter and moved forward, pushing through the group of onlookers with only a mild case of catcalling. Once inside, I peered at the stairs winding up the other two floors, the sounds of a crying infant and a man's laughter flitting down.

There were no numbers on the doors or any sort of directory, so I took another deep breath and went to the first and only apartment on the ground level. Knocking, I wondered what could have happened that landed Mark in such a place. Had he been punished for going after Tristan with me? Was he kicked out of The Order, too?

Guilt at having not written him bit at me. I hadn't been a terrific friend while I was gone. Part of me had been afraid to reach out, because of how things had been when we last saw each other. Tristan had confessed to stealing Templar treasure in the past and kidnapped Randall from prison, intent on finishing the villain his way. When Mark had found out about the theft and my husband's plan, he'd seemed to be of the opinion I should leave him. He couldn't understand why I would forgive my husband and keep the past where it belonged. My friend had left us and went to tell the Grand Master what we were up to, as Tristan requested.

That was the last I'd ever heard of him.

Nervousness grew inside me as I waited for the door to open and I knocked again, louder this time.

"I'm coming!" a voice yelled from inside, frustration in the woman's tone.

Pausing, a spark of recognition lit in me, and I grinned, the uncomfortable feeling inside me giving way to delight.

"Is that—" I began, beaming as the door was thrown open. "Abella!"

My longtime friend, accomplice, and Lady's Maid looked at me in surprise, her mouth popping open as her red lips formed an "O." Almond shaped eyes gazed at me in disbelief, her beautiful face a mask of astonishment. Long, black curls piled on the top of her head, covered by a small cap, a few of the strands having broken free from her pins and tumbled down her back. A stained, white apron covered her somewhat plain, yellow dress, with a dirty handkerchief and pair of scissors shoved into a pocket below her waist. Around her wrists, she wore a pair of off-white ribbon bands like bracelets, the fabric hugging her skin and making it look like she was sporting a pair of cuffs. However, I knew why she wore them; her father had tried to cut her hand off for stealing a loaf of bread when they were starving, hoping the action would restore honor to his name and bring him back into good favor with those above him. The horrible hack job had gone on unfinished, thankfully saving her hand and the use of it, but it left a mess of scars. Rather than draw attention to the one hand, she covered both sides, hoping passersby would leave the matter alone.

The injury was what had brought us together. I'd visited my good friend, Father Torres, at Notre Dame and he introduced me to her, hoping I would be able to employ her in my household before she was turned out on the street once more. As fate would have it, Abella turned out to be a perfect fit for me, both as a help in this strange time and a best friend.

Well, at least she had been one of my best friends before the whole Tristan kidnapping Randall and running off to Ireland mess. I'd not written her either, but it wasn't a surprise to find her here, working with Mark in his surgery. She was in love with him, or had been, and had started working as his nurse before I'd left the city.

All in all, I immediately realized what a sucky friend I'd been and regretted letting my fears keep me from reaching out. I knew nothing of my friends and their lives now, just as they didn't know anything about me.

"Samantha?" she breathed, the French lilt in her voice so beautiful and familiar to me.

Laughing, I threw my arms around her, pulling her into a tight hug. It had been too long since I'd seen her, my heart overjoyed at our reunion.

She seemed frozen for a second, her body stiff in my embrace, but then melted, wrapping her arms around me and emitting a sound that was half a laugh, half a sob. Michael whined, squished between us, and she pulled away, staring at him in surprise.

"You have a baby!" Giggling, her eyes lit up like a tree at Christmas, glancing at me and then back to the child.

"A little boy," I informed her. "Michael."

"Michael." Brushing her hand over the top of his head, she chuckled as his hair stood up in its regular fashion. "He is *magnifique*, Sam. Simply beautiful." Holding her hands out toward him, she shrugged. "How could he not be, with such a blend of his mother and father in him?"

The compliment made me blush, and I shook my head, glancing down at him. The boy was almost the spitting image of his father if you asked me. He had my nose, though, and my hairline, so I supposed there was some resemblance to me, too.

"Thank you," I told her warmly. Smiling, I met her gaze once more. "Abella, how I have missed you!" Unable to help myself, I hugged her again, laughing in happiness and contentment.

"Come inside," she said, patting my back with fondness. "Sit for a while and tell me why you've come back to Paris."

She ushered me inside, closing the door, and I took a moment to look around the small space. It wasn't much. There were a few chairs against the wall and what looked like a room with a bed across the way. A narrow hallway wrapped around the far right corner, concealing what I assumed was at least a kitchen area and decent sized bedroom.

"This is where Mark has his clinic, as he calls it," Abella explained, sitting on one of two chairs beside the window. "Every evening, he sees patients in that room there." She pointed to the glorified closet. "And everyone waits their turn with him in here, in these chairs."

"He's doing well?" I pressed, desperate to hear news of him as I sat beside her.

"Oh, *oui, Madame*. He makes house calls to his wealthier patrons during the day and assists the less fortunate here when he can." She sounded so proud of him, her face flushing as she sang his praises. "Mark has learned so much since you left. He is highly sought after by those of all classes. They say no other can match his methods."

"I suppose not," I agreed, smiling. "He is from the future, after all. We know a little more about the body and how it works there."

"Yes, his experience with medicine work from your century is wonderful," she asserted. "As well as his natural remedies from his time in Arizona and the skills he gained serving as a ship's surgeon for so long. He applied himself to the trade when he returned from Ireland, too, and the work has paid off for him in the grandest way."

Pride continued to radiate from her as she went on and I bit my lip to keep from giggling. Apparently, she was still infatuated with him, at the very least. However, there was no mention of the two of them being together, other than the fact that she was here when he was not.

"He's on a house call right now?" I asked, interrupting her.

Nodding, she leaned forward, grasping my hand. "I'm so happy you came," she confessed. "I have missed you so!"

"I am, too," I agreed. "I'd hoped to ask Mark if he could help me with something, but I guess I'll have to wait until he gets back."

Her expression fell as a flicker of doubt passed across her features.

"What is it?" I asked, alarmed by her change in demeanor.

She shook her head. "It's nothing. Only . . ." Pausing, she chewed on the inside of her cheek, as if trying to decide what she wanted to say. She let out a breath and released me as she stood and walked to the center of the room, folding her arms. Glancing back, she gave me an apologetic grimace. "I do not think Mark will want to see you, Samantha," she said, her voice quiet.

Pulling back, I tried to cover my surprise by placing a hand on Michael's back and checking on him. The fear I'd had standing out in the hall returned in an instant, my throat tightening as I realized the awful truth.

I could have lost one of my best friends and the only other person who knew what it was like in my time.

"He's still upset with me." My voice cracked as I whispered, unable to look up at her and see the reality of it in her face.

It was infuriating I felt like crying. I knew I'd made the right choice in sticking with Tristan—with my husband. He was the man I loved, and I'd promised to stand by him through thick and thin. The opinion of another man who claimed to love me didn't have any sway over that.

However, as I sat here, in Mark's shack of a house, hearing how superb he was doing and seeing how much Abella still cared for him, it hurt to think he could not want me in his life anymore. We had so much in common. In many ways, we were the only people who could understand one another. Pandora's Box had sent us both through time, and we'd each suffered much for it, in our ways. We'd been there for each other in our most exceptional times of need.

But, Mark couldn't seem to get past the fact I was

in love with and married to someone else, and now it seemed he had finally broken over that matter.

"Well." Abella hedged, the hesitancy in her voice making it obvious she didn't know what to say. "He was so mad when he came home, Sam," she said. "I'd never seen him that upset before, nor have I seen him like that since."

She came back to sit beside me, taking my hand once more and squeezing it. "I don't think he spoke one word for an entire week. All he did was sit in his house and refuse to see anyone. I would come to help him with his medical work, and he wouldn't acknowledge I was there. After a month, he told me he was moving to this place. There was no explanation or reason given me. I think, when he realized I remained resolute in my decision to work with him, he was finally able to share some of his grief with me."

She paused, clearing her throat. The expression on her face was hard to read. She seemed to pity Mark, but also feel his pain.

"He didn't tell me what happened," she continued, "only that you weren't thinking clearly. He said you were making a blind decision, refusing to see what was right in front of you. That was it. It took me hours to get him to say that alone. When he did tell me that little part, he was so upset he could hardly get the words out. He seemed convinced you were making the biggest mistake of your life."

My anger flared, and I took a deep breath, reminding myself Abella was only the messenger, not the face of such ludicrous notions. Sharing my reaction to Mark's fit throwing would do nothing but upset her.

The fact of the matter was Mark always felt like

he should have a say in what I was doing. To hear that he'd not only been spouting off what he thought I should do behind my back but that his anger was so intense he couldn't speak, ticked me off. His hermit act beforehand enraged me. To behave like a child and blame it on something he had no business being involved in was infuriating.

It felt like he didn't respect me or my wishes, continually trying to get me to change my mind. He was mad when he first heard I'd gotten married and was pregnant. Then he was upset I insisted on being a part of whatever crazy missions The Order sent him and my husband to fulfill. Finally, he was angry that I wouldn't leave Tristan after hearing about his past. Every single time, he'd lectured me, telling me why what I was doing was stupid, ignoring that the last thing he'd freaked out about had turned out okay.

Maybe it was a good thing I hadn't reached out to him while I was gone. He might not have responded. Come to think of it, I didn't know if I wanted to talk to him while I was here, either.

Standing, I smiled tightly at Abella. "I'm sorry he put you through that. I was hoping he could come look at Tristan's brother for me, but that doesn't sound like such a good idea anymore."

Eyes widening, she stood as well. "You're leaving? Already?"

Sighing, I nodded. "I sent Tristan away for a while because I didn't want to make things worse between the two of them. If Mark isn't coming for a visit, I need to go get my husband and bring him home."

Eyebrows raising, she grabbed my arm, stopping me as I made to leave. "Tristan's brother? I didn't know he had one."

Peering over my shoulder, I felt my brow furrow. "Mark didn't tell you about him? I assumed The Order would have filled him in on everything that happened."

"If they did, he hasn't said anything to me."

Blinking, I fell silent, not sure where to start in the story. Mark had heard of Callaghan, I knew that much, but did he know he was alive? Was he aware of what happened in the Otherworld? Didn't he know Randall had been in The Order's grasp for a year and escaped?

"This brother needs medical attention?" Abella continued, squeezing my arm as she smiled and brought my attention back to her. "I can come help him if you want. I've been working here with Mark the entire year, during his nighttime hours. I don't know as much, but I should be able to do something." Gesturing to the empty room, she laughed. "It's not like I have anything to do at the moment."

I relaxed some, my annoyance for Mark replaced by gratitude for my long lost friend. "That would be very helpful. Thank you."

She grinned. "It's nothing. You can tell me the story on the way, *oui*?"

I nodded as she released me and went into the small room.

"What ails this brother?" she called back.

Clearing my throat, I folded my arms, making sure not to jostle Michael in the process. "He's been cut several times, deeply. I stitched him up, but I'm worried he's getting an infection."

"Hmm." A rustling sound drifted out of the closet, the hem of her skirt visible as she knelt down and went through something behind the door. "The festering ones are the worst. If that is the issue, I believe we can catch it in time."

Scooting out from behind the door, she stood and brushed off her skirt and apron, hoisting a small satchel over her shoulder. Beaming, she motioned to the door. "Lead on, old friend."

The walk back took a little longer than the one there, since Abella kept stopping in surprise as I told her the story of what happened in the Otherworld. She'd gone on missions with us before, but she'd never been in the thick of something mystical and unexplainable. It was her preference to stay behind and tend to those in need, only joining the fight when necessary. Every time she heard of the crazy experiences we'd had, she was completely floored.

The excitement and misery of the Otherworld tale gave way to a recap of my life living in Ireland, which gave a much needed lift to my spirits. It was so easy to talk with her and share my dreams and reservations as a mother. Until that very moment, I didn't think I had missed having a female companion with whom to share my thoughts. Now that I had one again, I realized there were some things Tristan didn't seem to connect with or understand. However, Abella accepted it all, adding in her own opinions, until I realized we had passed the house and needed to backtrack.

Finally, we made it back home and inside. As we walked up the stairs, Abella told me of the work she'd been doing with Mark, sharing a heartening tale of a baby they delivered together.

"It had so much hair," she continued, walking down the hall and grabbing the handle of the door I'd pointed out. "Like your little one does. I have often wondered—"

Pushing open the entrance, she stepped inside, only to stop cold and emit a high shriek, immediately turning around and letting the entrance fall shut.

Inside, I heard Cal swear in Gaelic, the crash of something falling over and shattering slamming into my ears. Before I could ask what was happening, Abella flung the door open again, peering inside.

"Are you well?" she asked, her voice timid, only to be sworn at again.

"Get out of here!" Cal yelled. "Can't ye see I'm tryin' to put these damn breeches on?"

Covering my mouth, I laughed silently, watching as Abella slammed the door again and leaned against it, hiding her reddening face with her hands.

"I saw him!" she whispered through her fingers, a tinge of horror to her embarrassed tone.

"I heard," I replied, snorting.

"No! I mean, *oui*, I saw Callaghan, but not him, his . . ." Glancing around, she pointed to her nether regions, whispering fiercely. "His *virilité!*"

Pausing for a moment, I looked at her mortified face, lips trembling as I tried to keep from falling over from the hilarity of both their reactions. "And?"

Taking a step back, she sized me up, mouth open. "And what?"

"Well, you've seen one before, haven't you?" I asked, feeling like teasing her for a moment. Cal was probably dying of embarrassment inside, and I wanted to give him a minute to right himself, too.

Flustered, she nodded, a look of confusion covering her face. "I have, but not any like *that*. All the ones I've seen have been on sick men who needed help."

Deciding not to ask what she meant by "that," I nodded again, reaching around her and knocking on the door.

"Callaghan?" I called as loud as I could without shouting, not wanting him to mistake who it was. "Are you decent? Can we come in?"

A grumbling reached my ears as I waited, something else falling over inside the room, and he answered grouchily. "If ye must. I've at least clothes on, now."

Grinning, I paused, glancing back at Abella and her mortified face. They couldn't see the humor in the situation yet, but I had a feeling they would one day. In the meantime, I couldn't wait to tell Tristan about it.

Motioning for her to join me, I opened the door and went inside, noting the broken vase on the floor and knocked over chair. Cal had tucked himself back in bed, the blanket pulled over his legs, and his chest left bare. It looked like he'd been in the basin while I was gone, washing before we returned. Abella had been unfortunate enough to catch him before he was dressed.

Clearing her throat, she came in behind me, face flaming, and curtseyed. "My apologies, sir," she said. "I should have knocked before entering, but I'd become carried away with talking and didn't think."

Cal sniffed, his face red, and nodded. "Tis fine. Ye meant nothing by it, I'm sure."

She bowed again, a stiff, awkward air about her, and began rummaging through her bag, looking for something.

Walking over to the bedside, I sat down in the

chair and busied myself with feeding Michael, who had woken up during all the commotion.

"I thought ye were bringing Mark," Cal whispered, leaning toward me as best he could so Abella wouldn't hear.

Shaking my head, I smiled. "He wasn't home. This is Abella."

His eyes flashed with recognition, having heard me talk about her often in Ireland, and he smiled. "Is it now?"

Glancing at her, he relaxed. "It's a pleasure to meet ye, Abella. I've heard much about ye."

Stopping her digging, she looked up at him, meeting his eyes for the first time. A beat of silence passed between them, and she smiled, the blush fading from her face. "The pleasure is mine, Mister O'Rourke."

"Callaghan," he corrected her. "If ye're gonna be poking and prodding me, we might as well be on a first name basis."

Chuckling, she nodded. "Very well. May I sit with you and take a look?" Pulling a small pair of scissors from her bag, she stowed them in the pocket of her apron and stepped forward, waiting for his permission before settling on the side of the mattress.

The uncomfortable air returned to the room as she looked him over, reaching out and lightly touching a section that was redder than the rest.

"I'm sure to have these ugly scars for the rest of my life," he joked, a measure of discomfort in his gaze as he watched her.

She peered up from her visual examination of his wound, meeting his eyes once more. Slowly, she pulled the thick band off her scarred wrist, holding it up for him to see. "It's not the scars that make you ugly," she said quietly. "But the reaction you have to them. Those who truly matter won't care one lick about them if you don't."

He sucked in a breath, a weight seeming to leave him as he looked at her mutilated skin, the marks twisted and wound together, creating a web of scars. To my surprise, he grinned, staring into her eyes once more.

She smiled, laying the band down on his blanket, and returned to her examination. When she stood up and went outside to ask the cook for more wood for the fire and water to boil, Cal looked at me, completely smitten.

"She's wonderful isn't she?" I asked, laughing at his reaction to her.

Sighing, he shook his head, putting his hands behind it. "She's more than that. I've spent enough time among demons to recognize an angel when I see one."

I stared at myself in the dingy mirror, feeling another part of my time in Ireland slipping away.

It was a polished piece of metal I stood before, my reflection fuzzy and somewhat distorted, but it did the job. The fancy skirts resting around my waist looked as voluptuous as ever, cascading down from my matching bodice and jacket, one of the pins holding the stomacher in place catching the light as I turned toward the window some. Lace bunched around my elbows, spilling out from the sleeves like a waterfall. Even my hair, which I'd worn in a simple braid or bun for the majority of the last year, was carefully curled and piled on the top of my head, ribbon bows here and there to match my gown. It had taken well over an hour to shred the old rags last night and twist my locks into the strips of fabric, rolling them like overnight curlers.

Shifting my weight from one foot to the other, I grimaced, spanning my fingers around my waist. I'd gained some weight with the baby after all, not to mention from eating wholesome food and not ship's rations all the time. While the dress had fit like a glove the last time I was here, it was a little tight now. I wouldn't be surprised if everyone could tell either, from the way my full breasts threatened to spill over the neckline at any given moment.

Michael, who possessed a canny ability that alerted him the moment anyone thought about my boobs, began to cry, the sound his familiar begging for food.

"Hush now," I told him, walking the few steps to stand beside his bassinet. "Give me two more minutes and I'll be able to sit down with you."

His crying only intensified as I slid on my shoes, loathing the uncomfortable heel in them. But, as Tristan had said, we needed to look our best to visit the Temple. It had been a week since we first arrived and Grand Master MacDonald had yet to send for us. Deciding to take our fate into our own hands, we'd all agreed to go to the Temple and demand an audience ourselves, since we apparently weren't as urgently needed as we'd been led to believe. At this very moment, Tristan was out with Callaghan, trying to find him something suitable to wear without spending all of our money.

Personally, I didn't think the leader of the Templars would care what we wore to see him. He would most likely be in the same old kilt he always wore, carrying his giant hammer.

Smiling to myself, I recalled the time I'd spent as a member of William MacDonald's privateer crew. He was a stickler for rules and loyalty, which sometimes got him in more trouble than he planned. I'd liked him well enough as a captain, not so much as the Grand Master. Everything about The Order was turned on its head the moment he took office. Members who had been loyal for decades were forced to come in and testify to their commitment or face the dungeon with Randall.

Of course, there was also the whole Randall issue. MacDonald had insisted The Order let him live, in an attempt to discover more traitors. When Tristan and Cal were banished, he brought the snake back to Paris, where he vowed to take care of him.

Instead, we were all here again, trying to figure out how to recapture the villain and end him for good.

As my smile melted into a frown, I tried to brace myself for what this visit could entail. There was no guessing what MacDonald would want from us, or if he would call my husband back into the ranks of his men. I didn't know if he'd allow us inside the Templar hold without an official invitation. Whatever his decision, I was sure to find out today.

Having finished getting ready, I sat down on the bed and pulled Michael to me, glad I'd not laced the top of my bodice so tightly. As he latched on, there was a light knock at the door and it opened, the maid curtseying as she regarded me with wide eyes.

"*Madame*," she said. "You are beautiful!"

Blushing, I laughed, dipping my head in thanks. "You are too kind."

Smiling, she curtseyed again. "There is a visitor downstairs for you. He says his name is Mark Bell?"

Even with all the annoyance and anger I'd felt over hearing about his reaction to my past decisions, I couldn't help the grin that covered my face. "Really? Tell him I'll be right down."

She nodded, closing the door with a snap.

I let the baby nurse for a few more moments, knowing he wouldn't be happy with ending early, but I couldn't help it. I was so excited to see Mark again and ask how he'd been, not to mention introduce him to Michael. As it was, it took me another ten minutes to get downstairs, Michael drooling all over my dress as I tried to get him to burp.

"Mark?" Calling out as I reached the ground floor, I peered into the sitting room, beaming as I laid eyes on my old friend.

It was odd, how Mark could look so much like his old self and not at all at the same time. He was wearing something more sea-worthy than the typical, upper-class fashion of Paris, his hair swept back in a modern style with the sides short and top long. A calf-length duster covered his arms, hiding the skull and crossbones tattoo he'd sported since I met him, and the brand Thomas Randall had burned into him.

Most of all, it was his face that was different. Worn and tired, he seemed to have aged in my absence, his eyes dark and hooded as he stared at me. There was no excited recognition or happiness like there'd been before. Instead, as he stepped forward, I had the sudden feeling we were complete strangers, perhaps lost to each other forever.

"Samantha," he said stiffly, eyes darting past me to the hallways, agitation in his movements. His gaze dropped to the giggling, spit covered child in my arms.

"So, the witch was right," he muttered. "You were pregnant. Congratulations. She looks beautiful, from what I can see."

Frowning, I resisted the urge to ask him what was wrong. All the resentment and fury I'd felt toward him before seeped back in, his behavior telling me he was still upset with me. An entire year had passed, but Mark was going to continue to act like a child about everything. Why I'd expected any different was a mystery to me.

"It's a boy," I refuted with the same amount of

rigidity he'd shown me. "His name is Michael."

Whatever wall he was trying to hide behind collapsed as he heard the name of his deceased friend and my father. "Sam . . ." Hesitating, he met my stare again, conflicted. "Your dad would be so honored you chose to name your son after him."

The statement only made me angrier. I couldn't help the ire boiling inside me as I considered how he'd run back here, lied about his part in Randall's kidnapping, and his behavior when he heard I wouldn't be coming back. Even more so, I was angry that he stood here in front of me, acting like we were strangers one moment and talking about my father the next.

"What can I help you with?" I asked, rage laced through my words. "Are you here to tell us MacDonald finally invited us to a meeting?"

His eyebrows raised, but he didn't seem surprised by my words. In fact, it looked like he bit back whatever it was he wanted to say, instead opting for the path of least resistance. "I'm not here for The Order. Abella said you were back and I thought . . ." Shaking his head, he moved to sit down, staring out the window in silence.

"You thought what? That everything would go back to the way it was before?" I snorted, shaking my head as I sat in the chair opposite him. "It's not that easy, Mark."

"I know it's not," he replied, his anger surfacing. "That's not what I meant, either. All I wanted was to see how you were doing. That's it."

Brushing his fingers over his mouth, he slumped back in his seat.

Pursing my lips, I accepted his answer. There was

more I wanted to talk about, however, more we needed to clear up.

"You lied to MacDonald about what was going on in Ireland," I stated calmly, setting the baby on my lap. It was obvious he had—he remained here, in the city, no exile forced upon him. Whatever he'd shared with the Grand Master had been enough to save his neck while condemning all of ours.

He paused, his gaze moving to me, and I could tell from the way he was looking at me that he was deciding if he wanted to fight or not. Huffing, he sat forward as he rubbed his hands together, ready to get it all out in the open.

"You don't know what you're talking about," he replied. "I didn't lie about anything. Tristan told me to say I was forced to come along with him, to protect myself from blame. If anything happened to him, I was going to take care of you."

Ignoring the ridiculousness of that logic, I shook my head, gaping at him in disbelief. "And MacDonald just went along with it? No questions? No doubt?"

Frustrated, he shook his head, holding his hand up. "He was too busy going after your traitor of a husband to question me, which was good because I wasn't exactly ready to talk to anyone about it."

"Yeah, I know," I shot back. "Abella told me all about the hissy fit you threw when you came back.

"Hissy fit?" His eyes darkened as he stood, towering over me. "You mean the fact I was upset because you're too stupid to see you're in too deep?" Growling, he shook his head.

"You have some nerve—"

"I have them all when it comes to you!" he

117

snapped. "Don't you see that? My entire existence here revolves around you!" The words ground from him like they'd been forced upon threat of death, his eyes blackening with hurt and turmoil as he continued to spout off his explanation, not bothering to let me get a word in edgewise. "And you up and left without another word, despite the dishonest history you've been fed for years, leaving me behind to deal with the fallout." Looking at the ceiling, he sighed, a tremor of emotion skipping through his voice. "You left me alone in this time, again, and when you returned you didn't even come to see me."

Caught by the wounded tone and defeated look of him, I paused, a small amount of my anger dissipating at his confession. "I did come," I countered quietly. "You weren't there."

"I wasn't," he agreed. "But Abella told you when I would be and you still never came."

"You could have visited me sooner," I replied, defensive. "I'm not the only one capable of keeping up a friendship."

He laughed, rubbing his jaw. "There were no letters, no visits—nothing after you left. I don't think I was your friend, Sammy. Not in your thoughts, anyway."

Offended, I drew back some, scowling at him. "Again, I'm not the only one capable of writing a letter! In case you didn't notice," I gestured to the child in my hands, "I've been a bit busy with other things."

"And I haven't?" He laughed, motioning in the direction of the street outside. "The people of Paris are starving, Sam. They're dying of disease and poverty, yet the wealthy around them do nothing to help. Before

I opened the clinic, there was almost nowhere for those without means to go for treatment. I've been up to my eyeballs in boils, syphilis, and tuberculosis since the second I said I could help them.

"The Order's been no help, either. MacDonald hasn't let me leave the city once. I'm never assigned to guard duty or any other missions. They cut my pay, I lost my home, and yet I was expected to serve as a physician for any Templars who needed me. I've been a prisoner here, this whole year, struggling to make it through, and you were what? Frolicking along the coast, living out a perfect fantasy where you had no troubles and the family you always wanted?"

The words hurt more than expected, and I frowned, recognizing the pain he was displaying for me. A wealth of questions had bloomed inside me as well, but before I could interrupt him to ask, he went on.

"Why did you go with him, Sammy?" he asked, his voice breaking as he said my name. "Why did you stay with him after you knew the truth?"

Sucking in a deep breath, I met his stare, shaking my head. "Tristan is my husband, Mark. I love him. That's why I went with him. You know that."

Nose twitching, he sniffed, glancing away. "I know."

Hesitating, I considered telling him he had to let me go. We were never going to be together, no matter what happened. He knew that already, but for some reason, he couldn't seem to get over his feelings. Even with Abella, who had openly told him of her love, he was still stuck on me.

"It's so tiring, living like this," he admitted.

"Pretending to be something I'm not. All I want is to go home and leave it all behind."

"That's fine with me," I replied equally as soft, deciding not to push the subject further. "We can sort this all out later if you'd like."

"No," he answered quickly. "I want to go *home*."

The way he said it made my heart clench painfully. I knew what he meant. He wanted to return to our time. More than thirteen years had passed since he traveled to the past. As I watched him sit back in his chair, I suddenly found myself wondering if that was the only way Mark would ever be happy again. The slump of his shoulders suggested it might be.

The front door opened in the hallway, Tristan and Callaghan's voices filling the space as they entered the house.

"Excuse me for a moment," I muttered to Mark, leaving him to himself and his miserable confession. Hurrying into the hall, I shut the sitting room doors behind me, catching the brothers by surprise before they went upstairs.

They were both dressed in knee-length breeches and white stockings, with matching vests and jackets. While Cal looked a little worse for wear in his dark brown and green ensemble, Tristan appeared as excellent as ever in his black, his eyes shining as they found mine.

"*Mo bhean álainn*," he breathed, crossing the room in two steps and halting before me. Grasping my hand, he pulled it toward his lips, kissing it gladly as he continued to beam at me. "Ye are a sight to behold, love."

Blushing, I laughed, pleased with his compliments. "You don't look half bad yourself," I replied, grinning at him as I was distracted. "I'd almost forgotten what you looked like in court attire."

"I'd be remiss if I'd lost any image of ye in a dress such as this," he answered in appreciation. "Ye could have any man eating out of the palm of yer hand in that gown."

"Tis true," Cal agreed, smiling at the pair of us. "Ye look right bonnie, Sam. I couldn't be prouder to call ye my sister."

"And you look wonderful, brother," I responded in kind.

"Ach." He waved his hand in dismissal, grinning all the same. "They aren't new, but they'll do." He ran his fingers through his long, curly black locks, giving me a boyish, but thankful grin.

Tristan kissed his son on the head, cooing something unintelligible in his native tongue. "Why isn't Michael ready yet?" he asked quietly, glancing toward the shut doors I'd just left.

"Right." Grimacing, I closed my eyes for a beat. When I met his stare again, I exhaled slowly. "Mark is here."

Tristan's eyebrows rose, a look of surprise flitting over his face before he cleared his throat and his expression became a mask of politeness. "Oh? What does he want?"

"He only came to see how we were doing. But—"

Biting my lip, I glanced back at the entrance, the questions Mark's sharing had brought up swirling in my mind.

"Something isn't right, Tristan," I muttered. "He says his pay was cut and he was forced to move out of his home. MacDonald has kept him as a prisoner in the city, not giving him any other orders or missions to complete." Meeting my husband's contemplative gaze, I shrugged. "Should we ask him about it?"

"It can't hurt," Cal offered easily. "We could find out about the past year before we meet with MacDonald. Maybe it will help us prepare."

Tristan made an odd sound in the back of his throat, his eyes darkening for a moment. "Aye, we should ask. Mark and I may not have separated amicably, but I do not think he'd keep information from us for that reason."

"No, I wouldn't."

Facing the sitting room, I stared at Mark as he leaned against one of the doors, his arms folded and a frown on his face. For a beat, it seemed the two men were liable to burst into action, throwing fists at one another until they drew blood. But, thankfully, the moment passed, and we all moved into the sitting room again.

"Mark," I started. "Would you mind telling us what's been going on with The Order since we left?"

He shook his head, sighing. "I don't want to talk about it anymore, Sam. I came to see how you were doing and I've done that, so I think I'll go now."

Grabbing his wrist as he moved toward the door, I gave him a small smile. "Please?" I asked again. "We've no idea what's happened other than Randall escaping, and Captain MacDonald hasn't sent for us once, though he insisted we hurry and leave our home to meet him. We—I want to know what's going on."

He watched me for a beat, his arm flexing beneath my touch as he decided. "Fine," he finally breathed. "What do you want to know?"

"Sam says ye've been struggling," Tristan started straightforwardly, sitting on the long couch with his brother while Mark and I took our same chairs.

"You could say that," Mark answered with hesitance. "I wouldn't be the only one, either, what with all the changes MacDonald has made since becoming Grand Master."

"You mean how he called all the Templars to the city to prove their allegiance to him?" I pressed.

Mark shook his head. "That was where it started, yes, but not where it ended."

"What happened?" Tristan's gaze turned worried as well as angry, but I could tell it wasn't directed at Mark this time.

He was concerned for the organization to which he'd dedicated his life. If something were wrong, even if he weren't technically a member anymore, he would want to help fix it. It was just part of who he was.

Mark slouched in his chair. "After you were banished, and they brought Randall back here, MacDonald started changing everything. He kept saying we had too much and we needed to humble ourselves if we were going to take on the task of protecting these treasures."

Grimacing, I remained silent as he halted. If I knew anything about The Order and the men in it, I could quickly guess that all the changes were not received with grace.

"Everyone received a cut in pay," Mark started again, his voice revealing his poor opinion of the actions. "The funds were instead put toward purchasing privateering licenses from the king. Those in elegant homes were relocated or required to pay for their lodgings themselves. The ships were sold and downgraded to more manageable sloops. Empty treasure rooms in the Temple were adapted to hold storage and stockpile rations for voyages. Any treasure moved through the city is now subjected to a rigorous process, to ensure its safety and arrival to its final destination."

"How is the man still in command?" Tristan asked, interrupting him. Raising an eyebrow, he leaned forward, resting his elbows on his knees as he gazed at Mark. "The men cannot have accepted these changes without question."

"Not everything he did is bad." Mark laughed. "By turning away from piracy, he's enabled many of the men to walk freely in the city once more. Not to mention, his stockpiling of supplies has made the sailors better fed and equipped for the job he is asking them to do. Combined with smaller crews and more manageable vessels, those three changes alone have enabled him not to lose one boat the entire year. His focus is on the treasure, which is where it should have always been for each Grand Master, if you ask me."

"There has to be resistance to all this change," Cal butted in.

Turning his attention to the O'Rourke he'd yet to be officially introduced to, Mark nodded. "MacDonald has struggled to maintain control, for sure. I don't know how he's kept an all-out riot from happening. I mean, his own guards let Randall go, but—"

"What?" All our voices combined sharply as he revealed that nugget of information.

"What do you mean 'let go?'" Frowning, I stared at him, the hair on the back of my neck rising as I realized what had happened in our absence.

He bit his lip, pausing for a beat as he looked at me, regret in his eyes. "Randall didn't escape," he said, his voice quiet. "He was let go by the guards put in place to watch over him. They've turned to Black Knights because they don't like the changes

MacDonald has been making."

Cal swore under his breath, and I knew he was struggling with all of this. Black Knights hadn't been more than an idea when he was last here, serving The Order. The sect had grown and revealed itself after he'd disappeared to the Otherworld. To hear that his supposed brothers in arms were changing their allegiances over such trivial matters was sure to anger him. If the red color of his face was any indication, it infuriated him.

Tristan, on the other hand, looked as if he'd expected something like this to happen all along. If he had, he'd never voiced those thoughts to me.

"I mean, he should have seen it coming," Mark continued, swallowing hard. "It started with threats, then fighting among the ranks. For months, he refused to acknowledge it all, until about twenty-five members were locked in the Bastille for dueling. There was an attempt to make some amends, but, in the end, the split still happened. That's all I know, other than Randall did something in the prison after he escaped."

"What?" I almost didn't ask. There was no telling what a madman like Randall would do to another human being. I'd seen him eat someone, after all.

"All I know is what I heard," Mark offered. "No one has shared what exactly happened. They're saying he killed all the other prisoners. Slit their throats and mutilated the bodies."

Callaghan sucked in a sharp breath, his hand going to his chest and the still healing wound hidden beneath his shirt. "Mutilated," he breathed, rage entering his shaking voice. "Like he did to me, you mean? He carved his name in the bodies?"

Mark shrugged. "I don't know. Everyone who knows what happened has kept it as quiet as possible."

"That's why the Grand Master has called us back," Tristan muttered, understanding lighting on his face. "It wasn't his own name Randall carved in the bodies; it must have been mine."

"And he attacked Cal to make sure we got the message," I added, catching on to what he was saying in an instant.

"Damn it," Cal muttered, shoving to his feet and running a hand through his hair as he stood, turning from us.

Guilt at his mutilation filled me again. It was even more our faults he was injured now. If I hadn't known what horrors he'd faced in the Underworld, I would have thought he'd have been better off staying there than coming with us.

"Cal," I stated in a gentle tone, standing with the intent of going to him.

"The rat wants us to come after him. But why?" Turning around he revealed a tight but determined expression, whatever he'd been feeling only a moment ago locked away. "Ye think he's still after Tristan's blood? Why would he need more of it? He's already immortal."

Hesitating, I glanced at my husband, wondering if I should push the issue of his brother's attack. Tristan shook his head, closing his eyes for a second as he worked to absorb all the information we were receiving.

"He took your blood?" Mark asked Tristan. "Why?"

Tristan sighed, opening his eyes. "I am a direct

descendant of the first High King of the Éire, who was married to a goddess. Her blood runs in my veins."

Mark's eyebrows rose, surprise and perhaps a bit of appreciation in his stare. "That must have been one hell of a trip to the Otherworld you guys had."

"You have no idea," I replied dryly. Sitting back in my seat, I nodded toward my husband again, patting the baby's back as he played with the lace on my dress. "Randall bit him, that's how he got the blood."

"Probably would have killed me if ye two hadn't stepped in to save me." A weak grin flashed from Tristan's face toward me, gratefulness in the stare.

"He shouldn't need anything more from Tristan then," Mark continued, ignoring us. "All the other blood he took was only a small amount in a vial. He should have taken plenty with a bite."

"It was watered down," I countered, wincing at the use of the phrase. "Would Randall need more because Tristan isn't a full deity?"

"I don't think so." Callaghan shook his head. "But Randall must want him for something if he'd go through the trouble of marking me and leaving a calling card here in Paris."

We all fell silent at that, the possibilities of what Randall could be up to swirling in the air around us as if baiting us into action by their mere presence.

"Randall can't use the full power of the gods yet," I offered, changing the subject and putting an end to the uncomfortable quiet.

"Aye, that's why he was after Nuada's Hand in the Otherworld," Tristan agreed. "The power within him cannot be released if he's not whole." Grinning at me, he chuckled. "I suppose it's luck that ye managed to cut off his hand all those years ago, no?"

I shrugged. "Even if he were whole, he'd still be on the hunt for blood. He wants ultimate control and power. That's why he's taking some of each god and absorbing it into himself. Once he has everything he wants, he'll be more powerful than anything we've ever heard of or seen. We'll be dead before we can blink."

The admonition twisted uncomfortably in my mind. Randall was sneaky about what he wanted to share with us. He'd played with our minds and managed to get us to do precisely what he wanted more than once. Who was to say his summoning of us wasn't another attempt to force us into finishing his plans?

At the same time, Randall *had* changed since he first absorbed the blood of the Native American and Norse gods, all those years ago. His cunning leaned more toward madness as of late, and he seemed torn a million different ways as he battled the voices in his head.

There were two things I knew for sure. First, Randall wanted me and my family dead. We were the only ones who continually stood in his way. Second, he believed I had a critical role to play because I was a time traveler.

Whatever he was planning, he knew we were supposed to be a part of it. I could only hope that it wouldn't mean our deaths and his victory.

"That would suggest he's gone somewhere where he can not only get more blood but to a place where he can make himself whole," Cal said, drawing me back into the conversation at hand.

"But where could that be?" Tristan added,

stroking his chin. "Every treasure port he knows of has either been decommissioned and buried or is under heavy guard. The Hand of Nuada is destroyed. What else would he think to go after?"

Mark shrugged. "Beats me. I told you everything I know. The guards broke Randall out of his cell and ever since then Paris has been a madhouse where Templars are concerned."

A loud banging on the front door drew all our attention, and I watched as the maid appeared, hurrying to the entrance and opening it a crack, peering out to the doorstep.

"*Oui*?" she asked timidly.

"Where are they?" A voice with a Scottish accent roared into the house. "What do they think they're doin', comin' back here when I told them in no uncertain terms they are banished?"

The maid stumbled back with a shriek as Grand Master MacDonald shoved his way into the house, his anger reddened face peering into the sitting room, topped with a felt cap sporting a blue ribbon. The rest of him followed, his usual kilt and white shirt covered by a black vest marching into the room as he hefted his giant, two-headed, wooden hammer over his shoulder as if to threaten us with it.

Icy blue eyes glared at all of us from his sun worn and wrinkled with age face, the thin line of his lips barely visible beneath his long beard. "I told ye not to come back," he stated menacingly. "So, tell me, O'Rourkes—what are ye doing in my city?"

You could have heard a pin drop in the silence that followed the question, all of us staring at the burly captain in shock. Even the baby watched him in awe, the drool-soaked lace of my sleeve forgotten.

Captain MacDonald continued to glare at all of us, his eyes bulging slightly as he caught sight of Mark in the chair. Rage rolled off him, fingers twitching around the handle of the hammer as he waited for an answer that didn't come. He didn't seem to notice that we were all so surprised by his arrival that we couldn't put the words together to explain right away.

"Well?" he demanded. "Ye had best have one hell of an excuse for returning. I dinna want any of this petitioning to stay, either. My ruling stands, no matter what ye may think of it. I've not been so disrespected since—"

Tristan stood, holding up a hand and interrupting MacDonald's rambling. He stared at the older man curiously, his words hesitant as he spoke. "Ye didn't ask us here?"

The query only seemed to irritate the Grand Master further. "Dinna start that," he growled. "I'll not be treated like a fool while ye try to convince me otherwise."

"It's an honest question," I interjected as I found my voice again, not liking the way he continued to barrel through the obvious signs of our confusion. "We were told you wanted us to return. You didn't send that message?"

MacDonald's head jerked back some, an incredulous expression covering his face. "Of course I dinna." His ire gave way as he glanced between us all, taking in our varying stunned looks. It was his turn to be tentative as he sat his hammer on the floor. "Ye . . . believed I did?"

"We were brought here by a Templar ship, the captain of which insisted you had called us back to Paris because Thomas Randall had escaped."

The Grand Master appeared even more affronted by my words, his eyes locking on mine like he didn't quite know what to make of me. "I did no such thing," he stated quietly, frowning as his ridged posture relaxed a bit more. There was still defensiveness in his stance, but I could tell he no longer directed it toward us.

"Of course, we already knew Randall had escaped," Callaghan added rather coarsely. "Because he sent us a message just before yer runner arrived."

"It wasna my courier," MacDonald stated again. "I tell ye all I had nothing to do with yer return to this place. I assumed ye remained in exile on the Irish coast until one of my men told me they'd seen ye in the Paris streets this very day."

"Your spies are a bit behind," Mark mumbled, watching the scene unfold with little interest. "Abella told me three days ago they were here."

MacDonald's eyes narrowed. "And yet, ye dinna think to tell me, did ye?"

Mark slunk in his seat somewhat. "Maybe if I ever saw you," he muttered. "It's not like I'm called to the

Temple much these days."

MacDonald opened his mouth to reply and then shut it, annoyed with Mark's response but choosing to ignore him. Instead, he focused on Tristan, shaking his head and closing his eyes. "How long have ye been here?"

"A week," Cal answered for his brother with a frown.

"A week! How—"

"I don't think that's necessarily our biggest problem right now," I spoke over the group, confounded they could all focus on such trivial matters when there was a larger issue present. "Who brought us back here if it wasn't a Templar?"

Everyone fell silent, and MacDonald took a moment, confusion and frustration on his face as he considered the question.

"We were given the name John Roberts if that helps at all," Tristan added.

MacDonald's expression fell, recognition lighting in it in an instant. Covering his eyes with his hands, he laughed, shaking his head. Staring at us again, he pursed his lips. "Yer sure it was John Roberts? A young man, tall, with scraggly blond hair?"

Those of us who had met him nodded.

The Grand Master laughed, all humor gone from the sound. "John Roberts was part of the group that freed Randall from his cell. He's practically Randall's right-hand man, from what I've heard."

It was like I'd swallowed an entire bag of ice. So many emotions flitted through my mind as the truth sunk in, devastating all the prior assumptions about safety I'd had.

They tricked us into coming here. All that time on the ship, where I'd brought my child and let him sleep in our cabin, where I'd openly nursed, sang, and played with him, we hadn't been safe. The house we were in now wasn't protected. This entire city wasn't secure. Everywhere I looked was a war zone, filled with secrets and pitfalls meant to destroy us.

"Tristan," I gasped, feeling as if the room were suddenly spinning. I wasn't one to faint when presented with bad news, but this was hitting me harder than most times.

He was there at once, squeezing my hand and scooping the baby off my lap without question. "Breathe, love," he whispered in my ear. "All will be well."

"We were brought here by a Black Knight," I responded sharply. "It is not all going to be fine! We trusted him with our lives, with the life of our child, and he could have killed us at any moment. He was in our house! He was—" My eyes landed on Callaghan, and the room stopped rolling somewhat. "He was there when Callaghan was attacked," I whispered.

My brother-in-law's face fell as he closed his eyes, wrath boiling to the surface. "I was on the ship with the rat that carved me up and didn't even know it," he muttered, fingers clenching into fists. In a violent motion, he slammed one into the wall, leaving a small hole in the wood panel.

"Carved up?" The Grand Master stared at him in bewilderment. "What are ye saying, man?"

In reply, Callaghan flung his jacket off, undoing the vest beneath and lifting his shirt to reveal the angry wounds on his chest.

MacDonald stiffened, his lips pressing into a thin line.

"Just like the men in the prison." Mark shook his head, exhaling.

"It wasna Randall's name carved in the prisoners," MacDonald mumbled, his eyes meeting mine for a beat. "It was . . ." Clearing his throat, he stared at Tristan, nodding in his direction. "Tristan's. It was Tristan's name."

"I suspected as much," my husband confessed. "Though, I believed it to be the reason for our summons. Hearing that ye did not require our assistance now, I wonder why ye did not call us back, considering the key involvement we have with Randall."

"Exactly," the Grand Master replied. "Ye're involved in every crackpot plan the villain creates. Why would I call ye back and play right into his hand?"

I didn't care about the specifics at that moment in time. All I could think about was the danger surrounding my son. Every little thing that had occurred during our crossing from Ireland to France played through my mind, some of them blown out of proportion as I searched for any sign that should have warned me something was off.

"Could Randall have been on the ship with us?" Glancing back at Tristan, I tried to keep control over the fear I was feeling.

Most of it was for Michael, our sweet baby who had been put in harm's way by his naive and foolish parents. What had we been thinking, accepting everything and not questioning it first? Why hadn't we demanded more proof, or refused to leave until we had confirmation from Paris we really were expected?

Suddenly, Cal's attack made more sense. It wasn't merely a trick to get us angry about Randall again and to let us know he'd escaped. It was a tool used to frighten and move us along, to steal our sense of safety.

And it had worked, just as the bastard planned. Once again, we'd fallen right into his trap, without realizing what was happening.

Tristan shook his head. "If Randall were on board, he would have confronted us and taken whatever it is he's after. No, I think Roberts was working alone."

"Or at least under orders," Callaghan growled.

"A safe bet." MacDonald sighed, picking up his hammer and resting it on his shoulder again. "And whatever the reason, the plan obviously worked. No sense in fussing over it now. All we can do is right what's been done. I apologize for barging in as I did, but I assumed ye had gone against my orders. Again."

Mark snorted, smiling at me and clearing his throat. When I glared at him in reply, he shrunk some, his grin disappearing. "An easy mistake to make," he agreed. "But I'm glad that's not the case this time."

"Aye, as am I." The Grand Master pursed his lips once more, face pensive as he considered his options and exhaled, nodding his head. "Verra good. I have much I must attend to."

"What do ye plan to do about this?" Tristan pressed. "About Roberts and whatever Randall is up to?"

"And how can we help?" I added. "Since we're clearly a part of it?"

The Scotsman shrugged, eyes narrowing. "I will

take care of it, as is my duty as leader of The Order of the Knights Templar. Ye and yer family will return home."

"What?" Once again, everyone exclaimed surprise and disdain for the answer at once.

"It's not safe for them there. Surely you can see that," Mark interjected.

"I'll send a Templar to keep guard until Randall is captured again," MacDonald replied, unbothered. Pausing for a beat, he faced Mark, eyes narrowing, the shadow of an idea crossing his face. "Ye, for instance." MacDonald smiled as if he'd been waiting the whole year to find something to pin on Mark. Apparently, I'd been wrong in assuming my old friend was MacDonald's golden child. The way the Grand Master stared at him made it clear that he was happy to condemn Mark for whatever part he'd played in our escapades last year, even if it had taken this long to do it.

"Me?" Mark sputtered, shoving to his feet. "But, my work—my patients—"

"Will all get along fine without ye," MacDonald concluded. "And since the last attack was one that required the care of a doctor, it only makes sense to send one of my physicians along."

"You're only trying to get rid of me." Mark laughed, shaking his head. "You don't have any use for me anymore. That's why you've kept me here, in the city."

MacDonald's smile fell, his eyes uncaring as he stared at my friend. "Assuming that was the case, Bell—it's not—ye will serve me better among yer friends. I ken I can count on ye to keep them where they belong."

Frowning, I watched the old man, wondering what had happened to him in the last year to make him so unforgiving and uncaring. The captain I'd served under had only the best interests of his crew in mind.

Perhaps that was the problem now. William MacDonald had the whole of The Order to take care of, and it was killing him, trying to do what was best for all of them and facing opposition to his actions at every turn. He was a good man to have in charge, but a weak leader in this instance, forcing everyone to follow what he said without any thought to further consequences.

It made sense to send us home if Randall had worked to get us away from there. But who was to say the Black Knights wouldn't return?

"You can't exile me for nothing," Mark argued. "I've done everything you've asked of me since I returned. What—"

"It's settled then." The Grand Master stomped his foot on the wood floor, speaking over him. "Ye will all board a boat in the morning and be on yer way."

The rain was more of a mist as I stood on the docks the next morning, staring at the vessel that would take us down the Seine and back out to the open ocean. Surprisingly, it wasn't one of The Order's ships, the merchant crew busily finishing up with the loading of their wares, feet slipping in the puddles on the worn wood planks beneath their feet. It was almost like watching a dance, witnessing them glide up the gangplank and disappearing over the railing of the vessel, her three masts rising high into the sky like trees missing their green. The sails remained tied, shouts ringing out on deck as everyone followed their orders.

Pulling my cloak tighter, I huddled into the warmth of the fabric, briefly checking on Michael in his sling. Despite the bleak conditions, he remained asleep, sucking his thumb as his other hand twisted into the small lace edging of my bodice.

"Are the both of ye warm?" Tristan's lips pressed against my ear, the warmth of his breath causing a ripple of gooseflesh to spring up on my arms.

Nodding, I smiled, closing my eyes as I leaned on him, letting out a breath I hadn't realized I'd been holding.

"Good," he muttered, kissing the side of my head. "It'll only be a few moments more, and then we'll be locked in our cabin, savvy?"

"We're fine," I assured him. "Just . . . tired, I think." Pulling away some, I met his stare. "So much has happened and changed in the last week."

"Aye, I know it has." He pursed his lips, his attention diverted for a beat as he looked past me, his nose twitching.

Turning, I watched as Callaghan helped Abella with her bags, the smile on his face so broad you could have seen it from the other side of the river. He'd hidden his excitement well when we informed him Abella would be returning with us, too. Of course, her official reason for coming was to be my Lady's Maid and a governess to Michael, but we all knew it was only an excuse to get her back where she belonged— at home, with us.

I watched the pair of them happily conversing, noting the way she seemed to lean into him, her grin wide and bright. She'd been delighted when I asked her to join us. What surprised me most was learning she hadn't heard Mark would be coming with us as well, and I found myself wondering more and more if they had missed the chance to be with each other while The Order butted its way into every facet of their lives.

However, there was no mistaking Cal's intentions, observing the two of them now. It would be interesting, seeing how the three of them worked together on the island.

Frowning, I stared past the young couple, my gaze settling on Mark, who was several paces behind. He didn't carry much, only bringing two bags. I recognized one of them as his medical case and the other as his ratty knapsack his clothes were kept in. He watched the pair in front of him with a blank expression, the rain soaking into his hat and dripping off the rim.

"Some changes will be for the better," Tristan whispered, finding my hand in the folds of my cloak and grasping it. "Our family will be together. That's all that matters."

Remaining silent in my reservations about returning to Ireland, I bit my lip, a small sense of despair washing over me. He was right. There were a lot of good things that came from this trip. However, more bad news had found its way into the mix, and, here we were, about to go home and ignore it all.

I couldn't be the only person who thought that was wrong, could I?

Our three traveling companions approached us, an energy of excitement buzzing about the first two.

"You didn't have to wait out here for us," Abella exclaimed, her eyes rounding with concern as she stared at Michael, warm and dry on my chest. "You'll catch a cold in this rain!"

"We're fine," I assured her, pulling her into a happy embrace. "The crew is still loading the ship anyway. We would have only been in the way, watching for you."

"Abella is right," Mark agreed, his words tired and distant as he nodded toward me. "You and the baby should get inside. You'll catch the croup or worse in this weather."

I rolled my eyes. "I'm not any more breakable than I was before just because I've had a baby. You'd all do well to remember that."

Giving Tristan a playful smile, I pulled the cape around me more, moving to head up the gangplank as it cleared of crew members. Each step I took felt wrong, the opposite bank of the river coming into view as I paused beside the railing. All around us, Paris felt bleak and abandoned, as if joining in on the guilt I felt at leaving our problems behind.

Was it so wrong to want to escape everything and live happily ever after? Sure, there was a chance our lives could be disturbed by Randall and his Black Knights again, but that would be a risk until The Order finished them for good. We were no longer part of that organization. Why should I feel like it was still our duty to finish the villain off?

Michael stirred at the subtle rocking beneath us, breathing out as he nestled closer to me, burrowing into his wrap.

Placing a hand on his head, I faced the docks, pursing my lips as I watched the others board. Where I'd felt fear at returning the last time I stood on deck, this time I worried we were leaving too soon, abandoning the world to a tirade of horror.

"*Madame* O'Rourke?" One of the crew, dressed in a navy like uniform, addressed me politely, holding an umbrella over my head.

Dragging my gaze away from the stone and wood buildings, I nodded. "*Oui. Merci.*"

"Your cabin is ready," he said with a thick accent, his smile revealing a missing bottom tooth. "I can take you there now?"

"That would be wonderful, thank you."

Tristan joined me, placing a hand on my back and nudging me forward. With one final stare at the city, I turned my back on it and went into the bowels of the boat, wondering if and when I would ever see it again.

It was miserably dark in our cabin, with only one lamp allotted to us and almost no wick to keep it lit. The glass case swung back and forth from its hook in the center of the room, casting shadows every which way as the sea knocked us about however it saw fit. We'd been given an actual bed over a hammock, the head and left side of which pressed against the wall. Three wooden pillars stretched to the ceiling in each corner except for the one nestled in the crook of the space, a thick curtain stretched between them for privacy. However, all of that did nothing to stop the pitching of the water beneath us, and as I struggled to remain on the thin mattress, I pursed my lips, wishing we'd received a more seaworthy place to rest.

Tristan, who was somehow dead asleep, rolled to the wall with a thump that startled him awake, a low laugh on his lips as he realized what had happened.

"At least it's only a few days trip," he muttered groggily, reaching for me in the dim light. His hand wrapped around my bicep, squeezing reassuringly, and slid down my arm, brushing across Michael's head where it lay on my elbow.

Biting my lip, I nodded, staring at the wooden planks of the ceiling. The seconds seemed to tick by, my breath ringing in my ears, and I knew I wasn't going to be able to stay silent any longer.

"Are we doing the right thing?" I whispered.

He paused, his hand withdrawing back to his side of the mattress, and a substantial sigh filled the air. "When I think of ye and Michael, aye. I believe returning home is the right thing to do."

Swallowing hard, I remained still, blinking as moisture pricked at my eyes. Of course going home was the right thing to do. We had a baby now. We couldn't go gallivanting across the globe, throwing ourselves in harm's way, consequences be damned. It didn't make any sense, let alone sound like responsible parenting.

Tristan's voice wavered as he paused, his fingers finding mine and wrapping around them. "But if I consider the world and our place in it as a whole? Nay, love. I do not think we are on the path the gods intended us to take."

Sucking in sharply, I felt the first few tears roll down my cheek, a sense of both overwhelming relief and fear filling me in an instant. I gripped his hand back, squeezing so hard it made my joints hurt, but he didn't complain.

"What can we do?" I asked, my throat tight with emotion. "Leave as soon as we get back home? Where will we get a ship? We don't have any money as it is."

"Ye're sure ye want to do this?" he pressed. "It is true, Randall will likely come for us at some point. If we go after him now, we will be heading directly into battle. There will be no second chances at returning to the life we had this past year."

I glanced over, finding his eyes in the darkness. "I'm sure. Going home feels wrong, Tristan. We have a part to play in this. If we try and avoid it now, it will only be that much worse for us when Randall does come to finish what he started."

The craft rolled a little more sharply than it had been and I held onto Michael tighter, placing my free hand on the closest beam and keeping us on the bed. Tristan scooted over, slipping his arm beneath my head and cradling the two of us against him, the returning motion of the vessel pushing us together.

Brushing a strand of hair from my forehead, Tristan smiled, pressing his lips there. "Ye have always been so brave and strong, Sam." He paused for a beat, kissing the top of Michael's head too. "What will we do with the bairn?"

"He will come with us." I shrugged, frowning. "It's stupid and dangerous, but the only people I would trust with his care are here with us. Michael is part of our family, and we are going to stick together, as we agreed when we first left Ireland."

"Very well." There was a tiny bit of hesitation in his tone, but I knew he accepted and agreed to my terms. "The boy stays with us. Should it come to any fight—and I'm sure it will—ye will be the one to keep him safe?"

"I will do whatever it takes," I promised faithfully. "Even if it means leaving you strapped to the mast while it burns."

He chuckled at the allusion to one of our previous encounters with Randall. "Good. I can take care of myself, so long as I know ye and the babe are safe."

I nodded again, breathing away a bit of the stress I'd been keeping locked inside. "We can track Roberts, since we don't know where Randall is," I started. "He should lead us right to the rat." Shaking my head, I realized I was getting ahead of myself. "And what about a boat?" I asked again. "It's all fine and dandy that we agree we need to do something, but it's going to be difficult to get anywhere without something to do it on."

"Aye," he agreed. "I see yer point. We'll have to find something that will work."

"Something bigger than your little fishing rig," I continued, adjusting my position so I could lay on my back. "But not so huge we can't sail it ourselves."

"That's not a problem," he said in an offhand manner. "Most crafts can be crewed by only a few men if need be. A skeleton crew of sorts, should the worst happen and the majority of the crew is lost. It is a huge amount of work with only a few, but I reckon five to seven men could crew this vessel."

His voice trailed off, the expression on his face turning to contemplation as he rolled onto his back as well. After a few minutes, he laughed, moving to his side and propping himself up on his elbow.

"We could use this ship," he said happily. "It would work wonderfully."

"*This* one?" My voice squeaked as I stared at him, dumbfounded.

"Aye," he answered encouragingly. "Think of it— it is on the smaller side of most galleons, which means it's faster. Roberts won't be able to outrun us on his best day. We can take other ships if need be, build up our wealth, and eventually buy our own sloop, which will make for a quick hunt. If we make port in La Coruña, we can ask around and get a hint at where Roberts might be, then we—"

"Hold on," I said briskly, setting Michael down flat and sitting up. "You want to take *this* ship, the one that is currently fully manned and under the command of a merchant captain? How are you going to do that, Tristan? Surely, you don't believe the five of us can beat over one hundred sailors?"

"Pfft." He waved his hand, lying flat once more as he grinned up at me, putting his hands behind his head. "This crew would turn in an instant if they thought they could get away with it. The captain treats them horribly, and I imagine the pay is next to nothing."

"Mutiny?" My voice rose almost as high as my eyebrows. "That's what you're suggesting?"

He grinned again. "Aye, love. I've done it before. Why not now?"

"You were part of the crew before," I hissed. "And working for The Order! You weren't an actual pirate."

"I most definitely was," he countered. "My ulterior purpose does not change that fact, Sam."

Sighing, I rubbed my face with both hands. "I know that," I replied snappily. "But there was a difference between then and now. You won't have a powerful organization backing you if you get caught, Tristan. None of us will. We'll all hang."

Sitting up, he wove his fingers into my hair. "Then we'd best not get caught, savvy?"

"This is madness," Mark muttered, rubbing his brow in small circles.

"Better than nothing," Cal replied, grinning.

Shaking my head, I kicked the both of them under the table, motioning toward where Tristan sat with a few members of the crew, a bowl of broth and hard tack resting in front of each of them.

The galley had seemed the most likely place to start spreading ideas of mutiny. Every member of the crew except the captain and his officers came there at some point during the day, beaten and tired from their load. All they wanted to do was eat, and it made for the perfect spot to talk while they listened.

After Tristan had insisted the crew would turn, I started paying more attention to what was going on above and below deck. They were subjected to harsh rules and punishments, sometimes forbidden from speaking amongst themselves during specific times of the day. It became more and more evident the stress they were under, their faces tight and drawn as they went about their business. Somehow, Callaghan had gotten one of them to tell him how much pay they received for each voyage. It was mere pennies. Truth be told, I was surprised they hadn't ousted their captain and turned pirate on their own before now.

"We had a barrel of rum each night," Tristan said, his voice flitting over to our table as he chatted with the riggers who'd just come down from the sails. "And played cards until the stars lit up the sky. Then there would be singing and play-acting—ye know the like— until the bell rang and it was time to sleep. Best family I ever had, my shipmates."

Smiling, I bit the inside of my cheek to keep from laughing. It was true when Tristan had been captain his crew had been like his family. He ran a tight ship, but the men liked him. Perhaps it wasn't as laid back as he was insinuating now, but I knew telling the truth wasn't his point here.

He was buttering them up, for lack of a better way to put it. All the bragging he did about how great his boat was, how close everyone had been, was meant to make them realize how strained their crew was. He was trying to make them want something better out of their work. It was highly unlikely he would be voted into any position of power after the mutiny happened, though he was trying to suggest he was the right man for the job with all his tales of captaincy. In reality, we would most likely all have to work to prove ourselves and gain their trust.

"Is it true you let your men vote on everything?" The rigger seemed suspicious at best, tired lines around his eyes as he squinted in the dim light.

"Absolutely," Tristan replied without hesitation. "I'm no tyrant. Any captain who doesn't take the opinions of his men in stride shouldn't be one in the first place."

And there it was. Without explicitly saying the word, Tristan had planted the seeds of mutiny in their minds.

Mark picked up his cup and took a long swig of

his rum, coughing somewhat as the alcohol burned down his throat. "That's my cue," he whispered, rolling his eyes as he shoved from the bench and strode over to the unknowing sailors.

"Are you spewing fish tales again?" he asked, falling into his role without any effort.

Tristan laughed. "I'm doing no such thing! Only sharing stories about our adventures at sea." Turning to the riggers, he nodded toward Mark. "Ask him anything about what I've said, and he'll tell ye the truth of it. I've sailed on more voyages with this man than I can count."

"They work well together," Abella stated, smiling as she held her arms out to take Michael from me.

Michael giggled as he blew a spit bubble, the tiny human not bothered one bit by being at sea and loving all the attention Abella showered on him.

"Yes," I agreed, passing the baby over the table with ease. "When they get along, they do."

It hadn't been easy, convincing Mark to turn to mutiny. However, the more time he spent with Tristan, the more relaxed they seemed to become around each other. The animosity they'd held for the past year slowly melted, perhaps as they realized they'd each played up the others part in their falling out. However, in the end, it was Abella who'd convinced him to help.

We all agreed Randall needed to be stopped sooner rather than later. As underhanded as this move was, it was the only thing we could do to get the ball rolling.

In the three days since we'd decided on a course of action, the men in our group had been working to convince the crew covertly. Callaghan watched their interactions through the day, noting who he believed the weak points were in the captain's net of loyalty. We would be arriving in Ireland soon and out of time to do anything if our encouragement didn't take hold by tonight, though.

"I've been speaking with the surgeon," Cal stated, leaning closer as he spoke. "The boy's scared out of his mind something is brewing. I think it could happen tonight. We've hashed it out with enough of them for the idea to stick. I'd not be surprised if we woke with a new captain in the morning."

"Are we sure they'll turn to piracy?" I prodded, feeling my anxiousness over the whole affair rise. "What if they dump the captain but decide to return to their seller?"

Callaghan shook his head. "We've not been so open about it here, but trust me, Sam. The three of us have been singing praises to piracy these past couple days. If a mutiny is going to happen, they'll take the ship for themselves."

Closing my eyes for a beat, I sighed, not liking the chance of it all. I knew they'd been working hard to turn the tides in our favor, but there was still so much that could go wrong. Not to mention the time it was going to take to get any of us in a position of power where we could decide our direction.

"There's no need to worry yerself, Sam." Cal laughed, the sound of him standing up causing me to open my eyes. "We'll be after Roberts and chasing the rat before ye know it."

Sauntering away, he joined the group at the other table, his loud laugh combining with Tristan's as they listened to whatever it was Mark was telling them.

After a few moments, I found myself too nervous to stay and listen any longer. Motioning toward Abella, I rose and left the galley, heading up the stairs to the main deck with her and Michael in tow.

There was something about fresh sea air that made me feel more in control of myself. The breeze moving through my hair filled me with new life, like the caress promised adventure and freedom. It was soothing to listen to the ship's bell, too, as well as the wind in the sails. Everything about being at sea calmed me. We'd been through so much hardship beforehand I'd never really noticed that fact until I'd been gone for a while.

"Good day Madame O'Rourke, Mistress Abella."

Turning, I watched as the captain left his position beside the helm, traversing down the staircase that led to the forecastle with a smile. A crown of tangled blonde curls billowed in the breeze at his nape, the ribbon he'd used teasing his sun-worn face. He wore a mid-calf length jacket made of dark brown leather, his white shirt untied at the neck and tucked into his long, brown breeks. If I hadn't heard the way he berated his crew at almost every moment, I probably would have believed him handsome. However, personality played a large part in my attractions, and he'd destroyed that image the same day we'd met.

Unfortunately, he'd also destroyed any hope I had of not having to speak with him on a daily basis when he informed me he'd taken considerable interest in attending myself and my Lady's Maid during the voyage. He didn't often have women passengers and wanted to make sure he was doing everything he could to keep us comfortable.

At least, that was what he'd said. His wandering

eyes and lingering gazes spoke otherwise.

"Captain Sotherby," I said with as much warmth as I could muster, swallowing the curse I wanted to emit and curtseying out of respect instead, Abella following suit beside me. "How are you today?"

"Quite well, quite well," he replied, grinning at me. "And yourself?"

"Very well," I agreed, smiling. "This is a wonderful ship you have here."

"The *Prosperity* is my pride and joy," he gushed, always ready to brag about his vessel. "I built her up from nothing, you know. She'd sink this very day without me to captain her, out of pure loyalty."

Laughing at his joke, he didn't seem to notice we were not amused. He also remained in the dark about the angry looks the crew within listening distance gave him. It was apparent the captain did nothing but order everyone else around. He refused to touch any ropes or steer if needed. Without his crew, his ship would sink, but the man was too stupid to see it.

"Surely your men must be thrilled to work with such a captain," Abella stated artfully, biting her lip as he smiled, the joke going right over Captain Sotherby's head.

"Of course," he replied. "These sailors started out as nothing. I shaped them into the great men they are today. Without me, they would be naught."

Grabbing Abella's arm, I nodded, pulling her away. "We'll take a turn, if that's fine with you, Captain?"

"Oh." Caught off guard by my sudden dismissal, he took a second to compose himself, nodding curtly. "Of course. Take in the fresh air. It is so much nicer out now that the storm has passed."

Putting our backs toward him, I linked our arms and walked as fast as I thought would be polite. "Callaghan is right," I whispered to her. "With the number of people who heard him back there, I wouldn't be surprised if we didn't have a new captain come morning."

"God willing," she muttered back. "What will they do to Sotherby, do you think?"

Frowning, I glanced back at him, watching as he pointed out a significantly tiny spot on the deck the cabin boy had missed swabbing. His beratement of the boy brought tears to the child's eyes, and I felt a twist in my stomach at the sight.

"I don't know," I replied. "But I bet it won't be good in any way."

A rush of footsteps and angry voices jerked me from slumber, the swaying of the boat catching me off guard for a moment as I tried to regain my bearings. Michael remained asleep, cradled in a mess of blankets and pillows, while Tristan's side of the bed was vacant.

Wood splintered somewhere in the hall, the sound of a door crashing open echoing through the night. The swell of speech grew, a riotous roar spewing into the air.

"What is the meaning of this?" Captain Sotherby's voice rose over those of his crew, furious and groggy.

There was no discernable answer I could make out as I slipped from beneath the covers, checking to make sure the baby was secure in his spot. Quickly, I grabbed a dressing gown from on top of our chest, wrapping it around myself and tying a knot in the belt.

Something knocked on the door, the tide of sailors having changed directions now, flooding back toward the deck.

"Mutiny!" Captain Sotherby bellowed, the words mixed into the press as it forced its way out of the small hallway. "I'll see you all hang for this!"

I cracked the entrance to my room open, peering outside as the last few men rushed past. Across the way, Abella peeked through hers as well, surprise on her face.

"Now?" she whispered.

"Sounds like it," I agreed. "Tristan isn't in bed."

I glanced down the hall, to the smaller quarters past ours. The doors to both Callaghan and Mark's cabins remained shut, suggesting they were either asleep or with everyone else.

Swallowing hard, I pulled the edges of my robe closer together and slipped out into the moonlight.

A mob of people stood in front of me, some of them carrying lanterns and torches that cast long shadows over the proceedings. A few of them had taken to the rigging in an attempt to get a better view, others on the forecastle staring down. Those who weren't shouting curses and listing offenses had grim faces, acceptance in their eyes.

"You won't make it one day without me!" The captain continued to shout as the sailors shoved him toward the railing, setting him atop a crate they'd laid out and elevating him to a point where everyone could see. "I demand to know who is responsible for this behavior!"

It was like he couldn't tell the amount of trouble he was in. The angrier the crew became, the redder the captain's face grew, until spit flew from his mouth with each word he screamed out at them. The collar of his nightgown was turned up at an odd angle, his mass of hair billowing around his face like a damning halo.

"I demand to know the name of the bilge rat who drove you all to this poor decision," he continued, slapping away the hands that attempted to bind his wrists together.

"Look around!" One of the officers shouted from the crowd, his face angry. "You're looking at him. Each of us voted, Sotherby. We made this decision together."

The captain's face flushed as he looked at the young man, rage boiling in his eyes. "Johnston," he sputtered. "You are behind this? You . . . You . . . Judas!"

Johnston, the Quartermaster, pressed his lips into a thin line as he glared at Sotherby. Shoving his way to the front of the group, he stared up at his former captain. "You are charged with being unfit to lead, for enacting cruel and unusual punishment, and for underpaying your crew. How do you plead?"

"This ain't no trial, Johnston," one of the riggers growled, grabbing a rope and holding the end of it menacingly. "The captain knows what he did, like alls of us do. Let us finish the job and get on with it."

Captain Sotherby scanned the crowd, a small amount of panic entering his eyes, and laughed. "You mean to hang me for these 'crimes,' is that it?" Shaking his head furiously, he growled at the lot of them. "I tell you, if you make one move against me, I'll see you hanged as pirates."

Johnston paused, glancing at the men, and shrugged. Slowly, a smile spread across his face. "Then I suppose we're pirates now, mate."

The crew roared at that, shouting their approval as they surged forward, knocking the displaced captain from his perch, literally and figuratively. A bit of a scuffle ensued, fists flying through the air until I caught sight of Sotherby's bound wrists, hoisted above his head. His whole body followed, the men lifting him onto their shoulders and throwing him into the ocean.

For a beat, nothing happened, the rope connected to the man going slack as he hit the water with a splash.

A few of the men grabbed the end of it, pulling it tight, heading in the same direction they'd tossed him off.

Wincing, I turned toward Abella and frowned.

"What are they doing?" she asked breathlessly, her hand at her throat.

"Keelhaul," I muttered. "Dragging him across the barnacles below. Killing him."

It was the worst thing that the crew could have done to him. If he didn't drown first, Captain Sotherby's body would be sliced to ribbons by the shells on the bottom if the boat, causing him to bleed to death. Assuming he somehow lived through all that, he would most likely contract an infection, which would also kill him in the end. Whatever happened, the man's death warrant had been signed and delivered by his men this night.

Abella's eyes widened somewhat, but she nodded.

We'd all understood this could be the outcome of our meddling.

Peering over my shoulder, I searched the crowd for Tristan, finding him on the stairs to the right of me. As our eyes met, he smiled sadly, the guilt we both felt at our actions in his stare. It vanished as he addressed one of the crew though, his face becoming a mask of adrenaline and excitement.

A few minutes of anticipation passed, the men buzzing between themselves until Sotherby's body was yanked from the water and dangled above them like the day's catch.

A breath I didn't realize I'd been holding escaped me as I saw he was dead.

The corpse fell to the deck with a sickening crunch and thud, blood trickling from the gouges in the skin, the once handsome face and hair now a mangled mess of flesh and tangles.

Placing a hand on my stomach, I turned away, closing my eyes as I battled the urge to gag. I'd never forgotten the horrors I'd seen at sea before, but this felt different somehow.

Maybe because it was partially my fault it had happened.

The excitement around me seemed to die as the men fell silent, the waves lapping the hull the only sound for a beat.

"What do we do now?" someone asked.

"Ye nominate a new captain!" Tristan shouted back, laughing. "A man who will lead ye and keep yer best interests at heart."

"I nominate the Quartermaster!" A different voice rang out, followed by approval from the rest of the men.

"Aye, Johnston!"

"Give Johnston command!"

I watched the former Quartermaster visibly swallow, his eyes trained on the man he'd betrayed.

Another beat passed, and he nodded, smiling as he looked up. "I accept," he yelled over the rest of the crowd.

The new pirates crowed with delight, celebrating their bloody victory.

Captain Johnston held his hands up for silence, grinning from ear to ear as he stepped onto the crate their previous leader had occupied only moments before. "And my first order as captain will be to break open the rum in the galley, boys. Tonight, we celebrate. The ship is ours!"

Another raucous cry pierced the night, and the men swelled again, surging below as they clapped each other on the back, congratulating themselves.

"Time to go," I said brusquely to Abella, grabbing her by the arm and towing her into the hallway. "A couple of drunks we can handle ourselves, but not a whole crew of them. We'll leave the rest of the night to the boys. You and I will sleep in my room with Michael tonight."

As if to enunciate my point, a pistol fired into the sky, followed by a cheer below.

Shaking my head, I sighed, entering into the safety of our shared space and locking the door behind me.

Fanning myself, I watched the open ocean, wishing Captain Johnston would hurry up and get on with it.

After a night of overindulgence, the men had agreed they would start off by turning around and selling their cargo at a lesser-known port. Then, they would take their new supplies and make a name for themselves. Unfortunately, due to the enormous hangover most of them were nursing, we'd not made much headway on our course. The sails weren't out currently, a good majority of the day having been spent sleeping and moaning.

Abella hummed lightly beside me, cuddling Michael. "We'll be on our way soon enough," she said in a sing-song voice, smiling at him. "Glaring at the water won't help, will it?"

Snorting, I folded my arms. "I can't help it.

They've wasted all this time." Facing her, I glanced around, dropping my voice. "Time we don't have, Abella. Who knows where Randall is right now? He could have already taken another treasure, and we wouldn't know it."

Frowning at that, she met my stare, opening her mouth to say something. Before any words left her, her gaze moved past me, eyes narrowing.

Glancing over my shoulder, I watched as one of the crew approached us, his walk and leering smile making it clear he was still drunk, not to mention the bottle wrapped in his grasp. He appeared to have either peed himself or sloshed a drink all over his bedraggled shirt and breeches, his bare feet as sunburned and sickly looking as his face.

"Hello, ladies." He hiccupped, tapping the brim of his hat with two fingers, his breath so smelly it made my eyes water.

Not bothering to be polite, I linked my arm with Abella's and began to leave, only to be yanked back by the waist. Yelping, I turned in the man's embrace, leaning from his mouth as he swooped in toward me.

"Come now," he purred, in what I was sure he thought was a seductive manner. "All I want is a little kiss."

"Let go of me," I hissed, shoving him.

Surprisingly steady, he laughed, tightening his grip, grinding his pelvis into me and leaving nothing to the imagination.

Huffing, I slapped him. "My husband will have your head when he hears of this," I ground out, still trying to push him away.

"Who said he has to know?" His words slurred as

he laughed. "He's not here now. It can be our little secret." He made a shushing noise, giggling in his drunkenness, nose-diving into the crook of my neck and plastering his horrible lips on my skin.

He was right, of course. Tristan was nowhere to be seen, or Cal, or Mark. I was on my own here while they were off doing whatever convincing they needed to do to control the ship.

Funnily enough, I didn't care that they weren't there at the moment.

A sense I'd not used in some time wrapped around my mind and I growled, seizing the blade at his waist. In an instant, it was angled at the hollow of his throat, my free hand clutching him as tightly as he did me.

Pulling back, he ogled me in drunken surprise, a low guffaw emanating from him. "You think you could do it?" he asked, goading me. The look in his eyes said he didn't believe me capable of harming him, or anyone else. "Kill a man? Or does your husband do your dirty work for you?"

The anger inside me intensified at that, the idea of him treating others in this manner lighting like a fire. "Do not mistake the absence of a penis for the inability to defend one's self," I growled. "I've killed men before, and I could do it again, easily." Pressing the point of the blade against him a little harder to drive the idea home, I smiled. "I don't need my husband to protect me—I can do that quite well myself. It's not only the men who are pirates on this boat. You'd do well to remember that."

The sailor swallowed hard, his Adam's apple trembling as the blade nicked his skin, drawing a small drop of blood. The look of confidence and mirth faded from his eyes, replaced with fear as his hands released me.

"Very good," I smirked. "Now run along and get yourself cleaned up. You reek like the wrong end of a sick dog."

He nodded, stumbling backward, and ran, slipping below deck once more.

Taking a deep breath, I suddenly became aware of a few riggers perched in the ropes overhead. They all stared at me with guarded expressions, watching as I thrust the blade I'd stolen into an empty crate.

"Sam?" Abella asked timidly, drawing my attention back to her. "Are you well?"

Pursing my lips, I nodded, working to relax my shoulders.

She stared at me a moment longer as if assessing whether or not I spoke the truth, and smiled. "Pirates like to whore," she said humorlessly, moving to stand beside me again. "We should have thought of that before."

"Yes," I agreed in a tone just as dry. "I assumed we would make ourselves useful in other ways, but it appears not."

"They already have a cook and a surgeon. There's not much more we can do to help than that, is there?" She began humming again, swaying with Michael, kissing his nose as he giggled. "At least we have Michael to keep us company," she said happily. "What with his baby laugh and handsome cheeks!"

She kissed him again, blowing raspberries on his neck and he crowed with delight, his little eyes lighting up as she played with him.

Her earlier words stuck with me as I watched the

two of them, the sour meeting moments before slipping away with a smile on my face. She was right; there wasn't much else we could do as part of the crew. We were probably small enough to work the rigging, but I had no idea what any of the knots were or how to properly keep the sails as they should be. The statement gave me pause, and I decided to think about it further. Perhaps there was something I could learn, or a job I could fill that I hadn't considered yet.

"Good day, ladies." Callaghan's voice had us turning again, his smile serving to ease my tense mood further. "I wonder if you would join us men in your room for a chat? Tristan has news he'd like to share with us all."

"What's going on?" I asked as soon as we were all cooped up in the small space.

"I've good news," my husband said, swooping in and kissing me in greeting.

"Well, an okay update," Mark amended, folding his arms as he leaned on the now closed door.

"You've been allowed to join the crew?" Abella asked anxiously.

"Aye, all three of us," Cal responded with eagerness. "Captain Johnston said the men would have to vote on it, but I don't think they'll have any problem accepting us. We were the ones that pushed them to mutiny, after all."

"Don't be so sure," I cautioned him. "That may turn a few of them against you. They won't know if you can be trusted or not. And . . ."

Biting my lip, I glanced at Abella, knowing I should tell them what happened with the sailor a few moments ago.

"What's amiss?" Callaghan questioned, catching on as he looked at the two of us. "Has something happened?"

Sighing, I nodded.

"What?" Mark pressed. "You haven't had time to do anything."

Raising an eyebrow, I sat on the bed. "I . . . may or may not have threatened the life of one of the crew a few moments ago. At sword point. I drew blood, but he was otherwise unharmed."

"To be fair, the man kissed her," Abella added quickly, sliding into the explanation before any of them could say anything. "He was very drunk and wouldn't leave her alone. I believe she acted accordingly."

The three men remained silent, absorbing the information.

"Either way, I'm confident we're accepted," Tristan continued, smiling. "Lord knows I won't fault ye for defending yerself. However, that's not the best of what I have to share."

"Oh?" Relieved my actions wouldn't affect their plans, I leaned into him, wrapping my fingers around his. "What is?"

"Captain has agreed to head to La Coruña," Mark stated in a matter of fact tone. "He believes it's to drop you off with family, but he's approved none the less."

My eyebrows rose as I looked at Tristan again. "To drop us off?"

"He thinks it's bad luck to have women aboard," he said, waving his hand in dismissal. "It won't matter by the time we've arrived, though."

"Why not?" Abella inquired, asking before I could.

"Because." Tristan grinned, lowering his voice before continuing. "I'll be captain by that point."

I couldn't help but laugh. "I don't doubt your drive and ambition," I started. "But how exactly are you planning on doing that? You can't lead the men in a second mutiny, not without drawing their suspicions."

"He won't have to," Cal replied with confidence.

"He'll prove himself before then. The crew will see what a natural leader he is and vote him in on their own."

"Meaning you plan on helping them attack and raid another ship." I glanced at Michael, a thread of dread winding through me.

"It's the only way, love." Tristan's voice was comforting, but I could hear the hesitation in it as well.

"I know," I responded. "Everything will be fine. I trust you."

He smiled at that. "Good." His energy seemed to transfer to me as he kissed my forehead, his excitement at his plans coming to fruition contagious. "Walk on deck with me, savvy? I've missed you."

For the next four days, after we made port in England and slipped away into open waters again, that was how our lives played out. Tristan worked with the crew, I spent my time with Abella and the baby, and, in the late afternoon, my husband and I would walk around the ship hand in hand, talking about nothing in particular. It would have driven me insane if I didn't know we were headed in the direction we wanted to go.

Tristan, on the other hand, became more anxious with each day. We'd not yet come across a merchant to chase, and I knew he was worried we would make it to Spain before he could gain control of the boat.

Truthfully, I didn't know what he was planning to do that would turn the crew in his favor. It felt as if I were constantly looking over my shoulder for either Roberts or MacDonald, come to stop us from achieving our goals, too. I did trust that everything would work out the way it was supposed to, however, and so I said nothing, choosing to let each day pass by with as little stress as possible.

"Ye're awfully quiet." Tristan's hand tightened around mine, his smile lifting my spirits considerably as we made our slow, evening walk.

"Just thinking about . . . everything," I admitted. "It's been four days without anything happening, especially after the mutiny was so much more brutal than I'd imagined it would be. It feels like a change is around the corner."

He laughed. "It may be, love. How fares Michael? He is still holding up at sea?"

"Of course." Grinning, I thought of the boy and how fast he was growing. It was like he made changes overnight sometimes, becoming smarter and more able in the blink of an eye. He'd begun rolling over in the bed, prompting a much closer watch of his activities between Abella and I. It was crazy to think that in a few months he would be walking, beginning to talk, and leaving the tiny, helpless human he was now behind.

"And ye?" Tristan continued, slowing until we stopped beside the bow of the ship. "How are ye, *Grá mo Chroí*? Ye have put up with much in such a short time."

Sighing, I nodded, an instant weariness threatening to take over me. "I'm fine," I answered truthfully. "Getting back into the swing of things."

"Aye." His eyes sparkled with mirth as he stared at me, his lips twitching. "I heard tell of yer exploits on deck with the drunkard. Ye do not need me to protect ye, do ye?"

Laughing, I shook my head. "You know I don't.

Not when it comes to men putting their hands where they shouldn't."

He chuckled, pulling me into his embrace. "That and much more," he muttered, his lips brushing against my ear. "It's like I've always said. Ye are a fierce soul, Samantha. My brave heart. My pirate lass."

"And you are my everything and more," I muttered back, tilting my head until our mouths met.

Groaning, he wove his fingers into my hair, holding us together as he teased me. The kisses weren't long or deep enough, my breath catching as the need to delve into him overwhelmed me. For a moment, I forgot we were out in the open, my hands spreading across his chest, heart racing as I captured his bottom lip between my teeth.

A chuckle rumbled inside him as he gave in, covering my mouth fully and stealing my breath. His touch felt like taking flight and putting down roots at the same time, like the push and pull of the ocean, balanced and awe-inspiring.

Strong arms wrapped around my waist, anchoring us together. The smell of him, of sea salt and sweat, mixed with rum and a hint of smoke, surrounded me, threatening to consume me completely.

And I would let it. If every moment of every single day of my life were spent like this, I would be the happiest woman on the face of the planet. There was nothing that made me feel more at peace and loved than Tristan's embrace.

Breaking away, he rested his forehead on mine, grinning as he played with the ends of the loose strands of my hair. "I was thinking," he started, his tone low and seductive. "What if we had Michael sleep in

Abella's room tonight? I've not had ye all to myself in some time. Not the way I want to."

Blushing, I chewed on my lip, nodding. "I can ask."

His face flushed and he caressed me again, laughing. "Sometimes ye make me feel like a lad who hasn't got his head on straight."

"That's a good thing, right?"

His eyes burned as he gazed into mine. "Aye. Very good."

Inhaling, I leaned in, content with one more kiss for the time being.

"Sails!"

The cry drew our attention, our gazes turning toward the skyline. There, in the distance, I could barely make out the shape of a boat. It was hardly a pinprick, the blazing light of the setting sun almost washing it out. The eagle eyes of the watch had spotted it though, and there was no doubting what it was.

The crew excitedly gathered on the starboard side, pointing and searching for themselves as Captain Johnston emerged from below and took up his spyglass. After a moment, he lowered the instrument, a determined and excited expression on his face.

"Her sails are drawn," he muttered. For a beat, he thought to himself. Smiling, he exhaled. "Mister Wilcox," he stated to the navigator, loud enough for the entire group to hear. "Set a new course. We have a ship to catch!"

The men roared with delight, scattering about as they went to their positions, the sails billowing as we turned.

Grasping my arm, Tristan muttered in my ear.

"Take Abella and Michael to the surgery. It'll be the safest for ye, and ye can help the physician if need be."

Nodding, I moved to obey, surprised when he tugged me back, his face serious and grim.

"What is it?" I asked breathlessly, my heart still fluttering from the embrace we'd shared moments before.

"Take the sword from the chest." His lips barely moved as he spoke, his eyes looking past me, untrusting of those around us. "Should anything happen, use it."

Stunned, I gaped at him, the words stuck in my mouth for a beat. "I can't use Excalibur," I whispered back. "It's yours—you're the only one who can."

"I'm the only one who can pull it from stone, which is not where it currently resides, now is it?" He raised an eyebrow, giving me a small smile. "There's no one else I would trust to wield it, Samantha. It will give me relief to know ye have it. This fight . . . It will either bring us success or destroy everything. These men have never pirated before. I cannot say which way the battle will go. Take my blade and promise to defend yerself with it if ye must."

Blinking, I frowned. "What about you? Do you have another weapon?"

He shook his head. "There's plenty to choose from."

The idea still didn't suit me. I couldn't picture myself handling the legendary blade, let alone using it. But, as I looked at my husband's face, I knew I had no other choice than to agree.

Even if I only held it for his benefit, it would be worth it.

"Fine," I breathed. "I'll take it."

Leaning in, he kissed my forehead, his fingers pressing painfully hard into my arm before he let go. "We've time before we catch her. Gather the others and make yerselves comfortable. When all is said and done, I will come to ye."

I pursed my lips. "Stay safe."

His grin banished some of the worries that had filled me with his words. "Always, love."

Parting ways, I hurried toward the cabins, not sure where Abella and Michael were at the moment. When the rooms turned up empty, I went through the chest beside our bed, shoving aside dresses and tattered hats until I uncovered the blade Tristan wished me to keep.

My hands hovered over the pommel, and I swallowed hard. It was still difficult to accept this was a mythological weapon. Looking at it, bundled in its sheath, laying at the bottom of our belongings, no one would have assumed anything of it. However, I knew as soon as I pulled it free of its bindings, the blade would glow with a faint light, made up of magic and pure goodness, if what we'd been told in the Otherworld was true. All I knew for sure was that it was powerful and dangerous.

And that my husband wished me to keep it for him.

Steeling my nerves, I grabbed the thing and held it against myself, partially hiding it in my skirt as I hurried from the room. Anyone who did notice I had it quickly forgot, the crew eager for their first hunt.

"Samantha!"

Abella's voice cried over the din, her figure appearing on the steps to the galley, Michael in her arms. Her expression was worried, her grasp on him tight as she watched me walk toward them at a brisk pace.

"Mark said to go to the surgery," she said as soon as I was within speaking range. "He is fighting with the men, but the physician will be down there with us."

"I know," I stated calmly. "Tristan said the same."

Her eyes widened as she stared at the sword in my hands. "Do you think they will attack us there?"

Shrugging, I jerked my head toward the bowels of the ship. "I'm not sure. If we are, it's better to be prepared, isn't it?"

"Ready yourselves, men!" Captain Johnston's voice carried over the deck again, his command echoed by his officers. "Come nightfall, we will be the proud victors of this battle!"

Searching the crowd for Tristan, I found him on the opposite side ship, his eyes locking with mine before he smiled, encouraging me.

"Come on," I said to Abella, turning and pulling up the hem of my skirt so I didn't trip on the stairs. "It won't be long now before all hell breaks loose."

Water dripped through the floorboards above as we sat in the surgery, the physician anxiously tending to his instruments and muttering to himself. With only a few lamps to light the cramped space, it was hard to tell what he was doing, but I knew he was nervous.

"*Monsieur*?" Abella asked timidly, rising from our spot in the corner and rubbing her hands on her dress.

Startled, the short, young man glanced up at her, his scalpel falling from his hands and clattering onto the ground, beneath his operating table. Nervous eyes peered at her as he gulped, rubbing his palm over the short stubble on his face.

Stepping forward, Abella carefully picked the tool up, flicking open one of the lamps and laying it on the flame inside. Removing the man's leather apron from its hook on the wall, she held it out to him, encouraging him to take it on his own.

"The flame purifies all," she stated quietly, nodding toward the knife. "And you'll need this cover to protect your clothes."

He glanced down at his wrinkled shirt and vest, his trembling hands brushing against his thighs as he cleared his throat. Meeting Abella's eye again, he carefully took the offered item, sliding the neck harness over the top of his head and tying the back together.

"You've never been faced with this kind of work before?" She continued kindly, joining him on the other side of the table as she rolled her sleeves up.

"N-no," he stammered. "I mean, yes, I have, but not of this magnitude. This is my first voyage—I assumed working at sea would give me more experience and credentials when I return home to open my practice. But then the crew turned pirate, and Captain Johnston wouldn't let me retire when we made port, and my village needs a doctor. If I die today, they will—"

"Shhhh," Abella whispered. "All will be well." Her hand covered his, steadying it as she smiled.

Gulping, he looked at her in shock.

"I have seen many things like this before," she continued easily, her tone soothing and even. "It will be bad. Men are going to die, no matter what you do."

He made a sound of distress, pulling away from her.

Grasping his fingers in her own, she guided him back, smiling. "But I am here to help you," she continued, the phrase sounding more like an order than an offer of help. "If we work together we may yet save some who would have perished. *Oui*?"

Swallowing hard, he nodded. "*Oui*. I mean, yes. Thank you. Miss . . ?"

"Abella," she stated with a grin. "I was an assistant to a physician in Paris and have worked on a ship before."

"Very well." His head bobbed for a moment as he stared at his table again. After a beat, the worst of the nerves seemed to pass, and he straightened. "Does putting the blade in the flame not ruin the edge in the metal?"

"No," she responded. "But it will help keep the men from becoming sick after you work on them. You must cleanse the knife for every person, or it will be for naught."

Frowning, he regarded her. "Where did you learn this technique?"

"She's right," I responded roughly, drawing both their attention. "You have to clean it, or they'll get sick, maybe die. Wash your hands, too."

Above, the first sound of a cannon firing boomed through the ship, the responding splash distant and ahead of us.

The doctor opened his mouth to debate further but snapped it shut as I stood, Michael cradled in my arms.

"There's no time to argue about it now," I continued, my tone somewhat harsh. "Get them all in a flame, or you won't have time once the battle starts."

As the pair went about readying the room, I peered out the flap that covered the entrance. The deck was empty, hammocks swaying among the men's belongings. Waves rolled the ship from side to side, the floor pitching somewhat as we barreled forward, racing toward our prey.

Michael remained unbothered by everything, yawning and sucking his thumb as I held him, having no clue as to what was about to happen. Having him here made my heart clench in fear. There was so much that could go wrong, so many ways he could be hurt. But, there was no one else I would rather him be with at this moment than with his family.

Another cannon boomed overhead, the cheering of the men revealing we were at last in range to hit the target.

I didn't know if the other ship had tried to run.

Saying a silent prayer for the souls on board the other vessel, I let loose a sigh and turned my thoughts to the people going into battle. It was all I could do to hope that our ideas would somehow work out and we would all make it out of this mess alive.

"This is a crackpot plan," I muttered to myself, letting the curtain fall back into place and finding my seat in the corner once more.

After another half an hour, filled with cannon fire and not much else, I finally heard the telltale sounds of a ship boarding. Gunshots rang in the air, as did shouting and more cannons, the cracking of wood ringing in my head.

Flinching, I covered the baby's ears, rocking him gently as he cried, big fat tears rolling down his cheeks.

Suddenly, the curtain yanked aside, a man nursing a bloody shoulder stumbling into the room.

Abella and the physician burst into action, going about their business without hardly any hiccups. As soon as they'd removed the ball from the man's arm, another injured sailor appeared, this time gripping his stomach, blood dripping from his middle.

"This way," Abella ordered, all but shoving the other man off the table. "Wrap him up," she said to the doctor. "And sit him beside Samantha."

It felt like a blur after that. Soon, I'd given my chair up to someone else, swaying in the far corner as I rubbed Michael's back, trying to keep him calm. It sounded like an all-out war overhead, the battle lasting much longer than any other I'd experienced.

Slowly, I began to realize we were losing. There

were too many men here in the surgery, too many injured that were fleeing the fight for protection and assistance. If those who remained above weren't careful, we would all find ourselves at the bottom of the ocean before the moon finished rising.

The curtain moved aside again, revealing Mark and a slumped over body he was struggling to carry alone. Blood gathered around his midriff, soaking his shirt and dripping slowly onto the floor.

"Abella," I said sharply, looking for a place to set the baby that would be safe.

Turning at the sound, my friend's eyes widened as she saw Mark. "Are you hurt?" she asked, going to him in an instant.

"It's just a scratch," he grunted, hefting the person with him into the room with another step. "And most of it isn't mine. Captain Johnston, on the other hand . . ."

The man's head rolled back, revealing the new captain, beaten and bloodied, a saber slash across his face.

"What happened?" I asked, feeling like I was watching the grasp of death slowly steal the man from in front of us.

Mark shrugged. "He panicked."

"What needs to be done?" Abella asked, impatient as she helped to hold the man up on the other side.

"He's fading fast. I've got my finger against an artery that's been nicked here, in his armpit. If we can stitch it up now, he might still make it." Flexing his hand under the captain's arm, Mark revealed the spot that needed immediate tending. "Help me lay him down, will you?"

As he struggled to move farther into the room, I located a sailor who wasn't too injured and passed Michael to him. "Here," I ordered, not giving him any choice in the matter. "If you make him cry, I swear, I will cut you." Raising a finger up, I let the threat hang in the air for a beat before moving to help Mark and Abella.

"Tristan?" I asked, taking up the side Abella had been handling.

Mark grunted as we laid the captain on the table, a weak stream of blood spurting out onto the floor as he revealed the wound in full. Clapping his hand over the area, Mark shook his head, pursing his lips.

"He was on board the other ship, last I saw. The worst of it is over."

Another cannon boomed outside as if trying to prove him wrong. As a light layer of dust sprinkled down from above, everyone in the vicinity flinched.

"Give me a needle and thread," Mark commanded, holding his hand out to Abella. There wasn't an ounce of surprise when she handed it over before he'd even finished speaking, the two of them working together like a well-oiled machine as they tended to Johnston.

The ship's physician, noticing this, wandered off to the other men, checking their wounds and bandages and leaving the team to work alone.

Frowning, I fell silent as well, taking Michael back into my arms and moving to the curtain once more. As I peered out, I caught sight of movement on the gun deck, the sounds of a light scuffle flitting down to me. After a moment, there was a dull thud and the fighting ceased, the first beats of silence filling the air.

Hesitating, I strained to see anything through the

hatch, the golden sky marred only by a few strands of rigging.

A hand gripped the edge of the opening, its owner pulling himself into view, recognition covering his features as he saw me.

"Are ye well?" Tristan asked, his face blood splattered and sweaty. Slowly, the rest of him slid into the opening, his weary body resting on the steps, a gory sword in his other hand. His hair fell across his eyes some, the dark locks wet and dripping as his chest heaved, breath eventually returning to normal.

Nodding, I bit my lip, feeling the clenching of my heart as we stared at each other.

This was the life we were choosing. Danger. Death. Criminal. We had to be out of our minds to go this route.

But what other choice did we have? Surely, this was better than doing nothing, than letting Randall win and surrendering ourselves to his mercy.

"Are you hurt?" I asked, finding my voice as I spotted a rip in his trousers, the fabric dark and bloody around his thigh.

"Only a wee cut," he assured me.

"O'Rourke!"

The voice called from above, drawing our attention as the quartermaster appeared in the opening as well, concern on his features.

"Aye?" Tristan asked, shoving to his feet.

The man gawked at him for a beat, uncertainty in his eyes, and shrugged. "What do we do now? Take the lot?"

I caught the slightest hint of a laugh in Tristan's eyes as he sheathed his sword and suppressed my grin.

It was like we were on a ship with little pirate babies, all of which had no idea how actually to do the task they'd set out to perform.

"Ye'll take what's of value," Tristan explained patiently. "Yer hold is already filled with goods from port, savvy? Take only what will fetch a pretty penny when we dock again. Ye'll need the guns as well."

"Guns?" The quartermaster raised an eyebrow. "We already have guns."

"That ye do," Tristan agreed. "But not nearly enough. *Providence* is heavily armed as she is, but if ye intend to hunt down other merchants, ye're going to need more power than ye had today to make it quick."

"And what of the repairs?"

Tristan waved a hand. "Set yer men to it, Quartermaster. The faster ye can repair the damage to the hull, the sooner we can be on our way and making coin, no?"

The man nodded, rubbing his chin, doubt creeping into his features. "Perhaps I should speak with Captain Johnston about his wishes beforehand," he started, taking a step onto the first stair.

"There's no need."

We all turned at the voice, my chest clenching again as I heard the regret in the tone.

Moving through the curtain beside me, Mark sighed, wiping his bloody hands on a dirty cloth, his expression stiff and mask-like. He stared at us for a beat, blinking, his posture rigid.

Without him even saying anything, I knew what news he had to share. I'd seen him stand that way before, seen that look on his face. The other men seemed to know the truth as well, their faces falling as

he spoke the reality of our situation.
"The captain is dead."

"I didn't mean for it to happen like this, ye know that, do ye not?"

Leaning against the door to our cabin, Tristan ran a hand through his hair, exhaling. He'd cleaned up once he was done helping with the moving of the goods, revealing a shallow but extended cut on his leg. At my insistence, he'd allowed me to wash it, his expression pensive and lips silent as I worked.

Then, the news we'd both been expecting arrived. The crew needed to vote for a new captain, and Tristan was up for consideration.

I almost wanted to laugh, thinking about it. Again, this was what we'd planned. He needed to prove himself to them, to gain the men's trust and secure the highest position of leadership. However, the way it had all worked out—with several of the men injured in a nasty conflict and the new captain dead before he'd had the chance to try his hand at anything—was not what I'd envisioned.

For some reason, I continued to think that there would be a measure of propriety at sea. The good guys would win, and the bad ones would fall. We were pirates, but we were civilized. However, each time the ocean and I resided in the same space I learned over and over that this was a bloody and unforgiving profession.

And the crew of the *Providence* had learned that

hard lesson today, too.

In the aftermath of the battle, I'd learned how awful things had been above deck. Captain Johnston hadn't panicked. He'd completely lost his bearings, having no idea what to do once the fight began. The men had been just as frightened and confused, their blundering leading to the length of the battle and severity of their wounds. The entire plot to capture the ship had fallen apart in a matter of moments once the two vessels became lashed together.

Tristan must have seemed like a godsend. He rallied those around him, leading the charge and ordering them about with Callaghan's assistance. Those who had been beside him suffered the least and, ultimately, they took their prize under his guidance. Even afterword, they turned to him for instruction and advice, doing everything he said without question.

It was no wonder they were considering him as their permanent leader now.

"I know," I answered Tristan, continuing to feed Michael in the corner chair. "I wish it had gone down different, that's all. I feel like we're responsible for their deaths. All of them."

"Ye think I don't?" he asked, his voice rough as he shook his head in frustration. "What other choice do we have, Sam? Randall is out there, possibly looking for us as we do him and Roberts. Life was going to be lost no matter what we did."

"I know that," I responded sharply, giving him a brief glare. "I agreed to all of this. I'm not trying to blame you for anything." Sighing, I shook my head, closing my eyes as frustration picked at my raw edges. Softening, I met his stare again, shrugging. "I'm only trying to tell you the truth about where I stand. All of this—leaving our home and throwing ourselves back into this battle—it's been hard for me to accept. I know why we're doing these things. They *are* for the greater good. My mind and my heart are struggling to reconcile them, that's all."

Smiling, he nodded, understanding and recognition in his eyes. "Aye. It has been difficult, but I wouldn't have anyone else by my side through it all."

The reassurance worked, and I grinned. "You're stuck with me, whether you like it or not."

"Oh, I like it. Very much, love." His gaze smoldered as he stared at me, the teasing tone of his voice serving to lighten my spirits somewhat.

A knock at the door drew both our attention then and I held my breath, waiting as he cracked the entrance open and shared a few murmurs with whoever was on the other side.

The latch clicked shut as he faced me again, leaning against the wood.

"Well?" I prompted, nerves filling me at the prospect of how our future could change now.

Pursing his lips, he glanced around the room, a bit of humor entering him when he stared at me again. "Ye won't have to complain about a lack of light in our new quarters, what with all those windows along the back wall."

Relief filled me, to the point that it brought tears to my eyes. "They voted you in."

"Aye," he said in confirmation. "I am captain."

Smiling, I stared at the coast of La Coruña, easily recalling the last time I'd been here. The occasion appeared to be on Tristan's mind as well, his chuckle drawing my attention as he stopped beside me, peering over the railing at the green, Spanish town.

"Ye know, the last time we were here, I thought I would never see ye again." His arm wound around my waist and pulled me to him, words muttered into my ear as he continued, his lips brushing my skin and tickling me. "I wanted so much to protect ye from Rodrigues, and ye'd angered me by toying with him, but it nearly tore me apart, setting ye ashore here and sailing away."

Laughing, I leaned to the side, staring at him. "Toying with Rodrigues? I did no such thing."

He chuckled again, nodding in response. "Aye, ye did, lass. I remember the sight of ye on his lap with his lips at yer neck quite clearly. If I'd not possessed a Herculean amount of self-control, I'd have ripped him limb from limb right then."

"I was only trying to catch him off guard," I argued, giggling in spite of myself. "Or did you forget I only cozied up to him so I could knock him out and steal his clothes?"

Humming softly in the back of his throat, he kissed the side of my head, nuzzling his nose in my hair. "How could I forget such a thing? I found ye in them not a week later, after ye shot me, foolish woman."

"An accident," I countered, still laughing over the memories. "I assumed you were a pirate coming in to kill me, after all." Leaning on him, I placed my hands on the top of his, settling into his embrace comfortably.

"That was the first time you ever kissed me, when you found me on that ship with Father Torres."

"Aye. So much for Herculean self-control, eh?"

Turning in his embrace, I wrapped my arms around his neck and pulled him down to meet my mouth, his touch causing my heart to pound the same as it had that first time. His lips moved with mine, almost teasing me, but it didn't matter. Whenever we were together like this, I felt like I was floating on a river of happiness.

Contented, I faced the shore once more, observing the longboat being prepared to take us to the beach out of the corner of my eye. Ahead, several vessels were docked, leaving no space for our galleon to move all the way into the harbor.

An air of unease flitted over me, and I shifted from one foot to the other, frowning. We had our ticket to chase Roberts now, but what if no one had seen him since we parted ways? There was no telling how lengthy our hunt would be, and I could only hope for our desired outcome in the end.

Steeling my wandering emotions, I cleared my throat, resolving to take each day on its own merits. There was no use getting worked up over the future when it remained so frustratingly out of reach.

Glancing to the other side of the ship, I relaxed at the image of Abella and Cal playing with the baby, sitting close together as they tickled and kissed him. Each seemed drawn to the other, like gravity, their smiles shining.

Cal had been doing much better with all his stitches removed. Abella made quick work of them as soon as we'd left Paris and still checked on his wounds often, especially after his escapades during the battle. He'd healed nicely though and escaped any significant injury, prompting her to share how pleased she was with his recovery.

If I was honest with myself, I was beginning to wonder if her presence here was more for Cal or Mark.

Turning a little, I watched the latter as he hovered around the crew. Something was different about him these past couple days. I'd believed he was doing better after sharing his feelings with me in Paris, but it appeared the opposite was true. His eyes didn't shine with happiness anymore, and his speech was no longer upbeat and positive. The Mark I'd met in my own time and the man I saw now were two completely different people.

"He's not doing so well," Tristan remarked, his attention turning to our old friend, too. "Almost sickly, if ye ask me."

"Yes," I agreed, saddened both by the fact that Mark was suffering so and that I wasn't the only one who was noticing. "He's . . . homesick."

Tristan remained silent, the pair of us scrutinizing him a moment more.

Continuing to peer at Mark, I felt a sad twist in my heart. I'd never considered other options for returning home before. There was no need; I didn't want to. There was nothing left for me there. This time and place was my home now, with Tristan and my family.

Mark, on the other hand, had nothing here, it seemed. He'd bounced around from place to place, keeping to himself, stuck in a past from which he wished to escape. He refused to do anything that might alter the future unless he found it absolutely necessary.

Of course he would want to go home. Life would be easier there. He had friends, maybe family members who were missing him, searching for him, hoping he would turn up.

"Tristan," I started, hesitating at the last minute. How could I tell him I wanted to search for another way to travel time? Mark was a touchy subject for him. I also didn't want him to think I may leave him someday if we discovered how to do it. When Pandora's Box had been in our possession, the option of me going home was forever hanging over our heads, picking at our relationship like flies.

"Captain?"

The first mate's voice interrupted me before I could say anything else and I sighed, resigned to the fact that I would have to talk to Tristan about it another time. With any luck, he would realize the nature of my request and wouldn't make a big deal out of it. He knew I loved him and that I didn't want to leave.

Tristan turned to the man, nodding. "I expect ye all back by nightfall tomorrow," he called loudly across the deck.

The first mate grinned, facing the men as well. "All ashore who's going!"

An excited scramble started, and I laughed, stepping out of the way with Tristan as we watched the men eagerly head for the boats. Among them was the physician, his belongings grasped in his hands, permission to leave the crew secured.

"What about us?" I asked softly, watching as he found his seat, an expression of relief washing over his face.

Tristan hummed, wrapping his arm around my

waist. "We will ask around," he stated simply. "Roberts has to make port somewhere. We'll find him."

"And when we do?"

He paused for a moment, his face darkening some. Breathing out, he straightened. "He'll take us to Randall, one way or another."

Our time at sea seemed to fly by as soon as we set sail again, a few sightings of Roberts having been shared with us by disgruntled sailors in the pub at La Coruña. Most of the men we'd spoken to had made it clear he was a force to be reckoned with, sharing tales of woe and misfortune in regards to anyone who had been unlucky enough to cross his path. Without any findings of our own, we were forced to make port often, asking around for any clue to the direction we should be going. After a week or two, we came to the conclusion he was heading for the Strait of Gibraltar, for reasons unknown.

Tristan had convinced the men we were hunting an enormous treasure. However, after almost a month of no prizes, I was sure they were beginning to mutter the idea of mutiny between one another. All it would take is one vote and we could lose control.

The crew seemed to be establishing an opinion of dislike toward the women and child presence on their ship as well. As it was, we spent most of our day seated atop the sterncastle, observing the goings-on of the vessel with quiet ease. It was the best place to feel a part of everything, with Tristan by our sides every so often, giving orders and checking in on us. When he was busy elsewhere, we had no one to watch over our area but ourselves. Mark had taken up the position of the ship's surgeon when the last one left, and

Callaghan was always doing his share of the work. When the other men started looking at us with distaste and whispering about bad luck, I started bringing a sword everywhere with me. Sometimes, I wondered if my earlier altercation with the drunk member was the only thing keeping them from rushing us outright and doing whatever it was they wished to us.

We passed through the strait without any pause, sailing around the other side of France and into the Mediterranean Sea. The location gave me a strange thrill and excitement, being one of the places I'd yet to visit in the world. I'd often heard tales of how beautiful the land and water were here and imagined vacationing in Greece or Italy.

Tristan was quick to caution me. This place was not the same as it was in my time. The countries did not get along so well and, despite the fame of their brothers in the Caribbean, more pirates sailed the Mediterranean Sea than any other. It was as dangerous as it was beautiful, a fact he made sure to drive home with force.

Staring at the southern coast of France, sitting beside the table Abella and I had taken to playing cards on, I nodded in the direction of the wooded land.

"Do you think Randall escaped by road instead of sea?" I asked Tristan, observing as he examined the distant earth through a spyglass.

"It is possible," he agreed in an offhand manner, focusing on his task. "That would explain why Roberts came around this way."

"To pick him up, you mean?"

"Aye. He could head for Marseille." Sighing, he lowered the instrument, sliding the pieces together until it was small enough to stow in his pocket once more. "That doesn't make sense, does it?" Shaking his head, he took the empty seat at the table, absentmindedly nudging one of the soft, teething toys I'd made for Michael with the toe of his shoe.

The baby giggled from his blanket beneath the table, laying on his tummy, a string of drool connecting him to the various items I'd deemed safe enough for him to handle. It was a sound that seemed to soothe Tristan somewhat, but the concentrated expression on his face remained.

"Randall has the Norse boat, no?" He frowned. "Why not fly away with it then? Why travel by land or sea at all? He had the perfect escape plan. Why risk anything else, especially a trip that would involve him moving through the largest shipping port France has?"

"Perhaps Roberts is on a different mission?" Abella offered. "We've yet to find him. Maybe, once he is in your custody, his purpose will become evident."

Tristan remained silent, his frustrations evident as he stared over the deck of the *Providence*. I knew he was probably thinking many of the same things I was about the crew, his mind continually churning through the choppy waters that were his thoughts lately.

"Sails!" The lookout in the crow's nest waved his white handkerchief overhead, drawing everyone's attention. "Off the starboard bow! Black sails!"

"Black?" I said in surprise, rising from my seat as I strained to see what was ahead. To my astonishment, the ship was almost on top of us, barreling through the water as if it meant to ram right into the *Providence* without stopping. In the middle of each of the vast, dark sheets secured to the masts, a great, blood-red cross with a black circle in the center immediately drew the eye.

"Is that . . ?" I breathed, feeling both fear and relief seep into my bones. I'd seen the mark many times before—on Mark's arm, where Randall had branded him.

"The symbol of the Black Knights," Tristan answered quickly. Pulling the spyglass from his pocket, he extended it and examined the incoming vessel. "It's Roberts," he confirmed, snapping the telescope shut and tossing it onto the table. "The bastard's managed to sneak up on us. We'll be at arms within fifteen minutes, if not sooner."

Moving quickly, he leaned over the railing, shouting down to those on the weather deck. "Man the guns!" he ordered. "That's the one we've been hunting. We're in for a brawl, lads!" As the crew began to swarm and arrange themselves, he crouched down and scooped Michael off the floor, passing him to me.

"No," I replied, immediately handing the baby off to Abella. "I'm not sitting in the surgery again. That was practically torture, listening to all the violence and not knowing what was going on, all while injured and dying men stumbled into the place. Your quarrel with the Black Knights is mine too. I'm staying up here this time."

"Michael and I can help Mark," Abella said instantly, not bothering to argue or try to use my son to convince me otherwise. She knew when I said I was going to fight, I meant it.

From the look on Tristan's face, he knew it as well.

"Thank you, Abella," he conceded, frowning as he continued to stare at me. "Should anything happen—"

"We will be fine." She smiled, scooting around us and heading toward the stairs. "The best physician I know will be with us. Stay safe, *mes amies*."

As she disappeared down the steps and into the lower deck, Tristan let out a long sigh. "Ye're sure ye want to do this?" he asked. "I believe a child can stand losing one of his parents, but both . . ."

Taking his hand, I smiled. "I'm sure." My voice was steady and strong, the determination I felt to do this secure inside me. "And Michael won't be losing either one of us. I promise."

He snorted, glancing past me as his men continued to scramble to their places. "Don't make promises ye cannot keep, savvy?" His attention wavered, moving on to his duties as captain and he motioned for me to go. "Get yerself changed," he ordered. "Ye can't go into combat like a pirate if ye're in a dress."

Grinning, I turned, making my way to our cabin via the quickest route I could manage. All around me, men armed themselves, Tristan's voice shouting over the din and echoed by his boatswain as the helmsman frantically spun the wheel in his hands, trying to turn before being rammed. To the untrained eye, everything appeared disjointed and panicked. As a member of a few crews before and having seen how these men worked, I could see them for what they were.

Roberts and his crew of Black Knights were about to face a well-oiled machine of pirates under the command of one of the best captains on the seven seas. Sure, they only had one battle under their belts, but we hadn't been sitting around these past weeks. Tristan had been drilling the men, training them, transforming them into a team that could do what he required of them.

Slipping into our cabin, I quickly changed, throwing my dress on top of the bed and attempting to tuck my shorter shift into a pair of black pants I'd brought for an occasion such as this. However, there was too much fabric. Knowing I didn't have time to unlace my stays and change completely, I ripped the material until it was almost shirt length, tossing the extra to the side and successfully getting what was left to fit inside the breeches. Moving quickly, I donned the rest of what I needed, stopping in front of the dingy mirror for a beat as I headed for the door once more.

Laughing, I realized I looked like the female pirates Hollywood dreamed up, with their corsets over their shirts, belts slung across their hips, and tall boots hugging their legs. My long, free hair tumbled down my back, a sword in one hand and a loaded flintlock in the other. All I needed was a period appropriate coat and floppy hat with a feather in it and I would have looked like I'd walked right off a set somewhere.

Rather than be self-conscious about my appearance, I discovered that it made me feel powerful. The woman I'd used to be—the woman who wore pants daily and fought with men twice her size, who communed with gods and bartered with prostitutes, who did whatever was necessary to meet her goals, who was a pirate through and through—was present in that image. It was tough and fearless, which was exactly what I wanted to convey now, stepping outside and taking my place among the crew.

Striding from the captain's quarters, I hurried

down the hall, pushing out into the bright sunlight as the first cannon from Roberts' end splashed in the water only three feet off the bow. We'd managed to turn enough to avoid a collision, but it was apparent the Black Knights weren't going to give up that easy in their pursuit.

Finding Tristan beside the helm, I went to his side, touching him on the shoulder. "Where do you want me?"

He glanced at me for a split second, his eyebrow raising as he took in my appearance, and smiled. "Right here, with me."

Another cannon fired from the enemy, glancing off the railing below the bow and taking a chunk of the wood with it.

"Hold!" Tristan commanded, glaring at the ship as it sped ever closer.

The men shifted anxiously, watching as their attackers drew nearer, a red flag flying from their mast—a sign that no quarter would be given to anyone aboard the *Providence*. If we didn't win this battle, we would all die, whether we surrendered or not.

"Tristan," I muttered, warning in my tone as another blast cracked against the maidenhead, ripping the figure's face clean off in the process.

"Not yet," he replied, his voice tight.

Roberts' continued to barrel through the water, the sails pulled to full capacity as she bared down on us. Then, just as I thought we'd missed our moment to attack, Tristan's command shot through the air, loud and sure, confidence exuding from him.

"Fire!"

Across the whole deck, the cannons we'd taken

from the merchant vessel shot off, accompanied by the original ones below. A cloud of smoke rose into the air, the sound of the barrage enough to make me want to cover my ears and flinch away from it all.

Across the way, Roberts' craft cracked and jerked, its progress shuddered as her crew was taken out by the sheer volume of cannonballs raining down on them. Still, the vessel continued to move forward, coming up by our side crippled, but not unable to stay in the altercation.

"Board her!" Tristan roared. "Fight for yer lives, men!"

Grappling hooks flew through the air on both sides, the ships pulling together as each crew raced to be the first to step foot on the other's vessel. Swords glinted in the sunlight, guns fired, their smoke filling the air alongside the sounds of ferocious battle cries and eager growls.

Finding our place among the men, Tristan and I grasped hands for a beat, an unspoken bond of love between us. Letting go, I focused on the current predicament, knowing I would have to be fully aware of what I was doing if I wanted to survive.

Suddenly, we were surging over the railings like a flood, some men meeting in the middle, others falling by the wayside as the factions clashed. Without pausing for a second, I jumped over the edge, landing on the web of ropes cascading across the side of the Black Knight vessel and climbing my way to the top.

As soon as I was on the deck, I fired my pistol, striking the nearest Black Knight in the chest. The sailor beside him rushed me, his blade clanging against mine, and the rusty knowledge I held about swordplay surged to the front of my mind, taking over as our duel began.

Shoving the man back, I stepped to the side, avoiding his wild, downward slash, and cut across the back of his thigh, my blade digging deep. There was no time to celebrate the small victory, my attention immediately turning to the next opponent.

To their credit, no one seemed to care I was a woman, on either side. I fought as hard as anyone else, slashing and stabbing, pushing my way through the mob of men that waited to steal my life from me.

A bullet grazed across my shoulder, and I hissed, spinning around to meet the enemy who'd shot at me. He seemed surprised as I attacked, stepping back as I bore down on him, hacking with as much strength as I could muster. Finally, he found his feet and held his ground, pushing me back.

We traded a few more blows until I cut into his middle. Blood spurted from the wound, his eyes going wide as I yanked the blade free and pushed him to the ground.

I'd forgotten what it felt like to fight like this. It made you feel invincible, while still so fragile at the same time. Every step you took could be your last, so each one counted more than anything else you'd ever done in your life. It was like the battle was happening in parts, my conscious mind only really noticing a few key elements.

The Black Knights were like a wall, continually climbing from below and replacing those who fell. It seemed impossible for them to have such a large number, but the fact was as soon as one of them died, another took his place. They didn't appear to care for their wellbeing as much, either, eagerly acting out rash decisions that would end with them wounded or dead.

Another round of cannons fired from below, alerting me to the fact that there was still a sizeable force that we'd yet to face. The realization was cut short by a loud crack, and I turned, watching as the main mast of the *Providence* toppled into the sea on the far side of the battle.

Something cut across my hand, and I dragged my attention back to the conflict, jabbing toward the man who'd injured me. As I glanced around, I realized how awful this war was turning out to be. Blood covered the wooden planks, making it as easy to slip in a clear section as one littered with bodies.

The Black Knight in front of me disappeared, engaging with someone else and I paused, annoyed with my clothes. It was damn hard to breathe in a pair of stays while jumping and ducking around flying metal.

Tugging at the laces, I glanced around again, trying to gain my bearings.

And then I saw him. Captain Roberts stood beside the helm, engaged in combat with Callaghan, their blades clanging as they did a sort of dance, spinning and sliding across the top deck, hacking apart the railing and the helm as they battled.

My stomach clenched as I watched them. The last time I'd seen the Black Knight, I'd believed him our friend and ally. His blond hair had blood in it, but I couldn't tell if it was his or someone else's. The young man's face, which had been so peaceful and serene before, was angry and red now, his shouts loud and murderous as he swung his blade through the air, using his free hand to punch and slap whenever possible.

He was an entirely different person, the façade he'd worn before replaced by his true self. As I watched the two of them battle, the realization that he, too, was unlike the men I'd seen follow Randall in the past struck me. He seemed to operate without fear or regret, every movement he made as crazy as the look in his eyes.

Time froze for a moment as Roberts' blade struck Cal above the knee, my brother-in-law's face contorting with pain as red splashed from the wound, his form falling to the ground.

It took a second for me to realize the shouting I was hearing was my voice, my hands shoving aside the men in front of me as I tried to get to Cal, to save him from the death Roberts was about to give him.

The Black Knight's sword raised high in the air, angling down toward Cal, the point of it shining in the light.

Tristan materialized in an instant, his blade blocking the killing blow. Shoving Roberts, the two of them entered a battle as fierce as the one I'd seen seconds before.

Callaghan struggled to his feet, batting another Black Knight away as he haphazardly moved down the stairs, his leg bleeding freely as he limped along.

A flintlock fired close to my ear, and I ducked, sucked out of my spectating and pulled back into the fight. It was one of our men who shot this time, saving me from the person who had been about to cut me down.

Nodding my thanks, I did my best to regain my focus. As soon as I shoved away from my latest opponent, though, I found myself slipping out of warrior mode and back into a worried wife and sister.

Turning, I took a steadying breath, the excitement of it all fading as I pulled out of the action. More than just the elements materialized, fear wrapping its fingers around my heart and tightly squeezing as I realized what was happening.

The dead bodies were almost all our own crew. Black Knights pressed in on all sides, swarming, leaving a mass of dead and dying men in their wake. What I'd thought were cries of battle before were actually the moans of the injured, their lives fading from their eyes as I watched.

New cannon fire filled the air, and I jerked around, looking at the opposite side of the boat. Someone was coming to our aid—another galleon, with brightly colored sails, fired on Roberts', the crew shouting anxiously to us, not knowing it was too late to save the majority of our men. By the time they reached us, we would all surely be dead.

For a moment, the villains didn't seem to know what to do, their attention divided by the two groups. As one, they somehow reassembled, their cannons beginning to fire on the newcomer. It was as if they forgot we were there, Roberts' voice directing them.

Panicked, I searched for Tristan again, not seeing him among the crowd. Callaghan had disappeared, too, their absence sending a horrified shock through me.

Everything was spinning out of control. The confidence I'd felt earlier fled, replaced by the unknown. Somehow, we had lost, despite Tristan's training and the determination of the crew. Now, I was all alone, standing in an ocean of my foe with no idea how to get through it.

The ship tilted beneath me, leaning toward our craft and I slipped, grabbing onto the railing in a panic as I tried to sort out this new development. Bodies rolled across the deck as the tipping continued, the battle ceasing as everyone moved to address what was happening.

"Cut the lines!"

A voice shouted nearby, breaking through the ringing in my ears, and I glanced back at the *Providence*, screaming as I saw the waterline inching higher and higher on her hull.

She was sinking. The boat housing my son and friends was slipping beneath the surface, torn apart by the battle. White waves churned through the gun windows, pushing the wood down, stealing them from me without care.

The Black Knights began cutting the lines that held the two ships together, turning their attention to the new threat as they abandoned the one they'd squashed without hardly breaking a sweat. It was as if they held no regard for the men they'd slaughtered, their determination stronger than any group of dissenters I'd met in the past. With each rope they severed, their vessel settled more evenly on the water, escaping being pulled down by the *Providence*.

Surging forward, I pushed my way through them, swinging my blade, desperate to get to Michael and take him to safety. It was like everything was happening in slow motion, my eyes searching for some sign of him escaping to a longboat, but there was nothing but bodies.

The Black Knights held me back, their hands gripping my arms and hair, pulling me from where I needed to go. Shouting in frustration, I lashed out, hitting everything I could reach.

Something heavy smashed against my head, and I fell to the ground, the sight of my boat's remaining masts lowering in the sky the last thing my blurry vision took in before going black, and I knew the vessel was going to its new home at the bottom of the ocean.

My head throbbed, the ache in my skull bringing an image of little creatures trying to tunnel their way out of my ears to mind. With each pulse, the pressure grew so great I felt I might throw up, my innermost self desperately wishing I could return to the black void I'd been occupying. There was no pain in that place, no sickness, not even any hint as to whether I was alive or not.

The longer I lay there, hovering in a spot best described as halfway between light and dark, the more I knew I needed to pull myself back into life and figure out what was going on. There had been something important, something devastating that happened. As I remained on the edge of the pit, I couldn't remember what it was. It was too painful to try and step out of it, my consciousness burning with anguish so powerful I didn't want to touch it.

Figuring out what happened would have to wait until the headache ceased.

It was unclear how much time I'd spent in this state. Thoughts came and went, the world remaining empty at times like I was floating through space, without a care for anything.

Finally, something stirred inside me, and I reached out, touching the wall of emotions I'd been ignoring.

Memories came rushing back, the horror I'd bottled up filling me. The battle, the ship—Michael!

Gasping, I sat bolt upright, my eyes flying open and taking in the room around me. Sunlight filtered in through a small window, shining on the polished, wooden floor. A writing desk and mirror were anchored across from me, the hammock I resided in swaying both from my sudden movement and that of the ocean. Everything about this place was unfamiliar, right down to the shirt and pants I wore and the colorful blanket tucked around my legs.

The absence of my family only served to panic me further. Where were they? Where was *I*?

Uncovering, I slid to the floor, the pounding in my head increasing tenfold as I moved. The pain caused a moan to brush past my lips as I placed my hands on my temples, collapsing into a puddle.

Strong hands grasped me, sliding beneath my arms and hefting me up. For a beat, I relaxed, realizing Tristan was with me at last. As soon as he opened his mouth, I knew it wasn't him, however, and fear filled me as I tried to jerk from the embrace of the stranger trying to put me back where I'd started.

"*La, la, yjb ealayk albaqa' fi alsarir,*" he said in a language I'd not heard before. It sounded Middle Eastern if I had to guess, and the unfamiliarity of it made me panic more.

As I glanced over my shoulder, I caught sight of some black hair, tucked beneath a small, square-shaped hat that reminded me of a fez, the skin on his ear a dark brown. There wasn't anyone I knew who wore anything of that manner or was of that descent. Flailing, I tried to shove away, bile rising in the back of my throat as my body warned me of its dislike for all this movement.

"He says you need to stay in bed."

The new voice, warm and commanding, blanketed the room, filling it with a silent authority. There was also understanding and mercy in it, the words soothing in some way.

Going still, I gripped the edge of the hammock, held up by the first man as I moved to stare at the second.

To put it simply, he looked dazzling. He was tall, with a well maintained, chest-length beard. Brown, hooded eyes set beneath heavy brows observed me, offset by the white of the turban anchored around his temples with a gold band. Long hair, the same color as his eyes, tumbled down his back, brushing over a lengthy, dark purple vest that was lined with a pelt and had a delicate, golden pattern sewn into the side. It hung open, revealing a second, red vest with gold trimming on top of a plain white shirt. These tucked into a twisted, brown and green cloth belt, which had a brass watch on a chain looped around it. Black pants flowed out of the bottom of the belt, the fluidity of them like the air over the sea. Fabric gathered at his ankles, covering the trunk of his sturdy looking, black leather boots. It didn't seem like everything he was wearing should go together, but it did, miraculously. I felt like I was staring at a sultan, all dressed up in his most elegant clothes, putting on a show for his people.

"The wound on your head has not fully healed yet," he continued, his accent thick and heavy. "Our surgeon has been tending you this past week, but if you get up now, you'll be staying in this room for a while longer than planned."

"*Yjb ealayk albaqa' fi alsarir*," the first man said,

encouragement in his tone. He motioned to the hammock, trying to lift me, but I shook my head, closing my eyes at the pain the action brought.

"Where is my family?" I asked, my voice barely a whisper from lack of use. Clearing my throat, I tried again, determined to get answers. "What happened? What ship is this?"

The second man held his hands up, smiling. "There will be time for questions and answers." He nodded at me. "After you get back in bed."

Huffing, I frowned at him, not liking that I appeared not to have any choice in the matter. Still, sitting in bed and knowing what was going on had to be better than standing here and having no clue.

Grumbling some, I pulled myself back into the bed with assistance from the first man. He went about tucking me in, fluffing my pillow and helping me to sit up. Saying some other thing I couldn't understand, he hurried from the room, the brief glimpse of the hall beyond the door not giving me any inclinations as to what was going on.

The second man took the chair from the desk, sliding it beside me, and sat in it, crossing his ankle across his knee and leaning back comfortably, arms folded. "I am Raafe Zadari, captain of the *Lioness*, which is the vessel you are on board now."

He held his hand up as I opened my mouth to speak, chuckling. "Patience, *shakhs shujae*. I know you have many questions. If you let me, I will answer them all the best I can. You need only listen."

"What does that mean, *shakhs shujae*?" I asked, ignoring his plea for silence as the use of his native language distracted me. Was it something bad? Did it mean slave or prisoner? Was I stuck here, destined to live a life of servitude, never knowing what happened to those dearest to me?

The continued speaking amused him rather than drive him to anger, and he laughed. "It means 'brave one.' My men and I witnessed your battle with the pirates. You are quite fierce. We count ourselves lucky that it was not us who faced your wrath that day."

Realization lit in me. "It was you that came to our aid," I breathed.

"It was." Standing, he went to the window, running his palm over his beard. "I have yet to discover why pirates would feel the need to attack pirates." He gave me a pointed look, eyes sparkling with humor. "However, I am a Corsair myself, and I felt the need to come to your aid. Tell me, *shakhs shujae*, what offense do you hold with the men who sunk your ship?"

I shook my head. "It's a long story."

"We have all the time in the world."

Biting my lip, I sighed. "Where is my husband? I assume if you managed to rescue me, he must be here, too. He wasn't on the boat that . . . sank."

Tears filled my eyes, dripping onto my hands as I hung my head in despair. Michael was gone, as were Abella and Mark. If I'd not insisted we bring him, he would still be alive, possibly the others as well. Instead, they were trapped in the bowels of the *Providence*, forced to spend the rest of eternity at the bottom of the sea.

"Tristan is above deck," Captain Zadari said patiently. "With your brother-in-law, your two friends, and your son."

My head jerked up so fast that my vision spun.

"What?" I asked, desperate to get out of the hammock and go to them.

"Not so fast." Crossing the room, he kept me from falling, setting me back on the pillow and holding me there. "As I said, you have a nasty cut on your head and need to rest. Your family will be in to see you as soon as Akil—our surgeon—gives his permission. He's gone to fetch you water and food to eat. After that, you should be reunited."

"I don't want to wait," I insisted, pushing against him.

"What do ye mean I can't go in?"

Tristan's voice filtered through the door, muffled and annoyed, but the sound of it made my heart leap with joy.

"Tristan!" I yelled, my voice cracking as I struggled to attain the volume I needed for him to hear.

Captain Zadari made a somewhat annoyed noise and released me, moving to the entrance and opening it. On the other side, the smaller, first man stood with a tray of food and drink, Tristan towering over him, our baby in his arms.

Not bothering with any more words, my husband shoved past the two men, a broad smile cracking across his face, relief in his eyes. Stopping at my side, he passed Michael into my waiting arms, rubbing my leg as I practically squished the child and cried all over him.

"I thought he was dead," I whispered, peering at Tristan in horror. "All I saw was everything sinking, and then something hit me, and I went out. I believed they were all dead."

He shook his head, leaning in and kissing me on

the forehead. "Mark got them out," he muttered, resting his forehead on mine. "Loaded them into a longboat and shoved off before the rest of us realized what was happening."

"When we caught sight of him and saw he had a woman and child with him, we knew we had to come to your aid," Captain Zadari added, stopping by my side as well.

The doctor pushed his way into the group, babbling in an upset tone, motioning for Tristan to take the baby as he set the tray of refreshments on my lap.

"And Cal?" I continued as Tristan did what was requested of him, needing to know everything that happened. It was different, talking to Tristan about it. I trusted what he said and was able to focus, rather than try and decipher Zadari and his motives. "I saw him with Roberts. He was hurt when you saved him and—" Pausing, I considered something I hadn't before.

"How did we get away?" Glancing at the captain, I frowned. "You and your men took over the fight. Did you beat them?" Hope blossomed in my chest, and I looked at Tristan. "Is Roberts in the hold?"

Frowning, he shook his head.

Captain Zadari shifted uncomfortably, sighing. "They ran once your craft sank," he admitted. "We gave chase, but when they entered the Nile Delta, we were unable to follow, due to the size of our ship."

The doctor pantomimed eating to me, the actions frustrated, his reasons for wanting Tristan to wait to see me clear.

I waved a hand at him, not bothered by his insistence. "I don't understand." Ignoring the delicious smelling meal resting on my thighs, I sat up more, staring at him questioningly.

"If we were to track them down, we would need a sloop or smaller," the captain explained. "The Nile, while deep enough to accommodate the *Lioness*, is filled with sandbars and reeds, making it easier to run aground in a vessel such as this. I do not possess the exact reckoning it would take to maneuver her waters, nor does my navigator.

"And why would we continue to hunt them? They had no qualms with my men and me. Our chase was only a courtesy for those they so viciously tore apart. Now that we have parted ways, there is no need to press a battle unless our paths cross again."

Tristan frowned, eyes growing dark, but remained silent. He gave off the impression that he and the captain had already argued about this and he'd lost.

The look on his face kept me from voicing my displeasure at the statement, and I swallowed, peering at Captain Zadari. "Then where are we headed?"

The captain smiled, clapping his hand on the doctor's shoulder as the man threw his palms up in defeat. "Home, Mistress O'Rourke. Home to Gibelet."

Mark sat in the chair beside me, reading a small, leather-bound book, the only sound in the room that of turning pages every few moments.

I was still sequestered to my bed by the ship's physician, so the family had taken to ensuring someone was with me all the time. I'd no idea what the others did when they weren't in here—probably roamed the deck or slept or something—but I appreciated they at least tried to keep me company while I healed.

It was a wooden beam or pole that hit me in the head, splitting the skin open. No one knew for sure since I'd been scooped up by one of the crew of the *Lioness* and carried away without any investigation. They'd battled Roberts for a few moments before breaking off. My understanding was that the whole ordeal had been quite messy and rushed.

My care, however, was the exact opposite. There was now a small bald spot that stretched from behind my left ear to the center of the top of my head. Akil had been kind enough not to slice all of the hair off, taking his time in sewing me up and covering the wound. He'd made it to where I could hide any scar with the rest of my locks, happily noting my progress each time he came to check on me.

Much to my appreciation, I'd been told I would only have to stay in bed for another day or two. Still, Tristan insisted I have company at all times. He'd often bring Michael down to play and nurse, soothing me when I cried about how my milk was drying up due to lack of feedings.

My baby was growing up too fast. Not being able to cuddle with him as often, to experience that bond between mother and child, broke my heart. I knew he was old enough to get by with regular food and the goat's milk he'd taken a liking to, but I'd hoped he would breastfeed until he was more than a year old. It felt like I'd lost part of my role as a mom.

Mark coughed, bringing my attention back to him, though he continued to say nothing.

Chewing on my bottom lip, I fought the urge to sigh. When we were left alone like this, all I could think of was how awkward the two of us still were. We'd never really finished the fight we had at our reunion. It'd been weeks since then, and we'd talked fine with others present, but I was positive there was still some things we needed to clear up.

"Do you know anything about where we're going—Gibelet, I mean?" I asked, deciding to ease my way into whatever it was I wanted to say. I still wasn't sure where to start and needed a few minutes to sort it out. However, if I had to listen to him stay silent for much longer, I was going to lose my mind.

He paused in his studying, glancing over at me with a nonchalant expression. "In regards to anything other than piracy? Not much."

When he didn't go on, I sat up more, trying to prompt him. "Anything at all?"

He shrugged. "It's a port city. Possibly the oldest continually inhabited place in the world."

"So, ancient," I summed up. "Important. And part

of—"

"Modern day Lebanon," he supplied, nodding. "The Ottoman Empire, in this century. It's not called Gibelet in our time. I only recognized the name because of the Barbary Corsairs and the research I've done on them."

My eyes widened. "That's what these guys are? Barbary Corsairs?"

Even in my limited knowledge, I'd heard of the pirates called by that name. They were ruthless, unforgiving, and known for selling their captives into slavery.

The bubble of safety I felt aboard this vessel shrank slightly.

Mark seemed unbothered. "They're bound by several peace treaties right now. I suspect that's why they came to our aid; Captain Zadari is trying to uphold the deal with France by protecting her waters."

I swallowed hard, absorbing the information and trying to return to my perusal of his wisdom. "You said Gibelet has a different name in our time?"

His book snapped shut, and he sighed, realizing I was going to keep talking to him rather than let him read. "Byblos is the English name, I believe. I mostly scanned the information when I came across it. After all, I didn't know I would need to know the details in depth later on in life." His lips pressed together, but he smiled all the same, acceptance exuding from him. "There was a lot of it. Many names, theories, and histories tie to Gibelet. A researcher could probably spend his whole life studying it, and he would still never know all there is."

"Sounds exciting." I tucked a stray hair behind my

ear, grinning at him. "And these corsairs? I bet you've loved getting to study them up close."

He made a non-committed sound, glancing toward the door. "I focused more on the Caribbean pirates." Unable to help himself, he laughed. "So, yeah, it's been cool to examine the Mediterranean side of things."

"Maybe it makes up a little for you being stuck here?" I spoke with a soft tone, hesitating as I tried to gauge his reaction.

The mirth faded from him, and he returned to his book, shaking his head. "I guess." Frustrated, he huffed. "I shouldn't have said anything before, about how I was feeling."

"It's—"

"Don't worry about it, Sam," he said roughly.

"I am worried," I pressed. "We can all see you're unhappy. We want to help."

The volume clapped shut as he glared at me. "All of you. Really?"

Surprised, I leaned away some. "Yes, all of us," I answered in defense.

He snorted, rising from his seat. "I have a hard time believing that."

The shock inside me gave way to offense. "What are you talking about?"

Motioning to the world outside, he chuckled without humor. "You've done a fine job replacing me already."

Surprised, I raised my eyebrows. "What do you mean?"

Walking to the window, he shook his head in anger. "That's what Cal is doing, isn't he? He's

Tristan's right-hand man. You've had no problem telling everyone he's part of your family and that you love him like your brother." He folded his arms. "Even Abella seems to fancy him," he muttered, his face flushing.

"You think Cal is pushing you out?" The idea was almost comical. If it hadn't been for the hurt expression he wore, I would have assumed he was kidding. "Mark, no one is ever going to take your place. Not ever. You're as much a part of my family as he is."

He snickered, rubbing his face. "We both know that isn't the truth, Sammy. The only time you and I were part of the same family was when we were working on Oak Isle with the rest of the team. But as soon as we both came to the past, those people died, didn't they?" He shrugged as silence stretched between us.

What was I supposed to say to that? The words stung more than anything he'd ever said to me. But, he was right. The people we were in our century didn't exist anymore. We'd been forced to change to survive. The only difference was, I didn't mind the changing.

"This whole thing is ridiculous, you know?" he stated, an air of annoyance in his voice. "I'm in my late forties and I'm completely thrown off my game by the arrival of a man almost twenty years my junior. I should be at home, successful in my career, getting ready to retire. Hell, I thought I would be married with a few kids at this point by now, not single and a glorified pirate. My life is a twisted soap opera of crap."

Compassion surged through me as I recognized some of the feelings he was sharing, and a sad smile crept across my features. "You miss the life you had before. "I do, too, sometimes."

"Yeah, but you won't go back, even if you had the chance to."

"And you would?"

He stared at me seriously, his eyes taking on a shine of misery. "Of course I would," he answered, his tone uneven. "This isn't the life I was meant to have, Sammy. It never was."

"Until I showed up and set everything in motion." I leaned back on the bed, staring at the ceiling. "I suppose that's another thing I should apologize for."

Glancing at him, I pressed my tongue against the back of my teeth, feeling like a complete heel. He'd been damaged by more than my departure in the last year. It was almost like I was looking at a different man. I'd caused so much of his pain and discomfort, and it picked at my heart, whispering that I'd done more than screw up our friendship.

I'd ruined his life.

"I'm sorry my actions brought you here," I said, my voice quiet. "And that you are so unhappy because of it." Sighing, I rubbed my face. "I didn't mean to leave you alone either, especially after the rough time you had when you first came to the past. I should have written or done something to let you know what was going on, to check in on how you were. In my mind, you had The Order and Abella. It didn't occur to me you would consider yourself abandoned without me. I promise I won't do it again."

"Sam." The turmoil of feelings in his voice faded to just one—regret. "I shouldn't have fought with you the way I did before. It's not any of my business, making demands about what you do with your life. That's something for which I need to apologize. You're a grown woman and can take care of yourself. You've proven it many times over. I'm sorry I always stick my nose where it doesn't belong."

A weight lifted from me at his words, and I smiled. "We're good," I assured him. "But, you still have me worried. You look miserable, Mark. What can I do to help?"

He pursed his lips, slowly walking to the chair and sitting. "I'm only homesick. Give me a while and I'll be okay."

I nodded. "You know, if I can ever figure out a way to send you back, I'll do everything I can to make it happen. You believe that, right?"

Chuckling, he nodded, another layer of the hostile shield he'd been wearing disappearing. "If only. I've searched high and low for a way back, but as far as I can tell, you buried the only option beneath Oak Isle. Not that I blame you for that. I would have done the same thing in your place."

Grinning, I laughed. "Oak Isle," I breathed. "Do you think our letters ever made it to Scott? That he found Pandora's Box and got it to The Order?"

He shrugged. "I have no idea. If he did, I hope he's done with all of it and living out the remainder of his life in a nice retirement. He deserves it."

"And the twins, too," I continued. "I hope they're still making delicious pizza and living life to the fullest."

It was freeing, talking about them all. We didn't typically discuss our past, for some reason. It seemed to be helping Mark with his homesickness, so I went on, sharing memories from our time there and what I imagined to be happening in the future.

When a knock on the door interrupted our chuckling almost an hour later, I beamed at Tristan, welcoming him in with a wave.

"Ye sound like ye're having a good time in here," he stated, smiling. "What are ye speaking of?"

Mark exhaled, the most relaxed I'd seen him in a while. "Home," he replied.

"Ah." My husband nodded, raising an eyebrow in surprise. "I hate to interrupt then. However, I bring good news from the surgeon." Facing me, he grinned. "Ye are allowed to come on deck this evening."

Sitting up, I gasped in delight. "I can get out of bed?"

He beamed at me. "Aye. The crew is ready to tell stories and fish tales, and Akil has decreed ye are fit to join us all at last."

It was somewhat odd, exploring the *Lioness* for the first time. I knew virtually nothing about it, eagerly soaking in everything I could as I left my room.

It was one of the most beautiful vessels I'd ever sailed. Besides my cabin, there were four others, a wide hallway stretching between them with the captain's quarters on one side and the helm stationed outside the entrance. The polished wood in my room extended through the whole space, giving way to a more rough and seaworthy style outside. A maze of well-organized ropes stretched up the masts, holding aloft sails that were startlingly colorful. They were a patchwork of shades, sewn together with expert care. I'd never seen a ship with such different sheets and stared for a moment, taking in the sheer magnitude of it all. This was one of the more prominent ships I'd been on, almost as big as the man-of-war The Order possessed, cementing the belief that I was among very successful thieves.

Focusing on the men themselves, I found them as unbelievable as their captain. They reminded me of *Aladdin*, with their turbans and flowing garments. Each was as colorful as the patches in their sails, bright blues and golds peeking out from beneath fur-lined jackets. Even their shoes were different, some of them pointed, while a few had flat, rectangular wear. They were perched in the rigging or sitting on barrels, laughing together as they spoke a language with which I was not familiar. Many of them greeted me, chuckling at my expense, but there was no unwelcome feeling they gave off. In fact, the Berbers didn't seem to care at all that we were with them. It was as if we were merely part of the family they enjoyed at sea.

True to what I'd been told, we were treated to several stories and play-acting as the sun set, the pantomimed tales bringing laughter to everyone's lips. The sailors were skilled and well-practiced, making it to where we often didn't need to understand their language to know what was happening. They spoke in broken English for the most part though, trying to accommodate their guests, which I appreciated.

Sitting with my family, breathing in the fresh air and relishing the feel of the wind on my skin, I was surprised to find how utterly happy I felt in that moment. I'd been inside for too many days, missing out on what nature had to offer.

When the festivities were over, I decided to stay out for a bit, looking away from the deck and her lit lanterns to the night sky. Ever since Tristan had taken to teaching me the constellations, I'd found solace in the act of stargazing. It relaxed me to go over the names of each set, hearing Tristan's voice in my head as he told me their stories.

Sitting on a barrel in the very point of the bow, I sighed, folding my arms, laying them on the railing, and resting my chin on them. Everything seemed so . . . peaceful. In the background, one of the sailors softly sang a tune I'd never heard before, his voice adding to the perfect nature of the evening.

"May I sit with ye?"

Tristan's Irish accent broke through the haze of it all, and I sat up, smiling at him as I scooted over, patting the spot beside me.

Resting there, he wrapped his arm around my waist, kissing my head as his attention turned to the sky. "What were ye looking at?"

Gesturing to the heavens, I smiled, leaning against his shoulder. "The Little Dipper."

"Ah," he replied knowingly. "Little Bear, ye mean. The one ye never have any trouble findin'."

Laughing at his gentle correction to my modern knowledge, I nodded. "Yes, but I'm getting better. I can see parts of Great Bear, too—the Big Dipper. And of course, the North Star is in there. I thought I could see part of Draco coming out, but I'm not sure."

Gazing upward, he rubbed his thumb over my side. "Aye, the dragon's up there. He takes a while to make an appearance, even longer than in Erie since we're further south now." Turning his attention to me, he grinned. "Ye've quite the handle on the constellations now, don't ye?"

I beamed at him. "I do, don't I? I'm a bit rusty, but for the most part, I think I could find a particular set if I wanted."

"It's good to hear having yer head split open hasn't rattled yer brains too much."

He laughed as I swatted at him, kissing me in apology.

Chuckling, I returned to my gazing, listening to the singing and the soft creaking of the wood around us. The ocean lapped the sides of the boat, the wind blowing gently by, pushing us forward, toward our destination. Sniffing, I detected traces of cooking meat wafting across the deck, most of the smell carried off by the breeze.

Closing my eyes, I revisited the many times I'd been the one cooking in the galley, working to earn my keep among the crew. Already, I didn't like not having anything to do. Abella had Michael, insisting that she keep him so I could have time to myself. Cal was below, letting Mark look at his wound with the surgeon. They'd gotten into a lively discussion, filled with broken English and shaking heads, each trying to convince the other about how the cuts should have been handled. Yet, here I was, sitting around, doing nothing. It drove me insane.

"Tristan," I said, sitting up straight and turning to face him. "I want to do something helpful." At his bemused expression, I held up a hand, silencing whatever he'd been about to say. "Not just while we're on the *Lioness*," I stated. "All of them. I feel like everyone else has things to do, and all I have to offer is cooking now and then. I need to learn a new skill that will make me an asset, not a passenger along for the ride."

He raised an eyebrow. "Ye want to be part of the crew every time?"

Nodding, I grasped his hands in mine. "Yes. I'm tired of feeling like I don't do anything. Everyone treats me like I'm merely a woman."

"But ye are a woman," he pointed out, a teasing tone to the words.

"I am more than that," I responded, giving him a stern look. "And I know you know that. I've served as a member of the crew plenty of times before."

"Aye, ye have."

"But it's not enough," I insisted. "I don't want to have to fight for my right to come on the ship with you. I want to be invited of my own accord."

He stayed silent for a beat, regarding me with a small smile, and nodded. "Did ye have a particular task in mind to learn? I'd be more than happy to help ye study whatever it is."

Grinning at his acceptance, I leaned back in his arms. The truth was, I had no idea what I wanted to do. There had to be something I could excel at other than cooking and nurse work.

The railing gleamed in the moonlight as I stared at it. Carpentry, maybe? No. A lot went into building and repairing boats, plus there was heavy lifting required at times, and I may not be up to the task when needed. Not without practice anyway.

As I chewed on the inside of my cheek, my gaze traveled over the rigging, admiring the beautiful web of lines dancing around one another, threading through the sails. I contemplated when I'd spoken with Abella about finding new jobs. It would be possible to learn all the knots. I was small, too, which would be good for climbing and quick movements above the deck.

The North Star twinkled brightly beyond the ropes, drawing my eyes back to the heavens. Grinning, I recalled the nights in Ireland, watching the sky in wonder.

Suddenly, I had it. It had been staring me in the face all this time, waiting for me to discover it. As soon as the idea entered my head, I knew without a doubt that it was the path I was meant to take.

"Navigation," I whispered, pointing to the skies. "Teach me how to follow the stars, not only recognize them." Sitting up again, I met his gaze, noting the uncertainty in it. "You will, won't you?"

"Navigators do more than look at the sky," he answered with a serious tone. "Ye know that, right? There are calculations and measurements involved, which must be taken with special equipment."

"So?" I pressed. "You know how to use it all, don't you?"

He nodded. "Aye, for the most part. It's only . . ." His voice trailed off, and he frowned, pulling me back into his embrace. He chuckled, the sound rumbling in his chest. "Frankly, love, ye aren't the best with numbers. Are ye sure ye want to learn something that will focus so heavily on a topic ye yerself have said ye've no love for?"

The question caught me off guard, and I laughed, relaxing in his embrace. It was a fair point—I'd never been all that great at math. However, I didn't struggle too much with it. With perseverance and drive, I knew I could master whatever calculations navigation would require.

"I'm sure," I responded with positivity. "Especially if you're going to help me learn how to do it."

"Hmm." He was silent for a moment, eyes turned heavenward, and slapped his thigh. "Very well. We'll start with a lesson in terms for tonight, aye? I have a feeling I'm going to have to barter with our navigator before he lets me handle his astrolabe."

"Astrolabe," I said, trying the word out.

"That's the tool ye'll use to measure the angle of the stars or sun to the horizon. We'll need the man's declination charts, too, if he's willing to let ye pour over them a bit."

"Declination?" Separating myself from him, I crossed my legs, feeling an eagerness I hadn't in some time.

"The angle of any given star at a specific moment and location, in relation to the equator," he explained. "Such a calculation is difficult to make, so most navigators have charts with the angles already located."

"Okay," I replied slowly. "And how does that fit into navigation?"

He smiled, eyes shining with happiness as if he were not at all bothered by helping me. "When ye use the astrolabe, ye're finding the distance between yerself and whatever it is in the sky ye've fixed on. It's called yer zenith. That number, combined with the declination of that same object in the sky and a simple calculation, will give ye the latitude at which ye currently rest. To get where ye wish, ye must know yer latitude—"

"And the latitude of where you're going," I finished for him, excited. "So, as long as your latitudes match and you're heading in the right direction, you'll eventually end up at your final destination."

"That is correct," he agreed. "The process is simple but very easy to misconstrue. If ye measure one thing wrong, ye could end up miles from where ye need to be."

I shook my head, beaming at the stars as I thought over the phrases and explanations he'd given me. "I can do it," I said, surer than the first time. "And I'll be a valuable member of any crew."

"Ye were always a valuable member of the crew,"

he muttered, brushing his fingers over the spot where I'd been cut, my hair slipping through his touch. "To every man ye've saved and me. Cooking and helping in the surgery are not positions that need belittling."

"I know," I answered, staring into his eyes. "But I feel like I was treated as . . . Less than. Not by you," I amended quickly. "Other people. MacDonald never wanted me to do anything else. I couldn't perform any other tasks if needed. I want to learn this and prove I'm worth more than food and medicine."

Smiling, he nodded. "Aye. I understand, love. If this is what ye want, I will support ye in it. Ye'll be the finest navigator on the water, I'm sure of it."

The ship swayed back and forth, making it extra difficult to get an accurate reading on the astrolabe. The *Lioness's* navigator—a short, constantly happy man named Shafeek Al-Enezi—chuckled as he watched me struggle.

He peeled the outer layer of an apple off with a short knife, eating the skin separate from the flesh. Juice ran over his tanned and weathered skin, soaking into the tight ends of his white, billowy shirt. Every two slices or so, he would drag the back of his hand over his blue vest, stopping short of the black sash tied around his waist. He didn't seem to mind the sticky liquid that dropped on his tan pants and bare feet, but I found the entire thing quite distracting.

Sighing in frustration, I lowered the astrolabe to my side, keeping a tight grip on the top ring. "How am I ever supposed to get the right angle if this thing is too heavy to hold up for more than a few minutes?" I asked, glaring at Tristan as he smiled at me from behind Shafeek.

The navigator shrugged. "You get stronger, I suppose," he said, his accent thick. "That is what I tell my son when he is practicing. The sea . . . She is tough, but you must be tougher. The ocean is an animal that does not wish to be tamed, yet here we are, fighting the good fight each day. She will mislead you and put you in danger if you cannot control her."

Motioning for me to pass over the round, brass disk, he put his last apple slice in his mouth, slid the knife into his belt, and seized the ring on the top, lifting the instrument up to his chest level. With trained precision, he moved the arm connected to the middle, adjusting it until the far end lined up with the sun, directly overhead. Beneath us, the boat continued to move up and down, swaying with the waves, making it that much more problematic to get a reading. However, as I watched, he somehow managed to get the pinprick of sunlight shining through the first site on the spindle to match up with the tiny hole on the second. Keeping the piece in place, he checked the notated degrees around the edge of the ring, consulted with the roll of paper splayed across the crates beside us, and nodded.

"Here," he said to Tristan, passing the instrument over. "Raise it for her." Glancing at me, he smiled in encouragement. "Your arms will get there, *shakhs shujae*. You've been in bed with an injury. Your body needs time. Until then, your husband can help you. It is not uncommon for three men to work together on rough days." Pointing to the four cut out spaces in the ring that created a cross, he laughed. "That is why there are holes, see? The wind moves through without swaying the disc, but, at times, you still need the extra help to get it aloft."

Tristan took the piece without objection and lifted the astrolabe aloft as he placed his free hand on the small of my back, muttering a soft reassurance as I exhaled.

"If we were looking at the stars or the moon, you could raise it and look straight through the pinholes,"

Shafeek explained. "The sun is different. Watch the second sight."

He rotated the spindle for me, watching the progress of the tiny light as it moved across the small plate. "Let me know when you have them matched," he ordered as we moved up with another swell.

I held my breath, focusing on the thin beam as it danced across the small, brass plate. It slipped into place, and I exclaimed in excitement, relieved to have finally achieved a small part of my goal.

"Very good!" Shafeek pointed to the angle at which the spindle was resting. "Record your number," he stated. "I marked the stars at sunrise for you. Check the chart for their crossing and tell me where we are."

Nervousness blossomed in my stomach as I nodded, taking stock of the numbers I needed and turning toward the manual he kept. After a moment, I faced them, blowing air from my mouth in an exaggerated manner, and put my hands on my hips. "Thirty-eight degrees north?"

"Not bad, lass," Tristan said appreciatively. "I counted us at thirty-five earlier, when ye and Shafeek were talking amongst yerselves."

"And I made thirty-four," the corsair agreed. "'Tis common to have a couple of degrees difference. I believe we're on the right path for now."

Grinning, I watched as he plucked another roll of paper from beside the manual, unraveling it with a snap and smoothing it over the top of the barrel. A map of the Mediterranean Sea stared back at me, with handwritten notes in several places. Some of them advised sailors of shallow waters or swift currents, others detailing sightings or battles that had occurred.

"I reckon we have a few days yet till we reach Gibelet," Shafeek continued, tapping a spot in the ocean water where I assumed we must be.

"Then it is good we have all managed to get along, no?" Tristan laughed, clapping the smaller man on the shoulder, nodding his head toward the foot of the sterncastle.

Glancing in the same direction, I suppressed a chuckle, observing as Abella tried to politely disentangle herself from a group of sailors, including Callaghan and Mark. The men were quite taken with her, forming a crowd around her whenever she sat on the deck with Michael as she was now. Several times, I'd been sitting with her, only to be completely shut out of conversations until I had no choice but to take Michael and leave her to converse.

Pirates they may have been, but it appeared the Barbary Corsairs respected when a woman was with another man.

Unfortunately for Abella, it was apparent she was not spoken for, and the men had taken to trying to earn her favor. Sometimes they teased her, only to see her blush. Others, they engaged in in-depth talks about Paris and the dress scene there. Many asked her for fashion advice, creating a game she played in a happy manner. Truth be told, I didn't think she minded all the extra attention, even with Mark around to see it.

My smile faltered as I looked at him. At first, I'd assumed he was vying for her attention with the rest of them. The longer I watched, the more it became clear that he was caught in the crossfire. His head was bent over a book, back turned toward her, shoulders hunched over as he ignored the five other sailors stationed around him. He looked so sad I wanted to throw my arms around his neck and hug him until he was better.

"I'll inform the captain of our progress," Shafeek stated, drawing my attention back to him and Tristan. "You did very well today, Sam. Why don't you meet me at sunrise tomorrow and you can work with the stars for a change?"

"That will be wonderful, thank you," I replied with warmth. "I look forward to it."

He tipped his head, moving past me with a whistle on his lips.

My attention drew back to Mark, and I saw him get up and slip below deck, abandoning his infested spot.

"Will you help Abella with Michael?" I asked Tristan, squeezing his hand. "I'm going to go below with Mark for a bit."

He raised an eyebrow, a brief shot of surprise shining in his gaze before he leaned in and kissed me. "Aye," he muttered against my lips. "But ye know taking the bairn from her will only encourage the men to get closer."

"Cal won't let them," I said positively. "He's doing his best to show them she's his without actually claiming her."

"Of course. That would require talking to her about more than his wounds." Tristan snorted, shaking his head as he stepped back, folding his arms. "The man lost his ability to speak to women while he was in the Otherworld, it seems."

"Five hundred years alone in a place that continually hunted and killed him, only to bring him back to do it all over? I bet he lost more than his ability to speak with women."

My voice trailed off as we both looked at our brother, watching as he laughed and spoke with the group on the other end of the deck. They were swapping stories about dignitaries, no doubt quizzing Abella on her time at French Court once again. If I hadn't known better, I would have thought Cal was at ease in the group. However, after living so close together for a year, I knew when he looked over his shoulder it was a force of habit, as was his repositioning after two to three minutes. He was hardly able to stand still unless he worked at it. It was a cruel twist of fate that Roberts had managed to break in and wound him further.

Sighing, I put aside all the problems we shared. The five of us had been through a lot over the years. It was all I could do to take one issue at a time. Callaghan's problem wasn't something that could be solved in a single conversation. Plus, he looked content at the moment, despite his nervousness.

No, it was Mark that needed a friend the most right now. Smiling at my husband, I strode from him, content with having another conversation about home, so long as it would lift my friend's spirits.

"Land ho!"

Turning at the cry from the crow's nest, I held a hand up, shielding my eyes from the sun, and squinted toward the starboard side of the ship. There, in the distance, I could make out a strip of land, as well as several masts marking the skyline.

Tristan, looking as well, placed his hand on my back. "We'll have a new heading soon, hopefully," he muttered. "I plan on asking Zadari's assistance in securing passage down the Nile."

"We'll catch Roberts on the river," I agreed. "Where there's less space to run."

"Precisely."

The harbor was mostly surrounded by an old, brick wall, leaving only a small space for ships to come in and out. Each stone in the structure looked as if it had been there for centuries—maybe it had been. Along the manmade edifice, vessels docked, each of them as colorful and extravagant as the *Lioness*. Sails splashed with different hues dotted the masts, the hulls painted various shades, each stern bearing a name befitting of the boat it represented. Several of the crafts were being unloaded, the sailors calling to each other in their native language, waving as we dropped anchor a few hundred feet away, being too large to enter the cove.

Turning my attention to the shore, I took in the buildings lining the sloping hill off the beach. They appeared to be made of the same material the harbor was and were old as well, a few needing rebuilding. On the right side, a road disappeared down a tree-lined enclosure, the top of what I assumed to be the castle Zadari had told us about visible over the branches. It was back a way, the barrier hiding whatever it was that occupied the area between the edge of the beach and the edifice on the hill. A red flag that matched the one atop the *Lioness* flew over the tan building, the single bright color in a world of brown and dark greens.

"This way," Captain Zadari commanded, stepping onto the gangplank that had been put in place. "We'll leave them to unload."

He strode down the wooden walkway, stopping on the dock to wait for us to catch up. A few words were exchanged with the villagers as he raised his hand in greeting.

"It is good to be home," he declared with a laugh, beaming at us. "I hope you do not mind my friendliness with old friends. I've been gone for some time."

"Oh?" Cal frowned. "Ye and yer men were not on a trading voyage?"

"No."

The captain set a leisurely pace, moving to the end of the harbor and starting up the dirt road toward the castle. People from the village greeted him but gave us stares of mistrust and concern, our European clothes alerting them in an instant that we were outsiders. As we walked, the trees cast shadows across us, dampening the heat of the late day.

"My men and I were aboard the *Lioness*, set for Marseille when we were attacked by competing raiders," the captain explained, walking in front of us with Cal and Abella. "Luck was on our side, and we managed to save the cargo we intended to sell, but the ship was injured during the fight. We were forced to stay in France to complete the repairs.

"We'd been gone from home a little over a month then. I was eager to return home, but we chose to come to your aid first.

"That explains why the *Lioness* was so nice," Mark muttered to me under his breath. "She's fresh from the carpenter."

"All their crafts look fine," Tristan agreed, holding Michael as he walked on my other side. "They are well cared for."

"Aye." Zadari smiled over his shoulder. "They call us the Princes of the Sea. What prince sails in a poorly put together dingy?"

Nodding in agreement, I stared at the path ahead. The entrance to the castle was becoming visible as we came up the hillside, two guards standing beside the opening in the barrier. As we neared, they saluted Zadari, the edges of their hands touching the turbans wound around their heads. Each held a spear, their faces impassive as we walked by, our feet crunching in the dirt.

At once, we were surrounded by the castle, the path cutting through the courtyard of the tall building. It split off in a few different directions in the center, leading down another vegetation-lined alley to what looked like a garden on one side and a maze of ruins on the other.

The building itself was simple, made of the same stuff as everything else here was. It was old, too, the top crumbling in places and reminding me that, even though I was several hundred years in the past, this place had already been here for centuries. A few pillars that looked to be of Greek or Roman influence were nestled in the dirt and were worn enough to have been made by the long-gone civilizations. Everything else was mostly square, with slatted windows thrown in wherever the builder had thought necessary. The design looked peculiar to me, but I slowly realized this place had been built as a fortress. It was made to withstand attack and provide cover for those on the inside. Tips of cannons were visible on the rooftop, the guns pointed toward the harbor, defending their claim on the port to this day. The door we entered through was small and simple, with only enough width for us to pass through one at a time.

Inside the building was much the same as the outside, color wise. The hallway was peaked above our head and dark, our footsteps echoing as we traversed the empty walkways. At one point, we entered a large, open space that had several staircases in it. They were built along the walls and led into different parts of the castle, great windows letting the light in at last.

Zadari led us up one of these sets, taking us down another hall and depositing us in a meeting-like room. It had a table and chairs, as well as decorative cloth hanging over the open windows and cushions on the floor. The heat was sweltering, but a fire burned in the hearth all the same, warming the food trays that had been left beside it.

"Make yourselves comfortable," Zadari instructed. "The crew will come and eat with you when they're finished unloading. It is a tradition, to welcome us home. I'll have rooms prepared, and someone will be by to fetch you shortly."

"You aren't staying?" I asked, feeling nervous about being left in a strange place with no idea what to do but wait to be seen by another person.

"I must see my family," he explained, his face radiating joy. "My woman is expecting a child, and I am anxious to see how she fares."

Tristan waved for him to go, chuckling as Michael grunted and reached for the food behind us. "See to her then. I wish ye the best of luck and news in that regard."

Zadari bowed, his smile growing more substantial,

and wasted no time in taking his leave, his footsteps disappearing down the hall with almost alarming speed.

For a beat, we all stood there, unsure of what to do. It was odd, being left in here without any preamble or real explanation. It felt like we were prisoners in this room, forced to stay when all we wanted to do was leave.

"I'm famished," Abella confessed, looking over the food. "But what is all this they've put out? I see meat, but I don't know what this is."

She picked up an orangish brown item that looked like a raisin but bigger, holding it in the palm of her hand as she showed it to the rest of us.

"That's a date," Mark said, settling onto one of the seats beside the fire. "Try it. They're very sweet. You'll like them."

Unsure, she raised an eyebrow, watching him for a moment, and popped the fruit in her mouth, smiling as the flavor washed through her.

"You're right," she said, still chewing. "Very sweet. Would you like one?" Picking a few more off the tray, she sat on the cushion beside his and offered it to him, her face flushing as their hands lingered together longer than necessary.

"I'll try one," Cal said, reaching over and plucking one from the mound, breaking the contact between the two.

For the briefest of moments, I saw the look the men shared, each of them somewhat annoyed but polite. Then, as if I'd imagined the whole thing, they relaxed, chewing on their snacks in silence.

"This is lamb," Tristan stated, eating a small piece

of the meat and offering a morsel to Michael. "Whatever they've flavored it with is different."

"Bring me a little?" I asked, sitting at the table and motioning for the baby. "I'll eat while I feed Michael."

Soon, we had spread the food out amongst ourselves, trying the exotic cuisine happily. As the sun lowered in the sky, not quite beginning to set, there was the ringing of a bell, and a single voice began to sing somewhere inside the castle, the sound reaching us in our secluded spot.

Ignoring the scandalized expressions of everyone but Mark, I listened to the prayer as I fed the baby, finding the melodic chanting relaxing. While I didn't understand anything they were saying other than Allah's name, I knew they were only offering their thanks and asking for protection. They would all be following the prescribed movements of standing, kneeling, and bowing, too, as I'd witness during our trip here. The sailors on the *Lioness* had prayed several times a day, as was customary in the Muslim religion, but they'd never had someone sing what they were silently reciting. Shafeek had been kind enough to answer my uneducated questions about the practice, taking no offense at my curiosity.

The European companions of our group didn't seem to understand or be as accepting of the differing faith. Tristan had told me many times he believed there was truth in all things and therefore didn't care what religion anyone practiced. As the prayer continued for several minutes, however, he appeared uncomfortable, and I recalled the few times I'd witness him cross himself during prayer time on the *Lioness*.

Still, the three of them said nothing, continuing to

eat with Mark and me until the song faded and an air of unimportance filled the space. After another minute or two, footsteps sounded in the hall, and we all turned, staring at the new presence in the doorway.

The man wore clothes much like those of Captain Zadari, loosely fitted and adorned with color. His beard was much longer, almost tickling his stomach as he bowed his head in greeting and it was streaked with white, showing his age.

"I thank you for waiting through our prayers," he said, his accent so thick it was hard to understand what he was saying. "Unfortunately, we do not have much time, as Maghrib will begin in a few moments, with the setting of the sun." He gestured to the window, noting how close the orb was to beginning its final descent. Blinking, he appeared to be trying to decide what else to say. Sweeping his arm to the side, he backed into the hall, motioning for us to follow him. "I will take you to your quarters for the evening."

Rising to my feet, I held Michael close so he could continue to nurse and frowned. "We aren't waiting for the rest of the crew?"

"No, mistress," he answered, nervousness flashing across his face. "Captain Zadari said to bring you to your rooms now."

Tristan rose, his expression one of mistrust. "I think we'll find our own accommodations in town," he said, his tone careful. "Thank you for the offer."

The man made a panicked sound, shaking his head. "No, your rooms are already prepared here. You will stay the night."

"Are we prisoners here?" Mark asked.

"I knew it," Cal muttered, shoving to his feet.

"You Berbers are all the same! What, you think since your ancestors kidnapped mine and sold them into slavery, you can do the same to us?"

"N-no!"

Sympathy filled me as I watched the man fiddling with his belt, stuttering through an answer. "We're tired," I stated loudly, interrupting him and glancing over my shoulder at the group. "We've been through a lot these past weeks, without a proper bed to sleep in or bath to clean ourselves. I suspect Captain Zadari must have wanted to afford us some courtesy by allowing us to clean up and rest before we go our separate ways." Focusing on the poor messenger, I smiled. "Is that right?"

Relief flooded his features as he nodded, placing a hand over his heart. "Yes, Mistress. If you'll only come with me, you can rest for a time and speak with the captain in the morning, after Fajr."

"Fajr?" The words sounded even more odd with Tristan's Irish accent.

"Sunrise prayers," the man explained. "Our meetings here revolve around prayer times." Glancing out the window, he fidgeted. "If you could come with me, it is almost time for Maghrib. I would like to not be late."

"Of course," Mark agreed, speaking for the group before Cal could explode again.

Striding past me, he set the pace for the group, moving out into the hall and waiting with our escort for the rest of us to join him.

Slipping my finger into Michael's mouth to break his hold on me, I covered up the rest of the way and placed his head on my shoulder, patting his back as I went out as well. He burped as Tristan joined us, followed by Cal and Abella.

"Right," our guide said. "This way."

He set off in the direction we'd first come from, leading us back down the stairs and along a new corridor, his hands folded behind his back, footsteps marching down the stone floor.

"If you don't mind my asking, what is your name?" Hurrying beside him, I smiled, trying to show that we were friendly and he didn't need to be so nervous in our presence. There was no telling what the man thought of Europeans if he worked for a group that had terrorized their enemies into creating peace treaties with them.

"Hannibal, Mistress," he replied, the answer short and curt. His eyes stared forward as we moved around another corner and went further into the castle's depths.

"Hannibal," I repeated. "You aren't normally the messenger, are you?"

The question caused him to laugh, and he glanced at me sideways, smiling. "No, I am not. Most of my time is spent in the gardens and ruins, caring for the castle grounds."

"You've done a beautiful job," I complimented him, my interest peaked. "This place must have an incredible history."

"Yes," he answered with ease. "This place has been the seat of many different things. The castle itself is an old Crusader fort."

It felt like the floor had dropped out from beneath me. "Crusaders?" I asked weakly. "You mean . . . Templars?"

Tristan's hand was the only thing that kept me steady, his grasp tightening around my fingers as we waited for the man to reply.

"Aye," he said, grinning as he looked back at us. "They abandoned it long ago, after the crusades. It serves as one of our main shipping ports now. We do a lot of trade with Cairo—Captain Zadari's hometown—and Marseilles, but it is nice to have a place to call home."

The statement did little to relax me, but he didn't seem to notice the agitation his words had caused.

"I don't suppose ye see many Knights coming to reclaim it from ye?" Tristan sounded hesitant to me, but, again, our guide didn't notice.

"None whatsoever," he replied with confidence. "The organization remains as wiped out as it was at its end, leaving us to claim the spoils."

I wasn't so sure. Glancing at Tristan, I could see the concern in his eyes. The presence of it made me more nervous.

Swallowing hard, I stared ahead, any sense of safety disappearing. Despite Hannibal's insistence that there were no Templars here, I couldn't help but feel we'd somehow been trapped.

After a few more steps, Hannibal stopped and motioned to a row of doors on the left-hand side of the wall. "You'll be staying here. Someone will come and get you in the morning."

Bowing his head, he turned without another word and vanished down the hall, leaving us alone once more.

Where the rest of the castle had seemed drab and, frankly, uninhabited, our room reminded me more of the colorful ships I'd seen in the harbor. Bright ceiling to floor curtains hung in front of windows that opened outward like French doors, leading to a patio and adjoining courtyard. The sheer fabric made it to where anyone could see what we were doing, but it also provided a beautiful view of the night sky. Our bed was positioned close to the windows, covered with fluffy pillows and thick blankets with magnificent patterns that matched those of the cushions in the corner, the spirals and triangle shapes melding together in a wonderful, hypnotic form of beauty. In the opposite corner, nearest the door, a table with matching chairs rested, fresh desert blooms placed in a vase at its center. Between that and our bed was the focal point of the room. A large fireplace held a smoldering flame, the stone mantle carved into the shape of two trees. Each side was a trunk, the branches growing upward and entwining together overhead, creating the flat shelf that held a few books and more flowers. A woven rug sat on the stones in front of it, leaves embroidered across its face. Altogether, the room made me feel like we had escaped, shut away from our problems and cocooned in the embrace of luxury.

Tristan, flopping back on the bed from his position at the window, sighed and adjusted his position, sinking into the feather mattress.

"What do you think?" I asked, coming to lay beside him, Michael nestled between us.

"About?"

I shrugged. "Everything, I guess?"

He took my hand in his. "I don't rightly know, Sam." His lips pursed as he stared at me, and I knew he was thinking of Hannibal's words. "We would be wise to consider all of these men to be Templars. However, the time we've spent with them has made me more inclined to think they are not."

"Why?" I pressed. "Do you not recognize any of them?"

"There's that," he agreed, "but it's something more. These men do not act like the other Templars I have known. I believed our guide in the hall when he said there were no Knights here. If they are, they must be different, following their own rules and ignoring MacDonald, or they are simply pirates."

"Well, not simply." I motioned to the room around us. "Piracy has made them rich in a way I've never seen the Templars display. They're living like kings. Well, princes," I corrected myself. "Princes of the sea. That's what Captain Zadari said, wasn't it?"

"Aye, it was." Rolling onto his side, he smiled at me, reaching out and tucking a strand of hair behind my ear. "And ye? How do ye feel about it all?"

I shrugged in reply. "Something seems a bit off," I shared, lowering the tone of my voice. "Like they don't know what to do with us, but they don't want us to go. I mean, they sent the gardener to show us our rooms. Isn't that odd?"

He nodded, contemplating my words. "I do not

know that it's necessarily odd, but it did catch me off guard."

"And there were guards at the gate, but I haven't seen anyone else since we came inside," I continued. "Where is everyone? Shouldn't there be entire crews worth of men here? They weren't all in the harbor and it looked like most of the dock was full. Why haven't we seen more people?"

"They could live in the town, rather than reside here, in the castle," he offered, but I heard the doubt in his voice, too.

"So many questions," I muttered, looking at the sliver of sky outside, framed by the crumbled roof of the castle. In the distance, I could hear the tail end of whatever prayers were being offered, the singing voice not as present here as it had been in the meeting room. Twilight was fading from the sky, the first stars beginning to make their appearance as the sun fled into oblivion.

"And the Templars always at the front of them," Tristan mumbled. "But, for now, I think we are safe."

Glancing over, I watched as his eyes fluttered somewhat, sleep claiming him quickly in the comfortable bed. As his breathing evened out, I smiled, squeezing his hand gently before releasing his fingers. Michael slept snuggled between us, his thumb in his mouth, and soon, I found myself drifting, the scent of sweet desert flowers all around me.

Michael's fussing woke me not much later, his hands grabbing and squeezing anything he could get hold of. Tristan, still asleep, stirred, a soft breath moving past his lips.

Groggy, I scooted closer, offering my breast to Michael. In response, he cried louder, not hungry. As I groaned, I sat up, gathering him in my arms, and gave him a soft shushing. Not even the rocking motion of my arms calmed him, and he was soon so upset that I thought he might wake everyone in the castle if I didn't soothe him soon.

"What's the matter?" Tristan asked, words slurring together as he rolled over, looking up at me.

"Nothing," I assured him. "He's fussy, that's all." Glancing toward the still open window, I saw that the moonlight had lit the courtyard. "I think I'll take him for a little walk and help him calm down."

"Do ye want me to come with ye?" He sat up, resting on his elbow and rubbing his eyes.

"No, I'm fine." Sliding off the bed, I grabbed my cloak, wrapping it around myself and the child. "I'll be back in a bit."

"Don't leave the gate," he said seriously, waking up a little more as he warned me. "Stay where there are guards. We don't know what will happen if you try to leave on your own."

Smiling, I nodded. "I will. Go back to sleep."

Patting Michael's back, I continued to mutter to him as he cried, carrying him outside. The courtyard had an open walkway that led to the gardens, and I soon found myself strolling the path, taking in the beautiful plants and the crumbling edifice in the moonlight.

A lot of what had once been here was gone. Ruins occupied most of the land within the walls, tall Roman pillars reaching up toward the moon, native trees wrapping their branches around the structures. What was left of the majority of the buildings was represented by foundations and outlines that were no taller than my knees. The ocean glittered in the distance, only a sharp drop off protecting the castle from incoming invaders. The more I walked, the more beauty I found in all of it, the history of this place speaking without words.

Eventually, I found myself on the floor of an amphitheater, Roman in construction. The stones were dark and crumbled, creating an uneven floor. Along the back, I could still see the designs that had graced the edifice in its prime. Ahead of me, the rows and rows of seats looked as if they were still waiting for a show to start any minutes. They had crumbled in places as well, but I climbed them anyway, singing softly to Michael as I navigated the highs and lows. Finally, tired and ready to sit for a while, I pulled my cloak off, not needing it in the warm air, and laid it in one of the foot spaces, setting Michael down to play on it.

He'd calmed, for the most part, the noises he made now those of play as he rolled onto his stomach and bunched his fists in the fabric. As I lay down beside him, disappearing into the steps, I stared at the sky, looking for the constellations once more.

After a while, I came to, realizing we had both fallen asleep. The baby breathed deeply beside me, sucking his thumb in the crook of my arm.

A woman's voice reached me, hushed and anxious, amplified by the theater. She spoke in a language I didn't understand, the words melding together in a blend of nonsense. With a start, I realized

I wasn't supposed to be hearing whatever conversation she was having, but she had no idea I was there. Michael and I remained hidden in the steps, with nowhere to go unless we wanted to be found out.

Captain Zadari's voice answered, frustration in the mysterious words. It sounded like he was arguing with the woman.

The conversation went on for a few minutes, the both of them asserting themselves and their opinions, I assumed, until one word stuck out at me with startling clarity.

MacDonald.

Captain Zadari had said the name, his voice still moving quickly as he spoke.

My heart seized in my chest, my lungs shuddering to a stop as I strained to listen. There was no way it was a coincidence he'd said the name of the Grand Master of the Templars, not in a million years.

The shock gave way to anger as I realized where we were. This was another Templar hold, the base of operations for this region. Zadari was no pirate. He was a Knight, doing his part to protect the treasures of his organization. It just so happened that he'd been lucky enough to catch a family on the run from Paris.

Which meant we would be returned to MacDonald, our plans shattered and more punishments pushed on us.

Biting my lip, I tried to banish the images of what would happen to Tristan if The Order found out he'd disobeyed more orders. It was a miracle he'd escaped the noose before. Would he be able to do it again?

Blinking several times in succession, I tried to relax and focused on eavesdropping, hoping I would be able to glean a little more information from the conversation.

Silence filled the air. Freezing, I wondered if the pair had noticed I was here. I half expected Zadari's face to suddenly appear over my own, anger in his eyes. Instead, the woman began speaking, my presence continuing to go on unnoticed.

The pair exchanged a few more words, their voices fading, footsteps crunching through the gravel path until I was left alone with the stars once more.

Steeling myself for possible capture, I sat up, peering around the abandoned space as I bit my lip, not sure what to do. One thing was certain, though.

We needed to leave this place tonight before anyone expected us to try and escape.

Scooping Michael into my arms, I hurried from the amphitheater and through the ruins, looking over my shoulder for Zadari and the woman every step of the way. When I was finally back inside our room, hidden by the curtains and as safe as I could be in this situation, I sighed, watching the courtyard for a few minutes to make sure they hadn't spotted me and followed.

Confident I'd managed to sneak back, I went to the bed, shaking Tristan's shoulder. "Wake up," I whispered, stepping back when he sat up with a start, his hand curling into a fist.

"What is it?" he asked, eyes blurry and voice tired.

"We need to go," I stated in the simplest terms. "Zadari is a Templar."

That woke him up the rest of the way.

"What?" he exclaimed, lowering his voice when I shushed him in a panic. "How do ye know?"

"I fell asleep with Michael out in the ruins, and when I woke I could hear him talking with a woman. They were speaking their language, so I didn't understand any of it, but he said MacDonald's name."

He slid from the bed, fixing his clothes and putting the boots he'd shed back on. "Have ye woken the others?"

"Not yet. I came straight here and watched for a while to make sure I wasn't seen."

Nodding, he put his hands on his hips, letting out a long breath. "We'll have to move quickly, I suppose. At least they allowed us to bring our blades with us when we left the ship. We could dispatch the guards out front, but if we run into anyone in the hallway—"

"No," I interrupted. "There's another way."

The drop-off to the beach was farther than it had looked from the harbor. Standing at the top of the small cliff, staring at the abandoned cove beneath us, I wondered if we had to be crazy to try and escape by this route. There were no guards and it was left unprotected by the wall, though. Unless we wanted to alert everyone to our departure and try to fight our way out, this was the only way to go.

"It's not as high as it looks, methinks," Tristan whispered, his hair blowing in the breeze. "Twenty feet, maybe?"

"We can't jump that far without getting hurt." Shaking my head, I held Michael tighter. "What about the baby?"

"Here," Abella called, her voice barely a sound in the night air. As we all turned to her, she pushed aside a bush, revealing a bit of a slope on the other side. "We could slide," she suggested. "It looks too steep to walk, but it will be better than jumping."

"Good find." Cal grinned, striding over to her to get a better look at where she suggested. Facing us, he nodded. "It's a little rocky, but it will have to do."

He pushed through the shrub and sat down, inching his way in the dirt, slipping every few feet and sending a cascade of pebbles racing ahead of him. Disappearing for a moment, his form appeared in the sand below, well and good.

Relief coursed through me and I smiled, returning the wave he sent to us.

"Torches," Tristan hissed, pointing to a spot on our left.

A single flame bobbed along the edge of the precipice, following a path through the ruins. It stuck out in the night, the moonlight shrinking back from the bright blaze.

"It's a watchman," Mark guessed, grabbing Abella's hand and pulling her onto the slope with him.

Tristan motioned for me to hand him the baby and go ahead. "Ye watch yer head," he cautioned me. "If ye split it open again now, we're done for."

Swallowing hard, I moved to the pathway and sat down, scooting over the ground as fast as I could without losing control. The rocks and brush scraped across my skin, drawing blood in a few places, but I didn't stop, knowing we had to hurry and get out of sight.

When I reached the bottom, Callaghan grabbed my hand, pulling me against the cliff wall and putting a finger to his lips. Motioning up, he brought my attention to the guard, who was now walking across the expanse we'd all just occupied.

Tristan had stilled on the slope, rolling beneath another plant, his finger in Michael's mouth, muffling any sounds the boy was making. All of us seemed to hold our breath as the light overhead paused. As the guard continued to stand there, I believed we'd been found, until a small stream of liquid trickled down from above.

Disgusted, I shrank back, grateful to have not been discovered but horrified we were being peed on.

Thankfully, most of the stream went into the dirt, the guard aiming out far.

A few more beats passed, and the watchman began to whistle a tune, entertaining himself as he went on his way.

As soon as the man was gone, Tristan slid the rest of the way down, passing Michael back to me and drawing his sword as he motioned for us to follow him.

Going to the right, we crouched down and took in the ships docked in the harbor. They looked empty for the most part, but there would be no way to know for sure until we boarded one of them and tried to steal it.

"Which one are ye thinking, brother?" Cal asked. "One of the smaller ones?"

"Aye," Tristan answered, his eyes narrowing as he continued to stare at all the different boats. "I think the black. What say ye?"

Frowning, I searched out the one he was talking about. It was close to seventy or eighty feet long, by my guess. One large mast stretched up from the center of the sloop, a second, shorter one pointing out from the bow, the rigging on it webbing through the air, creating a maze of ropes. It appeared a little cluttered, but that was a good sign. It meant there were supplies on board, the vessel ready to set sail.

"It's huge!" I muttered, meeting his gaze. "Are you sure we can sail it ourselves?"

He nodded, looking back toward the prize. "Easier than a galleon, love. The only question now is if she's empty or not."

"There will be a guard watching the harbor somewhere," Mark supplied, his tone thoughtful. "If we divide ourselves, send one group to secure the sloop and another to take out the sentry, we might make it out without incident."

Abella huffed. "I was hoping we'd manage to escape without killing anyone," she confessed. "But, I agree. We'll move faster if we split."

"And there will be less chance of someone setting off an alarm," I added, agreeing to the grim circumstances without any more questions.

"Callaghan and I will find the guard," Tristan stated, motioning to his brother. "Mark, ye and the lasses get out of the harbor. We'll swim out to ye when we're finished. Do not wait for us more than five minutes once yer out, savvy?"

"What?" I asked sharply, frowning at him.

He chuckled, leaning in and pecking me on the lips. "If anyone is caught tonight, it'll be Cal and me. We're the ones MacDonald wants. Ye'll be free to go after Roberts and Randall and stop them. I've complete faith in ye, love."

He rose, dashing off with sword in hand, slipping onto the harbor path silently and making his way around the half-moon shape of the cove with Cal.

"Come on," Mark muttered. "We don't have any time to waste."

I watched Tristan for a second longer and stood, following Mark to the craft we intended to steal.

It looked bigger up close, but it was, in reality, smaller than any seafaring vessel I'd been on. The name *Jaguar* was painted in gold on her black hull, the deck silent and abandoned by all accounts.

Mark undid the ropes anchoring the sloop to the dock and climbed over the railing, helping Abella over and taking Michael from me so I could scurry up behind them. He took a moment to peer down the stairs, listening for any sounds, and nodded, motioning for us to get moving.

"Abella, undo those knots there and pull the rope here," he stated, giving instructions as he moved along the crowded space. "Samantha, you and Michael take the helm. I'm going up to release the sails. Whatever you do, make sure this line stays where it is until I give the signal."

Everything moved fast after that. As soon as we were ready, Mark helped me guide us out of the small harbor. We were met with no resistance, to my surprise. Perhaps the Berbers were so confident no one would try and steal from them that they didn't think to take precautions against such a crime. Or, if they did, Tristan and Callaghan had managed to get to them before we were found out.

I heard the first gunshots as we moved out past the *Lioness*, a crewmember shouting as he saw us going by. Another pistol fired in the distance, and I turned, watching as Tristan and Cal ran down the stretch of land jutting out toward us.

"Turn the helm a little more to the left, Sam," Mark instructed, working the ropes with Abella as we tried to move in closer to the two men.

With a huge leap, the brothers dove into the ocean, their heads bobbing in the water as they swam to us. Behind them, a somewhat bloodied guard jumped in too, the torch on the hillside moving to the harbor at an alarming speed. Lights came to life in the castle, and I knew our escape had been discovered, but it was going to be too late for anyone to stop us.

Abella tossed a line to our boys, and they pulled

themselves aboard, grinning and whooping as they shouted at the man swimming out after them.

"Come on," Cal screamed. "Come aboard, I dare ye!"

"Time to go," Mark yelled, letting the rope in his hand loose and the master sail unfurl completely.

Laughing, I steered away from the shore, a sense of elation and surprise filling me.

We'd stolen a ship from the most feared pirates in history. Without dying. The realization made me feel invincible.

A cannon fired from the *Lioness*, missing us by a wide margin and destroying my perception of immortality. Glancing back, I saw a few crewmen on board desperately trying to get their rigging undone, and the sails opened, planning on coming after us.

"She'll take too long to get underway," Tristan stated, coming to stand beside me. "All of them will." Kissing my forehead, his clothes and hair dripping all over me, he chuckled. "And we are headed where the *Lioness* cannot follow. Take us to the Nile, love. We've a pirate to catch."

"That's it, ye've got it!" Tristan helped to pull one of the ropes as Abella worked furiously to try and tie a knot over the beam she straddled. As captain of our stolen vessel, he'd graciously accepted all of us as the crew and instructed those who weren't as knowledgeable about sailing with patience.

Abella, however, was obviously frustrated, her fingers fumbling over the ropes, sweat dripping in her eyes as she muttered in French.

"Come on, Abella," Mark grumbled, straining as he grasped the sail that'd come loose in place while she tied it down. "It's not that hard."

"Maybe you should climb out over the water next time and fix it then," she growled back, glaring at him.

"I would," he retorted, "but you aren't strong enough to hold the canvas down while I do it."

"And your big bulky hands would never be able to tie the ropes in time!" she shouted, her face flushing.

"They're not so bulky that I couldn't teach you everything you know about surgery."

"Watch it," Callaghan growled, his rope going slack as he leaned out of the rigging, glowering at Mark.

"Trade with Sam or something," Mark continued to complain, stretching his back in discomfort. "This is taking forever."

"That's enough," Tristan commanded, his tone disproving but even. "Abella, ye're doing a fine job. Focus on the task at hand and ignore everyone else. We can hold it as long as ye need."

"It's done," she announced, huffing as she wiped the hair from her forehead. Staring at Mark with a hard expression, she folded her arms. "When I say I can do a job, I mean it."

He snorted, shaking his head as he put his rope back in its place. Storming off below deck after that, he shoved past everyone else with a sour expression in his eyes.

Surprised, I nodded at Abella from the helm as she approached me, her own face grim. "What was that about?"

"Nothing." Her voice was crisp and short, making it apparent something was the matter, but also that she didn't want to talk about it.

Resting one hand on Michael's back in the sling, I remained where I was as she went to the sterncastle and sat down, turning from all of us.

Tristan, joining me at the wheel, sighed. "That was new," he muttered, glancing upward to our friend. "Did she say anything to ye about what's bothering them?"

"No." Frowning, I adjusted our course, peering toward the heavens. "It's almost time to check our latitude."

"Aye," he agreed. "We should be close to the Nile Delta, and Rasheed beyond."

"You still think selling the *Jaguar* is the safest option?" I pressed, uncomfortable with his plan to remain out of the Templar's reach.

"I do," he confirmed. "We'll sell this one, find another in Rasheed, and follow Roberts to wherever it is he's hiding.

"And if he's left Egypt? What if he's somewhere in the Mediterranean?"

Tristan shook his head. "He's not. Roberts—Randall—wants us to follow him. If the last place anyone saw him was the Nile, that's where he'll be waiting for us."

Callaghan stood on the deck later that evening, his gaze trained on the horizon, watching the direction we'd come from. As he bent over, elbows resting on the railing, his curls moved with the breeze, the opening of his white shirt flapping gently against his skin. One of his black boots rested atop a small box, nestled beside a pile of cannonballs, his entire form framed by the rigging reaching up to the mast of the ship.

Behind him a few feet, Mark busied himself with a book about Egyptian mythology, borrowed from the small library in the captain's quarters. Tristan was in the crow's nest, having climbed up there almost an hour ago to watch for any sign of our destination. Abella was at the helm, humming to herself, her arms looped around the handles as she leaned on the wood frame. I'd laid Michael down to sleep, making sure he was secure in the tiny crate we'd turned into a type of bassinet for him.

I kept coming back to Cal, though. Something about the way he was standing seemed so ridged and angry as if he were suffering from an unspoken curse.

I came to stand beside him as the last remaining light of day kissed the sparkling waves. We stood in silence for a while, the breeze catching the collar of my own shirt, making me grateful for the long pants I'd tucked it into, the idea of a skirt caught in the wind not what I would have wanted to be struggling with.

The stars began appearing overhead, and he stared at them in the quiet, as if stuck in his contemplations.

"You aren't mad at me, are you?" I questioned, making sure the others couldn't hear us.

He straightened, turning in surprise. "What? No. Why would I be?"

I smiled. "If not for me, Mark and Abella never would have met. She wouldn't be on this dangerous mission. He wouldn't be standing in the way of you telling her how you really feel."

He frowned at that, his brow furrowing, and he returned to staring at the horizon, remaining silent for a few minutes.

"I don't understand," he admitted after a beat. "How she convinced anyone to let her come in the first place, how she's remained so poised in the face of danger, how she . . ." His voice trailed off, and he turned around, resting his backside on the railing. Folding his arms, he stared in Mark's direction, the emotion in his eyes conflicted.

"How she can care for a man who is obviously troubled by her feelings?" I offered, my voice low and void of judgment.

Glancing at me, his nose twitched as he gave me a curt nod.

Sighing, I leaned on the side with him, tucking my hair behind my ears. "You have to remember, Mark and Abella have a history. They've saved each other's lives on different occasions. Both of them have an interest in helping others. He's shared a lot of what he knows about being a doctor with her, and she's taught him things about this time that no one else has."

"He acts like he wants nothing to do with her," Cal countered, frowning. "They seem at odds all the time. Yet, whenever I try to speak with her, he comes to her side, as if I am a threat."

I bit my lip as I nodded. "Their relationship is . . . complicated," I stated, aware it sounded like a lame excuse. "Mark comes from a different millennium. Things aren't the same there as they are here when it comes to age and romantic interests."

Giving me a sideways look, Cal raised his eyebrows. "And he struggles with that fact?"

"More than I think he's willing to admit to most anyone."

"Hmmm." His attention turned back to the other side of the vessel, silence stretching between us for several minutes. Clearing his throat, he glanced toward the heavens. "What do ye think I should do, Sam? I care for the lass, but if she wants another . . . I could be happy knowing she was."

I stood up straight, gazing across the open water. "Honestly? I don't know, Cal. It's not my place to say."

Still, it warmed my heart to hear him say that my friend's happiness came before his own. If I was truthful with myself, I didn't think Mark had ever had that kind of consideration for her. It was that belief that compelled me to keep speaking, despite my hesitance to say any more on the matter.

"Abella has loved Mark for years," I stated, my voice so soft he had to lean in to hear me. "But I don't know that Mark will ever be able to get over the differences that come with being so far apart, age and time wise. He . . . He wants to go home. If he ever finds a way to travel through time again, I think he would leave here in a heartbeat."

Shocked, Cal stared at me, his mouth popping open. "He would just leave her here, alone?"

I shrugged.

Shaking his head, he glared in Mark's direction for a minute. A wave of sadness washing over him, he turned and stared across the water once more.

"Samantha."

Tristan's voice drew my attention, and I turned, watching as he sauntered across the deck from the main mast, having left the crow's nest. He wore a giant grin, his bare feet gripping the wooden floor as it rolled with the ocean waves.

"I've spotted the delta in the distance," he told me happily. "By morning time, we should be on land and purchasing a new boat."

Cal stood and turned to face Tristan as well. "Good. Maybe we can make some headway with this mission at last." Leaving without another word, he pushed his way past Mark and disappeared below, to the hammock he'd claimed in the crew quarters.

Furrowing his brow, Tristan watched him go and looked at me. "What's wrong with him?"

Smiling, I shook my head. "Nothing. Nerves, I think."

He shrugged. "But he's doing well? Ye haven't noticed him struggling as of late, like before?"

Frowning, I shook my head. After Cal had escaped the Otherworld, he'd suffered from nightmares for months. It felt like a lifetime had passed since we stayed up with him, convincing him he wasn't in danger or under a spell to make him think he was safe.

Ever since he'd been attacked and carved into, he seemed to be dealing with those problems again, despite our efforts to help him.

Abella and Mark had their history, but Cal had his own demons to deal with, too. Adding conflicted feelings into the mix was almost too much for him to have to handle at this moment in time.

"He's upset about the way Mark spoke with Abella earlier?" It was Tristan's turn to be covert in his speaking now, his eyes darting toward the man in question.

"I think so," I responded. "He has a lot on his mind."

"Who, Callaghan or Mark?"

I leaned on the railing, laughing. "Both? I don't know. It doesn't matter. Abella can take care of herself. I think that's why Cal hasn't said anything about it for her. And Mark . . . Well, he's Mark. Stubborn and opinionated."

"And worried," Tristan added. "Our group has been out of balance ever since we rejoined and he's the one throwing it off."

"He's struggling," I said once more.

"That's no excuse for him to take his frustrations out on the lass." He frowned, his gaze moving to the helm and Abella's shadowy form there. "Someone ought to say something if she will not."

Closing my eyes, I breathed out, knowing he was right. "Fine," I grumbled. "I'll do it."

Beaming, he pecked me on the cheek, his eyes filled with mirth. "I'll light the lanterns. It'll be full dark soon."

Waving the comment away, I straightened and

made my way to Mark, hedging as I neared him. It wasn't my style to play matchmaker, but I always ended up being the person who had to talk sense into Mark when it came to Abella. They'd fought before, and I'd been in the middle then, too.

"Hey," I said by way of greeting, sitting beside him.

He grunted, focused on his reading, and said nothing.

Drumming my fingers on my thigh, I pursed my lips. "So . . ."

Lowering the tome, he stared at me, frowning. "I know, I shouldn't have spoken to her like that. I was tired and frustrated, and I took it out on her. I'm sorry, I won't do it again." The book rose, covering his face as he turned from me.

Grabbing his shoulder, I forced him to look at me, taking the hardcover and setting it on his lap. "I am not the one you need to apologize to," I whispered, glancing at Abella as I spoke. "What is going on? You two have been together this whole time, running your practice and being in Paris. Why does it seem like you've done nothing but fight while we were gone?"

Rubbing the bridge of his nose, he shook his head. "I don't know," he confessed. "There's nothing between us anymore, Sam. There was, once. I've kissed her a few times, but not at all since you left us. We've stayed close friends, but . . ." Staring down at me, he chewed on the inside of his lip before continuing. "Too much is different," he said quietly. "I don't want to hurt her, but it isn't ever going to happen. I thought I could fool myself and let it be, but I can't. If anything, our year alone proved that."

The confession made my heart hurt for Abella. I knew how much she cared for him, how much she wished he could let his reservations go and choose to be happy with her. This news would break her.

At the same time, I understood what he was saying. Mark was my friend, too, and I wanted him to be happy. I only wished it didn't have to bring pain to another person I loved. "You need someone from your own time." I folded my arms. "Someone your own age."

"Not even you can give me that."

His light attempt at a joke worked, and I laughed. "That's true."

Peering toward Abella, the mirth faded from me. "You need to tell her," I muttered. "Stop dragging her along. Let her be happy with someone else." Focusing on him, I smiled. "Let both of you be happy, even if it is on your own."

His shoulders slumped. "You aren't mad at me?"

Snorting, I shook my head. "Am I sad that my two best friends aren't in love? Yeah. But am I mad at you for it? Never." Turning serious, I nudged his toe with mine. "You do need to tell her how you feel. Soon. What you're doing to her now isn't fair. Abella may be able to take care of herself, but she has a soft spot when it comes to you. If anyone else had spoken to her today the way you did, she would have ripped them a new one."

"I know." Resting his elbows on his knee, he put his chin on his hands. "I'll do it. Give me a little time to figure out what I want to say."

"And no more of this jealous act you've been pulling around Callaghan," I instructed.

He opened his mouth to protest or deny it, I didn't know which, and I held my hand up, stopping him in his tracks.

"Cal has liked her from the moment they first met," I explained. "If you're too stupid to win her yourself, you can't stop him from trying."

Snapping his mouth shut, he frowned and begrudgingly nodded. "Fine. I won't stand in his way."

Stifling a small laugh, I stared in awe at the city ahead of me. I'd never imagined it would be so green, especially after the array of barren, desert clad images of the place I'd seen in my own time. It made sense there were lots of plants—the river was a massive supply of water, after all—but to have my impression of Egypt challenged from the moment we'd entered the Nile Delta was both thrilling and worrying to me. Not for the first time, I considered how much I didn't know about the world.

This place was farmland, not an entire barren desert of nothing. People working in the fields had waved to us as we sailed the river, fisherman calling out in greeting as we sailed by. Everything was so lush and populated, making me feel like I'd escaped into an oasis in the blink of an eye.

After playing matchmaker to friends and family, the idea of going on a vacation in a beautiful country sounded delightful. However, this was no vacation, and I couldn't escape the love triangle going on right under my nose if I wanted to. However, I was able to distract myself from it, and so I set myself to work, hoping to lead by example rather than words for a bit.

Setting my foot on one of the crates beside the railing, I scrutinized the women I could see on the docks in Rasheed, noting the way their clothes looked and wrapped around their bodies. After a few moments, I undid the tie around my ankle and moved it above my knee, letting the fabric of my pants balloon down and cover the rest of my leg. From what I could tell, that was the only way to make it look right.

I'd discovered a trunk full of clothing that better matched the culture of this area in the hold a few days ago. At Tristan's suggestion, we all found ourselves an outfit, hoping to blend in better once we arrived in the city.

Thankfully, women wore pants here. It appeared there was a wide selection of fashions to choose from, the ladies striding by sporting skirts, coats, turbans, pointy hats, flat caps, sheer face coverings, and all other sorts of things.

I'd chosen to pair my poofy white pants with a green tunic shirt and brown jacket. The gold pattern on the thigh length cover matched the metal belt that held it shut, my pointed shoes the same color as my shirt. While it was apparent the clothes hadn't been tailored to fit me, they did a well enough job of helping me blend in, as did braiding my hair several times over and connecting all the plaits together with a single ribbon at the ends.

Abella was dressed in the same manner, the two of us fashioning a sort of tunic for Michael to wear. The men styled themselves much like Captain Zadari did, but less flashy and noticeable.

Tristan appeared in the crowd as if my thoughts had summoned him. For whatever reason, the more we made our own path in the world, the younger and happier he appeared to me. Handsome as ever, I couldn't help but study him, admiring the outfit he'd chosen before going to shore. The blue turban wrapped around his dark hair made me think of the ocean and its swirling depths, bringing a new light to his green eyes I'd never seen before. His matching jacket brushed the earth as he pushed through the crowd, the edges dragging through puddles and flicking water onto his red pants. In his hand, held close to his golden vest, a full coin bag was clutched. One look at his smile told me he'd managed to do the task he set out to accomplish.

"Tristan sold the ship," I remarked to the others, turning from my perch and nodding toward the gangplank. "We should meet him down there and get out of here before anyone recognizes it."

As disappointing as it was to get rid of the sloop, I knew we needed to cover our tracks to keep the Templars from finding us. With any luck, we would be able to purchase one that would suit our needs and be on our way soon.

Making sure we didn't leave anything needed behind, those of us remaining on the *Jaguar* made our way to dry land, merging with the bustling crowd and Tristan.

"I've bought us a new boat," he said as soon as we were all within hearing. "Down the road. We can sleep there and make a plan."

"Aye," Cal agreed, scratching his collarbone as he traded annoyed looks with a man walking by. "Anything to keep us out of notice."

"Europeans aren't exactly welcome in this area right now," Mark mumbled.

"You know some history about it?" I asked under my breath, holding Michael close.

He shook his head, smiling. "Nope. Just look at

their faces when they realize who we are."

Peering at those closest, I watched as their expressions scrunched up, distrust and suspicion in their eyes. They glanced over our outfits and shook their heads as if annoyed we were there at all.

Sighing, I nodded, focusing on the group.

"What about dinner?" Abella pressed, nodding toward a stand selling roasted meat.

"We'll grab it on the way, savvy?" Tristan answered, jerking his head in the direction he wanted us to go. "I've other news to share as well."

"Good news?" I asked full of hope, worried we would have a harder time here than I anticipated.

His eyes met mine, and he grinned. "Perfect news, love. I know where Roberts is."

The statement was met with surprise and prodding from the rest of us, but he refused to say anything more, insisting we get our food and move to the new craft instead of staying out in the open. Leading the way, a skewer of tender meat in his hands that he munched on, Tristan led us down the docks, the *Jaguar* falling out of sight behind. After about a ten-minute walk, he stopped beside our new vessel, smiling.

"It's not much," he stated, "but it will suit us fine."

Frowning, I stared at the craft tied to the dock. "It's . . . a rowboat."

Well, that wasn't true. The thing was maybe twenty feet long, with a removable mast and sail tied along the inside, starboard railing. Oars rested on the port side. In the center, there was a square shelter to protect people from the sun, with a table and a few cushions. There was no wheel to steer with, but I could see the tiller in the back, ready to direct the craft through the water.

"More like a longboat," Tristan amended, hesitation in his eyes as he watched our reactions. "It's flat-bottomed, so sandbars won't be an issue. The mast is only needed when sailing upriver, which is why it's so small. There are paddles, but we should only need them should we become stuck somehow."

"It was made to sail this river," Mark mused, rubbing his chin, a hint of laughter suppressed behind his hand.

"And cheap, I suppose," Cal added dryly, grinning at his brother.

Tristan laughed at that, nodding. "Aye, it was. I've a mind to get us all home after this, and the money I saved will be more than enough to book passage back to Éire."

"Then it's the best thing I've ever seen," Abella replied, the first to touch the handrail. "Can we go aboard now?"

Nodding, Tristan helped her step over the edge, assisting Michael and me next. Soon, we were all on board and sitting at the table beneath the sun cover.

Unhooking the lightweight curtains in the corners, Tristan gave us a small amount of privacy from the rest of the world before sitting down.

"Roberts?" Leaning forward, I folded my arms on the table, smiling as I listened to Michael playing on the floor beside me.

Tristan finished chewing the bite of food he'd taken. "He's in Cairo, downriver a few days or so. The man I spoke to said he stopped here and made repairs before heading on. He believed the Black Knights were missionaries—they were inviting others to come to a meeting in Cairo in a few weeks' time—about when we'll be arriving in the city if he remembered the correct date."

"Missionaries?" My eyebrows rose. "What message they were sharing? Or was it only the meeting invitation?"

"He didn't say." Tristan leaned back in his chair, his face troubled.

"It can't be anything good," Mark replied, glancing between the two of us.

"Do ye think Randall will be there?" Callaghan asked quietly, seriousness exuding from him.

"I do not know," Tristan confessed. "The whole affair is strange to me. In the past, the Black Knights have been secretive about their plans. To have them now openly trying to recruit others and drawing the fight to themselves is baffling."

"Could they be recruiting for the boat?" I asked. "I mean, we did kill a few of their men on Roberts' ship. Maybe he's trying to fill his crew again."

"Or he's building an army for Randall to try and destroy the world with," Cal responded, his tone sour.

"*Que Dieu nous aide*," Abella muttered, crossing herself.

"He's not building an army," Mark asserted confidently.

"Oh?" Callaghan frowned, his sticky emotions regarding Mark flaring to the surface. "And what would ye know about the Black Knights and the bastard's plans?"

"You forget, I was once a member of Randall's crew," Mark replied in a strained tone. "I was a Black Knight before I was a Templar. I understand how he works in a way that none of you ever will." Taking a deep breath, he shook his head. "He's not forming an army, not yet anyway. He's trying to convince them to listen to him."

"Huh?" Confused, I stared at him, thinking back to our time on Randall's vessel together. Mark had kept me safe by joining the forbidden order to spy on them. Before I'd arrived as a hostage, he'd been working beneath Randall's command. He was right; he knew the Black Knight side of him better than any of us ever would.

"Think about it." Mark shrugged. "Almost every man who's signed up with him in the past has died. Who's going to follow him now, when he has such a rough track record? Tristan and Sam keep beating him every time they get together. He's only managed to make off with the bare minimum of what he set out to steal. He spent the last year in a prison cell. He literally has nothing to offer anyone except the promise of something better. I don't know about you, but I don't think a promise is really worth that much coming from someone like Randall."

The group processed his assessment in silence. He made a good point; everyone who joined with Randall in the past was dead. Why were so many of them willing to let him lead them now?

"He always wanted people to follow him," I said. "Even before this whole thing started. He wanted to be captain of the *Adelina*."

"And when he was my captain he would hold meetings in his cabin where he made great speeches and convinced his crew to follow him into stupid and dangerous situations." Mark smiled at me, a hint of sadness in his eyes as we discussed our past. "He wants the power that comes from having a following."

"He's convincing them to help him," Tristan agreed, frowning.

"All the more reason to go out and stop him," Cal inserted. "We can't let him rally the troops against us. MacDonald's already done a well enough job of that on his own."

"But how is he doing it?" Abella questioned, her mouth turned down. "He'll have had to convince them that whatever he can give them is worth dying for."

The words brought our fight with Roberts to the front of my mind as I gazed at the tabletop. The men had battled without fear or second-guessing anything they did.

Almost as if they were unafraid of death.

"He's promised to bring them back," I whispered, the idea forming quickly as I put the pieces together. Glancing up, I peered around our small group. "They think if they die, he will bring them back!"

Tristan blinked, not understanding what I was saying.

"Think about it," I pressed. "The men we fought on Roberts' ship weren't afraid of anything. If one of them died, another one took his place without issue. There was no mourning or shock when they lost any of them.

"The man you spoke with here said they were missionaries because the meeting he heard about *is* a religious one. They're sharing that they've beaten death and inviting others to join the fold."

Tristan shook his head, his expression falling as I continued to explain.

"In the past, Randall got others to follow him because of the wealth it would bring them. He promised lands and money and power. This time, *he's selling himself*. He's convincing them to follow him because he is basically a god—he already has the powers of several of them. These Black Knights are different because they believe he can save them from whatever fate they meet on his missions."

"It wasn't just MacDonald's actions that forced the split among the Templars," Mark added, nodding as he accepted what I was saying. "Randall was already sowing the seeds among the men, convincing them that he deserves their loyalty and trust because of the things he's accomplished so far."

"He's still promising them riches and everything from before," I added, "but with the added idea that he is their god."

"Why would they openly welcome others to join them, even those that aren't members of The Order?" Cal interrupted, his brow furrowed.

Pausing, I thought it over. "The treasure is here," I decided. "Whatever he's after next is in Egypt, and he wants locals, people who know the land and its history, to help him find it."

"Why would the Templar base be all the way in Gibelet if the treasure cache is here?" my brother-in-law continued to press. "That doesn't make any sense."

"Because there is another Templar outpost here," Tristan replied grimly. "Somewhere along the Nile. Gibelet must be the base of operations for The Order in this part of the world like Paris is the base for most others."

"Ye believe this theory?" Callaghan shook his

head. "I do not know if I can, brother. If Randall has indeed put himself on such a high pedestal, we will never be able to knock him off it."

"Which is precisely why he put himself there." Closing his eyes, Tristan sucked in a breath, rubbing his temples. Standing, he motioned for the other two men to follow him. "We must get on our way now, lest we are found by whatever Templars lie in wait for us here."

"And go where?" Cal insisted. "We stand no chance against the Black Knights if what we believe is correct."

Tristan grinned. "To Roberts' meeting," he said, his tone simple but grim. "That is the only way we will discover if any of our fears are true."

It was strange, fleeing the group who had kept me safe for so long and purposefully running into the arms of the one that had tried to kill me many times over. I felt as if I were watched at every moment by either the Templars or Black Knights as we entered Cairo, uncertain in a maze of tall buildings.

This place fit my earlier picture of Egypt more. Desert surrounded the city, dust heavy in the air as it was kicked up by wagons and people. Stone streets did nothing to quell the dirt, the sand seeping into everything it touched.

And yet, the place was as magnificent as any other I'd been to. Apartment buildings and shops lined the walkways, colorful fabrics and exotic fruits sold from stands on corners and messenger bags their sellers carried. Voices rang out, happy and content, the people as mistrusting as those in Rasheed, but somehow more welcoming. It was a place of trade and growth, where educated peoples and those with only street knowledge intermingled.

Pulling the heavy veil I'd purchased across my face so that only my eyes showed beneath the cover, I continued my slow walk, glancing around every few minutes to see if I was being followed.

It hadn't been difficult to discover where Roberts' was holding his meeting. True to what our Rasheed informant had told us, his men were out in the streets, inviting anyone who could hear to come along. However, due to our relationship with the Black Knights, we'd opted to buy veils and dress in less colorful clothing, in an attempt to blend in when we infiltrated the gathering.

My stomach clenched as I thought of Abella and Michael on our boat, waiting for us to return. What if they were caught? Surely, neither organization we hid from would hurt a woman and child.

Pushing aside the knowledge that they'd hurt me without any issue, I focused on what I was doing. The building was ahead, a crowd gathering in front of it. Surprised, I wondered how many people had come because they were interested in what was going to be said or if they were curious as to what wild promises this new religion would try and sell them.

Somewhere in the mass, I knew Tristan, Callaghan, and Mark would be waiting, too, disguised and ready to defend themselves if we were discovered.

Patting the blade beneath my coat, I sighed, reassuring myself of my own sense of safety. If I were discovered, I would be able to get out. This wasn't a meeting of dedicated men. It was recruitment, which meant if a fight broke out, most of the people would scatter, leaving me ample time to escape and a stampede to disappear into.

Making my way through the press outside and into the actual building, I found a place beside one of the support beams that held the apartments overhead up. Most of the space was packed with those ready to listen, a fire burning in the corner and throwing shadows across the elevated area that was kept clear by a few guards. A curtain hung over a doorway in the back, and I was sure that was were Roberts would come from to deliver his speech.

As I waited for the proceedings to begin, I caught sight of Tristan on the other side of the room, Mark and Cal positioned throughout the people as well. We'd decided it would be best if we split up, to better help in not being recognized. Once again, I felt for the handle of my blade beneath my cover, allowing the heavy metal to give me comfort.

Suddenly, the curtain moved aside, and Roberts appeared, a hush coming over the crowd. He'd not bothered to try and dress in the fashions of this country, instead wearing his usual breeches and billowy white shirt, a sword slung around his waist and a gun belt looped around his torso, clasped over his shoulder. The guy looked more like a kid than a man with his mess of blonde curls, one of which dangled over his forehead. When he spoke, it became evident his maturity and brilliance were not to be argued with.

"Welcome." His voice, low and smooth, blanketed the room, its warmth deceivingly inviting. "I thank you for coming this evening. No doubt, you have heard our words in the street, and they have touched you in some way. With any luck, what you witness this night will convince you of joining those of us already on the path to greatness."

Roberts paused for a moment, tapping his mouth with the knuckle of his pointer finger as if trying to decide what to say next.

"I need not recount your history to you," he continued, giving us all a gracious smile. "But if you will indulge me for a moment, I would bring one occurrence to light."

This seemed to sit well with all those in attendance, no one interrupting him or moving to leave. With our permission, he continued, spinning the tale he wished to share.

"In the beginning, there was nothing." He said it as if he were not to be argued with, his face showing the easiness of his belief in this thing he asserted to be fact. "No earth, no sun, no moon or stars." Pausing, he let a tiny amount of mourning into his tone. "No life. No death. Nothing."

Slowly, he paced across his stage, weaving the words together, his tone rising and falling for dramatic effect, the crowd hanging on his every word.

"When water burst into existence, it covered the nothingness, creating land, bringing to the earth the Nile, the source of all life in Egypt."

At this, a few members of the audience nodded their approval, acceptance on their faces.

"The sun came soon after, showering this infantile place with its warmth and light, and with it came Ra, the god of the heavens and protector of Egypt." Roberts smiled, his eyes looking skyward as he paused, letting the words work his magic for him. "After Ra came his children," he continued, facing the audience. "And from them, his posterity grew until the main characters of our tale came into being. Osiris. Isis. Set. All gods in their own right, some sharing love, and others sharing hate." His fist clenched on the last word, the sound slipping through his teeth like a bad omen.

"Set, angry with his brother for past misdeeds and jealous of his throne, lured Osiris into a trap along the Nile's shore, where he murdered and dismembered him. Having scattered his brother's remains across the country, Set assumed the throne, thinking all was well."

Roberts paused, pursing his lips in quiet thought as his mood shifted from powerful vengeance to something much softer. His tone became reverent and flowing as he went on, his eyes misting as if he were genuinely touched by what happened after the brutal murder.

"However, Isis, Osiris' loving wife, vowed to give her husband a better end. Taking the form of a bird, she and her sister, Nephthys, scoured the earth, searching for the pieces of Osiris and bringing them back together. She wrapped him in linen and breathed the air of life back into his lungs."

Even I felt like I was frozen, waiting for him to continue as he stopped, nodding his head as he stared over the group.

"Yes, my friends. Isis held power to give life to those who had lost it. She did not shy away from what needed to be done or what was asked of her. She took her power, and used it for good, to save her husband and kingdom. To bring back the man she loved, who had died wrongfully and horribly.

"I stand before you this day and promise to you—this power still exists. The gods have left it here, for us to use!" The kind, peaceful feeling left his voice as he got worked up, until he was shouting at the group, releasing all the pent-up energy he'd saved for this moment.

"There are those who would tell you it is not for us, that it belongs to the gods only. But the gods created us to become like them!" Swallowing, he grinned, chest heaving. "This day, there is a man, nobler that Isis, superior to Ra, or Allah, or God, or whatever higher being you choose to believe in." Pausing, he let the startling statement settle, patient in all things as he gave his sermon. "He is a god among men, a being willing to do what must be done, to do what the world is asking of him. The greater good is his purpose, and the salvation of all is his calling. If you will but follow him, he will lead you to the Knot of Isis and grant you a life free from daily struggle and pain. Your wounds will heal, your life will lengthen, and all of your troubles will fall by the wayside."

Those Black Knights in the crowd called out their agreement, clapping their hands and riling up the newcomers.

As the crowd continued to eat up the conversion speech, a sense of uneasiness washed over me. The feeling that I needed to leave while I still could grew larger until I found myself looking toward the exit and the fresh air outside.

"You may find this hard to believe," Roberts continued to yell over the crowd behind me. "I understand the hesitation I see on many of your faces. I was once there myself. I lived my life in fear, knowing it would one day end, and I would be forgotten by those left behind. That is not a life I want to live. And then I met this glorious being, this god among men. He changed me in more ways than I can count, and all he asked in return was my service and gratitude. This day that is all he asks of you. Still, believing is seeing. And so I say, look upon him for yourself and witness his miracles this day."

Panic flooded me in an instant—he was here. Thomas Randall was in the building, possibly already on the stage. Somehow, I knew he would recognize me the moment he saw me, disguise be damned.

Not bothering to look back, I started shoving my way through the crowd, hurrying toward the exit, bumping into people as I tried to force my way free. They were reluctant to move, the space already cramped, and the action drew attention to myself as I pried my way by.

As it became clear I wasn't going to make it out before being discovered, I glanced around, searching for Tristan. When I found him, I felt the color drain from my face.

He was looking at me with hard eyes, a knife held to his throat by one of the Black Knights standing behind him. There was no chance he could move without being slashed, and the look on his face said he knew it.

Desperate, I searched for Mark and Callaghan, finding them similarly contained. Blood streamed from Mark's nose, and Callaghan had a bruised and swollen eye.

Gulping, I shrank back, hitting the wall as I fumbled for my sword.

A hand grabbed my arm, squeezing it tight, and I jumped, staring into the smiling face of Thomas Randall.

"Hello, Samantha," he muttered, pulling me against him. "I see you got my message."

"I, too, thank you for being here," Randall started, his grip on me ironclad as he faced the crowd. "As I stood here, among you, I recalled a time not long ago when I felt as you do now. Lost. Alone. Abandoned. Perhaps, like me, you are thinking—what have the gods done for us? They built this earth, gave us life, and then abandoned us to wars and petty fighting, refusing to use their all-knowing minds and powers to come to our aid when we needed it most."

A chill moved through me as he spoke. This was not the off-kilter, mad Randall I'd known. His ability to be smooth and personable had returned, the craziness in his eyes had faded, and he exuded command over everything as he moved and spoke like the world was already his. Those in attendance who did not know better were eating the words out of his hand, eyes wide with awe as they stared at him.

He'd cleaned up for the occasion, too. His black hair had been braided in several places, the plaits flipped over his shoulder on his dark brown leather jacket and gray cotton shirt, but that wasn't all that important.

No, what concerned me most was the sword at his waist and the gun nestled in the belt that stretched across his chest. There was a knife in his boots, too, the handle resting on his calf, blending in with the fabric that matched his jacket.

"The old gods are gone," he continued curtly, interrupting my perusal of him. "But they left behind a way for us to become like them. I started this path many years ago, searching and discovering the secrets left behind for the taking. I have lost almost as many things as I found."

He held up his severed hand with a laugh, showing off the shiny, new metal prosthetic he wore. The fingers were fused together in a slight cup, the thumb resting beside them.

To my horror, the crowd laughed with him. He was charming them without even trying, winning them over without any real effort. They'd no idea the atrocities he'd committed, the lives he'd destroyed while on his "path."

Unable to help myself, I tried to jerk away, shouting. "No! Don't listen to him, he's a liar!"

Randall chuckled, his grip tightening as he glared at me. "There have been naysayers," he continued, addressing the room as our eyes locked. "And those who have actively tried to stop me. They have failed at every turn." Looking back over the room he smiled. "They said the power of the gods was not for me, but they were wrong. Isn't that right, Samantha?"

Releasing my arm, he pushed aside my veil and ran his fingers over my collarbone, causing gooseflesh to ripple across my skin, and grabbed the leather chord I always wore around my neck. Slowly, he pulled the necklace free of my shirt, revealing the Atlantean focal point.

"Pretty," he muttered, his eyes flicking to mine for a beat.

Unable to stay still, I stepped back, the pendant

falling on my chest. "What do you want?" I asked with force.

He smiled as if he knew what I was thinking and faced the audience. "Your necklace," he ordered. "Give it to me." Holding out his right hand, his lips turned upward as he tilted his head to the side.

"What?" Raising my eyebrows, I wrapped my fingers around the pendant, taking another step back.

A flash of frustration lit in his gaze, a glimpse of the old Randall appearing for a moment. "Do you not tire of these games, Sam?" The words were hushed and filled with venom, jeering through his barely moving lips as he glared at me. "Pretending to be people we are not, living a life that is less than we deserve? We are both capable of so much more, don't you think?" Facing the crowd, he yelled. "We all are!"

"I like my life just fine," I replied coldly, fingers twitching to grab the sword at my waist and use it to end him. It wouldn't make any difference, though. Even if I managed to kill him—which I'd never done in a one-on-one fight with him before—he would only come back moments later and prove to the entire room he had the powers he was claiming to wield.

"We'll see," he sneered. Grabbing the necklace, he ripped it off me, snarling as he leaned in close.

One of the men in the room roared beside us, throwing off his cape and revealing a bald head, long beard, and tattered Scotsman's kilt.

Continuing to bellow, William MacDonald hefted his hammer into the air and smashed it against Randall's back, sending the villain sprawling onto the floor and erupting the room into chaos.

"Dinna let him get that stone!" the Grand Master

yelled to me, nodding in the direction the broken necklace had flown.

Nodding, I scrambled after it, falling to my hands and knees as I searched the ground. All around me, people were fleeing and clashing with one another, a firearm going off as screams filled the air.

Catching sight of the Atlantean piece ahead, I reached for it, only to have my hand stepped on by a frightened man bolting from the scene. Hissing, I pulled back, cradling my palm for a second as I inched closer to the rock. Finally, I scooped it off the ground, wrapping my injured fingers around it, and let loose a sigh of relief.

"Give it to me!" Randall screamed, grabbing my ankle and yanking my leg out from beneath me.

The air knocked from my chest, and I gasped, struggling to maintain a hold on the broken necklace as he rolled me over and straddled my waist. His metal hand slapped my head, and I saw stars, his fingers prying at my own as he attempted to take the piece of Atlantis from me.

"Get off," I growled, bucking my hips and dislodging him.

Catching himself, he emitted a breathy laugh and shook his head. "You think you're so perfect, don't you? Samantha O'Rourke, time traveler." Shaking his head, he continued to claw at my hand, kneeing and hitting me wherever he could. "You cannot fool me, Sammy. I've seen what your century is like." His grin turned sour, eyes narrowing as he paused,. "You may have had that rock to protect your mind from me, but the rest of your party did not."

The statement made my stomach fill with an icy

dread, my determination to get him off me fading in the revelation he'd unleashed. "You've been visiting other people's dreams," I said slowly.

"Correct." His words were labored as we continued to wrestle. "What good would it do me to summon you here and then never know if you came or not? I needed some way to make sure you were listening to your instructions."

Bucking my hips again, I made him rise enough to knee him in the groin, smiling as he groaned. The action allowed me to wriggle a small amount of the way out from beneath him, panting as I tried to escape.

Digging his finger into my thigh, he yanked me back, sitting on top of me and grabbing my wrist. "Of course, after I visited Mark and realized the things you two had kept from me about your own era, I spent a good amount of time with him, discovering it all. The twenty-first century is very technologically advanced, isn't it?"

My heart was beating so loud I almost couldn't hear him, my entire being not wanting to believe what he was saying. "Mark never said anything about you being in his head." I stammered, trying to find any loopholes I could.

"He wouldn't, would he?" Randall gave me another sickening grin. "I made sure to keep my presence hidden. I checked in on dear old Tristan, too. Your husband doesn't dream of much but open ocean and you. I was always uninterested with his mind, more so when you lot were in Ireland. The only juicy tidbits I ever got from him were a few glimpses of you beneath those clothes." He raised his eyebrow, appreciation in his stare as he focused on my body.

It was like the floor was falling out from beneath me. For many months, I'd felt safe and protected, hidden from Randall and the world he wished to create. However, with a few words, he'd managed to destroy the entirety of the past year for me, tainting every memory with the fear that he'd been there with us during it all. Even worse, his lingering gaze made me feel violated in a way I'd never experienced, horror rushing through me as I considered he might actually be telling the truth about what he'd experienced with Tristan.

"Did you truly think you were rid of me?" He laughed, watching as my expression continued to fall, my resolve failing more by the second. "MacDonald disowns you, and that's it?" Shaking his head, he leaned over me, lips coming to my ear as he whispered. "You'll never be rid of me, Samantha. Not while you have what I want."

Wrenching my wrist to the side, he twisted it, screaming in my face as I cried out until I was forced to open my fingers and drop the stone on my chest.

He released me at once, allowing me to pull my injured wrist back to safety, tears pouring out of my eyes. I didn't think it was broken, but he'd rendered it useless for the next little while.

"Tristan!" I screamed, blinking back tears as I tried to get out from beneath him.

The brute laughed, shaking his head. "It's too late, Sammy," he told me with happiness. "I have what I wanted."

He took the amulet from my chest, displaying it like a precious belonging he'd lost and found again. In one swift motion, he smashed it on the wall, the force of the attack causing the building to shudder.

Caught off guard, I froze, eyes narrowing.

"MacDonald was right to try and keep this from me," he gloated, revealing the now cracked rock to me. "You hadn't the faintest idea what you were wearing around your neck."

A small amount of clear liquid seemed to be coming from the inside of the trinket, dripping out into Randall's palm. It seeped from one crack, the rock having collapsed beneath the superior strength of the one attacking it.

Randall held the stone over his metal hand and let the liquid drip over his skin and the prosthetic, discarding the rock and licking the moisture from his palm once the droplets stopped.

With a sickening lurch, I realized what he was doing.

The talisman had been gifted to me by the Atlanteans, beside the Fountain of Youth—the essence of their goddess. The shaman had said it possessed the power to keep me safe, to hide me from Randall, but I'd never question how it was able to do such a thing. Now, it was obvious that it had possessed water from the fountain.

I'd been wearing the blood of another god around my neck for over a year and never realized.

And Randall had just taken it for himself.

The reality of what was occurring slammed into me like a pile of bricks, my feet kicking of their own volition. A scream shredded past my throat, my fingers flying through the air and digging into his eyes.

Yelping, he grabbed my wrists, tugging them from his face and rolling to the left. Pebbles dug into our skin as we wrestled a moment more, his elbow digging into me as he blindly attempted to escape. Finally, we broke apart, his form skittering back, showering me with dirt and little pieces of wood as he clutched his bleeding face. The sounds of pain he emitted turned to those of laughter as the wound healed quicker than any other he'd had before, and I had another sickening realization.

The Atlantean goddess was a healer. She'd protected her people and extended their time in the Otherworld with her life-giving essence. Now that Randall had absorbed that power, too, he was recovering from his wounds faster than I'd ever seen before.

He made a pained sound, bending at the waist as he clutched his prosthetic hand, trembling as he stared at the silver piece. The water from the talisman swirled over the surface, seeping into the metal and his flesh, a bright light wrapping around the point where both pieces touched. Randall groaned, eyes bulging, his body trembling as whatever magic he'd enacted took hold.

The frozen fingers twitched, breaking free from their solid state, until the entire metal frame twisted and turned, following his bidding. His moan turned into a laugh, and he held his repaired hand out to examine, triumph in his eyes.

He rolled his shoulders, staring at me, and made a fist, striding to me in two steps.

Steeling my nerves, I cleared all the thoughts from my mind and focused on only one thing—ending this all right now.

Grabbing my blade off the ground, I slashed it

down, meeting Randall's hand with a sickening clang that made my bones vibrate.

Grasping it, he yanked the sword from me and threw it out of reach, his amusement echoing off the walls, making him sound ten times bigger than he actually was. Iron fingers wrapped around my throat, lifting me into the air, choking the life out of me as he watched on in glee.

"Sam!"

Tristan's voice roared through the space, his form appearing behind Randall, murder in his eyes. With him, Callaghan and several Templars materialized, too, weapons drawn. There were men from Paris as well as members of the crew of the *Lioness*, each of them ready to come to my aid.

Suddenly, Randall had his own men, a whole group of them flooding into the room. Bloodied and worn, they held their heads high, throwing themselves into the all-out brawl of Templars poised to take them down.

Kicking my legs, I caught Randall in the stomach, and he released me, hurling me into the ground with a roar.

Scrambling, I grabbed a weapon and swung out toward Randall, surprised when one of his men threw theirs in the way. Suddenly, I was fighting other pirates, twisting and turning as they did their best to keep me from getting to their master.

In the din, Captain Zadari's voice bellowed, his lithe form slashing through the opposition with little effort. Within moments, he had fought off Randall's guard and engaged him in combat, displaying battle skills of epic proportions.

The floor beneath me turned red, the groups continuing to battle after they were wounded. It was as if an unspoken deal to brawl to the death had taken place, each man grim as they faced down those who would see them dead.

Shoving aside the pirate I'd been dueling with, I quickly scanned the crowd for Tristan, spotting him locked in his own confrontation. Blood trickled from his cheek, his lips pulled back, teeth bared as he dodged and parried, gaining the upper hand over his opponent.

Beside him, Zadari and Randall still danced, their blades glinting in the light. With a graceful twirl and the dropping of his sword like that of a guillotine, Randall slammed his weapon into the captain's forearm, cutting into the bone.

The sound of pure pain and anguish Zadari made caused almost everyone to turn, our faces a mixture of horror and elation as Randall yanked the edge free and repeated the action, cutting the arm completely off.

Randall pushed Zadari to the ground, triumph in his haughty stare, and nodded to his men. They began to slip away, abandoning the war without another word.

Zadari continued to scream, his remaining hand grasping at his stump of an arm as he stared at it in shock, blood spurting from the end of the wound.

"Oh my god!" Mark's face went a pale white as he scrambled forward, shoving aside anyone who got in his way. "I need a belt!" he shouted, sliding in the blood beside him. He held his hand out, grasping Zadari's elbow in an ironclad grip. "Now!"

In a flash, Cal slid the gun belt from his shoulder

and passed it over, the group watching as Mark cinched it around the captain's arm. The bleeding slowed considerably with the tourniquet, but it did nothing to ease the shock that we all felt as we watched the captain's eyes widen.

Mark's fingers fumbled over the knot in his fabric belt, until he was able to pull it loose and begin wrapping it around the site of the amputation.

"I can help him better in a surgery," he said, his voice shaking.

"No," Zadari spat through gritted teeth. "Go after Randall. Leave me be."

"Take him to the surgery," MacDonald ordered to Mark and Cal, breathing heavily. "Everyone else make for the ships. We have lost here."

"Go after them!" Zadari roared. "Or I'll have lost my damn arm for nothing!" Flinching as Mark tightened the bandage as well, his face paled. Blood seeped through the cloth, dark red and angry.

"He's right," Tristan stated, rising from his bent over position and wiping the back of his hand across the cut on his face. "At the very least, we need to discover the heading Randall intends to take and slow him down the best we can. Any man who wishes to follow, make haste!"

The Templars rallied the same as they had when he'd led them in the past, a group of ten moving through the exit after him and taking to the streets, ignoring the protests of their Grand Master.

I inhaled sharply. He didn't know about the stone—none of them did. Randall was much stronger than the other times we'd faced him, and they had no warning. It would be a bloodbath, possibly the end of all who tried to stop the Black Knights and their leader.

Scrambling, I grabbed the first weapon I could reach—a short sword marred with blood—and ran after my husband, hoping I would catch up before it was too late.

The streets were almost as chaotic as the inside of the building had been. Citizens ran every which way, a path of destruction pointing in the direction the Knights had gone.

Moving as fast as I could and ignoring the pebble that had become lodged in my shoe during my fight with Randall, I followed, sprinting like I was running from the end of the world.

The clash of metal meeting metal rang out ahead, and I rounded the corner, flying directly into the battle that was now taking place in an intersection. Tristan and his Knights were cornering a small group of the traitors, washing the pavement in their blood. Among them, I recognized the bruised and bloodied face of Roberts, his hair sticky with gore.

"The ship!" he screamed, slipping around the wall of men meant to hold him in place and running after the group of escaping Black Knights with Randall at their head. "Get *Skíðblaðnir*, my Lord!"

Freezing, I watched as Randall's hand dove into his jacket pocket, the superior look of satisfaction on his face making me sick.

How would we catch them once they'd flown away? We could assume they were headed toward the closest treasure cache. Was there a man among us that had remained loyal and could tell us where it was? The Black Knights would beat us there with their vessel, and we would be that much worse off in this war.

Randall's face fell as he paused, his hand delving deeper into his coat, a panic entering his eyes. He dug into the fabric for a moment, staring down into its depths before his head jerked up and he growled. Rather than produce the source of their escape, he balled his metal hand into a fist and raised it high, slamming it against the ground. A tremor moved through the earth, knocking most everyone over as the street rolled, windows breaking in the buildings and pots crashing down. A cloud of dust erupted into the air, obscuring my vision.

For the second time that day, I felt the air vanish from my lungs as I hit the dirt, stars popping in my eyes and ears ringing. The wrist Randall injured slapped the stones, sending a stinging pain all the way up my arm and I groaned, rolling to my side. When I was finally able to sit up, the Black Knights were gone.

Looking to the sky, I squinted, trying to find *Skíðblaðnir*, but there was nothing I could see through the haze. Frustration filled me, and I sighed.

We could now add Cairo to the list of Black Knight battles we'd lost.

Rubbing my face, I shoved to my feet as I coughed, feeling the sharp point of the nugget lodged in my boot. Allowing myself a moment to grumble over something so trivial, I flopped back down, intent on removing at least one of the sources of my annoyance.

Slipping my boot off, I turned it upside down and shook it, letting a beach's worth of sand and a good-sized pebble fall into the palm of my hand.

"Sam?" Tristan coughed and waved his hand in

front of his face, trying to clear the dust in the air as he came to sit by me. "Are ye hurt?"

Shaking my head, I continued to stare at the rock, heart thumping quickly.

"Come on," he said, rising. "We've got to get to the docks if we've any chance of catching Randall by the time he comes out of the air."

"He's not flying," I responded, my voice weak. Glancing up, I wondered if I'd hit my head hard enough to be hallucinating.

"What?" Confused, Tristan stared down at me.

Bemused myself, I went over my encounter with Randall. "We wrestled," I started slowly, closing my fingers around the object in my hand. "It was a real struggle. There were stones and dirt and other gritty stuff around us. It must have fallen out of his pocket. He had it folded so small, he didn't notice he'd lost it until it was too late."

Grinning, I shook my head. "It was pure luck it ended up in my shoe. Either that or Randall is losing his favor with the higher-ups."

Tristan folded his arms, scowling in his misunderstanding. "What are ye talking about, Sam?"

Holding the stone out to him, I laughed unable to believe what I was looking at. The pebble was not a rock at all.

It was Randall's mythological ship.

Boarding MacDonald's sloop, I felt a weight lift off my shoulders as I saw Callaghan and Michael waiting for us beside the bow.

"You got Abella and the baby," I said to him, hugging them with all the strength I had.

"Aye," he confirmed. "Mark needed Abella to help with Zadari. They're still below, doing what they can for the man."

"You must have run the length of the city to get them here so fast." I kissed Michael's head, closing my eyes as I let the stress over his whereabouts dissipate.

"Randall?" Cal pressed, looking at Tristan, expectations low.

My husband shook his head.

Frowning, I watched the Templars who'd accompanied us come aboard, too. They were split between three crafts, all of which appeared to be waiting for orders on what to do.

The Grand Master's bald head appeared in one of the hatches leading below deck and his eyes narrowed in on us before anything else.

"Ye three," MacDonald ordered, climbing out the rest of the way and moving toward the captain's quarters. "Come with me."

Once we were all behind closed doors, MacDonald let out a sigh and sat at his desk. "This is a mess," he grumbled. "And ye lot have only made it worse."

The three of us glanced among each other, and Tristan gave me the slightest shake of the head—asking me not to say anything about Randall's boat yet.

"Ye owe us an explanation," he stated, the words rough as he faced the Grand Master. "How long have ye been in Cairo? And how did we escape arrest, fleeing through the streets like common criminals?"

"We have a man inside the law here. Many of

them, in fact." MacDonald raised an eyebrow. "Or have ye forgotten how far reaching the Knights Templar are?"

"We want to know everything," Cal added, folding his arms and waiting for a reply.

"We received several reports of Randall's exploits in Paris when he first broke free," the Grand Master stated calmly, giving in to their demands. "They said he was forming a church or new religion, with himself at the head. Black Knights were flocking to him, accepting his powers as a sign of divine providence that he should be their leader."

"Ye knew about this when last we spoke?" Cal asked, his tone sharp. "Why didn't ye tell us?"

MacDonald shrugged. "It wasn't important at the time."

"I disagree," Cal countered. "Men who believe they're following a prophet or god are more willing to do dangerous, stupid things. We've all seen it—they aren't like the Black Knights ye fought in the past. Knowledge of what was spurring them onward would have been helpful in our planning his capture."

"Well, ye dinna exactly capture him, did ye?" MacDonald looked at him sideways, frowning. "And I wasna sending ye out to get him. So there was no need to share."

Unable to help myself, I laughed at how absurd it all was. "Of course we didn't get him," I countered. "We had no idea that his new followers were willing to risk their actual souls to help him."

Tristan's hand wrapped around mine, and he lifted it to his lips, kissing it, his anger dissipating. "Aye," he agreed. His eyes lingered on mine for a moment and went back to MacDonald. "I suspected ye'd not told us the whole truth when we met, but I never would have imagined it to be something like this. Randall has stepped across the line to full hypocrisy. Even if ye were not planning on us having anything to do with him, ye should have at least warned us."

MacDonald grunted as if it would answer all the questions we had. "I recognize the mistakes I've made as a leader. I dinna ken who to trust." Pausing, he stared at the three of us, eyebrow raised. "But I knew it wasna going to be the likes of ye. Not after yer exploits in Ireland."

"Why let us go to that meeting tonight?" Cal pressed, folding his arms as he glared at the man. "If ye do not trust us, ye should have put a stop to it."

The Grand Master gave him a somewhat depreciating look and stared out the window. "It was the easiest way to draw him out without risking my own men."

I could feel the sting in the words, the men beside me pausing in surprise. It had been so easy to believe we were part of The Order again, on board their ship and fighting beside them. In a single utterance, MacDonald had managed to shatter that illusion, reminding me that I had never been considered an equal to begin with and telling the O'Rourke brothers they were no longer welcome among the ranks their family had served for generations.

Floundering, I shook my head, squeezing my eyes shut for a beat. "Mark is one of your men," I pressed. "Why didn't you protect him? Do you consider him banished, too?"

He waved his hand in dismissal, shaking his head

as he faced us. "It is in the past, Samantha. Let it stay there. There are more important things for us to worry about where ye are involved."

"She's right." Cal's voice turned suspicious as he moved to walk beside us. "If ye were truly trying to keep those under oath protected, ye never would have sent Mark to Éire. What are ye not telling us, Scotsman?"

"Things have happened I dinna plan for," the Grand Master replied with a sharp tone. "Some things I tried to stop. The truth is they still occurred, and my reasons for being here in Cairo and helping ye escape the Black Knights are my own." He focused on me, his lips forming a thin line. "Where is the amulet, lass?"

Taking a shaky breath, I squeezed Tristan's hand, glancing at him for a beat.

"Randall got it," I admitted.

Shoving to his feet, MacDonald swore, going to stand beside the window. After a minute, he faced me, fuming. "What happened?" he pressed, his brow furrowed. "I saw ye grab it. I thought it was safe."

Shaking my head, I frowned. "He was . . . himself. Condescending and frustratingly monologuing. Strong. Stronger than I was able to deal with." Licking my lips, I felt a thread of fear slip through me.

"You are not protected from his magic?" Cal asked. "He means to come to you each night and plague yer dreams?"

I shook my head. "No. I mean, yeah, he could, but that wasn't why he took it. He's been checking in on us in other ways."

"What other ways?" Cal's stare was as hard as Tristan's grip, his mouth turning down.

I stared at the desk for a beat before answering. "He's been in all of your minds, visiting whenever he wanted." Meeting Tristan's appalled gaze I chewed on the inside of my lip. "We were never free of him."

The revelation struck all of them differently, silence filling the room as they absorbed what I'd said.

"Why take the trinket at all?" Tristan asked. "What did he need it for?"

I laughed, covering my face with my hands. "It had water from the Fountain of Youth—from Atlantis—inside it. The fountain is the essence of their god." Staring at him, I tried to keep the bitterness I felt toward myself for not being able to protect it show. "And Randall took it all."

Tristan swore, slamming his hand on the table. "He's absorbed more powers?"

Nodding, I blinked a few times, keeping tears at bay. I didn't want him to be disappointed in me, but I wouldn't blame him for it if he did. I already felt that way about it all. I should have been faster, quicker, smarter. How many times had I faced Randall now? Still, I hadn't seen the attack coming, and I'd been unable to win.

I was getting tired of losing.

"There's more," I stated, cutting off anything they were about to say and hanging my head. "The blood fixed his hand."

Cal swore this time, running his fingers through his hair. "That was why he wanted us to follow him. He didn't have any other way to get the essence."

"His hand came to life right in front of me," I muttered. "That was the only thing we've managed to take from him, the only advantage we had in our war up until now. And it's gone." Glancing at Tristan, I shrugged. "I didn't know," I told him, the words weak. "If I'd known there was water from the fountain inside, I never would have brought it with me. I would have had it locked up, where he could never get it or dropped it in the ocean."

His face crumbled as he leaned in and gathered me in his arms, cradling me. "I know ye didn't, love. No one did. Do not blame yerself for something all of us missed."

"I dinna miss it," MacDonald inserted, his tone frustrated. "I knew what it was as soon as I saw the thing around her neck. That stone came from my cache, my port to protect. Why do ye think I told ye to stay in Ireland, far from the rat and his plans? If ye would have only listened to me—"

"What?" Facing the Grand Master, I scowled at him. "You exiled us because of the necklace, not because of what happened with Tristan and Callaghan?"

Snorting, he sat back down, rubbing his face before replying. "Yer actions in the Otherworld and the events leading up to it gave me a better reason for sending ye away. I should almost thank ye if ye lot weren't so pig-headed and naïve about the things going on around ye. When ye showed back up in Paris, I did all I could to send ye back to safety before something like this could happen, but did ye listen? No." Fuming, he glared at us. "I dinna ken why I'm so surprised. Ye never listened to me in the first place unless it was what ye wanted to hear, be it truth or lies."

The rant shocked us all into silence as we absorbed the new information. Finally, Tristan spoke, his tone hesitant.

"What did ye lie to us about?" Frowning, he peered at the Grand Master, a calculating look to his eyes. "Ye told us what we wanted to hear . . . It wasn't my name Randall carved into the prisoners at the Temple, was it?"

Tristan's voice caught, and I turned, surprised to find fear on his face as he looked at me. At the same time, there was a clarity in his gaze that felt sure and calm, as if he'd always suspected whatever it was he realized now.

"It was Samantha's name," he continued. "Randall wasn't goading me to come after him. He wanted her."

Shocked, I looked at the Grand Master, taking his silence and thin pressed lips as a confirmation.

"Me?" I squeaked.

"Ye were the one with the essence," Tristan mumbled, a great breath leaving him. "He didn't need me for anything. Only ye."

"And he wouldna have trusted someone else to take it for him," MacDonald agreed, breaking his silence at last. "Not when it was so vital to his plans."

"So he set a trap to draw us out," Cal added, catching on to what he was saying.

"He decided to bring Sam to him instead," Tristan continued, grim. "Left a calling card on my brother and spelled it out for ye in the bodies."

Flabbergasted, I glanced at the three of them, my emotions battling inside of me. There was so much guilt surfacing over what had happened to Callaghan, not to mention the fact we'd left our home and uprooted the life we'd been building for ourselves. The idea of facing Randall now that I'd given him the one thing he'd wanted from me was frightening, too. Not to mention the horror I felt over all the people who had died so I could be summoned to meet my enemy. Underneath all that was annoyance, though.

"Why didn't you tell us the truth?" Facing Captain MacDonald, I put my hands on my hips, frowning.

He hesitated for a moment, regarding me carefully until his shoulders relaxed and he accepted my inquiry. "I dinna want ye to be afraid." He smiled, the kind, considerate man I'd known before showing through for a beat before he continued. "Ye have been through so much, and I ken ye liked the life ye had in Ireland. I believed it would be better to handle the situation myself, to keep ye and yer family protected, along with the stone. That is also why I sent Mark with ye. Should the worst have happened, and Randall arrived to take what he wanted, ye at least would have had those best equipped to protect ye at yer side."

Surprised, I clamped my mouth shut, touched by how much thought he'd put into the decision for my sake. He was underestimating me, but it was apparent he hadn't meant any harm by it. Somewhere beneath the hard, unforgiving Grand Master he'd become, William MacDonald—the man who had loved his crew like family and offered up his life in place of theirs—was still calling the shots.

"And that's why Randall had an attack orchestrated at our home." Cal's voice fell, weariness grabbing him as his hand went to his chest, fingers tracing the scars he now bore. "He wanted the message to get through."

"And he dinna trust me to give it to ye."

MacDonald's lips turned down. "I am sorry for the part I played in your pain, Callaghan."

Cal didn't answer, his mouth a thin line as he stared at the floor.

"Randall was after me this whole time." Shrugging, I laughed, overcome by it all. There were too many revelations happening, my previous reckonings and realizations changing. One stood out above all, like a bright red scar on white canvas. "He already got what he wanted. We fell right into his trap. Again."

Suddenly, a rage like I'd not felt in a long time filled me, and I turned, slamming my fist on the wall, breaking the panel. A sharp, stinging sensation shot across my knuckles, the skin scraping and letting a trickle of blood rush forward.

"Sam!"

The mixture of surprise and condemnation in Tristan's tone made me laugh more. Facing him, I shook my now injured hand, hardly feeling the pain from my action. "Is this going to be our whole life?" I asked, words sharp as knives. "You doing everything you can to protect me and Randall beating us at every turn?"

Glancing at the other two, I couldn't help the sound of disbelief I made. "We have to do something. Anything. Randall gets more powerful every time we come across him. He has to be stopped."

"I believe that is why we're all gathered here, yes." MacDonald, unimpressed by my reaction, folded his arms. "It's also why I've brought yer sword with me from Paris."

Caught off guard, I paused, pulling back. "What?"

"*Dáinsleif* is on this ship. Sheathed, of course, but it is yers to use as ye see fit." His nose twitched, the slightest hint of a smile showing beneath his beard. "I decided it was high time we stop acting like we're better than the bastard and beat him by his own rules."

"Which means using the treasure against him." Cal nodded, rubbing his chin, and smiled. "It could work. Level the field at least."

"Aye." MacDonald stood, heading for the door. "I must check on Zadari now. He is our link to the treasure here and the secrets it holds. Once he's well enough to speak, we'll know what Randall can use we meet next—and what we can use to stop him. Assuming we make it to the treasure in time to stop him from taking it completely, that is. Damn, bloody flying boat."

He continued to grumble, placing his hand on the doorknob.

"Wait," I called, glancing at Tristan. "There's something more."

Flustered, he faced us, motioning for me to go on. "Out with it then. It canna be any worse than ye letting the amulet go."

Snorting, I smiled and revealed the tiny magic craft in my pocket.

Tensions were high as we set sail an hour later. The crew gave our group as wide a berth as they could on the sloop, following the Grand Master's commands without question.

It was interesting, watching the way MacDonald handled the authority he'd been given. I'd always thought him a strict captain, but as leader of The Order he appeared to be even more tightly strung than before. Barked instructions shot across the deck, his voice harsh and unforgiving. Our current predicament had something to do with it, as well as my reveal of the *Skíðblaðnir*, I was sure, but seeing him so strained made me feel at odds over my impression of him.

I'd realized he was still the man I'd known before when he admitted sending us to Ireland had been for our benefit and less a punishment. The revelation he'd considered my emotional state when sharing information with us had only served to further that assessment. Examining him now, I was struck with the urge to speak with him, alone, and thank him for all he was doing, as frustrating as it was at times.

"Sam."

Turning, I glanced at the crew member who had ventured over to us, taking in his smile and sparkling eyes. The same old turban he'd worn before was on his head, with a few new patches here and there, his array of knives tucked into his fabric belt.

"Dagger!" Laughing, I wrapped my arms around him in a tight embrace. "How are you? I haven't seen you since . . . Well, since we came back from Atlantis!"

He chuckled, returning the hug before pulling away. "I am well," he assured me. "I'm in charge of my own vessel, though I'm obviously not on it now."

"Captain?" Grinning, I looked him over again. "I knew it. You were a wonderful Quartermaster for MacDonald—and it seems he knew it, since he has you here, helping with this mission now. Are the others here, too? Valentine? Smithy?"

He shook his head. "Just me. The others are with my ship, the *Emerald*. All voyages have halted for the time being, and I wanted someone I trusted to stay behind while I was in Egypt."

Beaming, I nodded. "I'm so happy to see you. Do you want to sit for a while?"

"I can't," he replied, apology in his tone. "I wanted to say hello while I had the chance. Captain MacDonald has offered his quarters to all of you, too. He will sleep below with the crew."

Biting back another laugh, I realized he was here under orders, not to say hi. It was so like Dagger, following everything to the letter. No wonder MacDonald had promoted him and given him his own ship. He was one of the most qualified and loyal knights in The Order.

"Tell the Grand Master thank you," I replied. "And promise you'll come say hello when you have time to talk about all the adventures you've been on?"

"I give you my word." Bowing his head, he took his leave, striding off to whatever task he needed to accomplish next.

We were left alone for the rest of the evening, retiring to the captain's quarters as the sun set and the Nile was plunged into night. Michael, however, refused to sleep, and I soon found myself outside, observing one of the starriest skies I'd ever seen while listening to the soft creak of wood and the motion of the river.

An arm of the Milky Way stretched across the heavens, bright and filled with pinpricks of light. They sparkled and flashed like usual, but they seemed purely magical tonight. Orion's Belt was made of some of the most brilliant, and I made myself comfortable searching out other constellations while Michael played beside me.

Every now and then I would glance down, making sure he was okay. He'd started getting on his hands and knees, rocking back and forth, and I knew crawling was not far off. Once that happened, he would need to be watched like a hawk, more so if we were on the water. There was an endless number of things for him to get into, not to mention the possibility of somehow falling overboard.

Heaven help us when he started walking and running.

"He's a strong wee lad," MacDonald's quiet voice said behind me. "May I hold him?"

Caught off guard, I twisted around in my seat, watching as he crouched down and smiled at the baby.

"Of course," I replied. "But, he's a little energetic right now."

"Ack." He brushed the warning off without a care, slipping his hands beneath Michael's arms and hoisting him into the air. "Most lads are. I remember

315

when Rowan was little. His energy got him into trouble more times than I can count." Chuckling, he sat next to me, bouncing my son on his knee and grinning as the child laughed in glee.

"I never pegged you as someone who liked kids," I confessed, my heart warmed by the sight of them playing together.

"I love bairns," he admitted. "It's the older ones that rile me up and make me wish they'd brush off somewhere. How old is this one?"

"About six months," I supplied. "If you can believe that."

"I can," he said, making a face and chuckling when Michael cooed back at him.

I watched as they entertained each other for a few more moments, saying nothing, a smile on my face. MacDonald seemed so relaxed and content as if he'd desperately needed something to help take the edge off his responsibilities and Michael somehow supplied that to him.

Remembering my earlier wish to thank him for all he'd done, I cleared my throat, peering back at the stars. "Thank you," I muttered. "For trying to protect us. I know it didn't work out how you wanted, but I'm grateful all the same."

He paused in his motions, his eyes surprised as we stared at each other. "Tis my job," he replied. "Ye and yer family are part of my crew, despite my desiring otherwise at times."

I grinned. "Still. You didn't have to do anything extra for us. I didn't appreciate it at the time because I didn't understand your motives, but I do now."

He huffed, setting Michael on his lap and allowing

him to gnaw on his hat. "Aye. Perhaps I should have told ye the truth, rather than try and protect ye from it. Lord kens it bit me in the arse when I attempted to do that with the rest of the men."

"It can't be easy," I offered, "doing what you think is right and having those you trusted most turn on you. Everyone blames you for the split, for pushing the men toward Randall. I think you were trying to make them better. You have such high standards. It only makes sense for you to lead The Order as strictly as you did your crew."

He didn't answer, his face turning stony as he passed Michael back to me, standing.

"I don't blame you," I hurried on. "Randall is as responsible for what happened, if not more. You were only doing your job. He was the one that set out to destroy everything."

"My job is to take care of those who look to me as their leader," he said. "And I will continue to do that, till the day I die, even if it means I sacrificed myself to save them."

"No dying unless you go first." It was a sentiment he'd often shared on the *Isobel*, promising the crew he would die before any harm came to them.

"Exactly." He smiled, recognizing the command, and moved to leave, tucking his drool-soaked cap under his arm.

"You're a good leader, you know," I called after him. "A bit stupid at times, but good."

Chuckling, he shook his head. "Have them write that on my headstone, aye? 'Here lies William MacDonald, a bit stupid, but good.'"

His eyes sparkled as he watched me, a hint of

sadness entering them. "Ye still remind me so much of her, ye ken? That's something she would have said. 'Ye're a bit stupid, Will.' I can hear her voice in my head right now, sayin' it."

"Isobel, you mean?"

He nodded. "Aye." Wandering back toward me, he sat, staring up at the stars. "I feel her with me at times, watching over me. See that star up there?" He pointed out one specific light in the sky. "That's the one I named for her. She picked the one by it for her mother."

Glancing at me, he smiled. "Ye're easy to talk to like she was. Fiery, too, and stubborn to boot. I forget that until I've had a chance to speak with ye alone for a while." He coughed as he stood, his cheeks flushing. "I apologize, I dinna mean to be so forward. Ye spend all yer time among men and when a lady comes around ye canna seem to shut up."

Snorting, I shook my head. "You're fine. Everyone needs someone to talk to sometimes, even the Grand Master of The Order of the Knights Templar."

"Aye, but I usually talk to her." He nodded toward the heavens. "Ye were in the spot I usually come to when I set out to have the conversation."

"Oh!" Grabbing Michael's blanket off the ground, I stood up. "I'm sorry if I'd have known I—"

He laughed, motioning for me to stay. "Dinna worry yerself on my account. This old man needed company tonight."

Falling silent, he stared overhead for a few moments as I resituated myself on the crates and set Michael down on the blanket again. Instead of striking up the conversation, I sat with him and gazed at the heavens, letting the warm night air blow past us as we sailed up the Nile. It felt like we were moving across the sky ourselves, venturing into a magical realm of peace and happiness.

"I thank ye," he said after a while, his voice so quiet I almost didn't hear him. "It hasna been easy. I've made mistake after mistake. My men have turned on me. The choices I followed were right, but the consequences have been more negative than I expected."

Aware that this was probably what he shared with Isobel each night, I listened intently, giving him my silent support.

"Every time I make a decision that will affect others, it turns out wrong," he admitted. "Often times, I dinna ken what to do." He gave me a small smile. "A bit stupid. More like plain dumb, if ye ask me."

Taking his hand, I squeezed his fingers. "Human," I added to his self-assessment. "And facing a task many others would run from. And you aren't alone. Many of your men have turned, but just as many have not. We will stand in front of your problems with you and follow you to the end. And I'm always willing to talk, should you find that your stars have nothing to say."

To my surprise, he sniffed, his eyes watering for half a second until he blinked the moisture away. I knew he was showing me a rare side of himself, one that his men would never see. At this moment, he was the kind and loving man I'd known, not the stressed and furious leader he'd become.

The similarities I had with Isobel, the Irish woman

he had loved and lost when he was a young man, allowed him to share more than normal, giving me hope for him and the path he was leading the Templars down. I'd met the witch's spirit in the Otherworld. It was an honor to have him hold me on the same level as her.

Clearing his throat, he bent down, picking Michael up, and smiled at him. "A good, strong lad," he commented, our conversation coming complete circle as he changed the subject. "Just like his mother."

Mark sighed, rubbing a hand across his forehead as he glanced back through the doorway, into the surgery the next morning. "He'll live," he muttered quietly, the exhaustion in his voice evident as he addressed me, the Grand Master, and Tristan. "But only if he wants to."

"He's struggling with the loss?" I pressed, peering into the space.

"Wouldn't you?" His gaze narrowed in on my injured hand and he grabbed it, holding it up to eye level. "What did you do?" he asked, his tone incredulous.

"It's nothing," I assured him, pulling my hand away.

"At least let me clean it," he argued. "You should have already. You know how easy it is to get an infection in something like that."

"Can Zadari speak?" MacDonald asked without ceremony, interrupting before I could answer. "I ken it's a bad time, but we need his input."

Pursing his lips, Mark shrugged. "Zadari's conscious if that's what you mean. Whether or not he'll be able to tell you anything is another matter. I've been giving him opium on and off since we boarded."

"I suppose we will make do." MacDonald slid past him, disappearing into the room without another word.

Following, I wrinkled my nose at the iron scent of

blood, trying not to gasp as I caught sight of the captain on the table. Mark had sewn his arm up the best he could, but the wound was still wrapped in blood-stained bandages and hard to look at.

"Whiskey," Zadari grumbled, reaching a hand out for the full glass MacDonald passed to him. He gulped down the brown liquid and exhaled, tilting to the side as he sat.

Sensing he wasn't ready to speak, I remained silent as he downed glass after glass of alcohol. I knew I should tell him it wasn't good for someone to drink that much, but he was liable to hurt me if I did so now. Everyone else was quiet too, all of us giving him whatever he needed.

Carefully, Mark scooted beside me, taking my hand and cleaning the cut I'd given myself when I punched the wall. By the time he was finished, Captain Zadari had set the cup in his lap and was watching the procedure with little interest, his eyes watery, amputated limb hanging at his side.

"Captain?" MacDonald asked, hesitant.

Zadari's eyes focused on him, and he became more alert. "Ink," he rasped. "Now."

Surprised further, I watched as Mark procured a bottle from one of the shelves, opened it, and set it beside him.

The man dipped his finger inside, stumbling in his drunken state and spilling the black liquid across the bed. He didn't seem to notice, trying to mark the cup in a clumsy manner. However, it wasn't turning out as he wanted, and he cursed, searching around the room, and his eyes landed on me.

"Come here," he ordered, the air of consciousness

growing around him. "Write the bastard's name on this cup."

Confused, I rose from my chair, joining him and taking the potted glass from him. It was unclear if he understood what he was saying and glancing at the others was no help in figuring it out.

"Here," Zadari insisted, offering me the ink. "Randall's name."

Still not quite understanding why he would want me to do such a thing, I dipped my finger in the well a couple times and wrote Randall's name in thick, bold strokes, covering the entire surface of the cup.

Zadari examined it for a moment, nodding, and took it back, letting the inkwell crash to the floor and shatter, bathing my shoes and ankles in black. Raising the cup over his head, he chucked it into the ground as well, smashing it to pieces with a yell.

He said something in his native tongue, spitting on the remains of the glass and laid down, staring at the ceiling.

"What was that?" I asked in surprise.

"A curse," he stated simply.

"Curse?"

"An old one," he confirmed. "But a good one. Randall will pay for this, whether by my hand or that of Anubis. May the Jackal of Death find him and tear the flesh from his bones."

A stunned beat passed, the four of us staring at him with mild alarm.

"Verra well," MacDonald stated, leaning over him. "How are ye, man? Will ye be awake enough to talk for a while yet?"

"I don't know how I am," Zadari confessed. "But,

yes, I can speak."

"We need to know what's in yer treasure," Tristan stated. "What Randall could use against us."

Zadari snorted. "What could he not? There are weapons, books on magic, gold, jewels—he wants the Knot of Isis. We all heard Roberts say it." He groaned as he shifted, his face bunching in pain.

"The Knot of Isis?" Confused, I looked to see if anyone else knew what that was.

"It's blood." Zadari moaned. "The blood of Isis. The essence Randall is after."

Shaking my head, I pushed back the frustration I felt over everything. "He already has so much. I don't understand why he has to take more. It's almost like he's so consumed with greed he has to have it all, or he thinks he can't do it."

"What all has he taken?" Zadari asked, his interest peaked. "I've heard reports of his ship. It does not meet the description of any vessel I've seen before. Pointed on the ends, slender, with one mast. It sounds most like—"

"A Viking boat." Interrupting him, I nodded.

"One he took from another treasure vault," Tristan added, crossing his arms as he smiled. "Tis a powerful tool that we should not underestimate."

"What do you mean?" Zadari asked, confused.

"*Skíðblaðnir* can travel over sea, land, or air," Mark stated, recalling the name without issue. "It's a mythological vessel. Randall has used it to escape many times. He used it yesterday." He glanced at us for confirmation.

MacDonald shook his head. "The Norse craft is no longer in Randall's possession."

"What?" Mark asked. "How do you know that?"

"Because," Tristan told him, grinning. "Samantha took it from him during their duel."

"More like he dropped it and I was lucky enough to get it stuck in my shoe," I asserted.

Blowing air out of his mouth roughly, Zadari raised his eyebrows. "That changes things," he muttered. "We may yet beat him to Luxor and the treasure." He faded for a moment, his eyes fluttering, but came back, shaking his head to stay awake. "Does the villain possess any other artifacts?"

Mark held his hand up, stopping anyone from going on. "You should rest, Captain," he said with a quiet voice. "Your body needs every ounce of sleep you can give it now."

"I will not," Zadari growled back. "Not while I can be of service to my order and my Grand Master. I may have lost an arm, but I haven't lost my mind along with it. Tell me, what other items has Randall taken?"

Mark breathed in a frustrated manner, giving in without further argument. "Thor's belt. It gives the wearer the strength of the lightning god."

"We've not seen him with it since he first took it," Tristan added, thoughtful. "Not to say he doesn't still possess it, but there may be a reason he hasn't brought it back with him yet. Personally, I think we all should be grateful he didn't manage to take the Aegis with him from Oak Isle."

"Or anything from the Otherworld," Cal added, nodding.

"But he still has all the blood."

The group fell silent at my words, an uncomfortable air filling the space.

"Ichor, from the Greek gods. The essence of both the Native American and Norse gods." Glancing at Tristan, I frowned, imagining I could still see the teeth marks on his shoulder. "The Irish gods." Touching the now necklace free spot on my neck, I closed my eyes. "Atlantean." Staring at MacDonald, I bit the inside of my lip. "Every single time we've encountered Randall, he's managed to make off with what he wanted most. We can't let that happen again."

"How did he get Irish blood?" Zadari pressed, surprisingly still lucid after all the things he'd taken.

Tristan moved his shirt, revealing the scars from Randall's bite. "The goddess is part of my family," he said in hushed tones. "Randall took the blood from me."

Shaking my head, I confessed the opinion I'd been keeping bottled up for months. "He's become too strong. We might not be able to beat him as it is. Not without gaining power of our own first."

Zadari laughed. "How do you propose we do that? The man is practically a god. He has the power of five of them. Stole my arm with only two swipes." The alcohol was getting to him, tears leaking from his eyes. "I am ruined."

"You aren't ruined," Mark offered with soothing comfort. "You can learn to live without your arm."

"What good will it do me without a way to defeat the madman ahead of us? Taking his ship hasn't made him any less powerful."

Glancing at Tristan, I pursed my lips, nodding.

"We do have *some* power on our side already," he said.

He undid the tie around his scabbard, sliding the

sword out into the open. Excalibur lit up the room, shining like the moon on a clear night. It seemed to hum in Tristan's hands, recognizing the touch of its master, the one true king of the Éire.

MacDonald swore in his native language, shoving to his feet at once as he stared at the sword and Tristan as he held it. "Is that what I think it is?" He pressed. "Retaliator? I thought ye left it buried in the stones in the Otherworld."

Tristan nodded at the Irish name, sheathing the blade once more. "I pulled it free," he confirmed. "While it may not be the most help in our current battle, it will aid us against darkness." He glanced at me, smiling. "Both real and imagined."

MacDonald swallowed, shaking his head as he gazed at the legendary item. Glancing around the group, he sighed. "Even with a sword such as this, we are very much underhanded. Are there any other artifacts ye've taken I should ken about?"

"We aren't really in the habit of taking treasure that isn't ours," Mark responded, his lips turning down in distaste.

"We have another blade," I offered.

"*Dáinsleif*?" Mark supplied easily. "Isn't it in Paris? I haven't seen it since Runs With Wolves gave it to you after the battle in Arizona."

He gave no indication that the mention of his friend from long ago was painful, but I knew it must have been. The Apache warrior had been among the group that found him near death in the desert after he'd traveled through time. For years, Mark had lived with their tribe, trying to maintain who he was and figure out what had happened to him. While the pair remained friends to this day, I knew they hadn't spoken to each other in several years.

Anything that reminded Mark of the hardships he'd had here was always cast to the side.

Everything but me that is.

"I brought it," MacDonald supplied. When Mark stared at him in shock, he laughed. "It's time to fight fire with fire if ye ask me."

"So, we have a man with the blood of a goddess, but no powers," Zadari stated, staring at Tristan as if he expected to be shown an array of magic that would save the day. When nothing happened, he motioned to the sword in my husband's hand. "A few swords that may be of use, the Norse ship, and . . . what else?"

No one said anything.

Zadari frowned. "That's it?"

I shrugged in response, watching as the others did the same.

Swearing, Zadari struggled into a sitting position. "How have you lot managed to defeat him in the past at all?" he asked incredulously. "What does the brute even want from you? You have nothing!"

With a start, I realized Captain Zadari had no idea that Mark and I were from the future. I'd assumed MacDonald told him, but with that one question, it became evident that he didn't understand the entire situation.

Glancing toward Tristan, I saw the same revelation blooming on his face, while Mark drew in a sharp breath beside me. MacDonald stifled a small cough.

"Randall thinks I'm . . . special," I explained. "They found me washed up on the beach when I should have died, before he ran off and started recruiting Black Knights."

"He's wanted her ever since," Tristan added, bitterness in the words. "Though his obsession with my wife has changed somewhat over the years."

"Yeah." I snorted. "First he wanted me dead, then he wanted me to join him, and then he insisted we were soul mates." Rolling my eyes, I folded my arms. "I think we're finally back to the wanting me dead phase, thank heavens."

Tristan shook his head, frowning. "I wouldn't be so sure, lass." He moved to stand behind me, wrapping his arms around my waist and pulling my back against his front, holding me close.

"Whatever his intentions toward Sam," Mark cut in, his hands balling into fists as he stood before the Grand Master. "We shouldn't underestimate him. We have, several times, and it came out worse for us in the end."

"He is conniving, is what you mean to say?" Zadari asked. "In what manner has he tricked you in the past?"

"His kidnapping of Samantha was meant to draw me to him, to use as a sacrifice," Tristan growled.

"And he manipulated me into doing whatever he wanted when I was a member of his crew," Mark answered. "When it came to Sam or anything else."

"The dreams he visited me in were meant to make us think he was hurting." I shook my head, closing my eyes. "And his willing arrest was a ploy to get Tristan to break him free and take him to the Underworld."

"Where we all saw with our own eyes how insane he was," Cal added. "Until it came to the fight at

Avalon, that is."

"What happened at Avalon?" Zadari pressed, peering up at us with a mixture of interest and dismay.

"He slaughtered them," I whispered, the memory of bloody, body littered streets filling my mind. "All of them. In a manner of minutes."

"It was all a trap," Tristan shared, mourning. "Predictable. That's what he called me. He'd planned the whole thing from the beginning."

"And he's probably done the same this time around." Mark ran a hand through his hair. "Right down to his year spent in the Templar prison."

A sense of despair seemed to fill the surgery at that. It pricked at my heart, my body weary at the thought of having to go through another trial with Randall. How many more times would we face him? Each encounter we'd had was the last one, in my mind. But the villain kept coming back, like a bad smell you couldn't quite escape. Who was to say that this time we wouldn't fail completely?

MacDonald made a good point. We were massively under armed and ill-prepared for the upcoming conflict. Randall was stronger, smarter, faster, and hungrier. He wanted to meet his goals more than we wanted to stop him.

"What are we going to do?" Turning in Tristan's embrace, I stared into his eyes, hopeless.

Brushing his palm over my hair, smoothing it from my face, he kissed my forehead, squeezing me. "Whatever we can," he answered.

"What's our plan?" Staring at the map on the table, I waited expectantly for someone to answer, nervous energy pulsing through my veins.

We were only a day or so from our destination. The Grand Master had ordered his three ships lashed together so he could conference with his captains and decide their course of action once we made landfall. He'd allowed our family to join them, minus Abella and Michael who had opted to stay outside, giving in to the fact we were going to be a part of whatever happened no matter what he did or said.

"The cache is here, outside of Luxor," MacDonald supplied, touching the scroll. "Buried away among the rulers of a people from long ago. It will be easy enough to reach the treasure before Randall now we ken he's being forced to travel as we do. However, keeping him out of it when he arrives may prove difficult."

"And why is that?" one of the Templars pressed.

"Have you met him?" Zadari answered from his spot in the window. Grimacing, he held the bicep of his shortened limb and gazed out over the water, falling silent. He knew he wasn't going to be able to come with anyone to fight, not while he was still weak and healing. His presence here was a courtesy to the title he held, his command already taken over by one of the other men in the room.

"Isn't there a way to block it up for good?" Mark

queried, his nose scrunched as he studied the map. "If you're talking about the place I think you are, I know we could conceal whatever we want and not have it be found for hundreds of years."

Callaghan gave him a warning glance, which I was sure was meant to remind him not everyone here knew our secret.

"The problem willna be if we can hide it in time or not," MacDonald continued," but the number of men Randall has in his employ. My sources have suggested those we faced in Cairo were only a small amount of his true force."

"And there are not many of us," Tristan concluded, pursing his lips as he folded his arms and studied the course before us. "What is this place ye speak of, where the treasure is buried?"

"The Valley of the Kings," I said with a quiet voice. "Where many of Ancient Egypt's rulers are buried."

Surprised, MacDonald glanced at me, an impressed smile covering his features. "Aye, that's it."

"This portion is special." Zadari interrupted the conversation again, rising from his seat and joining the group. "There are things kept there my ancestors put into position. It is a sacred place, home to their gods, and deserving of respect."

"Of course," I hurried to say. "It's a graveyard and should be treated as such."

"I thought many of the tombs were raided in antiquity." Mark raised his eyebrows, peering at Zadari. "You're saying more chambers weren't bothered?" He gave me a sideways glance, and I bit my lip, knowing what he was thinking.

King Tutankhamen's tomb would be discovered in the twentieth century, bringing fame to the Valley of the Kings and revealing the wealth he'd been buried with. The Boy King was destined to become a household name, lighting the hunger for more searches and digs for decades to come.

Was it possible the treasure Zadari spoke of and that of King Tut were one and the same?

Swallowing nervously, I looked to Zadari, hoping that wasn't the case. If so, I was going to have to explain to MacDonald why we needed to leave it be.

The captain shook his head. "The cache is not in the valley. It's within *El Qorn*—The Peak."

Relieved, I sighed, letting my shoulders drop, ignoring the questioning stare Tristan gave me.

"This mountain, here?" Callaghan touched the location on the map. It was above the valley, the top of it shaped like a pyramid.

"Yes. The door is hidden and can be guarded, but we do not have enough men to stand at each corner of the mountain and watch for incoming threats, nor do we have enough to hold off the Black Knights for any amount of time at the entrance." Zadari sat in MacDonald's desk chair, leaning back and closing his eyes for a moment.

"Aye, he's right," the Grand Master agreed. "Which is why I propose we hide inside and wait."

"Why not take the Knot of Isis and remove it from the cache?" another one of the Knights asked. "That's what Randall is after, isn't it?"

"Trust me," Zadari said, his voice rough. "You do not want to remove the vial from its pedestal." Gazing at the group, his expression fell. "The blood is one of the things that has been in the mountain for thousands of years. It's cursed, protected by that which safeguarded the goddess herself."

"Which is . . . what?" Hesitating, I stared at the other men in the room, watching as they, too, looked on with discomfort.

"Anubis," Zadari breathed. "Should anyone disconnect it from where it sits now, I do not know what consequences they would face."

"Surely that is only a tale meant to dissuade robbers." Mark frowned, not believing it.

"Perhaps you should take it and find out," Zadari snapped.

Mark held up his hands, showing he'd meant no offense, and turned to MacDonald. "I think we should have a backup plan if this doesn't work. How will we get out if Randall gets the blood and has all his men there to fight us?"

"We won't," Tristan answered. "They'll kill us all before we can escape."

The sword in my hand felt heavier than I remembered, the sheath tied tightly around it as if to warn anyone who wished to pull it free not to do so. A knot formed in my stomach as I imagined how I would draw it later, unable to place it back in its carrier until I'd given someone a life-threatening wound.

The knowledge of the power *Dáinsleif* held was both a burden and a boon when one considered going into battle. On the one hand, it was a powerful blade that would protect me. On the other, someone was going to die after I used it. Even knowing the person was my enemy and would kill me if they had the chance, I still felt guilt over taking another life. I tied it to my belt, letting the worried contemplation circulate in my mind a bit.

The light of Excalibur shone from its place at Tristan's hip, a thin strip of the metal shaft showing beneath the pommel. By contrast, it was a weapon that seemed to be all good, wielding power that was both fair and just.

"Stay safe, *mo bhuachaill*. Abella will watch over ye until we return." Tristan kissed the top of Michael's head, cuddling him a moment longer before begrudgingly handing him over to me.

Smiling, I squeezed the baby, marveling at how much he'd grown in the short time since we left Ireland. What would we miss while we were separated from him? "I hate leaving him, too," I muttered to my husband, shooting him a heartbroken look. "But we agreed, this is what's best for him for now. He's nearby and safe."

"Aye," he concurred, the word rough. "We need only finish this business with Randall, and we'll never have to leave him again."

"Exactly."

Kissing the baby's cheeks, I closed my eyes, trying to soak up every moment I could with him. I wanted to remember what he felt like in my arms, how he smelled, what it was like for his wild hair to tickle me in the morning. Michael's continued safety was more important than my need to cuddle him though, and so I handed him over to Abella, feeling like my heart was breaking in two.

"We'll be fine," she said, her tone reassuring. "You'll be back before you know it. Michael and I are *copains*—we will get along fine while we wait."

Smiling, I grasped Tristan's hand in mine, resisting the urge to cry.

"Mommy loves you, Michael," I whispered, brushing his cheek with my other hand. "We'll all be home soon."

"That we will." Tristan ruffled his hair, the strength of his grasp on my hand the only sign he was struggling with the farewell.

Clearing my throat, I took in the stone dock and the boats tied to it for a beat. Mark and Callaghan stood at the edge of it all, staring at Abella as she bid each of us farewell. It had been decided she would stay here with the baby, where they would be safe from harm and could escape if the worst should happen.

It wasn't enough for me. Grabbing her hand, I passed the Norse ship from my palm to hers, shaking my head as she opened her mouth in surprise. "Keep it," I whispered. "I took it from MacDonald's cabin for you. If anything happens, open it up and fly far from here. Randall won't be able to catch you." Tears pricked at my eyes, and I sniffed. "You are our family. I wouldn't trust anyone else to take my son if Tristan and I couldn't do it ourselves."

Touched, she did cry, a single tear rolling down her cheek as she took the offering and pulled me into a tight hug, squishing our tiny companion. "All will be well," she muttered. "I know it will be. However, I will do as you ask if I must."

"Thank you," I muttered.

Pulling back, I wiped at my face and smiled at

Michael, taking Tristan's hand.

Mark approached her next, awkward and uncertain, but wanting to say his piece all the same. "Thank you, for all you have done for me." The words were uneven, but he smiled as he said them. "I want you to know you meant a great deal to me, especially this past year. I couldn't have run the clinic without your help."

She blushed, adjusting her grip on the baby. "It was nothing."

"It was everything," he insisted. "I'll never forget it."

Chuckling, she smiled at him. "Why does it sound like you're saying goodbye forever? You'll all be back, I know it. God is on our side."

Glancing my direction, he frowned, regret in his eyes.

Taking a deep breath, I realized what he was about to do and removed the baby from Abella, using the excuse I needed more time to hold him before I left. Stepping back, I took Tristan to stand by Cal, leaving the two of them to have their own moment. Their words flitted to our turned backs, the bare amount of privacy we could offer not enough to keep their conversation secret.

"Abella," Mark said, her name drifting through the air filled with regret. "There's so much I feel I want to say to you, but I can't put it into words."

She must have understood the tone with which he was speaking, but she laughed, the sound forced, like she was pushing through her reservations about him. "Think about it while you are gone, *oui*? You can tell me when you return."

"If I return," he amended.

"You will," she encouraged him. "I have faith. Randall will be beaten. We will be triumphant in the end."

"And we'll stay friends, no matter what happens?" he pressed.

"Friends." She paused, the awkward silence between them making me cringe for the pair. "What do you mean, whatever happens?" She was suspicious now, her tone rising as she questioned him. There was a hidden dare in the words like she was betting he wouldn't say what she thought he was about to.

Unfortunately, Mark didn't seem to be catching on to any of the clues she was giving him. That, or he was determined to say what he wanted and get it over with.

"I could be going to my death, Abella. If I am, I want you to know, you shouldn't mourn over me. What we had—what we tried to have, anyway—it's not ever going to happen. We don't work, no matter what we try. I love you, but only as a dear friend. I know it's cruel to say this to you now." He laughed, the uncomfortable sound of it making me wince. "But it's the truth. If I die today, you should move on. Choose to be happy. Go home and live life."

"I see," she responded, her voice tight.

The stillness that followed was filled with an array of emotions. Despite wanting to look back and see what was happening, I focused on the land, trying to preserve what alone time they had left.

Mark was suddenly walking past me, leaving her in the background without another word, his hands balled into fists and face flushed.

Turning, I felt my heart break as I saw Abella's

face, devastation and fury burning in her eyes. Fingers clenched against her palm and knuckles white, she faced away from us.

Callaghan, sensing this was his moment, went to her, placing a hand on her shoulder. "Men are often terrible at goodbyes," he muttered. "More so the ones that have bad news to share before going. But this will be over soon, *grá*. Then I'll see ye home safe and sound myself."

She turned, focusing on him and frowned. "*Vastu?* You are so confident in your own abilities and of those around you that you dare to promise me you will return back safe?"

Surprised by the sudden force and venom in her tone, even I took a step back. At first, it seemed she was about to vent her anger over Mark on him, but I realized it was something more, in addition to the pain he'd caused her.

I'd believed she'd been content staying here with the baby. She'd given me the impression that was what she wished to do. Watching her now, I realized it was hurting her to watch us go to battle without her. She worried for us, for the man she had loved, and for the family she'd found in our company. It wasn't surprising she'd never said anything—she loved Michael, too, after all, and wanted to keep him safe no matter what—but I'd assumed I was more perceptive. Somehow, if something had been wrong, I'd always believed I would notice, without her needing to say anything. However, Mark's announcement had hurt her, and she was lashing out, as I would have expected anyone to do in her situation. To her credit, she managed to keep Mark out of her conversation with

Cal, but it was clear she was struggling to do so.

"You have not seen the destruction an army led by Thomas Randall can leave behind, Callaghan." She shook her head, brushing off an angry tear as it slipped down her cheek. "Nor heard the cries of those left in its wake. I, however, have." Her expression turned stony as she stared into his eyes, a frown marring the lower half of her face. "Believe me when I say, it is not a sound I wish to ever hear coming from one I love." Her gaze flicked toward Mark, giving away who she'd been speaking about in an instant.

Clearing his throat, Cal nodded, his own expression turning grim. "I have seen what he can do," he reminded her. "I do not fancy reliving blood washed streets and bodies strewn everywhere." He remained silent for a moment, his expression calm as he watched her stare at another man. Sighing, acceptance washed over him. "Ye told me once it wasn't physical scars that make a person ugly, but the ones buried deep inside, twisted and angry, refusing to heal." Stepping closer, he lowered his voice, his hands moving to her waist. "I have those scars. Ye do as well. No doubt, ye've earned some new ones this very day. But I do promise ye, Abella, I will be coming back to ye. I will see ye safe, no matter what. Ye'll not be left here alone, forever."

Her lip trembled as he spoke, her stare softening as the words penetrated the unyielding façade Mark's had left behind. Then, as if a dam were breaking, she sobbed, throwing her arms around his neck and clinging to him like a lost child to its newly found mother.

Surprised, he froze for a beat, glancing at me as if

to ask for guidance before he wrapped his arms around her, holding her as he buried his face in her hair. They stayed like that for a moment, neither of them saying anything until MacDonald called for everyone to gather.

Pulling back, Cal cupped her cheek, wiping her tears with the pad of his thumb. "I would see ye happy every day, *grá*," he said, his voice quiet. "But I know ye'll cry yer tears while we are gone. If ye'll let me, I'll help ye dry them when I return."

"You shouldn't say such things," she muttered, toying with the edge of his vest, not meeting his eyes. "Even when you think I don't understand what you are saying."

Raising an eyebrow, he gave her a crooked grin. "Oh?"

"*Grá*," she repeated, peering up at him. "That is what Tristan calls Samantha from time to time."

His eyes shone as he gazed at her. "So it is."

Taking one of her hands in his, he raised it to his mouth and kissed it. Then, leaning forward, his lips lingered on her forehead for a second longer before he turned and joined the group on the shore.

Mark peered at him for a beat and turned to watch the harbor, whatever feelings he had over the exchange kept silent.

Realizing the time for my own departure had arrived, I kissed my son once more, hugging him tight enough that he squealed and squirmed, giggling as I tickled him.

"I love you," I whispered again.

"Me as well," Tristan hummed, doing a little tickling of his own. With gentle hands, he disentangled

Michael from me, pecking him on the cheek, and passed him to Abella. His shoulders fell as he released the boy, an air of sadness surrounding him for a beat before he shook it off.

"Stay safe," Abella ordered, smiling through the tears in her eyes. "And come back soon." Her gaze flicked to the group for a brief second, and she sucked in a sharp breath. Bottom lip trembling, she glanced at Mark, the pain at their shared words obvious on her features. "All of you."

In my mind, I'd always thought of the Valley of the Kings as someplace buried in the sand until someone from the modern age discovered it. Egypt was such a wealth of knowledge and secrets, new discoveries happening there daily it seemed. I would hear about it every now and then in my own time, pleasantly surprised by the news.

It became clear as soon as we arrived at the valley to the west of the Nile that such a perception was not possible. This place had never been forgotten to begin with, several of the tombs open and in plain view of anyone walking through. It was all a mess of destruction and pillaging, though, with broken pottery pieces scattered about and obvious tampering around the entrances.

"To think," I muttered, shaking my head in a mixture of surprise and disgust, "there is a treasure unlike anything ever seen beneath this sand, and all of these graves were desecrated by people trying to get a piece of wealth."

"Money makes people do crazy things," Mark agreed. "But we know not all of it is missing. Somewhere here, King Tut's grave is waiting to be discovered."

"Tut?" Tristan asked out of curiosity.

"Tutankhamen," I corrected him, smiling. "The Boy King. For whatever reason, his crypt was buried and never ransacked. They'll discover it in the future, along with all his treasures. He'll become one of the most famous, if not *the* most famous pharaoh of all time."

"That's all fine," Cal remarked, jerking his head toward the valley stretching out before us. "But we should not talk about it now, agreed?"

Frowning, I stared across the empty expanse of dirt and the cliff face. He was right. MacDonald led the Templars ahead of us, most of them unaware of our secret. The hot sun beat down from above, baking us all as we marched with what weapons and armor we had, a small army ready for war.

"Where is Zadari's man?" one of the Knights asked as we came to a stop, setting his shield on the ground. "Is he not leading us to the entrance of the vault as planned?"

"I dinna ken," MacDonald replied, glancing at the cliffs surrounding us.

"Something isn't right," Mark muttered, gripping his own weapon.

Glancing around, I caught sight of a glimmering point on the plateau closest to us, the light raising up and flashing in the sun. A whistling sound pierced the air as the beam shot forward and I grabbed Tristan, pulling him out of the way as an arrow dug into the sand behind him.

"Look out!" I shouted.

The man in front of us went down, pierced through with another of the projectiles, a whole swarm of them suddenly raining from the top of the cliff.

"Shields up!" MacDonald's voice roared through the ensuing panic. "They're over yer heads, men!"

A ceiling of metal began to form as the men who had carried in shields raised them, blocking the rest of the arrows.

"The crypts!" Someone in the middle of the group shouted, everyone's attention turning to the various openings in the cliff, the scraping of swords leaving sheathes filling the air.

In the blink of an eye, it was war.

Black Knights poured out of the ruined tombs, blades gleaming as they slammed into the wall of Templars gathered in the center of the valley. There were more of them than I ever could have imagined, a never-ending wave of them moving in from all sides. Within a matter of moments, the entire area was awash with blood and battle cries, the clanging of metal meeting metal making my ears ring.

"Tristan!" I yelled, feeling his presence next to me still.

"Fight, Sam!" he shouted back. "Fight for yer life!"

Sucking in a deep breath, I pulled *Dáinsleif* from its sheath, grasping the pommel in both hands as I raised it up, swinging it out to meet the attack from the traitor aiming at me.

There was no time to worry about being rusty or to wonder if I was going to be able to beat him. In that single second, I'd accepted there was no other outcome for this battle than for me to make it out and protect the treasure, as I'd been instructed. It was like being filled with holy purpose, creating a calm sensation in the sea of chaos around me.

Stepping to the side, I let my weapon slip down the edge of my opponent's, parrying his next attack and following with my own jab. The flowing clothes I'd taken from the *Jaguar* only served to enhance my range of movement, allowing me to twist and turn in a way the Black Knight couldn't. It was almost like we were dancing, kicking up the sand, slipping and sliding, our arms creating the graceful movements of a dance of death.

With a sickening squelch, my sword slipped past his defenses and slid between his ribs, claiming the wound it needed to be sheathed once more. The Black Knight regarded me, wearing a crazy smile, and laughed, blood trickling out the corner of his mouth.

"Victory or death," he muttered, his attention turning to something behind me.

The saying—Randall's saying—made me freeze, my skin rippling with gooseflesh. Hesitating, I turned, focusing on what my dying opponent was so happily and reverently staring at.

Randall appeared through the dust as if he were a magician making his grand entrance. A blade in each hand, he cut down anyone who tried to face him, his eyes locked on mine as he crossed the space, a smile on his lips.

My own mouth set into a grim line and I yanked *Dáinsleif* free, blood dripping into the sand from its tip as I met the bastard.

Swinging one weapon over his head, Randall jumped forward, instantly engaging me in battle. Where the first duel had felt like I was soaring through the moves, concentrating on what needed to be done, this one was clumsy and cautious, myself not used to clashing with someone who was wielding two swords.

Slipping in the sand, I ducked, cursing myself as

he nicked the hair on the top of my head. Forced to roll to avoid being skewered, I struggled to keep out of his way, fear beginning to grasp me the longer it took to escape his onslaught. Then, in a rare show of mercy, he paused, taking a step back.

"Now, Sammy," he said breathlessly, a laugh in the words. "You have something I want. Hand my ship over, and I'll let you live."

Grabbing the shield of a fallen Templar beside me, I scanned the crowd for Tristan. He was locked in his own battle, battling anyone who got in his way. Unable to call out or take a moment to survey how he was doing, I shoved to my feet, settling into a battle stance.

"I don't know what you're talking about," I growled.

Randall chortled, surveying me with amusement as I struggled to keep the shield up. "You are the only one who could have taken it. The only one I touched."

"How fortunate for everyone else." My lips curled back as I snarled at him, hatred oozing from every pore of my body.

Glowering at me for a beat, he appeared to be deciding if I was telling the truth or not. "You never were one to give up," he finally stated, raising his weapons. "I will give you that."

Lunging forward, he stabbed toward my unguarded side, the blade pinging off the shield as I barely managed to move it over. The force of the attack made my bones rattle, and I tumbled back into the sand, the air knocked from me as the cover fell on my chest. It was all I could do to cower behind it as Randall tried to stab me, his swords clanging and smashing against the metal.

An opening appeared for a split second, and I took it, kicking him in the ankle as he lifted his weapons over his head. He howled in response, losing his balance and falling backward.

It was all the leeway I needed.

Shoving to my feet, I used both hands to hold the armor in front of me and barreled into him. Throwing my weight into the attack, I shoved Randall as hard as I could, slicing down with my sword as he stumbled backward. Each step I took was forward after that, my mind and body refusing to let him gain another inch. It was a struggle, the pommel of my weapon slipping in my hand as it became covered with sweat and the shield so heavy I worried my arm might fall off if I didn't set it down soon.

"Give me the boat!" Randall bellowed, lashing out as he dug his feet into the ground, refusing to move back any further. "You can't beat me in a fair fight, Sammy. We've proven that many times over."

"Who said anything about fair?"

Spinning around at the voice, Randall growled as his eyes met Tristan's. In a flash, their swords were clashing against one another, the pair of them leaping around as if they'd rehearsed it.

Grinning, I threw my own body into the mix, the two of us taking on Randall with ease. It was as if we were the ones who knew each other's thoughts this time around. Our bond was built on trust, and it showed when we tackled our enemy together.

Grabbing the shield from me, Tristan flung it around and smashed it into Randall's face in a show of pure strength and hatred.

Blood poured from the villain's nose and mouth,

his eyes wild with fury as he backed off. The expression he wore gave me no doubt he planned on killing at least one of us before this battle was over.

"If you won't give me my boat, I will have to take it from your corpse." Randall spat, a gory mess of red leaving his mouth.

I snorted. "Do you honestly think we're stupid enough to bring it here, where we knew you would be?"

Randall paused, his stare turning calculating, and he smiled. "Of course," he muttered. "Your baby and his nurse. You left it with them, didn't you?" He clicked his tongue, shaking his head. "That was a poor decision on your part as a mother, Samantha."

My stomach clenched, and I realized too late I'd told him right where he could find his missing vessel.

"Roberts!" Randall boomed, his voice carrying over the crowd. "Our vessel is with the baby. Fetch it for me, will you?"

"No!" Screaming, I moved to run past him, catching sight of Roberts as he broke from the struggle and began running in the direction of the city.

Randall's blades swung up, aiming for my middle, only to be stopped by Tristan's sword.

"Go!" my husband ordered me as he shoved Randall back. "I've got him—you make sure Abella and Michael stay safe!"

Nodding, I put them behind me, pushing through the crowd in a panic, trying to keep a tab on Roberts as he ran on ahead.

"Sam!" Mark's hands caught me, locking me in place despite my attempts to get away.

"Let me go," I ordered, trying to yank my hands

free from his.

"We need to get up the mountain and into the vault before Randall does," he insisted, nodding to my brother-in-law beside him. "Cal will come with us. Tristan can join later. Roberts isn't important right now."

"He's going after Abella and the baby," I screamed, succeeding in breaking free. "They know I left *Skíðblaðnir* with them!"

"What?" Cal's face paled and contorted with rage.

He didn't wait for further confirmation. Before I could say another word, he'd taken off after Roberts, racing toward the river and the family I'd inadvertently put in danger.

Following after him, I sniffed, terrified tears dripping down my cheeks. I should have known Randall would guess who I left it with if I didn't have the ship on me. He'd been reading everyone's minds. It would have been nothing at all for him to locate it.

"Samantha!" Mark yelled behind me, catching up and grabbing me again. "Come on," he insisted, his voice rough as he watched Cal go. "Abella and Michael will be safe with Cal. He won't let anything happen to them."

I shook my head, trying to escape. "They are more important than the treasure," I hissed.

"And they'll die anyway if Randall gets what he wants!" Mark roared. "Think about the bigger picture, Sam! We have to get in the vault and protect the blood, or everything happening right now will be worthless. Randall will kill every Templar standing and then go to the docks and murder Abella and Michael. We have to stop him from getting the Knot of Isis."

Crying, I glared at him, still leaning toward the city and my endangered loves.

"I saw the way Cal held Abella," Mark added, the words clipped. "He'll die before he lets anything happen to her. He loves Michael, too. They will be safe with him."

The reassurance did little to calm me, but I knew he was right. Cal would protect them, but it would mean nothing if Randall got to the blood before anyone could stop him.

Glancing back toward the valley, I could see Tristan still working to hold Randall at bay, doing his best to make sure everyone was safe, despite knowing others he loved were in danger.

"Fine," I agreed, facing Mark. "Let's get up there and find the hidden door."

The wind whipped by us when we finally reached the pyramid shape of the summit, The Peak rising high into the sky. While the sounds of battle were audible below, it was peaceful where we stood, gazing across the blank rock walls.

"Alright," Mark said, breathless from our hurried climb, "if you were going to hide a door up here, where would you do it?"

I shrugged. "Maybe where there's a lot of rocks, so it would look like a little indent instead of a huge cave?"

"That could work, I guess." He put his hands on his hips, still trying to recover. "These mountains are full of caverns, which is why they buried so many rulers here. It was less work to cut out stone already tunneled out of the mountain by nature."

"So, start searching?" Shrugging, I banished the frustration and fear I felt, refusing to think about Michael and Abella. Callaghan would protect them, I knew it.

I needed to do my part here, or it would all be for naught.

Inching along the surface, I surveyed every nook and cranny I came across, anxious as the minutes ticked by. After what felt like an eternity, I found a rectangular boulder with perfect corners, almost invisible among the others.

"Check it out," Mark said, brushing off sand caked on the face.

I could just make out the faint markings he'd discovered, but I had no idea what they said. Beneath them, there were three finger sized indentations. It was all the proof I needed this was the correct way to go.

Putting my fingers in the holes, I pushed, a small clicking motion ticking against me until a blast of air moved through the cracks, and the door rolled up out of sight. A narrow tunnel I couldn't see the end of stretched into the darkness.

Facing Mark, I smiled. "Do you have anything we can light for a torch?"

He shook his head. "Hopefully there's something in there we can use."

The thought of going in blind made me uncomfortable, but I shrugged the sensation off, bracing myself as I stood in front of the entrance. It was only wide enough for one person to pass through at a time and short enough we would have to crouch to make it through. I was sure it would open up—this was supposed to be a grand treasure vault, after all—but I couldn't help feeling I was walking into a coffin I could be trapped in forever.

Dragging my palm on the surface, I entered the shaft, moving as fast as possible, the light of day fading behind me. The tunnel turned at a sharp angle, and I soon found myself in complete black, only the sounds of mine and Mark's footsteps giving any signs as to whether I was still alive or not.

As we traveled further, heading at a small, downward slope, I began to notice twinkling stones in the ceilings and, like stars stuck in the mountain. With a start, I realized that's what they were—glowing rocks arranged like the stars above the Nile. Several constellations stuck out, leading us onward, the path twisting like the river until the pathway opened into a large cavern covered with the glittering rocks.

It was hard to tell what all was kept here. I could see some dim shapes and paths through the area. The ceiling sloped upward in a pyramid shape, fitting into the form of the mountain.

"I smell oil," Mark commented, his shadowy figure stopping beside mine. "There must be a way to light it and see what's in here." He fiddled around, sniffing here and there, until, there was a sound like a flint being struck and light filled the room, flaming down a narrow trough that wrapped around the cave.

Gasping, my eyes rounded as I beheld the artifacts displayed before me. It was as if I'd stepped onto another movie set, only this time it was for a film set in Ancient Egypt. The walls were covered with colorful hieroglyphics. Statues of pharaohs and goddesses lined the walkways, emblems hanging around their necks on dainty chains and decorated with precious gems. Gold pieces filled chests, canopic jars rested on elaborate tables, and beautiful death masks glittered in the fire. There were shelves and shelves of papyrus rolls, stone etchings, books, paintings, and more miniature figures. Boats, complete with oars and sails, waited to be taken on the water, thrones were ready to sit on, all the artifacts gleaming as if they'd been cleaned that very day. The items were arranged around the edges of the carved cavern, leading inward through square paths.

In the center of it all, there rested three pillars,

simple in nature, but beautiful all the same. On the one farthest to the right, there was a plain, wooden box, the contents a mystery. On the left, an hourglass sat, also not extraordinary by any means. In the middle, a small vial filled with red liquid waited, the image of a jackal resting beside it.

It was evident these three items were the most prized among the whole collection. Of course, I knew what was in the vial. The others were a mystery to me.

"And hourglass?" Pointing to the object, I stared at Mark. "Got any clue as to what that might be?"

"None what so ever," he replied, focusing on the vial. "Where should we hide it?" he asked quietly. "In here? Randall would have to search for hours. It would buy us time, at the very least."

"What about the curse Captain Zadari spoke about?" Hesitating, I stared at the dog watching over the blood. There was a chance its presence could be here to scare robbers.

Or there actually was a curse.

"Truth in all things," Mark mumbled, thinking along the same lines. "What choice do we have, though?"

He reached for the vial, holding his breath as he did so, eyes flickering to the small Anubis for a split second.

And then a gun fired.

The hourglass shattered, spilling sand out onto the floor, the bullet having missed the both of us.

Shrieking, I ducked, seeing Mark do the same as I searched for the source of the shot. Another bullet bit into the base of the pillar on the right, and I skittered from the center of the room, backing up against one of the statues looking over the sacred pedestals.

Coughing, Mark brushed some of the sand still pouring out of the hourglass from his hair, using the pillar it had rested on as a shield from any further attacks. His back pressed against it, facing from me.

"Sam?" he called, glancing over his shoulder, searching for me.

"I'm okay," I responded, the racing of my heart slowing as no further shots rang out.

He nodded, still trying to shake the dust from his face. It gathered in a heap around him, covering his feet and rising up his legs like a flood covering land.

Frowning, I realized there was more sand than could have possibly been inside the glass, the shattered pieces still releasing a steady flow of dirt despite the small amount it had held.

"Mark?"

He coughed again, wiping at his eyes, unable to escape the onslaught. It followed as he tried to scoot away as if he were a magnet drawing it to him. Pieces lifted into the air, circling around him, a low howl growing in strength as wind rushed through the room, spinning like a twister around his body.

The sound made my blood run cold. I'd heard it before, the last time Pandora's Box had been opened. James Abby had unscrewed the lid on the vase, producing a horrible, screeching wind that not only killed him but threatened to take me with it.

"Mark!" I shouted, grasping the statue beside me with everything I had. The storm grew in strength, bellowing through the room, the dust rushing to my friend. It felt as if I were about to lift off the ground, the earth shaking, sound slamming into my ears.

On his knees, Mark attempted to move out of the vortex, but he could not. It was as if he were trapped in a box, his hair whipping around, eyes screwed shut, the granules cutting across his arms and drawing blood. No matter what he did, he couldn't escape the attack, a sense of desperation entering his movements as the scream of the storm increased.

"Hang on, Mark!" I shouted, still clinging to the statue for dear life. I worried if I let go I would be flung around the room like a house on its way to Oz, but I also knew Mark needed help. He couldn't get out on his own, but I could maybe pull him free.

Moving to lay flat on my stomach, I inched toward him, my braids stinging me the same as the sand. It was hard to see where I was going, tears filling my eyes as grit pecked at them. When I was, at last, close enough, I reached out, digging into the earth the best I could.

"Take my hand!" I shouted over the din.

Mark turned, blinking through his own tears and the swirling storm around us. "Sam?" he called, his voice distant like he was speaking to me through a closed window.

His hand gravitated toward mine, our fingers brushing.

And he was gone.

I froze, staring at the place he'd been a second before. The storm had not become thicker, blocking him from view. He'd vanished, like the flame on a candle being blown out.

For a beat, the sand seemed to pause, the air filled with sparkling dust. Ever so slightly, I felt as if an invisible chord seized my wrist and started tugging me inside the vortex.

Screaming, I pulled back, refusing to let whatever this was drag me off. The sensation was one I'd felt before, as recognizable as the earsplitting sound of the wind. It was the force that had pulled me through time, almost killed me, and had set me on this path in the first place.

I hadn't known what was happening the first time I felt it, but I knew exactly what would happen if I entered the sands. They would deposit me in another time, maybe my own, destroying everything I'd worked for the past five years. Going back was not an option, not ever. I would cut my arm off before I left my family.

Getting off my stomach, I sat, digging my heels into the earth, refusing to budge but somehow still inching closer. The pressure around my wrist increased as I was sucked in up to my elbow and I shouted in frustration, the joint in my shoulder stretching as far as it could without dislocating as I fought back.

"Samantha!"

Tristan's voice roared over the sound of the storm, and he was suddenly there, arms wrapping around my waist and tugging me back, anchoring me to him, to this time and place.

Tears of joy leaked from my eyes, and I continued to yank myself free, assisted by my husband. After what felt like a lifetime, whatever was seizing me snapped and I jerked backward, knocking Tristan over.

The wind stopped on a dime, the sand falling to the earth like a dirty rain. It rolled back to the broken hourglass in a wave, pulling pointy shards of the housing with it, the pieces gliding back together until all that was left was the hourglass, intact and holding the small amount of sand it had in the beginning.

Coughing, my body trembling from the amount of force it had taken to keep from being sucked up, I sat up, blinking the moisture from my eyes as the grit cleared from them and gaped at the place where Mark had been.

My friend was gone. The sand had carried him away, taking him who knew where. He'd been forced to endure the painful attack, succumbing to it when I was unable to reach him in time.

He was as good as dead to us now.

My ears were still ringing. "It took Mark," I breathed. "He's gone." Looking at my husband, my lip trembled, my tears turning to those of sorrow. "Forever."

It felt like I'd been stabbed in the heart. Wrapping my arms around Tristan's neck, I cried into his shirt. "I didn't get to him in time," I lamented. "He was right there—our fingers touched, and then he was just gone."

Tristan smoothed my hair as he held me in his lap, remaining silent as I sobbed.

It was my fault. If I'd gone to Mark sooner, rather than stay by the statue, I might have pulled him free in time. He vanished, and it was entirely because of me.

What would I tell Abella? How could I face her and tell her the man she loved disappeared?

An overwhelming sense of abandonment filled me, my hands twisted into fists in the fabric.

I was alone. Mark had been my only link to the century I was from, the only person who understood completely what it was like being swept to the past.

But he was more than that. He was a member of

our family, the man who had saved me when I was in trouble, the one who made sure we were all taken care of. Without him, how would we be sure of the historical aspect of our travels? Who would practice modern medicine on those who needed it most?

Tristan sniffed, and I pulled back, surprised to find tears on his cheeks, his lips turned down in a frown.

"I'm sorry," he muttered. "I should have been here to help ye pull him free." He shrugged, despair in his eyes. "We've lost him, Sam, and it is my fault."

Shaking my head, I dismissed the notion. "No, it's mine. I should have acted sooner." Pausing, I remembered the reason the sand had been set free in the first place. "What were you shooting at?" I asked.

"He didn't fire the gun." Randall stepped out in front of us, the Knot of Isis in his hand and a smile on his face. "I did."

Randall examined the vial, his lips curled into a twisted grin. All the wounds he'd received while fighting in the valley below were already healed, the only sign he'd been hurt at all the blood stains on his shirt. The two swords he'd tried to kill me with earlier were tucked into his belt, his head cocking to the side as his attention turned to us once more.

"I was hoping for a distraction, but not quite of that magnitude," he confessed. "The sand wanted nothing to do with me. Pity." He held out the Knot of Isis, shaking it. "Would have stopped me from taking this without issue."

Anger flashed through me, and I jumped to my feet, not knowing exactly what I was going to do, but he needed to be stopped right now.

"Ah, ah, ah." Randall shook his finger, stepping toward the hourglass. Eyes never leaving mine, he bent down, picking it up with his metal hand. "What would happen, I wonder, if I threw this at your feet and broke it open again?"

Tristan sucked in a sharp breath behind me, his hand coming to rest on my back as he stood, careful not to move too fast and spur Randall into action.

"It's a tempting thought," the villain continued to muse, resting the edge of the glass on his chin. Holding it toward me, he chuckled. "What would O'Rourke do without his time traveler?"

Shouting from the tunnel drew his attention for a beat. The sounds of the Templars and Black Knights battling at the entrance, some of them pushing their way toward the cavern, seemed to make whatever decision he was mulling over come to a head and he glared back at us, his smile vanishing.

"Which is more important?" he asked quietly. "Your wife, or stopping me?"

Lifting the hourglass over his head, he threw it toward the ground as he popped the lid off the vial of godly essence and tilted it toward his mouth.

All I could hear was my inhalation as I dove to him, hands outstretched to catch the glass before it broke and whisked me away from this place.

At the same time, Tristan leaped forward, grabbing Randall's fist and covering the opening of the bottle with his other palm, grappling for control of it.

Courage surged through me as I hit the earth, grabbing the hourglass before it shattered on the stones. Randall had underestimated us this time; we knew how to work together as a team. While he'd supposed we would both move to save me, he hadn't counted on Tristan trusting me to take care of myself.

Rolling, I cradled the container to my chest, taking it out of Randall's reach.

The villain roared in frustration as he and Tristan continued to wrestle. Leveraging his forearm against my husband's neck, Randall pushed him back, tripping Tristan as he stumbled backward, his hands still battling for control of the vial.

Everything was happening so fast, but it was as if it were in slow motion as I watched the next part. Tristan was rushing to the earth, Randall pushing him down and back, their legs tangling together.

The bastard's expression was one of triumph and glee, a throaty laugh leaving him as he won. It wasn't Randall's expression that scared me at that moment, though.

It was Tristan's.

I knew as soon as I saw him what he planned to do. There was no other way to stop our enemy, no path to freedom other than what he was going to do right now. He wore a look of determination and acceptance, his eyes focused on the vial still grasped in their overlapping grips, covered by his palm. As he fell back, he forced Randall's wrist to turn, uncovering the opening and allowing the liquid inside to pour into his mouth.

The blood splashed on Tristan's lips, splattering across his face and neck, sliding down his throat as he hit the floor with a heavy thud. Quickly, he wiped the back of his hand over the droplets he hadn't swallowed, smudging them in the gathering and licking them from his skin, his chest heaving as Randall glowered down at him.

It felt like I couldn't move as I watched the two of them, everything frozen.

"What have you done?" Randall breathed, fury rolling off him as he continued to stand over Tristan.

"What I had to," Tristan replied with a growl.

Randall shook, fists pressed to his sides, chest heaving as they glared at each other. "You will not take this from me," he hissed.

Shrieking, Randall stepped over Tristan, raising his metal hand high into the air and bringing it down fast, punching right through Tristan's chest.

"No!" I screamed, scrambling to get my feet beneath me. Before I could move, a hand grabbed my arm, keeping me in place. Turning, I beheld the horrified expressions of William MacDonald and his men, their battle with the Black Knights finished as both the loyal and traitorous sects watched the scene unfolding in front of them.

Staring at my husband, I tried to escape from the Grand Master, succeeding in only being gripped harder.

Tristan's eyes bulged, a closed-mouth groan leaving him, his hand grasping the arm shoved between his ribs, fingernails digging into the flesh until they drew blood. The gore dripped down Randall's wrist, adding to the mess flowing from my husband's wound.

Randall growled, twisting his grip, and with a great yank ripped the heart clean out of Tristan's body.

My *Grá mo Chroí* cried out, his head turning toward me, a tear leaking out the corner of his eye and sliding down his skin. As our eyes locked, he smiled, the love he had for me evident even then.

His chest sputtered, struggling to rise, and the air left in a slow leak, his hands sliding to the earth, body going still as the light went out from his gaze.

The sound of my sobs echoed in the cave, two of the Templars assisting MacDonald in holding me back. My energy was quickly expelled as I fought to go to Tristan, to murder Randall for what he'd done. Reduced to a crying heap, all I could do was scream, until my throat was raw, the taste of blood in the back of it.

The only hope I had was Tristan had swallowed

the essence. He had power inside him now that should keep him alive, just as Randall succeeded in doing each time he met his untimely end. The longer I watched his unmoving body, the more desperate I became, wondering if something had gone wrong and if he had been stolen from me forever.

Chest heaving, Randall straightened, glaring at the heart in his hand. He glanced at me, smiling, and rose the organ as if toasting my health. Bringing the flesh to his mouth, he revealed his teeth, sinking them into the object in his hand.

Fury ripped through me, and I bellowed at him, the sound like the war cry of an angry animal. Pain like I'd never known laced through me, my vision blurry as tears cascaded down my cheeks. As the sound I couldn't control continued to soar from me, it was as if a whole pack of dogs was crying with me, their barks vicious and hungry.

Something snarled in my ear, and I jerked back, gaping into the countenance of an actual dog as it slid through the rows of statues. Our gazes met for a beat, and I was struck with the impression the animal possessed true intelligence, his gaze calculating and calm. Its head swung toward Randall, growling as it stalked forward.

The noise from the rest of the pack increased, as if it were all around us, howling and circling, sneaking among the treasures, sniffing us out. Emerging from the shadows, at least ten jackals padded into the center of the cavern, haunches raised and stares judging.

Zadari's warning flashed into my mind. *The blood is cursed, protected by that which protected the goddess herself.*

I could still see the tiny image of Anubis on the pillar, his head the same as the creatures now closing in on Randall. For a moment, the figure's eyes seemed to sparkle with the same life the dog I'd encountered had possessed, a whisper of a breath brushing through the space, words I didn't understand creating little more than a murmur in my ears.

One of the dogs jumped at Randall, only to be backhanded by his metal hand, Tristan's heart falling to the ground. Before the bastard could recover himself, another sunk its teeth into his leg, ripping the flesh of his calf off like it was nothing.

Randall screamed, going down, a different beast grabbing his shoulder and shaking its head viciously, the cracking of Randall's bones audible beneath its growls.

"Help me!" Randall cried to his men, his eyes frantic as he scrambled, pulled every which way by the pack.

They fought over him like a fresh steak, snapping at each other and pulling him to pieces in front of our very eyes, ignoring Tristan's body and heart completely.

An arrow shot through the air, fired by a Black Knight, and struck one of the jackals in the flank. Rather than whimper or fall because of the injury, the dog turned, barking at the group, and launched its own attack on all our enemies.

MacDonald hauled me to my feet, pushing me around the other side of the statues and out of the way of the fight. His men followed, scampering as everyone else was mauled.

Randall's frustrated scream drew my attention,

and I peered around our protective shield, watching as he tried to bat another dog away. He was healing fast enough to hold his own, but I reveled in the fact he was constantly being torn apart.

The pack pulled him across the room in slow motions, dragging him in pieces, stealing him from the scene of his crimes. The Black Knights who were able followed him, disappearing down the tunnel, the sounds of the attack fading until there was nothing left but the Templars and myself.

Only then did MacDonald release me, allowing me to collapse on the floor and crawl to my husband. His eyes stared lifelessly at the spot where I'd been, his body void of life. Finding his abandoned heart, I picked it up, the sound that left my lips not human as I pressed it to my own chest.

Tristan wasn't healing. He'd taken the blood, but his body remained broken. My love was gone, and despite his best efforts to keep Randall from getting what he wanted, he'd failed.

We all had.

Sobbing, I leaned over his body, cradling the heart, my tears dripping over the bloody mess that was his chest. I couldn't stand to see him so torn apart, part of his body taken from him. With my shaking hands, I slid his heart back between his ribs, blind with pain and sorrow as my fingers brushed his bones.

Laying over him, I gave in to despair, not caring MacDonald and his men watched on. My entire earth was shattered. If I'd known it was a choice between being taken by the sand and saving Tristan's life, I would have gone back to my own time. My fears and ambitions felt silly now. I'd only been thinking of myself and what I wanted, not what was best for the ones I loved.

Twisting my fingers in his shirt, I pressed my forehead to his collarbone, not sure what to think anymore. It was all too much to handle.

Ever so slightly, the chest beneath me twitched, rising, lungs filling with air, and a hand brushed against my back.

"Samantha," Tristan's voice murmured, joyful and loving. "Why do ye cry so, love?"

Sitting up in surprise, I gazed into his eyes, wonderful and full of life. The image made me bawl harder, relief flooding through me as I shook my head, unable to speak.

His arms wrapped around me, pulling me to him as his lips brushed my forehead. "I wouldn't leave you like that," he swore. "Not ever."

"You weren't healing," I whispered, my voice lost after all my screaming. "I believed you were gone for real."

"Aye, I did too, for a moment or so. It was as if I were trapped in the dark, unable to move or breathe, stuck in limbo. Then, all was whole, and I came back." His hands continued to rub comforting circles on my back, our forms pressed together as tightly as they could be. "Whatever was missing returned, and my body began to mend."

Wincing as he sat up, he looked around the cavern, his features falling. "But it was all for naught. Randall got away."

I nodded, sniffing as I wiped the back of my hand across my nose. "He took your heart," I shared. "Bit right into it and took some of the blood for himself."

Pausing, a realization lit in me. I watched him, going over everything that had happened, making sure I was right.

"You didn't heal until your heart was replaced," I stated. "The thing you felt was missing, the object that kept you from coming right back, was your heart. It wasn't in your body, so you were unable to do what you needed to."

He frowned, mulling it over, and understanding lit in him. "We can kill Randall for good," Tristan declared. "So long as a vital part of him remains missing."

I nodded. "He was dragged out of here by dogs. If we go now, we might be able to catch him."

"That won't be possible now," MacDonald called, his figure materializing out of the tunnel. "The dogs killed him, but there were enough Black Knights outside to beat them off and recover the body. They left as soon as they had him, running like mice from a housecat. By the time we track them down, it will be another war, and we aren't equipped for that."

He motioned to what remained of his men, all of them injured, weary, and staring at Tristan with a sense of awe and respect.

"I think it is time we clean up this mess, return to Paris and regroup." MacDonald rubbed his face, tired.

"Roberts," I said suddenly. "Randall sent him after the ship—after Abella and Michael. Callaghan followed him, but I don't know what happened." Shoving to my feet, I grabbed Tristan's hand and pulled him up. "We need to go right now. Are you good?"

He nodded, grinning. "I feel better than I have in

a while, truth be told."

Smiling, I turned to MacDonald. "Let's get back to the harbor and stop them from retaking the Norse vessel."

The Grand Master shook his head. "We'll go back to the boats, aye, but I must see to my men now. Whatever plans ye make are yer own, O'Rourkes. This is where our paths part."

Frowning, I resisted the urge to fight with him. There wasn't time for it anyway. Whatever his reasons for not wanting us around, they would have to wait to be discovered.

"Fine," I replied, my voice clipped.

Jerking my head toward the tunnel, I urged Tristan on ahead of me, the two of us running the best we could through the small space until we were in the open air.

Sand whipped off the mountain, bathing the sky in brown. I couldn't even see the valley below anymore, a trail of blood leading down the side of the mount, accompanied by messy jackal pawprints.

"This way," I said, pointing to the decline. "Roberts took the road heading out the south of the valley. If Cal caught him, they'd be somewhere in that direction."

Tristan didn't answer, prompting me to glance back, watching as he stood in the mouth of the tunnel, clenching and releasing his fists.

He stared at them as if he'd never seen them before, his focus locked on whatever he was experiencing. Satisfied with his fingers, he looked at the sky and the earth around us, taking in everything like he'd never seen it before.

"Tristan?"

His attention focused on me, and he blinked, shaking off whatever he'd been taken by.

"Are you okay?" I pressed.

"Aye," he confirmed. "Only . . . I feel . . . odd. I do not know how to describe it."

"You can work on it later," I answered, snapping somewhat as I moved in the right direction. "We need to find Callaghan and Roberts before it's too late."

A gust of wind pushed past us, throwing dust in my eyes and mouth and I coughed, squinting as I watched something rising from the valley, hovering beside The Peak, straight across from us.

Caught off guard, I took in Callaghan's grinning face as he leaned over the railing of the airborne *Skíðblaðnir*. Beside him, Abella and Michael stood, smiling and waving to us.

"The Black Knights swarmed the docks," Cal yelled, waving us over. "It's on fire, but we managed to escape. Thought ye might fancy a flight yerselves. I feel like a damn bird up here!"

Abella laughed, nodding her agreement, excitement exuding from the pair. Her face fell as she gaped at us, the life sapping from her in an instant. "Are you hurt, Tristan? Whose blood is that?" The color drained from her. "Where's Mark?" she asked.

Swallowing hard, I glanced at Tristan.

He sighed, gazing back at them. "Much has happened," he stated simply. "Throw us a ladder, and we'll tell ye once we're aboard."

The boat rocked with the waves, the scent of sea salt strong on the air and new horizons waiting for us to find them. It had been six weeks since we left Egypt, and there was still no sign of Randall and the Black Knights. I was beginning to wonder if we'd chosen the wrong direction to travel in our search for them, but it would be pointless to turn back now. Our enemy had to resurface somewhere, and when they did, we would find them.

Sitting at the helm, I watched as Tristan and Callaghan worked with the rigging on the sloop we'd bought in Rasheed. It was smaller than the *Jaguar* but would work fine as a hunting vessel. It was also to be our home for the foreseeable future, and they treated it as such. At times, I considered if it would have been better to use *Skíðblaðnir* in our chasing of Randall, but I always decided it was better to keep the vessel tucked away and safe. We would draw attention to ourselves no matter how we used it and that was exactly what we didn't want to do if we were going to catch the villain unaware.

Beside me, Abella snipped herbs for dinner, quiet and contemplative. She'd not said much after I told her of Mark's disappearance. In fact, she didn't speak to anyone anymore. Often, I heard her sniffing in the dead of night, saving her tears for when she assumed no one would notice. Mark's request she not mourn him had gone unheeded.

We all felt his loss each moment, his memory locked in our minds.

"Mama," Michael said in his little baby voice, reaching for me as he stopped crawling across his blanket and sat down.

"Hello there," I cooed, obliging by scooping him up and setting him on my lap. "See Daddy out there? Wave hi to Daddy!" I moved his hand for him, grinning as Tristan beckoned back, blowing the two of us a kiss.

I'd worried he would be different after the blood like Randall had been. Instead, he seemed the same as ever. Once in a while, I saw a mysterious look in his eyes like he remembered something from long ago, but then the expression would fade, and he'd be himself again, laughing and planning how we would go about accomplishing our mission. It reminded me of how he'd been when he first left the cave in The Peak, the memory unsettling for some reason.

We'd not really talked about what happened. I had the sneaking suspicion he wasn't telling me something on purpose, but he would speak when he was ready. I was content to wait if it meant he stayed with me and was his regular self.

Sighing, I gazed up at the sky, trying to decide if I needed to check our location or not. It would be a while yet before we made it to Madagascar, and was not noon, but I was determined to do the best job possible as our navigator.

Hopping down from the bottom of the mast, Tristan padded over to me, kissing my cheek and ruffling Michael's hair. "What are ye thinking?" he asked, his voice pleasant.

"I'm wondering if the sun could move any slower," I joked, grinning at him. "You?"

His fingers brushed against my knee, his eyebrow raising in what I supposed was meant to be a seductive manner.

Chuckling, I shook my head, gazing back at the sky.

For the next couple days, it almost felt like we were returning to our old life in Ireland. There was a sense of security and contentment among the family, so much so I could almost forget we'd decided to go after Randall ourselves.

When we made landfall to get a few supplies at the halfway point of our trip, a familiar face was waiting for us on the shore. His sultan like clothing hadn't changed a bit, save the fabric that should have covered his missing arm being hemmed around his elbow, revealing the freshly scarred stump.

"You lot are hard to track down," Captain Zadari stated, smiling as he offered his hand to Tristan in greeting. "I've been following you for some weeks now."

"Oh?" Tristan grinned. "And why is that? Had enough of life as a Prince of the Sea?"

Zadari laughed, shaking his head. "Not quite, my friend. I'm here to bring you back to Paris."

"What?" I asked, panic filling me. "Why? MacDonald said we were free to go."

"I'll not consent to be yer prisoner," Tristan added sharply. "I may have taken the blood, but it was the only choice I had."

"No." Zadari interrupted him. "You are not to be

374

locked up. You and Callaghan have been voted back into good standing by the members of The Order."

We stared at him in silence, Cal and Abella gaping in surprise.

"I've your orders here." Reaching into his jacket, Zadari pulled out a sealed letter, passing it to Tristan.

He broke the stamp and read the contents, eyes going wide as he unearthed whatever information he was being given.

"They've not just voted us back in," he said, swallowing hard as he looked up at me. "They've given me the position of Master. I am to be one of MacDonald's advisors and generals. There is a ship they want me to command. This is a request for us to return to Paris as soon as possible for further instructions."

Dumbfounded, I took the letter from him, glancing at it. "Why would they do that?" I asked. "After everything you did before we were exiled and our disobedience recently?"

"They heard of your sacrifice inside *El Qorn*," Zadari answered. "The Templars who witnessed Tristan doing whatever it took to stop Randall and then being left alone by Anubis' dogs told anyone who would listen how he was the man they needed on their side in this war."

Tristan snorted, doubtful. "I did what any man would do in that circumstance," he replied humbly. "Nothing more."

"No," Zadari asserted with confidence. "You did not. And that is why the men have called you back to help lead them."

Frowning, Tristan glanced at me and the others.

"You will return with me, won't you?" Zadari continued, his voice eager. "I had to fight for the opportunity to come and fetch you. It would be disappointing if I had to tell everyone I failed in my convincing."

I continued to stare at Tristan, silent as I thought it over. It would be much easier to go after Randall with all the assets of The Order. We wouldn't have to run from the Templars any longer. There would be extra protection, should we need it. Tristan would be calling the shots with MacDonald. Overall, it felt like the right step to take now. Our lives were changing so rapidly, a bit of order was needed.

The uncertainty in his face made me pause. The impression he was hiding something from me surfaced, and I cleared my throat, addressing the captain. "Could we have a minute to speak about this alone?"

Zadari tipped his head in acceptance, moving to speak to Cal and Abella, and I took Tristan's hand, walking back to our boat and boarding it with him.

"What's going on?" I asked under my breath, turning to him.

"We can't go," he said instantly. "It's not safe."

Surprised, I frowned. "Why not? If you're a member of The Order, they will protect us all."

He closed his eyes, shaking his head. "I'm not worried about ye. It's the others—the Templars—I'm worried about. I can't promise they'll be safe if I'm there."

The words only confused me further.

When I didn't answer, he sighed. "I need to tell ye something."

I nodded, remaining silent as he glanced over his shoulder to make sure no one was trying to listen in.

"When Randall . . . killed me," he began, hesitating, "I cut him and his blood mixed with mine." He pursed his lips, a small laugh escaping him. "I can hear them, Sam. All of them. The gods Randall has absorbed over the years are in me, too, now, and I don't know if I can control them if we go back to Paris." He held his hand out, stopping me from speaking and continued. "I trust myself around ye, around our family. There isn't a force in this world or any other that could make me harm ye. But strangers? Men I have no connection with, save being their designated leader? I do not know if I can do it."

Swallowing, I let the words wash over me before replying. "Why do you think you'll lose control?" I asked carefully. "Do these voices tell you to do things?"

He shrugged. "At times." Frowning, he ran his hands through his hair. "We saw what they did to Randall, how they turned him inside out and forced him to do unspeakable things. I don't want to be like that."

For the first time, I realized the thing he'd been hiding from me all these weeks was fear. He was scared of the power he'd taken, of the beings residing in him, and what the future held for him now. Tristan had become a shadow of Randall, the very man he'd been trying to beat. They were both members of a secret organization, searching for treasures, and housing the gods within them.

And they couldn't be any more different from each other.

"You are not Randall," I said, my voice gentle as I touched his cheek. "Where he is weak, you are strong. His evil is outshined by your good. In every instance, you have proven you are a million times more a man than he is. If anyone had to bear this burden, to stand toe to toe with him and refuse to let him win, I'm glad it could be you. I believe you can do anything, even this."

His fingers brushed mine as his shoulders fell, a sense of relief wrapping around him. Eyes closing, he stood there for a moment, letting the air brush past us, the cries of birds in the distance.

"Whatever you want to do, I will support you," I added. "If you want to go home to Ireland and ignore everything, we'll do it. I want what you want."

He grinned at me and nodded. "I know ye do."

"What do you want?" I pressed, stepping closer.

He paused, grinding his teeth as he thought it over, conflicted emotions flashing across his features before he let out a long breath and nodded.

"I want a life free from this turmoil," he stated, twisting his fingers into my hair. "And that is why we will return to Paris with Zadari, and I will accept my role as Master within The Order."

"Are you sure?"

He nodded. "Fate saw fit to give me these powers for a reason. Randall isn't the only one who can escape death now. The Grand Master is right—it is time to fight fire with fire."

The Story Continues . . .

Be sure to follow Kamery Solomon
Books for more information on *The
Swept Away Saga #6*, **coming soon!**

About The Author

    #1 Bestselling Genre Author, Kamery Solomon, has been delighting readers with her God Chronicles series, featuring modern day adaptions of Zeus, nominated for Book of the Year and Cover of the Year, Poseidon, Hades, Adrastia, & Exoria. Kamery has also wooed her readers with her #1 bestselling fantasy novella, Forever, and her contemporary favorites, Taking Chances and Watching Over Me. Her most recent blockbuster series and #1 bestseller in Time Travel Romance, The Swept Away Saga, has had readers captivated on the high seas of romance and adventure! Kamery currently lives with her beautiful family in The White Mountains of Arizona and can often be found singing something from a Broadway musical with her siblings.

www.kamerysolomonbooks.com

Made in the USA
Columbia, SC
04 January 2019